Born in Zimbabwe, Tina Marie completed her primary school years at boarding school in Bulawayo, but on weekends and holidays she explored their family ranch in Nyamandhlovu, normally on the back of her horse. Her teenage years were totally different to her idyllic childhood. After her father died, the family of five women moved to Kokstad, a rural town at the foot of the Drakensberg Mountains in South Africa, and the boarding school hostel became her home. In winter she walked to school in the snow and could never get warm, and in summer she sweated, having to wear an impractical (but smart) blazer.

She began writing fiction in the UK while a stay-at-home mum to her two sons and she hasn't looked back.

Now living on a small island near Brisbane in Queensland, Australia, Tina Marie combines her passion for storytelling with her love for Africa.

Her first book, *My Brother-But-One*, was shortlisted for the Queensland Literary Award 2014.

Readers are welcome to find Tina on social media:
Facebook:facebook.com/pages/TMClark-Author/130010083845439
Twitter: @TinaMarieClark2
Website: tmclark.com.au

Also by T.M. Clark

My Brother-But-One
Shooting Butterflies

TEARS OF THE CHEETAH

T.M. CLARK

First Published 2015
First Australian Paperback Edition 2015
ISBN 9781743693100

Tears of the Cheetah
© 2015 by T.M. Clark
Australian Copyright 2015
New Zealand Copyright 2015

This is a work of fiction. Names, characters, places, and incidents are either the product of the author's imagination or are used fictitiously, and any resemblance to actual persons, living or dead, business establishments, events, or locales is entirely coincidental.

Published by
Harlequin Mira
An imprint of Harlequin Enterprises (Australia) Pty Ltd.
Level 13, 201 Elizabeth Street
SYDNEY NSW 2000
AUSTRALIA

® and TM are trademarks of Harlequin Enterprises Limited or its corporate affiliates. Trademarks indicated with ® are registered in Australia, New Zealand and in other countries.

Cover design: Squirt Creative
Cover image: © Nigel Pavitt/JAI/Corbis

National Library of Australia Cataloguing-in-Publication entry

Creator: Clark, T. M., author.
Title: Tears of the Cheetah / T. M. Clark.
ISBN: 9781743693100 (paperback)
Subjects: Man-woman relationships—Fiction.
Cheetah—Fiction.
Poaching—South Africa—Fiction.
South Africa—Fiction.
Dewey Number: A823.4

Printed and bound in Australia by Griffin Press

NAMIBIA

Windhoek •

Walvis Bay

•Luderitz

BOTSWANA

Francistown •

Musina
(Messina)

MOZAMBIQUE

Polokwane
(Pietersburg)

Nelspruit •

Pretoria •

Maputo

Johannesburg •

Mbabane

SWAZILAND

• Upington

Richard's Bay •

LESOTHO

Crystalberg*

Durban

Port Shepstone

Margate

SOUTH AFRICA

Stellenbosh •

Cape Town

Port Elizabeth •

*Fictional Town

As always, to Shaun, my love, my life.
And to my sons Kyle and Barry,
because we all share a total obsession with cats.

'We owe it to our peoples to join hands to fight poverty and disease, to protect the environment and to cooperate in the quest for a better world.'

Nelson Mandela

PROLOGUE

A million years of evolution quivered, her instinct strong to kill. To survive. The cheetah mother crept forward, concealed by the tawny grass. Puffs of mist rose as she controlled her breathing in the cold morning. She dug her claws into the solid African sand, and exploded towards the unsuspecting impala. A baboon barked a warning as he spied her from a perch in a nearby thorn tree, but his alarm call was too late. The second it took for the impala to react was too long. The cheetah was already right up behind the buck, and despite its acceleration in speed to dodge the predator, the cheetah was faster, her lungs specifically designed for just this scenario. As the impala turned a sharp right, the cheetah used her tail as a rudder and adjusted her trajectory accordingly. The cheetah expertly closed the distance between the antelope and herself. One more zigzag to the left, and the cheetah extended her paw outward, tripping up the fleeing impala. In a second she had it pinned by its exposed throat. She hung onto its neck, her iron-clad bite cutting off its life's air, suffocating the buck.

Within moments, the kill was over, and the cheetah quickly pulled her trophy to a scrubby bush to recover. After the short exertion, she needed to cool down, fill her lungs with fresh air and regain her breath. Then she could feast. Once her belly was full, she would return to her cubs and call them from the bushes where they were hidden, and she would share her meal with them. At six weeks old, they were now grown enough to accompany her on her hunts, but were still very dependent on her for milk.

Slowly, the African bush returned to normal, the hype of the danger over. The doves resumed their relentless cooing, wooing each other. The baboons continued to eat the soft tips from the tree they sat in, one grooming another as the sentry on watch picked at his yellow-stained teeth. The cheetah forgotten, the death of the impala was simply another passing within the bush. Survival of the fittest. This time, his troop were safe. They would continue their day.

The cheetah chirped, calling the cubs to her from their hiding place. Three gorgeous spotted babies. Their white manes, which disguised them as ferocious honey badgers to any unsuspecting passer-by, acted as a temperature control, providing a sunscreen in the heat and warming them in the bitter cold of the early Highveld mornings.

Chirping, she called the cubs again. A loud, high-pitched sound that carried across the grassland. They should have heard her, she hadn't run so far away from them.

But they didn't come.

She retraced her steps at a trot, chirping again, looking at the bushes, knowing they should burst out at any time, their eyes bright, and their fur as beautiful now as it would be when they were adults.

But her offspring didn't come.

She ran into the bushes, her senses alert. And that's when she smelt him. Man.

The top predator of her food chain. The reek left behind saying that he had been there, and there was no sign of her cubs. Their scent had simply disappeared, and all she could now detect was the acid stench of the unwashed man.

The mother cheetah searched in circles, scanning. She climbed on a fallen tree to see if she could spot her babies, and despite having perfect view for twelve kilometres, she could not see her cubs, nor the man.

Her forlorn calls of distress disturbed the quiet hum of the Highveld, but she continued calling for her cubs.

But they didn't answer.

CHAPTER

1

Cole waited for Mackenzie to appear. Soon she'd come around the corner and begin her race along the kilometre-long stretch of tarmac that ran alongside the fence line of *nTabaGrequa* Wildlife Rescue and Cheetah Conservation Centre's exercise pens. He looked across the double cat fence on the roadside and single Bonnox square mesh fencing separating that enclosure for the next cats, giving them ample space to stretch their bodies and flex their muscles. The dust track inside was already well worn and no mountain grass was able to take root on the cats' racing track along the fence line. Three extended length, large enclosures were on the right-hand side of the visitors' centre, dotted with small shrubs. On the left were three smaller ones, being only two hundred metres long. All of them were a standard two hundred metres wide.

The cats were rotated between enclosures four times daily. This ensured they never displayed unwanted captive behaviour and it helped to keep the intelligent animals from getting bored. A few of the enrichment pens had balls in them or long ropes with knots that were used to hone the growing cheetahs' hunting skills. Boxes were a favourite toy, ripped apart in no time as the cats looked inside for the treats – meat, or feather dusters which could keep them entertained for an hour or so as they tore them to pieces feather by feather. Others simply had more trees and fallen logs, mounds and different natural features for the cheetahs to explore, and learn to use to their advantage.

In another pen a similar track cut deep into the earth, where an area was cleared of bushes and grass from many claws eating deep into it for traction as the cheetahs chased bait attached to a quick-winding winch.

Mackenzie rounded the corner and prepared to pit herself against the fastest cat in the world. Sasha, born on *nTabaGrequa* two years ago, bounded into action. Her agile body stretched to its maximum length, then bunched as her feet whispered to the ground. Her unsheathed claws created traction. Her oversized nasal passages allowed oxygen into her lungs, as her metabolism kicked into higher gear – zero to sixty-four kilometres per hour in two and a half seconds flat.

Mackenzie pushed her bicycle to overdrive. Neck on neck they sprinted, a pure adrenaline rush. Cole smiled as he watched Sasha use her long, flexible spine to spring-load each stride, out-racing the bicycle. Sasha's body was supple and majestic as it streaked ahead to its maximum speed of one hundred and nineteen kilometres. The Ferrari of the cat world.

Mackenzie wasn't bad either. But Sasha won with her three-hundred-metre sprint at the end.

The cat used her tail as a rudder to perform a fast-paced turn when she reached the end of her enclosure and pranced back a step or two as Mackenzie zipped past, then stared after her. Triumphant. Waiting for the rematch she knew was coming in about half an hour.

Watching Mackenzie on her daily exercise routine from afar was always exhilarating. Cole wondered if she noticed that he'd switched the cats again, that she didn't race just one cheetah, but half a dozen of those closest to full rehabilitation on a rotating basis.

It had been Nama's change in behaviour that had brought the cyclist to his attention at first. Usually his most foul-tempered cheetah, his unexplainable character transformation was remarkable.

His spiteful behaviour had shifted to that of a happier cat. He'd become more approachable, less moody and not as mean. Cole soon realised Mackenzie was responsible. He'd made a mental note of the time she was riding past his farm, and had watched her movements ever since. When Mackenzie showed signs of keeping pace with the old cheetah, he'd switched the cats. Sasha, who'd been watching Nama's daily race through the fence, and mimicking it in her own enclosure, was moved into the outer one. Sasha had immediately taken up the cyclist's challenge.

Soon a rotation with the cheetahs had begun, with Mackenzie helping to exercise all the cats without even being aware of it.

He watched Mackenzie as she cycled away, pushing her body to its limits. She'd done well today. He wished he could tell her how well she raced. He wished he could stop her in the street in Crystalberg, look right into her velvet-blue eyes, and tell her how beautiful she looked racing his cheetahs, streaking across the earth, so free, so full of life, but he couldn't.

Although they had a kindling friendship, she was as skittish as a newborn zebra foal. The entire town spoke of the American on the hill, an artist, they said, and a loner. How she let no one close, such a city-girl trait, and when she hadn't changed in eighteen months, the talk became more about the snobby American or the eccentric artist on the hill.

But he knew there was more to her.

A single white American woman moving to Africa. Buying the old Joubert house, which had been for sale for so long and overpriced by its deceased estate, yet the distance with which she held herself from that community didn't add up.

Almost a year ago, she'd warned him off trying to deepen their friendship into anything more. He respected that, and knew how much courage it took to admit you wanted to be alone. Hell, he himself lived by that same rule.

No attachment. No commitments. No strings.

If he was being honest, she scared him. Made him want things he didn't have the right to have. So he'd kept his distance after that, a platonic friendship, a wave here and there. A coffee at Duduzo's Kofi Shop, looking over the majestic Sani Pass, its craggy grey stone sometimes covered in snow in the winter, sometimes green with sweet tufts of veldt grasses in spring. Not that he looked at the scenery when he was constantly distracted by her long dark hair that she had a habit of pinning up with a pencil or a paintbrush in a makeshift bun, which would then slowly escape with each movement, loosening more, until it begged him to reach over and pull the pencil out completely. But he never did.

Her coffee was always a strong black with no sugar, with Duduzo constantly present as a chaperon, his big face sweating into his pristine white chef's hat, and he was always hawking his pastries and cakes. Cole often bought more and took them home in a 'doggy box' for his staff. Mackenzie always refused with a polite smile, sticking to a single buttered croissant. He died a little every time he watched her pink tongue lick the flaky pastry crumbs off her fingers.

Even then he could see that when she smiled it didn't reach her eyes, she was simply being polite. Perhaps it was that inner sadness that attracted him to her, or the fact that he was known for collecting strays. Perhaps he just wanted to fix her and remove the haunting, replace it with laughter. Help her make her life better, but she wouldn't let him closer.

Who was he kidding? For the first time in a long time, he felt a real attraction to a woman. He was pulled to her, like a butterfly to nectar. Except she reminded him of everything he still wanted and could never allow himself to have.

Cole sighed as he watched her end her first race of the day, and turned around on the tray at the back of the *bakkie*.

'She's getting better,' he said.

Siphiwe grinned, his teeth shining in his dark face. 'Aw, *Baas*. She'll never catch your cheetahs, they are too fast for her.'

'She's giving it a good try. We'll see how her rematch goes.'

The two of them jumped off the *bakkie* to the ground and began unloading the heavy bags of lime onto the dam wall.

Cole wiped his forehead with his khaki sleeve. 'Dammit, it's hot. Tell me again why I'm doing this instead of one of the workers?'

'You love your trout, *Baas*,' Siphiwe said, 'and your water test said lime was needed.'

'Smart mouth!'

Siphiwe laughed.

Together they worked for another half hour before all the bags were unloaded. Cole called a stop and threw down his soft leather gloves, then checked his watch.

He walked to the back of the *bakkie* and hopped up. 'Show time.' He looked for the cyclist, but the road was empty. He could see Sasha sitting patiently, waiting, and Cole knew she chirped expectantly, poised for flight once more. 'Strange, she's normally like clockwork on the return journey.'

'Look,' Siphiwe pointed to the section of the road further away.

Cole's body chilled.

*　*　*

Mackenzie heard the vehicle coming up behind her and checked on the road to make sure she was well within the emergency lane. As it whooshed past, the minibus taxi driver hooted madly.

One thing she'd learnt early since coming to South Africa was to never catch a local taxi. The emergence of 'Black Taxis', as they used to be called, began way back during the apartheid era, when the lack of public buses available to transport the black and Indian population created a thriving enterprise for private buses for the masses. The minibuses began transporting people around the countryside and through the cities faster, and were more accessible than the government buses.

The convenience of this style of transport was that they could stop anywhere, not just in the government-designated bus stops. So like a taxi, it could be hailed anywhere along its set journey, but you got to share your ride with many others, all going to a similar destination. The taxi drivers catered for their clients by starting routes where government buses wouldn't travel, and they would travel more often, usually for a fee not much more than the bus. Drivers would load as many people into their vehicles to make a maximum profit. The black taxi trade had flourished, a cash-based business that wasn't policed much, and many taxi owners became very wealthy.

Although the government changed, the taxis remained. Along with the overcrowding, the excessive speed and the violent wars that occurred between the different carriers over the routes that each person was allowed to take. It was safer to hire a car, or better still, buy one. The newer taxis that had been rolled out were much safer than the older-style Hi-ace buses, and they were better maintained to a point, or so everyone told her, but the lawlessness of the drivers was still a problem.

She wasn't comfortable with a minibus this close to her. Like the territory disputes of the gangs in America, the shadow of corruption and greed had contaminated the village. Just the week before there had been a shooting in Crystalberg between two rival taxi owners. The townsfolk said it was a 'faction fight', a 'tribal squabble', and she needed to be careful for a while when cycling outside the town. She shivered despite the sweat dripping from her. She had waited a week, but now she was out again, experiencing freedom. She would never be a competitive professional athlete, but she loved being fit, keeping her body supple, and it felt good to be exercising after she spent so many hours indoors on her art.

The wind cooled her skin and the stiffness eased from her legs as it worked its way from her system. Back up to twenty-five kilometres per hour. Training speed.

She saw that the taxi had pulled onto the curb, sitting half in the emergency lane just ahead. The driver hooted as she passed, the loud blast unnatural in the quiet bush. Ignoring it, she carried on pedalling. Within moments she heard the vehicle behind her. Revving, then slowing. Revving again, all the while hooting. Panic began to eat at her. She dropped a gear and pedalled faster, moving closer to the edge of the road to give them more space to overtake.

The taxi kept pace, harassing her by coming closer. It backed off slightly and then came alongside her. Its windows were tinted dark. The idiot passenger reached out his arm and attempted to push her off her bike.

Her heart thumped in her chest, every breath burning as she inhaled the acid taste of her own fear. She sneaked a quick look at him. His front teeth were missing and his tongue wagged out of his lips like a dog, and a multicoloured Rastafarian-style hat held back his dreadlocks. Heavy bass boomed from the open window. She shuddered.

She'd heard stories of women being raped and killed just for being in the wrong place at the wrong time. Of taxis that had stopped to help women change flat tyres, who then robbed them and left them on the side of the road, beaten …

Shit, she was in trouble.

Mackenzie knew the worst thing she could do was stop, so instead she looked forward. She could not afford to panic.

Her best course was to get to safety. She had to keep calm. She swallowed the saliva in her mouth but almost choked on the terror as it stuck in her throat. She took a deep breath through her nose, blowing it out of her mouth, slowly squeezing shut the lid on her panic.

If she pedalled flat out for Cole's cheetah rescue centre and reached it before the taxi got to her, she could find refuge there once again.

They had first met a year ago when she had sought sanctuary from a storm in the entrance to his wildlife rescue centre. He'd driven his *bakkie* to the gate to invite her into his ranch to shelter in comfort. When she'd declined he'd stayed with her and they had waited out the storm in his *bakkie*, talking not like strangers but friends. Sometime during the storm she'd asked him to respect her privacy and keep his distance and she was surprised later when he'd done as she'd asked. When the lightning had passed and the thunder had rolled away down the mountains, she'd left.

The ranch buildings weren't yet in sight but she knew she was close. The way was flat, not uphill, so she could increase her speed.

She knew the taxi would maintain its speed, but the closer she got the better chance she had. It might work if she pushed herself enough, gave it everything she had and somehow avoided being shoved off her bike. The game guard at the gate was armed. If she could get into his sight, he would notice her, perhaps call for help, and the taxi would back off and leave her alone.

Her hands worked the gears carefully, trying to reach the maximum speed. Flattening her body into the silver metal, she wished this once she had a mountain bike instead of a road one, which meant she couldn't even attempt anything cross-country. She put her life into cycling as fast as she could back towards the ranch. She zigzagged across the road, trying to keep the taxi behind her. She glanced up to check her distance to the entrance.

She tried to remember where he was that morning, if she'd waved at him? Close to the visitors' centre or far away? She couldn't recall. Perhaps he had been watching for her from somewhere on his farm.

She shook her head, thinking of how ridiculous she had been all those months ago when at first she hadn't waved back. Then he had stopped waving. She'd missed it. So she'd begun to greet him once her race with the beautiful cheetah was over.

Maybe he'd see her now and realise that she was in trouble.

If she could only get to his gates …

Suddenly, the taxi was next to her again, and the passenger lunged out of the window and pushed her, hard. The road swayed in front of her, and she knew she was losing her balance. Instead of falling, she let go of her handlebars as she felt her bike and her body part ways. Ducking her head in, she rolled in the grass as she had been taught at the Taekwondo lessons her mother had insisted she take as a child.

When the world righted again, she saw the passenger scrambling down the small incline of the road towards her. Re-orientating herself after the tumble, she glanced around for a weapon of any sort to help her gain an advantage.

Nothing. Not even a rock.

She ran up the small incline for a firmer footing, and to distance herself from him and the taxi. He followed and came barrelling towards her. Holding her upper position, she gave him a round-house kick in the stomach. He reeled backwards. She went in with a triple punch, and then stepped back, creating space. She flexed her hands, her knuckles burning from the solid impact. Her breathing was deep, mostly even, despite the terror she felt. Years of training had made her think: assess the situation. React. Remain in control.

If he couldn't get to her, he couldn't rape her. She drew her right foot backwards, positioned her hands defensively in front of her body and centred herself. Ready to strike.

He straightened and spoke to her in an African language she didn't recognise before lunging again.

She knew how to do this if she could just stay calm. She knew martial arts and could defend herself in a fight.

An upper-cut punch to his jaw, then a step back and another roundhouse kick. This time to his crotch, and a knuckle smash to his throat to stop him.

He didn't even get to hit her or grab at her clothes. He clutched his throat and dropped to his knees.

One down.

The driver was out of the vehicle and pointing a gun at her.

Shit. If these men got her into that taxi, she was dead.

She backed away, putting distance between her and them.

She stared at the driver. He wasn't tall, he was just an average build, yet his arms spoke of an unnatural strength from hard physical work, muscles that could sustain a lot of strain. His skin was a lighter brown than the Sotho and Xhosa peoples in the area, like a cappuccino. The expression on his face held total contempt for her. As if just having her share the same air hurt his nose. His lips were over-full and he had a deep scar under the left eye on his cheekbone. He face was smooth and his hair was knotted into knobs around his head, like the spikes of an old-fashioned war club.

He was her superior in the muscles department. And he had a gun. She crouched down and grabbed a handful of gravel from beside the road, her nails scratching in the rough. It was time to run and keep running.

Mackenzie threw the gravel into the driver's face, turned and gave her last ounce of energy into running away from him towards the ranch entrance. Her martial arts trainer's voice echoed inside her head: *Move. Just move.* A moving target is harder to hit and the odds of a shot in a vital organ were small.

Without warning, all hell broke loose around her as shots were fired. The noise was deafening as if they came right over her head. She ran faster.

She heard the taxi start up, revving madly and smelt burnt rubber as the driver dropped the clutch in his haste to get moving. As she glanced over her shoulder she could see the taxi's taillights retreating. She looked forward again – Cole's distinctive safari vehicle was hurtling towards her. She slowed her retreat and faced her saviour.

She saw Cole step out of his vehicle before it had stopped, and run towards her.

'It's okay, we saw. You did well. You're safe now, Mackenzie, you're safe, I've got you,' he said, as he reached for her.

'That taxi,' she said, when it hit her.

It was over. Cole had her wrapped in his strong arms. She was safe.

Relief flooded through her and all the oxygen was sucked from her lungs. She pulled away from him, fighting with the strap as she undid her helmet and let it fall to the ground just as her vision blurred. Then she bent over and began to retch. She couldn't stop as huge heaves of acid bile mixed with her breakfast spewed up, over and over.

Eventually, she realised that Cole's leather boots were still standing next to hers, splashed with vomit, as he continued to gently pat her back in comfort. Mackenzie fought back tears and thanked all the gods in the universe that she was not dead.

'Hi, Mac. You are okay now, I've got you,' Cole said and she saw his teeth flash in his handsome face.

'Hi, yourself,' she said, and attempted to return the smile, but grimaced instead as panic set back in and her stomach clenched. Bile rose in her throat again.

'I'm going to—'

'No you won't, there's nothing left in your stomach. You're going to be okay. It's the down after the adrenaline rush.'

Yeah right! She could feel a little more now, comprehending her situation. Cole, the rancher, was still patting her back with one hand, and the other was securely holding her under her arm.

'You can relax. I'll take you back to *nTabaGrequa*, let you catch your breath, okay?'

'Sure.' Her voice came out breathless and not at all as she wanted it to. She cleared her throat. 'I mean, sure,' she repeated bravely, but she couldn't stop the trembling that rattled her teeth.

'You okay to walk?' Cole asked.

She blinked and broke contact with his eyes first, before taking a deep inhale of fresh air. 'Yeah, I'm good.'

His hands immediately dropped away. She missed their strength and the warmth, but acknowledged silently that once again, Cole was being the perfect gentleman. Her pounding heart missed a beat, the same as it had the first time she'd had the pleasure of meeting him.

She needed to swallow her fear and move on as fast as she could, and to that end she would need to get home.

'Thank you for coming to help. Again,' she said.

'No problem. Next time you want to start a war with a taxi, can you at least do it in a car?'

'I didn't start it. He did,' she protested, and glared at him when she realised he was joking, having seen his raised eyebrows and lop-sided smile lurking on his weather-beaten face.

'Ah, it's always the man's fault!' he added, laughing softly. Turning towards his *bakkie*, he said, 'Mackenzie, meet Siphiwe, game guard, and the good shot who chased off your new friends.'

Mackenzie extended her hand up towards the black one reaching down from the back of the safari vehicle. 'Thank you.'

He nodded, then took her hand firmly in both of his and shook it in a traditional greeting. 'Miss Mackenzie.'

'Come on, let's load your bike up and go home,' Cole said.

She watched silently as Siphiwe, with his rifle hanging from his shoulder, jumped down and was soon carrying her helmet and bike towards the vehicle, lifting the bike as if it was as light as a child's tricycle. The front tyre had buckled. Her heart sank at seeing her new bike mangled.

'We can straighten the wheel and buff the scratches. Make it shine again, Miss Mackenzie,' Siphiwe said.

'Thanks for the offer, but really it's too much trouble. I can take it back to the bike shop ...' she faltered as she noticed Cole had the truck car door held open for her.

'Use the step to get in.' His hand lingered near her back, but he didn't touch her as she would've expected. Once she was seated inside, he closed the door firmly, and walked around to the driver's side. She watched him, admiring the slight swagger and the way he moved, as supple as his big cats. She shivered again. If he hadn't come what would have happened?

What if she had taken a bullet? She ran her hand through her hair and noticed that it was unsteady. She knew that she could have died.

Only once before had she known the type of fear associated with being shot at. Of trying to do anything to keep alive. Only this time, the outcome had been different. There had been no death. She took in a deep breath and exhaled slowly, controlling her breathing.

Cole started the engine. Shaking his head, he put on his indicators, executed a neat U-turn and headed back towards the ranch. 'You sure you're alright?'

'Yeah, I'm good. I was a little overwhelmed, but I'm almost back to normal. Sorry for—'

'Don't you dare apologise,' he cut in, his voice a little louder than necessary. 'You fought like a wildcat there and were holding your own against that taxi gang. You did great!'

She swallowed her words and kept quiet, keeping her hands together to try to stop the shake. Logically, she knew it was probably a simple case of a taxi-war turf dispute, but she feared it was something more. That despite being out of the media for two years, someone was trying to put her back in the spotlight, creating their own headline news with her as the subject. The possibility of having the media interested in her life again terrified her. She sniffed, trying to control the dread racing through her veins, trying hard to quieten the illogical side of her brain's reasoning, because she knew that after all this time, the likelihood of it being anything media related was zero.

Despite the warmness outside, Cole switched on the heater and turned up the fan to blow on her. She almost put her hands out to receive the hot air like one would to a fire.

Cole asked, 'What the hell happened that a minibus was after you?'

She glared at him before she answered. 'Nothing. I swear. I'd stopped because I saw a blue *duiker*, and the taxi passed me. When I came around the next corner it was waiting. I was riding to your ranch for safety when you came to the rescue.'

'I'll call the police when we get back to *nTabaGrequa*.'

'Don't worry about that. No real harm's been done. Just my pride's as dented as my bike, that's all. I probably owe you a new pair of boots.'

'They'll come clean, don't worry about them, they have seen much worse. I've got to report the incident. Neighbours will've heard the shots, they echo off the mountains. They'll wonder what's happening.'

Uneasiness made her sit upright. Making herself taller for the fight that was about to come. Cole could unintentionally expose her real identity. If people knew who she was, then her anonymity would be shattered into a billion pieces. And this time, she might not survive the three-ringed media circus. Choosing her words with infinite care, she asked, 'Can you leave me out of the call? Like not mention me at all?'

'Why?'

'I don't need to attract any unwanted attention. In this town they already call me the cuckoo American on the hill. Can't you make something up about why you were shooting at the taxi? Please.'

He lapsed into silence for a moment, as if contemplating her request.

She knew it was a huge ask for him to lie for her, but she'd told the truth. Police involvement meant having the town know more about her, and essentially she had done everything she could so that no one related her to her famous husband or parents.

She kept her distance from everyone in the small town, and knew she had the reputation of the loner American. Watching life from a distance and not getting involved was hard, but it had given her a new edge in her art. Her productivity was high and she poured every bit of emotion into her bronze statues instead. Being friends with anyone would have meant potentially exposing them to the world she had left behind.

The unnatural silence was making her sweat. 'Please?' Even to her own ears, her words sounded pathetic. She remembered the last time she had pleaded with her own father to get the media to respect her privacy, but it hadn't changed the outcome. Her father had been too filled with pride to believe that he'd made a mistake, that his judgement was off-centre. All media was good for a politician, he'd said, and she just needed to grin and bear it. Her father had turned away from her when she'd needed him. When she'd needed his power he hadn't wielded it and stopped the media from stalking her.

Now she didn't trust easily. She worried that she didn't know Cole well enough, and that he would probably do the same if he knew who she was. He might think publicity for his centre was worth the loss of her newfound freedom. Her independence.

She took a deep breath, waiting.

'No problem, I'll think of something. Here we are,' he said, as they turned into the front gate of the cheetah rescue centre.

She looked out the window. The guard on the gate smiled widely at her and said, 'Hello.'

'He-ll-o,' she stammered, still stunned that Cole was going to conceal her involvement. She looked past him, through the high electric fence to the beautiful spotted cheetah still peering in the opposite direction, as if waiting for something. She could hear a *chirp-chirp* sound, almost bird-like, but foreign to her ears.

Cole said, 'Sasha's waiting for your return, she's calling to you.'

It was so ironic. Here a cheetah waited for her to finish her race, full of life and vitality, welcoming her in its life. But in her world, there was only emptiness.

CHAPTER

2

The visitors' centre was a rustic African-style building that appeared to sprawl across the front section of the property, its large thatched roof dominating the architecture.

'Come on, if you can't race Sasha today, at least you can come and meet her. After we call the police from the office,' Cole said as he switched off the engine of his *bakkie*.

'Do we have to, can't it wait?' Mackenzie asked.

'It will only take a minute, don't stress about it. Do you know that yesterday you raced Bartholomew, and the day before Nama had his turn? That's who started racing with you. You've pretty much raced all the cheetahs here old enough to run.'

'You're kidding, right? You change them? I thought it was always the same one!'

He shook his head with a grin. 'It's good exercise, and they all love you already, so come on in and meet a few of my kitty-cats.'

She smiled then and opened her door. How could she resist? Slowly, she clambered out of the high Toyota 4x4, and within moments, Cole's hand was there, reaching out to her in a welcoming fashion.

She looked at his hand and knew she'd reached a crossroad. It had become so hard to remain divorced from society. It was hard to live in a void, closed off from human interaction. After her experience today, she really could use someone to share her life with. To live life with again.

She put her hand inside his large callused one and felt his fingers close gently over hers. Her gaze drew up his body, across his broad chest, over the khaki shirt he wore, up to his tanned face, and looked into his green eyes. He was at least six-foot-two compared to her five-nine.

The fear evaporated and a new sense of awareness settled around her. She stared at him, her curiosity piqued. Her skin broke out in goosebumps, and her breathing deepened, but it was a natural awareness, not only an attraction for the handsome man standing in front of her. A sensation of rightness and safety.

She blinked, trying to shake off the rush of emotions, as they stood together in the centre of the cheetah reserve.

She watched him smile, the slow curve of his lips that spread to his eyes and revealed the small dimples in his cheeks. *Stupid, romantic fool*, she chided herself. *The man should package that smile and sell it*, was her first thought, *man-oh-man I wish I could sculpt it*, was her next.

'Thanks,' she said, and they started to talk at the same time.

Mackenzie felt herself blush, a hot flush that heated the slopes of her breasts and ran up past her neck, across her face.

'Come on, my centre office is this way, and Sasha awaits,' he said, breaking the tension, and tugged her along behind him.

She entered the busy visitors' centre, walking next to Cole. She noticed the reception area with the rustic wooden counter, a mounted cheetah behind it. She shuddered to think that while a member of their family was stuffed and put on display, just on the other side of the wood, real cats lived and breathed. The stuffed cheetah's eyes followed her as she crossed the room. The hair on her arms rippled, uneasiness settling in her belly. She glanced at the cheetah again, its eyes unchanged. The dead cat was creeping her out.

The general noise of the tourists buzzed around her as she followed Cole past the leather chairs and benches that provided the day-trippers a place to rest and enjoy the hospitality of the restaurant to the right. The cold stone floor squeaked as her trainers walked on it, its glossy finish astounding, considering the number of tourists she knew visited the centre. Unconsciously, she looked behind to see if she'd left footprints. It was an eerie feeling walking down the long corridor, and she was glad that Cole walked purposely beside her.

They turned into a doorway that had a sign on it – 'No Admittance. Staff Only'.

'Here you go,' Cole said, keying in the combination to the locked door. While she waited, she looked upwards. A moth flew inside the cathedral space above the fluorescent light, making shadows dance across the black creosote rafters of the roof, and further on to the natural grass thatch. The coolness of the centre surrounded her. Goosebumps formed on her arms and legs. She rubbed her arms vigorously.

'You cold?' Cole asked.

'A little, but I'm blaming these goosies on that dead cheetah in reception. Please tell me it wasn't you who had a taxidermist stuff it and make it into a display item? What about the cheetahs that see it, doesn't it upset them, too?'

'Never me. Digger died of natural causes about twenty years ago. He was already stuffed when I bought him from a collector. He's used extensively in the educational program in the schools and villages around here, as it's easier than taking a live cheetah in for the first few trips, until everyone is settled with the idea. Then we introduce an ambassador cheetah for them to stroke and form a connection. We've found that once they've met one in person they are a lot more enthusiastic in supporting the anti-poaching programs.'

'It's actually really amazing that you do that, but he seems to watch you as you walk through reception.'

'It's the glass eyes. The taxidermist who mounted him was renowned for his ability to make wildlife appear alive.' He pushed open a door on the left that said, 'Private Keep Out'. 'Do you need something warm? I have a jacket hanging up here.'

She shook her head as she looked around his impressive office. It looked out through a large glass wall at the cheetahs on the other side, and was decorated in a contemporary theme of white and black. Lots of overhead light accompanied the natural light streaming in from the window. The large, overstuffed black leather couch to one side suited the man perfectly. His enormous mahogany desk, which was obviously an antique, dominated the room, despite the white built-in shelving units and cupboards, and the white tiled floor.

She stood as she listened to Cole talking in an African language on the phone, then he hung up.

'The Police Member in Charge isn't there, I'll chat to him later. Now, we were on our way to meet Sasha, get you outside and back in the warm sunshine,' he said as they walked out of his office, bypassing the centre reception this time, with its busloads of noisy schoolchildren and tourists visiting with the ambassador cats, those that were tame and on leashes, interacting with the humans.

They turned down another passage and out of the side of the centre. The path led directly to the cheetah pens. She twirled around, getting her bearings. They were between the main road and the centre itself.

'This way,' Cole said, making his way to the furthest enclosure. 'I'll enter first because she'll get a bit excited, then you come in when I say it's alright.'

She watched as he unlocked the gate. The cheetah that she had seen at the other end of the enclosure ran across and jumped on Cole.

'Heel,' he instructed and gestured for her to sit down next to him.

Mackenzie held her breath as the huge cat dropped to the ground, and as he fussed her, she turned over for her tummy to be rubbed.

'You can come in now,' he said. 'Just make sure the gate latches closed after you.'

She entered, and shook the gate to make sure it was secured.

'Come sit next to me,' Cole said. 'She won't hurt you, she'll be curious at first, and try to make friends with you.'

She crept nearer to him, and then sat crossed-legged beside him. The cheetah got up from where she was and came to say hello to her. Face to face with Sasha, Mackenzie lifted her hands and touched the coarse fur. It felt smooth as she stroked the cat.

Sasha took a step forward and butted her head into Mackenzie's, and began purring. Loudly.

'Oh my God, she's just like an overgrown house cat,' Mackenzie said.

Sasha sat down in front of Mackenzie and rubbed her head against hers.

Cole leaned over and blew in Sasha's face as she attempted to lick Mackenzie's. 'Go on, get out of here.' The cheetah moved her head and continued to sniff at Mackenzie. 'Don't let her lick you. The first few times it's nice, in a painful, sandpaper-taking-your-skin-off type of way, but then it gets really sore. Sasha was born right here, and I'll be using her for my breeding program soon. Nama is her father.'

Mackenzie reached out her hand again to stroke the cat, and she continued to pet the cheetah for a little while, before noticing that Cole was quiet. He'd shifted his position, and now lay on the ground, with his legs stretched out in front of him, crossed over at the ankles. Breaking the silence would be hard, because she knew what was coming. No way could anyone not want their own curiosity satisfied.

Cole smiled. 'I always visit my cats to get rid of the stress. They're soothing, just being around them, having them come and talk to me, to touch them. It's as if what happens outside of the gates doesn't matter anymore. As long as they're well, and their warm bodies press into mine, everything's forgotten, and I relax.'

She looked at him lounging on the dirt patch, his eyes greener than the grass around them. She could no more read his eyes now than a year ago, when she'd first met him.

Her hopes of perhaps getting out of the pen without a question session reached as high as the trees that shaded part of the enclosure. He didn't seem to want to talk about her incident with the taxi, but just forget about it. She shivered.

'Still cold?'

'No, someone just walked over my grave.'

In the silence that followed she could hear the deep purring of Sasha as she lay down flat, putting her head on Mackenzie's feet the moment she changed her position, as if they were a pillow. Looking down at the cheetah, she smiled.

Cole gazed out of the cage, into the distance for a long while, before he reached over and gently put his hand on hers. 'I'm here if you need someone to help or to talk.'

'I can't. Because—' She stumbled in her excuse.

He let go of her hand to fuss Sasha, who was now attempting to sit on his lap.

Oxygen rushed into her lungs in a quick breath. She wasn't aware exactly when she stopped breathing. 'I can't tell you. I can't involve you.'

He shook his head. 'I think you should give me the benefit this time of allowing me to make that decision. A year ago, you told me I didn't have a choice, I needed to stay away from you. Keep a distance, and I did. Today, that changed. Seeing you fight a man larger than you, seeing you in danger, I had no choice. I had to get involved. I had to help you, and I think that deep in here,' he pointed to her chest, 'you know it, too. That's why you were trying to get to my ranch, to safety. Mistakes are made in life, they can't always be erased, but they are not necessarily always bad, and can often be fixed.'

'Have you ever made a mistake?' she asked.

'Plenty! Who hasn't?'

'The type that will never go away, but be with you always?'

He stared at her. 'A few. I no longer allow them to dictate my life.' He lifted her hand to his mouth and dropped a light kiss on the back. 'Let me in, Mackenzie. I can't stand here waving daily to you as you cycle past and not be allowed to at least be a friend.'

She looked at him. He was so gorgeous, such a man's man. He would be at home on the cover of any magazine, so strong, and yet he had just asked her to be his friend. Not 'tell me what is going on'. Not demanding, just a simple statement that had broken her heart even more.

She wanted to tell him. She wanted to scream about the injustice of life.

She might have been born with a silver spoon in her mouth, but growing up in Texas hadn't been easy. Growing up as 'the state's darling' under a microscope had been hard. Yet she had survived it, but losing her husband, Sebastian, had nearly killed her. The media hype and reading about it every day in the news, seeing his death replayed again and again on the television, had almost destroyed her soul.

Walking away, leaving that life behind, had been the only way she knew of keeping herself sane. Starting a new life far away from her high-profile family had seemed like a good idea, but two years later it felt like forever since she had spoken to her mom. She couldn't remember when she'd last talked to her dad, and although they knew she was safe and in South Africa, she had never told them where she lived. She was not ready to lose her newfound freedom that she had taken such steps to gain.

And there was no way she was going back to the United States.

She had found a place where she felt comfortable with who she was. Far away enough from the big cities and their absurdly high crime rates, but still within driving distance of a decent airport in case she wanted to flee. Far away from the five-star hotels that she would have frequented once, and the ball gowns of the political world, far from the glittering red-carpet world of Sebastian's, where fans screamed and the music ruled the night, to the quietness of the mountains. The tranquillity of nature and the preciousness of being alone.

So what if she had to remain aloof so that the town never found out who she once was. This way they would all be spared the cameras and the reporters who could descend on them if they knew she now lived there. True, they had lost interest in her, but she didn't want to do anything to reignite that type of scrutiny ever again.

She couldn't let anyone know how she wanted the man in front of her so badly that she dreamt of him nightly. A year ago it had been too much, too soon after losing Sebastian to begin any relationship, but now she knew she was just hiding behind her widow's robes. She was comfortable with her new life and uncertain of how to merge the two halves of herself back together.

Cole looked at her. 'You know, whatever it is, it's easier to face it with someone by your side than alone, less scary and certainly more fun.'

She smiled.

He hesitated for a moment, then spoke. 'Come on, let me introduce you to my other babies, they all want to meet you.' He pushed at Sasha, who resisted him at first, before relinquishing his lap and standing up.

Mackenzie looked deep into his eyes. When she really looked, they held sincerity, promise and wariness, but they held something else, too. Passion and lust. Her breathing shortened. Suddenly, his eyes cleared and were unreadable again. Guarded.

'When we're finished, I'll give you a ride home,' he said.

'Thank you, but no. I really appreciate the offer, but I'll be fine.'

'Don't be stubborn. Anyway, your bike's in no state to ride.'

'I'm not stubborn—'

'You are,' he said.

When she saw his smile widen, she let out a sigh of relief. Her green-eyed guardian hunk was fast becoming in danger of also becoming her hero.

Give it up, Ms Independence! she chided herself silently. Cole had already twice stepped in to rescue her, maybe this one time she would let him help. After all, it was a long walk back into town.

'You're right, I'm being stubborn. I'll accept the offer, thanks. Perhaps you'll come in and I can cook dinner, as a way for me to say thank you for today, to begin again, to a newer type of friendship?' she said, her voice quiet.

'It'll be my pleasure,' he said with a cheeky grin that set his dimples showing.

CHAPTER

3

Two weeks later, Mackenzie watched the arrivals board at King Shaka Airport. The brand-new airport at La Mercy on the north side of Durban had replaced the older Louis Botha Airport just before the 2010 Soccer World Cup. She had spent some time looking at the beautiful work of sculptor Andries Botha that graced the outside entrance. Admiring the formidable *nguni* cattle, knowing that once King Shaka's bronze had stood there, too, but had been removed within a month of the installation for depicting the king as a herd boy. She still didn't understand a lot of the internal politics of the South Africans, how King Shaka had been immortalised in bronze and yet removed because the current Zulu king didn't want him standing there. But she did understand Africa time, and as usual, there was a delay with the incoming flight from Cape Town.

She noticed the mechanical *tick-tick* of the clock above the general quietness as she waited. She stood up, arched her sore back, and sat down in the overused seating area once more. She smoothed her hand over her stomach again, adjusting her T-shirt over her jeans, and resumed her people watching.

A man with an overloaded trolley emerged from behind the glass partition, and as he came inside the stainless-steel barrier, he was mobbed by four suddenly really loud children and a wife who looked relieved that he was there. Harassed by the energy that bubbled freely from the four of them. The man's face was filled with awe and delight at seeing his children, and when he got a chance to hug his wife, he closed his eyes as if he had finally arrived home.

Mackenzie smiled. She should have averted her eyes from the private moment, but she didn't, instead she pulled her sketchbook out of her oversized bag and quickly drew the reunion. Her hand flew across the page, the pencil shading in areas swiftly so she didn't lose the image from her mind. She wanted to capture the expressions on their faces.

'Still stealing people's souls in your art?' Lauren's voice came over her shoulder. 'Just as good as ever, I see.'

Mackenzie clamped her pad and pencil to her chest and jumped up to greet her long-time friend, who was now her art agent. 'Lauren! So great to see you.'

They hugged each other. Eventually, Lauren stepped back. Still holding Mackenzie's hand, she looked her up and down. 'Wow, look at you! You look about twenty-two instead of thirty-two. South Africa suits you!'

'Thanks, but believe me I feel every day over thirty.'

Lauren raised one perfectly manicured eyebrow.

'Okay, I'll admit it, I'm alive and free and loving this place. It's so filled with inspiration,' Mackenzie said as she put her sketchpad away in her bag. Then she looked at her friend. A grey pencil mark was drawn onto her white blouse. The mark looked out of place on the perfectly groomed lady.

'I'm sorry, I've drawn on you,' Mackenzie said.

Lauren dabbed at it half-heartedly. 'It'll come out in the wash. Truly, it's fabulous to see you at last.'

'Madam, I push your trolley?' A young black man had appeared at Lauren's elbow and was attempting to take control of her luggage trolley from her. His body odour was so ripe that Lauren let go of the trolley and put her hand over her nose to block it out.

'*Tjhee. Tjhee. Ke a leboha,*' Mackenzie said, reaching for the unmanned trolley. The boy looked at her in defiance at first, but she stood her ground. Defeated, he left the trolley and moved towards the next tourist coming from behind the partition.

'What did you say to him? He seemed to move on quickly enough.'

'Just that we would manage. I've learnt a few words in Zulu and Sotho since coming here. These boys have been known to steal tourists' luggage. I know they need work, but they will rip you off as swiftly as you can blink. But don't think I don't feel for them,' Mackenzie said. 'They need work and they are trying hard, but because of a few *skabengas*, they all get tarred with the same brush and not trusted. Seriously though, we can manage your bags.'

'Oh my, he could've done with some deodorant,' Lauren said, fanning her face.

Mackenzie shook her head. 'Get used to it, this is South Africa. Body odour is part of the charm.'

Lauren grinned. 'I'll remember to carry smelling salts then, just in case.'

Mackenzie laughed. Lauren had always been like this, filled with energy, with a go-get-everything spirit. They had known each other since they were kids, and while Mackenzie had the slim figure of an athlete, Lauren was more curvy, and dressed to accentuate that rather than her lack of height. Her long brown hair was highlighted with multiple colours, which turned heads in a conservative country like South Africa. Her thick midnight-blue-rimmed square glasses made her look businesslike and intelligent, rather than nerdy.

Lauren had intelligence in spades. She had spent countless hours helping Mackenzie with her homework while they were in school and university, never letting her quit, and it was that same determination that had propelled her forward in the art world. She instinctively knew the difference between good and excellent art, the art you could hang the huge price tags off in any gallery around the world. It was why she was Mackenzie's agent and the second reason for her visit.

Mackenzie felt a flutter in her belly thinking of the new collection she so wanted to share with Lauren before anyone else.

Soon they were on the road.

'So how far is the drive to Crystalberg?' Lauren asked.

'It's only two hours and forty-five minutes usually, but we'll stop outside Pietermaritzburg for some dinner before it gets dark. There's a nice little stop just off the beaten track that has the most amazing meat pies, and for your vegetarian self, spinach and cheese that you will adore, the pastry is just perfect. And they serve it with gravy and fries, although they call them chips here, and a salad.'

'Pies? Fries? Seriously? I'm here on holiday, but I can't go back looking like a horse. You know pies will go right to the hips,' Lauren said.

'Believe me, with what I have planned for you to do, there'll be nothing sticking to your hips.'

Lauren shook her head. 'No. No cycling for me. I'm not going anywhere except maybe walking from your lounge to your pool, hopefully with a cocktail in hand!'

'You haven't changed at all, you know that? It's a bit cold for the pool, it's winter, and some mornings we have ice around the rim.'

'Thanks for the warning. I see lots of change in you though. You're so much more confident, more independent, and just look at these wheels. You drive a huge 4x4, and it rocks. The Mackenzie I know would've driven a Smart car to conserve gas and save the environment.'

'I know, so much has changed, and for the better. A lovely little Smart car isn't really practical here, a ton of art supplies doesn't fit on the roof, and I sometimes have to drive quite a distance to get those. I know that Thomas here will never let me down. I can load him up, and this baby eats the kilometres up easily, and safely, loaded or unloaded. My Toyota Hilux was a sound investment.'

Lauren grinned.

Mackenzie negotiated traffic out of Durban and then up through spaghetti junction, and then they were on the N3 freeway.

An hour later, Mackenzie took the turn-off into Pietermaritz-burg, and stopped outside a shop that proudly stated 'Bake House' on its roof. 'We're here.'

The coolness of an inland winter kissed Mackenzie as she jumped out of her *bakkie*. 'You'll love the food. I just need to move your cases inside the cab, so they're safe.'

'Right,' Lauren said as she helped with her larger bag. 'Now that's done, hit me with dinner, I'm ready to experience it all!'

Mackenzie threaded her arm through Lauren's and they walked into the shop arm in arm.

They were seated outside near an outdoor heater, and while they waited for their order, they watched the sky turn from brilliant blue, to deeper azure, and finally to black as night-time quickly took over, the birds noisy as they found roosts within the trees.

'Already this place is surprising me. I never thought of it getting dark so early here. It's like five o'clock, and the sun just went down. For some reason when I think of you here in South Africa I always see you in sunshine. I know it's logical, winter, cooler temperatures and darker earlier in the day, similar climate to Buenos Aires, but in reality it's all so different to anywhere, isn't it?' Lauren said.

'It is, but it's beautiful. Africa gets under your skin, give it some time,' Mackenzie said.

'If it changes me at all in the same direction as you, I'm going to enjoy these next three months with you, enormously.'

Their dinner arrived.

'*Siyabonga*,' Mackenzie said as the waiter put their plates on the table. She watched Lauren tuck into her food, and she followed suit, realising that she was in fact starving, having eaten nothing since breakfast.

'This was worth stopping for. This pie is amazing and the fries are perfect,' Lauren said, pushing her salad to the side of her plate.

'Told you!' Mackenzie said, sounding like a five-year-old. 'There are a few places that you can eat at all the time, and the food is fabulous. You can also get really sick if you eat at the wrong place, like from a street vendor at a market.'

'I take it that one is from experience?'

'Oh yes. When I first got here I moved around a lot, and I ate at all sorts of places, but food from a street vendor in Port Elizabeth almost made me admit myself into hospital. Never again.'

'Lesson learnt?' Lauren said with a laugh.

'Oh yes,' Mackenzie said, nodding.

They sipped their after-dinner coffees in silence and watched the other patrons as they came in and out of the busy takeaway area that was attached to the shop.

'You must be dead on your feet,' Mackenzie said.

'Actually, I slept really well on the plane. I'm dying to see your house and what you've done in your artworks. Itching to see it!'

'Well then I'll pay and we are out of here. We've still got nearly two hours to drive.'

After dinner they rearranged the suitcases again and climbed into the *bakkie*.

'Crystalberg here we come,' Mackenzie said.

'You sound like you love it here.'

'I do. At the moment, I don't think anything could drag me back to the US,' Mackenzie said, and she meant it.

Lauren stretched her neck to the right, then back to the centre and left again. A loud popping sound echoed in the front of the *bakkie*.

'Can't believe you're still doing that after all these years. I'm surprised you don't have to wear a collar and aren't crippled from arthritis!' Mackenzie said.

Lauren smiled. 'I still can't believe I'm here at last. That you finally caved and let me visit. It's been too long since—'

'You didn't really give me much choice.'

'I would've come earlier, you know. I would've come with you for the adventure when you first moved if you had let me,' Lauren said.

'I know, but I was so paranoid about the media hounding me, and photographing my new life for the front pages of some tabloid magazine. I needed to do it alone, for the peace, the space.'

'And no one deserves it more than you. So tell me about your new pieces of art. I'm sure that those pictures you sent me don't do them justice, as usual.'

'I can't be good at everything, and while I can capture pictures in my camera, I feel things in my art. So there is a difference,' Mackenzie said as a car drove close up behind them, and flashed its lights on high beams.

'Shit, just wait, you can't pass here, it's a blind rise,' she said, and put her foot on the accelerator to try to get to the passing space she knew was coming up. Despite the double white line with the red cat's eyes, the taxi flew past and weaved back into the correct lane, before quickly picking up speed again.

'Idiot!' Mackenzie cursed, and then let out a sigh of relief.

'Impatient, aren't they?'

'You have no idea. Taxi drivers here are madder than in New York.'

Lauren watched her friend. 'There were no markings on it, how do you know that was a taxi?'

'Most minibuses here are taxis, and they cause more traffic accidents and kill more people than anyone else on the roads. The buses have an overloading problem, but it's the taxis that help add to the almighty death toll in this country each year.'

'Noted. Don't get in a taxi here. But there's more to your reaction. I've seen you in worse traffic than this and your hands are shaking. This is about the attack? Do you need to pull over? I can drive.'

'I'll be fine, anyway we can never pull over on this stretch. There's a shack town just to the right here so it's not safe,' Mackenzie said, hugging herself with one arm, before returning it to the steering wheel. 'You're right. It's all about that attack. It's about realising that despite my newfound independence, I'm still not in control. It's about having to rely on Cole and Siphiwe to save me, and it's about ... I've just been uneasy around taxis since the incident.'

Lauren reached over and squeezed Mackenzie's arm. 'I'm glad you told me about it, and I'm glad I insisted on coming. I needed the holiday, I needed to see for myself that you were okay. So, who are Cole and Sipi …?'

'Cole and his game guard Siphiwe. Remember I told you Cole owns the cheetah rescue centre.'

'Right. Him. You know we should've spoken more about him on the phone. The way you say his name, I take it you like him?'

'I do,' Mackenzie said. 'The whole fiasco with having my line bugged after Sebastian died has tainted me against using a phone. And I guess towards the media in general, too.'

'You know, after you left, they took about a week to stop camping outside my door, hoping for a glimpse of you, then they simply dropped out of sight. There was one story about you disappearing, but they didn't print anything else about you that I saw. I'm sure that now they have moved on to torment someone else, and you can forget about them,' Lauren said.

'That's just it, I can never forget them. I'm conscious of them always. No one knows who I am here and I actually think that no one cares, they have enough of their own problems going on. I think that's what makes me love this place the most. The lack of interest in lives other than their own. The majority of the people here are just trying to get along. No airs and graces, just simple people.'

'So you love being here but hate its taxis?'

'I guess I do hate taxis, but only because they threatened my peace and quiet!'

'Fair enough,' Lauren said as they slipped into a comfortable silence for the next hour and a half.

Mackenzie flicked her signal on and turned right. 'Almost home, another ten minutes or so and we are there.'

'Perfect, I was beginning to think these hills would continue going upwards forever.'

'We can go higher up Sani Pass into Lesotho to see the view from the top of the world, but we're done for tonight.'

'Good, I can hear your art calling me,' Lauren said.

'Before we get to that I want to say thanks for coming out. I didn't know how much I needed to see a friendly face until you walked into that airport.'

'Hell, it's my pleasure, Mac. Besides, a few months out of New York will do me so much good. I'm planning on scouting for new unknown talent, continuing collecting for my galleries and expanding my horizons while I'm here, after a week or two of doing nothing to get over my jetlag. My assistant, Nadia is looking forward to taking on more responsibility.'

Mackenzie grinned as they entered Crystalberg. 'I wish you were seeing this town in the light. We're in a valley, but the Drakensberg mountains are high and craggy here. They're grey and old and magnificent.'

They drove down two more streets, and although there were streetlights on, only every second one worked and there was a general deserted feeling about the place.

Lauren said, 'It looks like a bit of a ghost town at night. Uninhabited and a tad creepy.'

'It does look like that, especially with the clouds so low and the mist swirling around.'

They turned again and drove up a steep road, then turned into a driveway. The lights on the house suddenly lit up, illuminating it in cold white light and almost blinding the women. 'Oh good, no load shedding tonight.'

'What's load shedding?' Lauren asked.

'There are too many power consumers and the electricity company can't cope with demand. So they switch off certain places at certain times. We're deemed low risk to switch off because it's basically a farming area, so we often have no electricity at night. Basically, the electricity companies instruct the councils to reduce the demand by load shedding or the entire grid will collapse causing a national blackout. They should be following a schedule, but they don't. It's so unpredictable. They can switch you off anytime they need to load shed quickly to avoid total collapse of the whole of South Africa's electricity grid.'

'A whole country could go dark? Incredible. So we could have come into a dark house? No lights? Have they seen that outside it's really black in these mountains?'

Mackenzie smiled. 'I have a petrol generator to take up the slack. Most people who don't want to be inconvenienced do. If there is no Eskom, mine will switch on automatically when any of the electricity in the house is used. So if my fridge needs power, it draws it. I had it installed after about a week here when I was left sitting in the dark with candles. They can be romantic, but not when you're alone and scared in a dark mountain house! Can you imagine if I put on the kiln then had the electricity go off halfway through baking? My ceramic stage would be a disaster.'

Mackenzie pressed a button and her automatic gates opened. She drove through, and then watched them close behind her. Only once they closed did she roll forward to the garage door, and pushed another button to open the garage. They inched in and it closed behind them.

'Home sweet home,' she said as she switched off and opened her door. The automatic light remained on, illuminating the garage enough for her to reach the opposite wall and switch on the main lights. A fluorescent tube in the ceiling flickered once or twice, then flooded the whole area in light.

A loud meow could be heard on the other side of the door and scratching, as if the cat wanted the door opened.

'That would be your cat, I take it?' Lauren asked.

'Farren, yes. She adopted me, and kind of now rules the house, and the studio, and my life. She just likes to be fed and fussed over every now and again.'

Lauren shook her head. 'I never thought you'd get a cat, a little dog maybe that you could carry around—'

'Hell no. No dog.'

Lauren laughed as she watched Mackenzie flip down the back door on the truck, and climb in to pass her the largest of her cases. Farren meowed loudly and scratched at the door again.

'We're coming, Farren,' Mackenzie said to the cat as she jumped down off the back and took the case from Lauren, putting it at her feet. 'Come on, this way, we can get the others later. We have to walk through the studio to get to the house and I know you're dying to see my latest bronze,' she said, then unlocked the inter-leading door into the studio part of her home.

Farren instantly wrapped herself around Mackenzie's legs, pro-claiming loudly that leaving her at home for a whole day was too long. Mackenzie bent down and stroked Farren, who climbed up into her arms, her front paws on her shoulder and her back legs and weight supported by Mackenzie. She rubbed her face into Far-ren's black-and-white fur. Farren's loud purr of happiness vibrated through her.

'She's so affectionate!' Lauren said as she reached out her hand and stroked her.

'Here,' Mackenzie said, 'Farren, this is Lauren. Be nice.' She handed her cat over to her best friend, who welcomed the small feline.

'Nice to meet you, cat,' Lauren said, snuggling her for a moment. Then she put her down as she followed Mackenzie. She took a few steps into the studio before her eyes focused on a small statue of an animal about half a metre in size. 'That is stunning. Please tell me that's coming to one of my galleries! I don't care what creature it is – it's amazing!'

'Thanks. It will be when it's done, that's the first of the *Nagapie* series, the Bushbaby range. I saw them when I was up on the Botswana border at Madikwi Game Reserve. There were two that got into my treehouse at Jaci's Lodge and spent a few hours catching the moths and insects. They left a bit of a mess, but when I explained to the reception that I had been taking too many photos to realise, they weren't worried, they said they'd rather them inside than the baboons and the monkeys. Anyway, I decided that they don't get enough publicity because everyone focuses on the big five, so I started these "Little Creatures of Africa Series", and they're the first in the range.'

Lauren drew her hand over the bronze in a caress. 'Look at this detail of the face. Look at what you've done with these eyes. There's colour on this bronze! This is new.'

'It's a technique that's used a lot at the local Goodwin Foundry that I've been visiting.'

'You changed foundries? I didn't realise there was more than one in this country.'

'No, added another. I'm still using the Workhorse Bronze Foundry in Johannesburg. The Goodwin Foundry is much smaller. Different. I've worked with a few of the local artists there. It was divine to be in a working studio with other artists again. It's been a while since I did anything like that. See the trees, with just a touch of cupric nitrate – copper – in the chemical patina, I've made the trees whisper to the *nagapie*, and adjusting it a little here, too, changing the colour tones. It's fun to play with.' She smiled as just talking about her art made her feel so alive. 'Oh and I bought another new gas torch to fire it on a rotating table. Bigger gas bottles, too.'

'You are amazing, you know that?' Lauren said.

Mackenzie shook her head. 'I don't think so, but I tell you, Lauren, I'm loving it here, and I feel that this local influence helps my statues to have depth. I'm seriously pleased with them and can't wait to get the others out of their castings.'

'Depth. You always had depth. Now you've created magic. This one looks alive. Oh my goodness. I knew when you didn't stop me coming that you probably had something special to show me. How many are still cast but not taken out? How many are ready? How excited am I?' Lauren clapped her hands together.

Mackenzie laughed. 'Great to see you haven't lost your infectious energy.'

Lauren grinned at her and poked out her tongue.

'There are ten ready for you to ship immediately if you want them and another fifteen or so that'll be ready to go when you leave, depending on how much I get done while you're here. My process has become very different here to what I did in New York when I was working and not touring.' She thought back to a happier time, of her teaching Sebastian how to weld and how useless he was at it, but they hadn't cared. She missed him all over again.

'It's driven by the distance to the foundry. I've taken to doing a batch of clay sculpting, a whole collection, and only when I've finished those do I get the lost-wax moulds done. When they're all ready I pack them into those forty-four-gallon drums so the foundry can just unload and pour. Then when I return, they simply load them onto the back of my *bakkie* and I drive home again.' She walked over to the next sculpture and began taking off its sheet.

'You drive from here to Johannesburg with those in your truck?'

'I do. It's a six-hour drive but they're so good. They get what I'm trying to achieve with my statues, and they're careful. It took a few trips to various foundries before I picked these guys. I even had one piece couriered to Port Elizabeth, but it wasn't the best, it was filled with bubbles.' The sheet now completely removed, she looked at Lauren, who again reached out to touch her statue.

'It's worth it. Your work has leapt ahead of the pack about a million dollars' worth! Seriously, your work is more alive than ever. You are going to make me rich, my friend.'

'Thanks,' Mackenzie said. 'I couldn't do this if I was in New York. This place is so peaceful and every time I take castings to the foundries, I get to fill up my creative well in the game reserves and sometimes in the local markets. I often people watch there while I shop. We have to go to the Soweto Market, it's on the "must do" list.'

'So you're not just planning on staying home, working the whole time while I laze around in the sun?' Lauren asked.

'No way, you need to get out and see South Africa. It's amazing. We can start local, do a few things here, but we have to do at least two of the main game reserves. And we have one gala event to attend while you're here, too. I've promised a HIV orphanage in Pietermaritzburg a sculpture to raffle off on their big money drive for funds. I need to deliver it soonish. I was kind of hoping that you'd help with the marketing of the auction and get involved so they make decent money? Say please, I could do with your help here?'

She walked to another part of her huge studio and pulled back a sheet that was draped over a pedestal.

'Oh my God. Tell me that there will be more of those!'

'There will be. They're waiting to go to the foundry. I had this one poured locally just to see how it would come out, and I loved it, so I did a few more. They just kind of fell out of my fingers.'

They stood looking at another coloured bronze, only this time it was of a child, playing with a wire-sculptured car. Her clothes were tatty, and she wore no shoes. Every perfect toe was sculpted, every piece of wire perfectly cast. Flawless little fingers gripped the wire with precision, and the face of the girl radiated happiness. 'Meet Shoebox.'

'Shoebox?'

'Her real name. She's one of the children at the orphanage. She was so premature that she could fit in a shoe box, but she's a fighter, she survived despite being HIV positive from her mother, who died shortly afterwards. She's now eight years old. I found the orphanage last year when I had some old clothes to get rid of, and I didn't want to sell them. My maid, Maria, knew about it because her sister works there. So I took a drive and what I found was amazing. The children and young people there are in need of everything.'

'So, now you've become a patron of the orphanage?'

'Just a supporter.'

'Do they have any idea who you really are? The power that you have to attract money if you put your mind and name to something?' Lauren asked.

'No. And you're not going to tell anyone either. Here I'm just another American artist. No one knows who I am. I've worked hard to keep it that way.' She thought about Cole keeping her secret and not naming her when reporting the incident to the police, and she couldn't help smiling when she thought of the change between them in the last two weeks. The shift from acquaintances to genuine friendship that had occurred so quickly.

'Well then I guess we'll make a mint for that orphanage with this stunning Shoebox. And as long as this intensity in your art doesn't stop now that you have your Cole just up the road …'

'It won't stop me working on my art. You'll be happy to know that we've been to dinner a few times and he calls often. We talk for hours late at night. He took my bike to the shop for me and then he brought it around. I've even told him you were coming,' Mackenzie said.

'Does he know who you really are?' Lauren asked.

Mackenzie shook her head. 'Can you imagine the pressure that would put him under?'

'Maybe you should let him make that decision himself,' Lauren said.

CHAPTER

4

Tobeko Ntuli, known to all in the Johannesburg underworld as maNtuli, checked her wristwatch. It was almost three o'clock in the afternoon on the last Saturday in August. She stood up, eagerly awaiting the virgins' procession, on the sixth day of the Umhlanga Reed Festival, the first day of dancing. The girls had already been separated into age groups, with the younger ones visiting Bhamsakhe Farm, near Malkerns, a small town about ten kilometres from Lobamba, where the royal residences were found. It was here in the Luyengo Chiefdom that the headman of the area looked after the reed beds to ensure that there were enough for the girls to harvest for the traditional ceremony, fencing them off so that cattle did not trample them beneath their hooves and wild pigs didn't destroy them. The rural town of Malkerns was not large, and relied on tourism and agriculture of sugarcane and pineapples to sustain itself.

The older girls had travelled to Mphisis Farm in the Ntondozi area, roughly twenty-three kilometres away from Lobamba, and had arrived in darkness. It wasn't far by Africa standards.

The next day they had each harvested about twenty reeds, long elegant sticks with tufts on the top. They were either tied together with plastic bags, or those who continued the more traditional ways would cut grass and braid it to secure the bundles. The girls and their precious reeds would then travel on the backs of large open lorries to signify the end of their long journey taken. In the dark they would return to the Queen's royal village in Lobamba. The first day back was always quiet, used in preparation for the celebrations about to begin. The girls would complete their costumes, braid their hair and ensure they had enough feathers if they chose to decorate in the traditional Swazi manner, with the feathers completing a full circle around the tight bun at the back of their heads.

She watched as each passed her, their hair braided or brushed. Their breasts bare, with their dark nipples showing proudly as they bounced unhindered, dancing to their steps. Many wore short skirts of traditional printed cotton, which barely covered their fanny area, others had spent time to thread bottle tops through string and wrap that around their bare ankles, so that they could make a shaker noise when they stamped their feet. Some had beads covering part of their backsides but leaving most of their butt cheek showing, as they would have in the days past. Their necklaces were handmade with glass beads, the girls having spent hours with their mothers or grandmothers making them. Their tassels, bright yellow, blue, black and white.

Some bought commercial knock-offs from China, produced on machines, which weren't as intricate as the Swazi or Zulu traditional designs.

Much had changed in the years of maNtuli's life. Her country of birth was not the only African land now flooded with Chinese junk. Even in South Africa where she had the majority of her business, there were so many cheap corner shops popping up that were flooding the markets. The government didn't seem to understand that the Chinese immigrants were taking the money that the locals needed, stealing their jobs. More than half of the Chinese imports didn't even pay taxes. That she detested. Even she had to pay the South African Revenue Service her dues. It was right. It was what gave her the authority to call up the municipality and complain when they left her businesses in the dark with the ever-present load shedding, and when the water didn't flow. It gave her the right to drive her Mercedes-Benz on the streets, where she wanted and how she wanted to. It gave her the right to use her passport and travel in and out of her country whenever she needed. Like to Swaziland.

She paid her taxes. She smiled, admitting to herself that she didn't pay as much tax as she could, but that was what good businesswomen did. They saved their company money. They made money. And they kept it. Businesswomen didn't give it away when it was not necessary.

The girls danced past, chanting as they went on their journey to the Queen Mother's quarters to present their reed bundles for her to fix to the screens around the houses within the traditional Ludzidzini Royal Compound.

A tall girl, wearing a white feather in her hair, strutted within the horde, not dancing along with the other virgins, despite carrying her bush knife and her reeds.

MaNtuli hoped that the girl failed to catch King Mswati III's eye and be invited to the Royal Palace harem, or become yet another bride to the polygamist king.

'Hey, you!' maNtuli called to her.

The girl looked up to see who was calling, then cast her eyes downwards as maNtuli walked into the crowd. While the girls were all dressed in beads with their young flesh flashing, she was in the traditional clothes of a mature woman. Her hat flat on her head, and her skirts a bit shorter than others who wore theirs to the knee. Her breasts were covered. She didn't show those to anyone anymore. No one got to touch or carve anything on her body these days. Her gun was holstered on her hip, just as many men had theirs pushed into the waistband of their skins and clothing hanging off their frame as they danced along, chaperoning.

'You,' she repeated, and gripped the girl's arm, her long acrylic nails biting into her young flesh.

The girl stopped and looked at her.

'Take this. If you want to work in Johannesburg, come and see me. I can provide for you.' She passed the girl her business card, and the girl took it and tucked it into her black panties without hesitation. Flat against her bottom.

Oh yes, this was a working festival for maNtuli. Where else could she see beautiful Swazi girls parading around, claiming to be virgins? She could smell the heightened excitement coming from them for the orgies about to happen afterwards. Girls who were of age often found out exactly what to do with their fannies and those tight little nipples after the reeds had been passed on, and the dancing before their king and his entourage ended. Once the fanfare was over and the cameras were switched off.

She sneered at the irony that she had danced in this exact spot so many years ago. At thirteen years old she had been taller than the other girls who lived near her in the shacks in Alexandra in South Africa. Although her best friend, Dominic, and his simple brother, Noah, had touched her a little bit when she had felt sorry for them, Tobeko had kept herself pure. Never allowing even Dominic more than a stroke and perhaps a tiny fondle.

She had always dreamt that one day she would dance at the Swazi Umhlanga ceremony, where the virgins danced for their king. Back during the 1950s, the ceremony had been an age-ranking ritual, where the young maidens wore large tassels signifying their virginity, and then finally when they came of an age to marry, they were allowed to remove it or use a much shorter one. That had fallen by the wayside years ago, and now they all danced together in height order more than age groups, and little girls of five wore the same dress as those ready to enter into matrimony or just ready to have sex.

She knew that the tradition wasn't ancient, that it had been born from the old *umcwasho* custom, where, if a young unmarried girl got pregnant, her family would be fined a cow by the local chief, and she would provide free labour and be 'in service' to the Queen Mother, until such time as the girl was at the right age to marry. When the time of free labour ended, there was a celebration with dancing and feasting. The whole practice had been brought about to try to preserve the Swazi maidens' virginity and to provide free labour for the Queen Mother.

Today the officials spouted off about it creating solidarity among the women by working together. MaNtuli smirked at that and shook her head.

She had seen a faded black-and-white photograph of the ceremony when she was young, when she and her mother had planned for a trip to Swaziland one day to take part. It was what had kept her going in the shack township where she lived. Dreams of something in the future. She had thought of it when she used to walk miles to school. She had thought of it when her teachers praised her, because she had known that she was different to the other teenagers who didn't have any expectations or ambitions in life. She had been proud.

But it wasn't easy to take the high road in Alexandra. There were always men offering money for tricks and proposing to teach her. Living with her domestic-worker mother was hard, and the money would have been helpful to them both.

Dominic got more than one black eye when he tried to stop men touching her during that time. Men who would wait while the girls walked to school, then ambush them. Noah, having had polio as a young boy and a limp because of it, often walked with her, because people underestimated his slow-wittedness, but he had an uncharacteristic strength. He gave many other boys black eyes and loose teeth doing what his brother asked of him: protecting her.

Army soldiers who would camp nearby and patrol their areas in their large armour-plated trucks would line girls up and have their way with them. She was lucky then. Still wearing the clothes of the primary school, the army men didn't approach her. Dominic stole and then gifted her the first knife that she kept on her all the time, to walk to school and to sleep with. A large bush knife. The handle was wooden and it had pop rivets holding it onto the steel blade, but it was sharp. Dominic had spent many hours rubbing it against the concrete with water, ensuring it could cut hair in a whisper and flesh if need be.

Then it happened. One of her mother's many men-friends tried to climb under her blankets on her sleeping mat and touch her. That knife, it cut him nicely, and he fled.

Soon afterwards, her mother said that it was time for their trip to participate in the Reed Dance in Swaziland, and it was a dream come true. Not only was she at last out of Johannesburg, but she was travelling in a bus.

A real bus. Where the chickens were in their crates and thrown up on the roof, where cases bulged over the side, tied on with thick ropes, and the driver packed them all in so tight that she had to sit with her legs over her mother's knees to fit on the seat. That was how the black buses of that time were. Crowded, and only for black people.

She met other girls her own age who were going to the virgin celebration on that bus, too. They shouted across everyone, talking loudly and with their hands to ensure everyone knew they didn't *skinner* about them. Her mother, who was always so sad and so stern, was suddenly filled with hope and talked about her finding a future and getting out of the shacks because of their journey. The excitement rubbed off on her, and she looked forward to the ceremony. Singing songs that her mother had taught her as a young girl.

That was before she knew the truth behind her mother's happiness. Before she knew that she had caught the eye of a fat old businessman named Samuel Ntuli somehow during the cutting of the reeds, and the washing of herself in the river, and when she had danced for her Swazi king. All that time Samuel Ntuli had been watching, and he had bought her as his.

After the last day when the king had danced with the girls, and the royal regiment also had danced, her mother introduced her to Samuel. He asked her to walk with him and her mother encouraged her to go, so she went with her elder as was expected of her. After all, respecting one's elders was an integral part of their traditions.

He took her to a hut nearby and she discovered that night exactly what men did with their cocks and what they expected girls to do with them.

In the morning, she rose early and ran away from him. She ran back to where her mother was staying. She found her mother drunk and hungover, a strange man in her bed who held his head when she spoke to her mother and kept telling her to '*Tulla*. Be quiet!'

She cried as she explained to her mother what had happened. She was so proud for getting away from the man who had ruined her. Her mother slapped her face then. For the first time in her life she struck her.

It hurt, stung, and she was ashamed because she didn't understand why her own mother took her hand and marched her back to Samuel Ntuli.

As she was dragged down the street, the truth had slowly been revealed. Her mother had sold her to Samuel Ntuli, a man of fifty. She now belonged to him. Six fat cows had been given to her mother as a *lobola*. Her mother had already sold one and celebrated, washing her hands of her daughter.

She never got to collect her ration of meat from the royal slaughter for the virgins, a thankyou from the king for keeping themselves pure. She was no longer pure.

But Samuel Ntuli, he was proud of his new plaything. That same night she learnt what a *sjambok* felt like as well, as it sliced through her young skin, leaving his mark on her body.

She tried one last time to return to her mother, convinced that she would take her home to their small shack in Alex when she saw the welts. Only her mother had gone. Abandoning her with the old man.

Samuel Ntuli found her sitting on the edge of the pavement, staring at the room her mother had rented for the reed festival.

'You can forget about your mother. Now you are mine. You belong to me. Come, we can go home, to my house in Pietersburg.'

This time she travelled in his taxi. The people were not as squashed as on the bus, but still there were over twenty when there should have been sixteen. Thankfully, she was seated in the front, between Samuel and the younger man Simon, who Samuel introduced as his number two. The way that he introduced her had Simon sweating, and not one inch of his body touched hers for the whole journey.

No one questioned how a man so old suddenly acquired a teenage daughter. He called her 'daughter' in the day when she went to school in the township, and she wore her white shirt with its black pinafore like every other girl her age. But he fucked her behind those closed doors at night when he got home from his work.

There were others like her in his house, too, older than her at first, but as she neared her sixteenth birthday, another joined them who was younger, like she had been: Esther. Now there were two 'daughters' under his roof. She would walk with Esther to school as if they were normal schoolgirls, trying to be educated in a hard society, but all the time knowing that they would never again be normal. They were sex slaves.

They would all sleep with him in his house. He liked to watch them together, and he liked to put his fat cock inside her, while the wives would play with her, too. Sometimes his associates would come and watch, she would be 'lent' to them, for a price, and if she made them happy, she would return to his cock at the end of the night.

Then it changed. On her sixteenth birthday, the older wives told her excitedly that she would marry him. She was now going to be wife number four and live with them always.

The only problem was that she didn't want to marry him. He was an old man, and he wasn't even kind. Beatings happened often, and she had learnt to do as he said, or his *sjambok* would lash her back causing painful welts. His associates liked to watch those beatings, too.

According to the older wives, he was a good provider, and they constantly told her how lucky she was that he was keeping her and he would look after her. Others who hadn't pleased him had been passed to his business associates, and they would make the sign of a cross over their chests whenever they were mentioned in whispers.

Tobeko wasn't an idiot. She might have been inexperienced three years ago, but she was intelligent. She knew what that meant: it was a death sentence to be passed to another. So she was married to Samuel Ntuli. She became maNtuli.

As a wife she was then expected to service only his needs, no other man's. She was expected to be at his house all the time, tending to the family, no more school. He expected her to give him a son, something none of the other wives had done so far. Someone to take over his business one day.

She begged him to allow her to do more. She was good at maths and accounting, so she could also learn about the family business that her son would take over one day. At sixteen she soaked up everything about his taxi business, and how he ran his two shebeens. For two years she learnt everything she could, and because she was so eager, he showed her.

At eighteen she got her own licence for driving the taxi to help make money and she became privy to even more about his enterprise. Almost nothing was recorded on paper, and the *kaffirbank* held his money. She now knew who he owed favours to and who owed him favours, and for what. She began to understand that in business, it was all about the money, and nothing was personal.

His other wives knew nothing of his business dealings, instead choosing to grow fat on his food and decorate his house for him, have more children. All of them girls.

She learnt how to stop having any of his children. She would never give him a child, and never a son. And now it was time for another change. She began her revenge.

As well as getting to work each day at the desk in the back monitoring his business, it had become her job to take him a coffee early each morning, even if she wasn't in his bed that night. She began putting just a little crushed *siphahluka* in his cup at a time. She knew the bulb of the Sore-eye Flower was poisonous, the old sangoma had told her that when she visited her for muti to take to not fall pregnant, and the *umkhokha*, the lucky beans, to take if she did fall pregnant. Soon he became sick, and she took over more of the running of his business. His colleagues already knew her, and she gained their trust. She slowly increased the poison's amount, and he became bedridden. She stepped up over his number two, Simon, who was still driving the taxi and still working for her husband. When he died within the year, she took over his business. She was nineteen.

She paid each of the other wives a dowry to settle them someplace else, and she put Esther into a boarding school and paid her fees so that she could finish her education and never be dependent on a man again.

And, despite tradition, she moved all the business money from the *kaffirbank* into a commercial institution, ensuring that there was the correct amount given to her, and that the local business-man who had held Samuel's money didn't steal from her.

Tobeko soon began to expand her enterprise.

She went back to Alexandra and fetched Dominic from the shack he still lived in with his brother, Noah, on their grandmother's property. He remained by her side as she grew Ntuli's business into an empire. Dominic was her number two, the fists and the brawn, but she was the brain.

The noise of the festival crashed in on her once more, and she turned away. Now, she hunted those virgins there that looked like they wanted something better from their life, arranging for them to be her working girls. She sold their virginity to the wealthy, and then she made money from their bodies for a few years afterwards. When they had had enough they could leave, but most of her work-ing girls stayed, running her shebeens throughout the country and working in her whorehouses.

She made sure they got paid well and that they were looked after, and girls were good at working when treated right. When trained right. She made sure they knew how to handle money and were educated.

Drawn reluctantly from her memories, maNtuli watched a girl bounce along the line, her big tits dark, her stomach and thighs rolling with fat. She had a special client looking for someone like that, someone of a more traditional frame and proportions. The girl was perfect. She walked into the girls to give her a card, too.

Eventually, the lines of dancing girls had stacked their reeds in front of the royal residence. King Mswati III walked down into the crowds. The music changed from just the women singing to the men joining in and the party began.

For a moment maNtuli clapped along, caught up in the atmo-sphere, enjoying the celebrations.

Dominic stood beside her. 'I wish I had seen you dance as a virgin here all those years ago. I bet you were the prettiest girl here.'

MaNtuli smiled. 'I was. That's what took me out of the shacks. That's why I could be who I am today. I come here to remind myself sometimes.'

'I wish things had been different for you. For you and for me.' Dominic touched his hand against hers.

She moved her hand away. 'Why wish for silly things, Dominic? We can't change what happened, but we can make money now because of it.' She looked back over the dancing women as they chanted together, their knives wheeling above their heads, their feet stamping the ground and their anklets of bottle tops making noises.

Dominic shook his head. 'Why is it always money with you?'

'Why do you ask me that when you know that we both had nothing, we were nothing until I got my hands on Samuel Ntuli's money? Now I sleep in a nice house in Sandton. I bought you that good house nearby. No more shacks for us, ever. Yet you still ask why money?' She shook her head. '*Eish*, Dominic, sometimes I think you never grew up in your shack and you are still as wet behind the ears as when we were thirteen! Without money, you and I, we are nothing in this world, just another black face in Africa.'

CHAPTER
5

Hope attempted to move her fingers. Slowly they reacted. At least her hands were not broken. She flexed her toes and moved her legs. Her head felt as if a thousand rhino bulls had run over it, and then turned and run back. She reached for her forehead to try to quieten the throbbing with her fingers, but something ripped at her hand. She opened her eyes. She attempted to focus, but the blurry image wouldn't clear.

She blinked. Once. Twice. Nothing. She tried squeezing her eyes shut tightly, and then slowly relaxing the lids and the muscles around her eyes. Slowly she let them open. The blurry object now had an outline, dark in the centre, but she could see blue around the edges.

That was a good sign.

Once again, she attempted to move her hands. Ignoring the pain of tearing flesh, she jiggled her wrist up to her head, then poked at the vision. It moved slightly, and came into better focus.

A thorn bush. *How on earth did she get under the weight of all this thorn bush?*

Taking a deep breath, she attempted to use both hands to remove it. It didn't budge. She lifted her head to see if she could wiggle out. *God her head hurt. Big time.*

Gently laying her hand on her forehead, she felt the bump. Raised to the size of a large chicken's egg above her right eyebrow, and it ran from there, across her temple, and into her hairline. She dropped her hand away, it was too sore to touch.

Okay, I'm alive.

Hope took stock of her small surroundings. She could smell something like burnt ash and melted plastic, the stench suddenly strong in her nose. She brought up her wrist to cover her nose, only to find the smell was on her sleeve. A light-green linen sleeve. Why would she wear such a colour? It reminded her of an old-fashioned safari suit.

Blank.

Try, Hope.

Blank.

She rotated her head around as best she could within the confines of the bush. She couldn't see much, except more bush, and thorns. Large white ones, with black tips.

She could hear soft footsteps scurrying around outside the bush. She didn't know if it was friend or foe, so she kept quiet. Ignoring the sting from the thorns as she moved her arm, she felt on her side for her trusty .9mm Glock. It was still there. She removed it from its holster and dragged it up to her chest. She was grateful that she still remembered about her weapon and the movements that seemed to come naturally, as if they were part of her.

The weight pressing down on her legs lifted. Someone was dragging the bushes off. She could feel their heaviness diminishing, as slowly the burden was gone from her upper body, and the cruel African sunlight flooded through.

She cocked her weapon, putting a round in the chamber as the thorn bushes parted.

'*Ukhuluma isiZulu na?*'

She looked at his hands in a surrender position, they were dark, their pink underside callused, and quickly ascertained that they held no weapon.

No threat to her.

She glanced at his face. Dark black, with ancestral roots somewhere in the Sudan or Northern Africa.

'O a bua Sesotho?' He seemed to try a different language.

'I don't understand you,' she said.

'Take it easy. Take it easy!' He switched to English. 'I was just trying to figure out what language you spoke.'

'Sure,' she said. 'English, and I'll take it easy just as soon as you get the hell away from me.'

'I'm no threat. I thought there was a poached animal hidden in there.' His voice was soft and reassuring.

'Really? Now back up slowly,' she instructed, still lying flat on her back. Something about poaching and dead animals pinged in her brain but was gone again just as quickly.

He moved away. She could no longer see him. Using one hand, she forced her body upwards, her other hand maintaining her hold on her Glock, trying to keep her neck as still as possible to stop her head from throbbing. She got into a sitting position, then she dragged herself upright. She looked ahead and saw his face again, and its frown lines, his mouth moving in slow motion, calling something out as everything around her closed inwards, and went blissfully black and pain-free behind her eyelids.

*　*　*

Mandla rushed forward to catch the woman, but trying to do so while dodging the gun didn't quite work. She hit the ground hard, her gun flying from her hand, thankfully not discharging, much to his relief.

He checked her pulse: steady and strong. Quickly, he retrieved the wayward gun, disarmed it and dropped the magazine into his waiting hand. Other than the dust from the fall, it was spotlessly clean. He liked people who took care of their weapons, it showed integrity. He pocketed the ammo then shoved the polymer-frame pistol into the waistband of his pants, before he returned to the unconscious woman. Her long hair drew his attention for a moment as it fanned in the dirt.

Although she was out for the count, he wasn't taking any chances. Someone had covered her with those bushes, someone with local knowledge, and that someone could return at any time. He pulled the rest of the thorn bushes off her, then ran his hands over her body. Nothing appeared broken. He turned her over onto her side, and carefully his fingers swept from her delicate light brown neck, down her spine, and hovered over her small tight backside. Deciding against touching, he carefully moved her onto her back. Looking around the site of the small aircraft crash, he could see no other evidence that anyone else had been with her.

He walked over to what was left of the small white plane and peered inside. The front dashboard was one melted tangle of plastic and wires. He lifted his arm up over his nose.

Doing concentric circles around the plane, the only other footprints he could see looked small enough to belong to a child. About the age of seven or eight only. They came inwards, went to the plane, then dragged the woman away from the wreckage a little to the side. The tiny steps then constructed the *boma* to protect the body from hyenas and other scavengers of the bush, before they walked out in the same direction they had started from.

He looked for anything personal, like a purse, a passport. The few words she had spoken to him had been with a British accent.

Nothing. The plane was clean. *Too clean.*

He smelt a rat, and it wasn't a natural, furry, tasty-to-eat bush rat either.

He returned to the woman. She was still out cold. Shit, he would have to take her back to his base camp where he had stashed his heavier equipment, and radio the company for a chopper to airlift her out. He was going to lose the trail of the cheetah, and there was a chance it could cross out of Ndumo and into Mozambique. *Shit!*

Lifting both of her arms, he hauled her over his shoulder, as if she was a dead impala, and adjusted his bearings, going back in the direction he had just come from. Praying he didn't damage her head any more than it was already. Knowing that he couldn't leave her here at the site of her crash.

*   *   *

Hope woke up slowly. Her head didn't hurt so badly, and her body was definitely not trapped under any bushes. She was warm, a soft blanket wrapped around her, a hot male body snuggled closely into hers, his arm holding her close.

The man!

Her eyes flew open in an instant. She sat bolt upright, hugging the blanket tightly to her chest. *Oh my God, I only have my vest and pants on!*

'Wait, don't move fast, you'll pass out again,' he said from next to her, as he lifted his hands, showing he had nothing in them.

'Who are you?' she asked, pulling the coverings around herself. She wished her voice sounded more in control, but it was lodged halfway up her throat.

'Mandla. Who are you?'

'Hope.' It hurt to say her name, her heart thumped alongside her vocal cords. *Isn't it supposed to be in my chest!*

'Nice to meet you, Hope. You are safe with me, I will not hurt you. I give you my word,' he said. 'Your body was in shock, going into a hypothermic state. I warmed you up with mine. That's all.'

He cleared his throat and lowered his hands as he reached next to him for his clothes. He stood up and she saw a flash of some strong muscular thighs. The stretcher they had been lying on to keep them off the cold ground of the bush rocked with the change in weight and she yelped.

He pulled on a black T-shirt. 'Where were you going in your plane?'

She looked up into his dark-brown eyes with their deep lines at the edges. He had really long eyelashes, not at all curly. A strong, chiselled, handsome face, with a nose that had obviously been broken at least once, as it had a small imperfect lump at the bridge.

'Ummm,' she said, her brain still a little fuzzy. Why couldn't she remember where she was going?

'Okay, let's try this. If you can't tell me where you were going, can you tell me where you came from?'

She thought hard. 'No,' she said quietly. 'I—I can't remember ...'

She watched him frown, the lines marking his beautiful complexion. 'Can you remember anything at all?'

She took a second before answering. 'Very little.'

It's quite a bruise you have there. Now that you are properly awake, I can give you some medication. All I have is aspirin, do you know if you have any allergies? Can you remember that?'

She gave it some thought. 'Not that I remember. I don't think I'm allergic to anything.'

Panic began to clog her throat. She was alone, in the dark with a stranger. She was half naked and she had no memories.

'Don't panic, calm down. I already told you I mean you no harm,' he said, but he didn't reach out his hand to try to reassure her. It was as if at that instant he knew she didn't want to be touched as she attempted to wrap the thin blanket around herself tighter.

She glared at him.

'It's alright. The helicopter will arrive as soon after first light as they can this morning. Charl has the coordinates already. Then they can take you to hospital for a check-over. My company is looking into who you are from your plane registration. At least I could still read that in the wreckage. Do you remember what happened to make you crash?'

Nothing.

'This is bad,' she said, and then she took a deep breath. 'I know my name is Hope Anderson. I'm a British citizen, and I'm thirty years old. I'm definitely not married. Which is good, given I woke up next to an almost naked man I don't remember climbing into bed with. And my mum keeps telling me to settle down, and my dad says I have an adventurous spirit, but other than that, I'm blank.' She shook her head. 'Ouch,' she said as she moved one of her hands to hold it.

'Try not to move your head too much. You have a hematoma on your forehead that hasn't gone down.'

She tentatively ran her fingers over her eyebrow and found the sore spot.

'Don't prod it, you will make it worse,' he said, gently pulling her arm away. 'Do you remember anyone else being with you at the crash site?'

'No. Nothing.'

'There was a child's footprints, do you remember a child at all, or a person who covered you with bushes?'

'No. Do you know where my clothes are?'

'Drying, they were pretty bloody, so I washed them for you last night,' he said. 'You can either wear damp clothes or you can wear my spare. It's not a hundred percent clean, but it's better than cold clothes.'

'I'll take the shirt for now. Thank you for washing mine.' She watched as he reached over and tossed his shirt over to her.

'It will be cool when you get out from under the blanket,' he said, turning to lean over the fire pit nearby and begin to work there. 'Once the sun comes up, your clothes will dry really fast. It's just cold at night, in the day it's already pretty warm, despite it only being August. It looked like whoever was there before me was trying to protect you. They covered you well, must have taken them some time to cut those bushes and make that *boma*. Do you remember what time of the day you were flying at?'

'No. We already covered this ground yesterday,' she said as she shrugged into his khaki men's shirt. It was cold against her skin, and fell to her mid-thighs. She was suddenly grateful that he had shared his blanket and his body warmth with her. She wrapped the blanket around her like a poncho.

'I'm dressed,' she said, giving him permission to turn back.

'I know that I'm repeating things from yesterday, I'm trying to check your memory, if it's recalling short term. It seems fine. Hopefully your other memories will return soon. I've seen it happen before, when I was younger ...' His voice trailed off and she watched as his face took on a distant look, which soon turned into a scowl.

Obviously not a good memory!

Soon, a small fire was blazing, and he put a billycan into the flames. 'I only have coffee, so I hope you drink that black.'

'Coffee would be great. Thanks. What time is it?' she asked.

'Four, the sun will come up soon. It will burn the chill out of the air and the morning mist. Come six o'clock we will be sweating again.'

It was morning? 'What day is it?'

'It would be Tuesday twenty-ninth of August. The chopper should be here by seven-thirty to collect you.'

Something about a meeting on Tuesday flashed in her mind.

'Why, where am I going?' she asked, a little confused that the chopper was only fetching her, and not them.

'To hospital. You need to be checked over by a doctor.'

'I had a meeting today. I can't remember what, or where, or why!'

'I guess you aren't making that meeting,' he said as he dug in his small backpack and produced a spoon for the coffee, which he ladled into the billycan.

'I can give you aspirin for your head,' he said, taking the painkillers out of his pants pocket.

He shook four aspirin into the palm of her hand. 'Here.' He offered her the green water bottle and watched while she swigged them down. 'Right, now coffee and food.' He passed her a tin mug of coffee followed closely by a dry muesli rusk. 'Don't drop it in the coffee, you will land up with sludge, but if you dunk it, they are edible.'

She removed the biscuit from the cellophane it was wrapped in.

'Trekking rations are not exactly five-star service,' he joked. 'Just keep your fingers off the sterling-silver serving dish.'

His mouth crinkled at the side, and his eyes narrowed when he laughed. It made him look like a naughty schoolboy caught out doing something he shouldn't be.

'Thanks,' she whispered as she blew on the warm liquid. Tasting it, she found it was incredibly sweet.

'Wild honey,' Mandla said, before she even had a chance to ask.

He drank directly from the billycan, and they lapsed back into silence over the coffee and small ration of rusks. When they were done, Mandla offered her the toothpaste tube, a canteen of water and a toilet roll that was squashed flat.

'Some things you still have to do in the bush. Pee and brush teeth. If you go just behind that tree, I can still protect you if any wild animal comes near. Please don't go further away.'

'So where exactly are we that I'm in the middle of the bush?' she asked.

'In the Ndumo National Park, northern Zululand, so keep your eyes peeled.'

Taking the toiletries offered, she headed for the tree. She remembered that going bush was nothing new to her. It certainly didn't feel alien. After she had obeyed the call of nature, she stood and kicked some sand over the toilet paper, covering it completely. Somehow she had known what to do. A memory or some type of survival training? Her mind reached further inside, looking for an answer.

Nothing.

'Dammit,' she swore as she came back into camp.

'Problem?'

'No, just no memory of where I learnt to pee in the bush,' she said, giving him back the loo roll.

He had his bag packed up already, and after stowing it into the top, he hoisted the rucksack onto his back. The stretcher as well as the blanket were gone and the camp was as neat as if no one had been there. She couldn't even see the sign that a fire had been burning enough to make coffee just a minute before.

'You pack up fast!' She turned around with an exaggerated slowness. 'Nothing, anywhere.'

'That's the idea. Leave only footprints, and not even those if we can help it. Come,' he said, tucking the toothpaste into a pocket in his pants. 'We need to walk a bit to where the chopper can land safely.'

'But, I'm still wearing no pants!' she said.

Mandla laughed. 'My shirt is almost a dress on you. You will be fine. I will try to keep out of the longer grass so your legs don't itch until you can put your own clothes on again. Rather let them dry or you could chafe.'

'Fine,' she said. 'It's not like there is a stadium full of people to see me walking in just a shirt.'

'Hope, I have seen mini skirts shorter than that shirt. Do you want your damp pants?'

'No.'

'Good, then it is time to get moving.' He set off. Within moments he stopped and then slowed his pace, keeping more to her sedate one.

'Thank you,' she said when she realised what he had done.

'Not a problem, we have plenty of time. It's not that far,' he said as he held out his hand to help her over a small washed out rut in the ground.

They left the shady cover of the denser trees and broke into more of a scrubland, with knee-high golden grass and only the odd acacia tree dotted here and there within the landscape to break the monotony.

He held up his hand, indicating for her to stop.

She did as instructed, without questioning, as if she knew that following orders meant life or death.

Mandla pointed. In front of them were three giraffe nibbling from a tree. Beneath them, a few brown impala grazed.

'See that tree, it's a common cabbage tree, we call it *umsenge* in Zulu,' he said. 'The black rhino in this park, they eat the roots and the bark, too, it's one of their favourites.'

Something about the rhino flashed in her mind, something important, then it was gone.

'Come, we can walk nearer. There are no rhino near the tree today. The place we are going is just beyond it.'

She couldn't believe that they could get so close to the animals. It was within thirty or so metres. A bark went up from one of the impala on sentry duty, and they all bounded off, their white tails flashing in their wake. The giraffe followed in the same general direction, although not before looking at the pair with a bit of 'what a bother' in their eyes, their long legs quickly eating up the distance.

They stopped under the tree.

'We can rest here for a while, there are no predators about.'

She sank to the soft ground, putting her back against the trunk of the tree, and lifted her face up to the welcome shade. Already she was sweating, just as Mandla had said, and the sun had barely begun shining over the horizon in the east. Its pink-and-gold hues were spectacular as its bright light danced across the grasses and over the tree, stretching beyond, as the African sun rose higher into the new day.

He passed her the water.

'Drink, you need to keep your fluids up.'

'Thank you.' She drank a little.

'More, it's all yours.'

'What about you?'

'I'll refill it when you are on the chopper,' he said as he checked her clothes, which were hanging off his backpack. 'Right, they are as dry as they are going to get before we have company, so if you want to put your own clothes back on, you might be more comfortable for an audience.'

She took her clothes and watched as he turned his back for her. She pulled off his shirt and scrambled into the green linen pants suit. It was still damp and clung when she was trying to pull her legs through, and she cursed it taking so long.

Eventually she was done. 'Thank you for the loan of your shirt,' she said, holding it out to him.

Mandla took it and stuffed it into his pack.

She sat back down and drank a little more water. When she screwed the lid on, he put his hand out to take it from her. Once again he hung the bottle from his shoulder, across his back.

'You should have a hat to cover your head, but I'm not sure it won't make your headache worse. That bruise isn't looking so good.

At least you'll have a bit more protection on your legs and arms now with your own clothes on. Come, I know you haven't had much rest, but we need to move again,' he told her, extending his hand out to help her.

She took his hand and stood up, relying on his strength, before reluctantly letting go of his hold.

Her head didn't feel worse, but he was right, she would hate to apply any type of pressure to it. Not having a mirror in the middle of a game reserve had its good points – she couldn't see how bad she really looked and how big the bruise above her eye was.

She walked as quietly behind him as she could. They saw kudu with their long twisted horns jumping gracefully along the tree line in the distance and passed a herd of zebra grazing in the morning sunshine, who just looked at them and snorted, while the wildebeest foraged alongside them.

Soon, they came to a clearing near a waterhole. Mandla stopped. 'We wait here,' he said. 'Charl will bring the chopper to us.'

He found them a fallen log to sit on, after he had checked it wasn't infested with ants or hiding any snakes. Removing his pack, which he dumped on the floor, he motioned for her to join him.

They sat together in silence, watching the goings-on at the waterhole. Birds came down for their morning drink. A turtle bobbed its head up at the edge of the water, sending a skittish pack of hunting dogs which had also come down to drink scattering away. They slowly returned, their thirst overcoming their fright at the aquatic animal.

No sooner had they resumed drinking, when she felt Mandla put his hand on her arm. She looked at him. He had a finger over his lips, indicating for her to remain quiet as he pointed towards the far side of the pool.

Two white rhinos had ambled down, their large horns jutting out proudly from their armour-plated bodies. They drank heavily from the water, then the larger male waded into a big mud patch near the edge. He tested the mud with his lip and his horn, then sank into it up to his knees. After using his head to toss the mud around a bit more, he knelt down and sat, hind quarters first, before lying totally submerged on his right side. He stood then proceeded to complete the mud bath on the left side. Now looking distinctly like a black mud ball, he walked calmly out of the shallow pool.

'It's unusual for the rhino to wallow at sunrise,' Mandla whispered. She noticed that while her attention had been focused on the rhino, he had removed a small laptop from his bag and she looked over at it.

Again she realised that somewhere in her mind, she knew this and she knew that they wallowed to cool their bodies, remove parasites and protect their skin from the sun.

How did she know all that? Was it important?

'What are you doing?' she asked.

'These two are known as Hugo and Millie. Two of the park's most successful breeding pairs. Millie is now almost eleven months pregnant. They are fitted with GPS transmitters so we know where they are at all times, what their vitals are, or if they are experiencing stress at all. They are monitored 24/7 by our company.'

She stilled. She knew the computer, knew its interface and what the markings on the screen meant.

She didn't know this man, of that she was certain. She took a deep breath, and although Mandla continued to read the computer screen, she looked away, trying to remember, trying to force her mind to work.

Her head ached. She massaged her temples, careful not to touch her forehead. She shooed a fly away from her face. Giving up on fighting with her uncooperative brain, she turned her attention back to watch the rhinos.

The male came out of the mud after a long while and ambled over to the female. He nudged her with his wet head. They walked away together but stopped at the edge near a broken tree, where he proceeded to rub and scratch on the wood for a good twenty minutes. He turned his bulk this way and that, paying special attention to his groin and axilla areas, as well as his big underbelly, the inside of his legs. Special satisfaction seemed to be taken as groans and squeals echoed across the water as he rubbed his neck, head and flanks on the smooth wood. Content with his belly scrub on what was obviously one of his favourite rubbing poles, the rhino moved off, back into the bush. As he trotted away, he snorted at a red-billed oxpecker that landed on his horn.

'Majestic, aren't they?' Mandla said.

'Yes,' she said, 'that they are.' She took a while to formulate her next words, because if she confronted this Mandla and he didn't like what she asked, she could be in trouble. Only every fibre in her body screamed that he would never hurt her, to trust him. 'What do you do that you have a laptop that works out here and can track the rhinos?'

'I'm looking for one of our cheetahs that should have been in the Hluhluwe National Park but who bleeped in Ndumo, then its GPS tracker went off line again for some reason. There are no longer cheetahs here in Ndumo because of the lack of adequate fencing and they tend to eat the goats and cattle of the informal settlements on the outside of the park. So our cheetah shouldn't have made it over farmlands into Ndumo. Some of the game rangers seem to think that its tracker is faulty. So I'm here waiting again for it to bleep me and give me a coordinate. Or if I can track it myself, I can call in the vet to dart it and take it back to the right park. Because until my company can prove that our equipment isn't failing, we are being held responsible for the animal going AWOL.'

'That's amazing. How long have you been here in the bush?'

'Almost two weeks. I had tracks yesterday, so I know he is here. I'll find him again, just need the time and patience to track him. Listen …'

She listened but could hear nothing.

'The helicopter is coming.'

She still couldn't hear anything. A full two minutes later, she could hear a distant *throb-throb* of a helicopter. *Man, he had hearing as good as a desert fox!*

She said, 'I'm lucky you were doing what you do here. Thank you for saving me and calling for help.'

'My pleasure,' he said.

The chopper drowned out anything else he might have said as he motioned for her to follow him. The sound pulsated in her head, the pain almost unbearable.

One of the chocks of her plane wasn't right as she had left it, it had moved from being centred. She saw a white man walking away from the plane. She'd purposely ignored the evidence that someone had fiddled with her aircraft, calculating the risk was worth it, to save something, and now it was going down. Her foot pedals wouldn't respond. Pain flashed in her head.

She suddenly knew she was the only person between *something* and certain death and she had just had her plane turned into a pile of scrap metal.

An ache pressed in her chest and a huge sob rushed from her throat.

She had failed her mission.

She never failed.

She began to back away from him, shaking her head. She screamed as the memories of the crash flooded in, the sound of the wind as it rushed past, and there was nothing she could do to slow her plummet to earth. The smell of the instrument panel burning. She grabbed for her Glock at her side, but it wasn't there.

Mandla looked at her and frowned. He looked confused at her sudden change in behaviour.

He stood up tall, signalling with his hand across his throat repeatedly to the hovering chopper. It landed soon afterwards and immediately cut its engines.

The silence was deafening in her ears. She sat on the ground, her arms wrapped around her knees, hugging herself.

'Hope. Hope?' he said, bending down to her. 'It's okay now, it's okay, I won't let anyone hurt you. It's okay, you are safe.'

'I'll never be safe. Someone sabotaged my plane, and now something is going to die and I can't remember what, and it's my fault I didn't get there in time,' she said, her voice shaking.

'Anything else? Can you remember their face? Did you know them?' Mandla asked.

The vision that had been so clear was gone.

'I failed. I had to save something, but I don't even know what.'

'Your memories will return,' Mandla said. 'This is our private helicopter and you are safe now. Charl will shoot back if someone tries to harm you. We will protect you. You need to get onto this helicopter, you need medical care.'

She looked into his face. 'Come with me?' she asked. She didn't know him, but he had saved her. She knew deep down that she could trust him. 'I'm scared to leave here.'

'I understand. But you need to go to hospital and I need to be here. I have to finish my mission.'

Mission – the terminology was so familiar.

A male voice boomed out nearby. 'Howzit, Mandla, what's up?'

'Charl, meet Hope Anderson,' Mandla said as he parted from the hug that he'd shared with Hope, when the helicopter pilot came into view.

'Ms Anderson. Glad to make your acquaintance. Your boss was sure glad someone had found you. He's calling HQ every hour wanting an update on you,' Charl said, then stepped towards Hope and held out his hand.

'My boss?'

'James Williams.' He lowered his unshaken hand to his side.

Hope just stared ahead. She turned and looked at Mandla, pleading for him to help her.

'Nothing?' he asked.

Slowly she shook her head.

'So, what company does Mr James Williams own?'

'Seriously, Mandla? CEO of Global Wildlife International. Special Agent Anderson is apparently one of his top field agents for anti-poaching of threatened and endangered species, specialising in big cats. You have been spending too much time in the field and not enough behind that desk in your office lately.'

'You are just jealous it's not you in the bush,' Mandla said.

'Darn straight,' Charl said.

Mandla looked at Hope. 'Hope has amnesia. Other than her name, she doesn't remember much else.'

'*Ag*, that explains a lot. Mandla, you want to jump in the chopper, too and accompany Special Agent Anderson to the hospital?' Charl asked.

'Would love to, but I'm on the trail of that cheetah. I saw tracks yesterday before I found Hope, so I'll circle back today.'

'Alright, well, Ms Anderson.' He turned and spoke directly to Hope. 'It's just me on duty as your sky chauffeur, then.'

She looked at Mandla.

'Go,' he said. 'You need to make sure everything is alright in that head of yours. You can pick up the pieces of everything else later. I'll return to your plane and search it again now that I know who you are, look for a reason you were flying over Ndumo. If I find anything my company will get in touch with you via your boss.'

She hated to admit it but he was right. She had to fly again. Nodding, she turned her back on him and walked to the chopper. The men behind her were talking quietly, their voices a low rumble in her ears as blood rushed to her head and sweat broke out on her upper lip.

She knew she loved flying, it ran in her blood. Getting up there again was going to test the level of strength in her to the maximum. She ran her hand over her head, then regretted the movement as pain shot through her forehead and into her hairline again.

Charl materialised by her side and opened the chopper door, while Mandla helped her in. He lightly placed the headphones over her ears. She smiled at him. They were uncomfortable but bearable. He buckled her belt. She gave him a thumbs-up. He touched his hand to his lips, kissed it and waved it to her. She laughed at the childish gesture of kissing goodbye as she watched him jump down nimbly. Charl slammed her door shut.

Then Mandla turned and walked a distance away as Charl jumped in next to her, switched on the chopper and the blades slowly rotated, getting faster and faster.

She kept her eyes on Mandla, the man who had saved her life and who they were simply leaving in the middle of nowhere. Only when she could no longer see him for the trees did she close her eyes.

CHAPTER

6

The telephone rang at 00:03. Cole was instantly awake.

'Hello,' he barked into the receiver.

'It's Michelle. We have two baby cheetahs rescued by customs at Richards Bay. Koos and I are already on our way to fetch you.'

'I'll be ready.' He put the phone down and climbed out of his bed in one motion. He lived for moments like this, when he knew he could make a difference. He stepped into his en suite and was dressed in *veldskoens*, jeans and a soft T-shirt, complete with a tracksuit top in his hand, and he was ready. When he looked at the clock it was 00:10.

He grabbed his cell phone off its charger and the keys off the hook in his garage, and climbing into his *bakkie*, he headed for the visitors' centre, with his windows wide open. His neighbours wouldn't take long to get to him. The night was dark, yet the African wildlife danced in his high beams. Moths the size of small teacups flapped against his windscreen and crickets whistled outside. Somewhere in the distance he could hear a jackal calling. Closer to him, he could hear the crow-like call of the night heron as it fished for frogs or fingerlings in his newly stocked trout dam.

'Damn,' he cursed, knowing that this rescue was going to be a hard one.

Michelle did a lot of work privately for other game farms in her large animal veterinarian practice, but whenever it was a rescue, she was the vet on call for *nTabaGrequa*, because they were the ones licensed to attend the animals in their province of KwaZulu-Natal, by Ezemvelo KZN Wildlife. And the government body had tightened up its licence in the last few years.

'*Sawubona, Baas,*' Dumisani, on night-guard duty, greeted him just as he snagged two cub cages from the storeroom, blankets, a few toys, and two baby rescue kits they kept at the ready, filled with electrolytes and protein powder sachets, bottles and formula milk.

'*Sawubona*, Dumisani, here grab these,' he said, passing them over.

'*Kubili? Ingulule?*' Dumisani asked.

Cole nodded. 'Yes, two cheetahs. Rescued in Richards Bay. When you hand over to Siphiwe at six o'clock, tell him to call me on my cell phone if I'm not back.' He locked the door behind him.

'*Yebo, Baas.*'

He realised that he might also miss Mackenzie's race with his cheetahs that day, then remembered she and her friend Lauren were visiting the HIV orphanage in Pietermaritzburg. He would be able to chat to her later.

They were outside waiting when Koos drove up in his 4x4 king-cab.

Koos got out of the driver's side. He was six-foot-eight, built like a tank of pure muscle. His khaki pants and short-sleeved shirt strained against bulges and every fibre stressed at his bulk. Cole smiled that even in a middle-of-the-night call-out, Koos wore the traditional Afrikaner farmer *veldskoens*, with no socks. The soft suede leather ankle boots didn't have room for socks around the tree-stump-like legs.

'Howzit, Cole,' Koos said, nodding once.

'Could have done with more sleep, but hey, these babies are worth waking up for. And you?'

'Same,' Koos said.

Dumisani loaded the cages in the back of the *bakkie*, and Cole climbed into the rear seat as Koos opened the driver's door and got in behind the wheel. Michelle was seated in the front.

'Thank you. *Hambani kahle*,' Cole said and closed the door.

Dumisani saluted him as Koos drove off.

'Hey, Michelle. What's their chances?' Cole asked, breaking the quietness inside the vehicle.

'Slim. Transnet National Ports Authority at Richards Bay had a reliable tip-off and found them together in a cat transporter on a ship, *Al Ihsaa*, bound for Bahrain, marked "live export". The transporter wasn't on the manifest. Customs thinks that one of the wildlife smugglers must be on the ship as a crewmember, because someone was trying to feed them – there were bottles filled with cow's milk. They are still checking the people and holding the ship.'

'Shit,' Cole said.

'I just hope that the cubs haven't aspirated the milk into their lungs,' Michelle said, a clear sign that she was worried.

'It's alright, Michelle, we can start them on the electrolyte solution as soon as we see them,' Cole said.

Michelle grunted. 'I just hope that they will be okay. They sound like they are really tiny. When will these darn poachers learn not to take cubs out of the wild and try to ship them overseas? I get that there is a market, but there are humane ways to get your hands on healthy cheetah cubs these days, they don't have to be stolen anymore.'

Cole frowned. 'Another Bahrain ship. Until they sign the Convention on International Trade in Endangered Species treaty, they will remain the back door into Saudi Arabia and Iran.'

'*Ag*, those CITES people need to hurry up and get them to sign up before we have no cheetahs left,' Koos said.

'Agreed. It's as if we are back in the 1920s. The demand by those blasted Middle Eastern yuppies using them for hunting and keeping them on gold, diamond-studded leashes is growing daily. Poor cats are being used as a fashion accessory,' Cole said.

'I know, but they don't see that for every one cub that makes it, about four die trying to get there,' Michelle said.

'Did they mention what state the cubs are in, if they are awake or active?' Cole asked.

'They said they seem weak and were constantly calling. They have quietened down now. Oh and you are going to love this part, the customs harbour master has changed, so they didn't call us right away, they called DeWildt, who instructed them to call us because we are closer.'

Cole laughed. 'Good to know we are not the only ones awake at this hour. They must have wondered what was happening that they got that call.'

'That cheetah refuge changed their name, remember. It's The Ann van Dyk Cheetah Centre now,' Koos said, reminding her gently.

'It's an old habit calling it that, the name change was sweet, but it's now a mouthful,' Michelle said. 'So everyone there is also awake and waiting to hear about our cubs. I'm just glad they were still vocal. We might have a chance, they might survive.'

Koos patted her arm. '*Liefie*, we'll be there as soon as we can, you'll save them.'

Cole smiled at the intimate exchange between the couple. He didn't need any interior light illuminating their faces to see the love passing between his friends. He could hear just how much Koos idolised his little wife.

Koos continued. 'It's only four hours to Richards Bay from here, we'll be there as the sun rises. If not before, if we get up some speed on the freeways.'

Michelle put her hand over her husband's larger one. 'I know, but it's going to be a long four hours' drive until we get there.'

Cole nodded. 'Come six am, we need to call the team at Bushman's Software Company to let them know we have another two cubs. I bet they were taken before Parks Board got GPS tags into them, too, just like the others. I talked to Brian yesterday and he was saying that they had one of the GPS trackers on a cheetah blank-out. They have Mandla up in Ndumo looking for spoor. He always was the best tracker between all of us. I seriously don't envy Brian with his part in our company. On days like this, I remember why I wanted to start saving cheetahs in the first place, but I'm glad I remained on the farm when the company relocated into the city.'

Koos said, 'That's scary, because so far you guys have had the best stock-control system on the market. Hope the disappearance of the adult isn't related because there seem to have been an influx of cubs either coming into rescue centres or found dead over the last six months. Something big is definitely going on, and the sooner you guys get to the bottom of it the better.'

*   *   *

The sun was just coming up over the Indian Ocean, turning it liquid gold as it peeked out over the horizon. The harbour never slept. Men walked here and there in the area lit with flood lights while machines dumped coal onto conveyer belts that spewed it into waiting ships.

Cole stepped out of the *bakkie* as it stopped. He already had the rescue kits in his hand by the time the customs officer greeted them.

'This way,' the officer said, and led them to a room right on the waterfront side of the modern building.

'I put them in the site office,' he said.

They entered the small room. The cubs were in a cardboard box under the desk. The officer only had a desk lamp on, and an iPod played soft instrumental music. Cole was impressed at the care that this man had taken to try to settle the cubs.

Michelle flicked the light switch and the stark fluorescent light flickered on. Only one of the baby cheetahs opened its eyes at the intrusion.

'That's not a good sign,' she said.

Koos closed the door to the office as Cole checked the windows. They didn't need the cubs to escape and they would be unpredictable at that stage. He went to stand next to Michelle, who had just opened the cage, and one small fluff ball hissed at her. Her hand already clothed in a pigskin glove, she gently lifted it out of the transporter and handed it to Cole.

Cole took the cub and cradled it to him, like a child. He lifted his T-shirt and placed it against his chest, then pulled the fabric back over around it and shared his body warmth with it. At first it didn't move, didn't react.

Michelle reached for the second one.

'It's still breathing, but it's weak,' she said as she laid it down on the cleared desktop that they would use. She got her stethoscope and listened to its heartbeat.

'Too weak. Koos – saline.'

Koos took a bag of saline out of the large medical kit he had carried in, and passed it to her, along with a line and a pack of needles.

Cole held the cub down on the desk with one hand, as she quickly shaved the area on its front leg and put a needle in, attaching the saline. 'Right, we can give this one half an hour before I do anything else. It's badly dehydrated and it needs warmth.' She placed it in Koos's hands. He followed the same procedure that Cole had, warming the baby quickly with the heat from his own body as Michelle attached the saline bag to a drip holder. Then she adjusted the drip to a flow at a faster rate, and covered Koos's hand, which was cradling the cub, with her own. 'It has a chance,' she said.

She turned her attention to Cole.

The cub inside Cole's T-shirt hadn't stayed limp for long. Once it was warm, it had popped its head out, and was watching the goings-on with interest, although it wasn't fighting with him and hadn't attempted to run away. As if it knew that it was in a safe, secure place.

'Your turn, darling,' she said as Cole lifted his T-shirt and delivered the cub back into Michelle's hands.

The cub chirped, and Michelle, Cole and Koos smiled.

'This one is a fighter,' Michelle said, putting it on the table. It lay down where she placed it, weak but not defeated, as it watched her closely.

Cole put his hand on it to keep it from any sudden movement and from struggling should it suddenly feel it was in danger.

Michelle listened to its heartbeat, and checked its teeth and mouth. She felt its whole body, checking for bulging and breaks, checking for any damage and any heated spots, but couldn't find any. She spent extra time on its belly, making sure there was no distortion. Finally, she shaved its leg, she put a needle in and took a blood sample, then she inserted an IV, wrapped the little paw with bandages, and hooked up a saline bag. The cub barely moved.

'Cole, can you just stay with this one, put it back in your shirt?'

Cole stepped forward and took his cub, and waited while Michelle set up another drip stand. The three of them were a practised team, they worked well together in their rescues. They had been together for many years, and it showed.

They hadn't always been so organised – when Cole had first started, no one had known much about the cheetahs at all. The first time they had taken one into their care they had all stayed up through the night, and the next, so terrified to even sleep in case they missed something and lost one. But soon they learnt to relax and took shifts, ensuring they didn't all get exhausted at once. He remembered how much his own father had loved cheetahs, and it was because of that love of them that Cole had even taken notice of the big cat in the first place. It was one of his clearer memories of his dad before he died, visiting Kruger Park and spending hours just watching the reintroduced cheetahs. He remembered his father telling him that his children or his children's children might never see a cheetah in the wild, only in zoos, as their numbers were dropping, and that it would be a sad day when they became extinct.

After he finished school and inherited his money, the first thing Cole did was look for a farm where he could one day save them, in his father's memory, because he couldn't see a future without cheetahs.

Feeling the cub's warm body resting against his reaffirmed that he had made the right decision. The cheetahs needed a champion, and he was there to help pull them back from the edge.

'Mich, this one is too still,' Koos said quietly.

Immediately she was by her husband's side, checking the little cheetah. The tears that welled in her eyes told them the news already.

For that one, they were too late.

'It's gone,' she said.

The cub inside Cole's T-shirt chirped again as if it could sense that something was happening and it began to struggle. Cole held it firmly and spoke softly to it, and it poked its head out of the top of his shirt again. Then it settled. It tucked its head against his chest and slept.

Koos gave Michelle the cub, and she removed the now useless saline bag. She wrapped it up in a blanket and put it into the transporter. 'It can travel on the back,' she said, 'that one can stay where it is. We can put it in a cat cage on the back seat if it becomes active by the time we get home. It's as stable as we are likely to get it, so let's head west. I want an ultrasound of its chest and stomach, and we can start feeding electrolytes in the *bakkie*.'

Koos and Michelle packed up their equipment. Koos made two trips to the *bakkie*, first with Michelle's bag and then with the transporter carrying the deceased cub. He had obviously informed the customs officials of the outcome, as one looked sad when he came to help with the small transporter cage. When he saw the one baby with its head sticking up and resting on Cole's neck, he smiled. 'At least you got to save one.'

'We wish it had been two, but the other one was desperately dehydrated, and he was sick, too. I'll know more once I get to do an autopsy on her back at *nTabaGrequa*. For now our first concern is getting this little fur ball back there, under some nice warm red lights and getting some sustenance into its stomach. This cub is about eight weeks old. It's the age that many are stolen from the wild. The hunters think that if they take them when they are still small, they will domesticate easier, but they don't realise that they still drink milk until they are at least three months. And at three months old, they will already outrun a human trying to pick them up, so it's a catch-22 situation for both the cheetah and the poacher. These two look like they have been away from their mum for about a week or so, which means they were taken when she first brought them out of hiding and on her hunt.'

'We followed protocol. We called CITES and reported to Officer Van der Weisteshuisen. Hopefully they find who's responsible during their investigation. I feel sorry for those officers, they seem so busy these days. Our wildlife is in peril, and we don't catch enough going out to make those poachers give up trying,' the customs officer said as they walked to the *bakkie*.

'No one can save every animal,' Cole said, stroking the cheetah's head. 'But as long as we each try to save at least one animal when we see it in need, we can, with any luck, keep them preserved for the next generation.'

'I agree. You take care of it!' the customs officer said as he closed the door behind Cole and pointed to the cub. 'I'm glad I swapped shifts and was able to find them. Please keep us updated, we like to know what happened to those that we have a hand in saving.'

'Will do,' Michelle said, before she got in the back with Cole. She had her stethoscope ready to monitor the cub on their journey home again. 'We are ready, Koos.'

Cole switched his attention from the waving officer to the cub that slept on his chest. To its shallow breaths on his chin and the rise and fall of its tiny body under his hand. He smiled and said, 'This one is going to make it, Michelle. We can save it.'

CHAPTER

7

Mackenzie checked her reflection in the entrance-hall mirror to make sure there was no clay smeared across her face.

'Just get the door,' Lauren said. 'You look fine!'

Mackenzie stuck her tongue out at her friend, smoothing her hair just in case. 'You might want to check yourself ...'

As Lauren went to look in a mirror in the lounge, Mackenzie opened the door. 'Hey, you.' She stepped back to allow Cole into her home.

'I know I'm late,' he apologised.

'It's fine, seriously. Gave me a little extra time to work on something and for Lauren to finish cooking. I don't know where the afternoon went.'

Cole smiled as he bent his head to kiss her cheek. 'It's good to see you. These are for you,' he said as he gave her some sunflowers wrapped in cellophane. 'They have to be hothouse grown because they don't flower naturally at this time of the year up here. I thought you might like them.'

Mackenzie buried her face in the soft yellow petals. 'Love them, thank you.'

Lauren walked into the entrance hall.

'Cole, this is Lauren,' Mackenzie said.

Lauren stepped forward. 'Lovely to finally meet you in person,' she said, holding his hand. 'Oh, Mac, he has strong hands, you can keep this one, he's really—'

'Lauren!' Mackenzie shook her head, amused because Lauren hadn't got to know Cole yet, and already she was teasing him like a good friend.

Cole smiled. 'I'm what?' he asked as he withdrew his hand from Lauren's.

'Um … actually, don't worry about that at all,' Lauren said.

'Mackenzie has been telling me about your visit and how much fun you guys are having together. Sorry it's taken me so long to get here and to meet you but it's been hectic in the last two weeks,' he said.

Lauren raised her eyebrows. 'Should I be worried about what tales she's telling?'

'No,' Mackenzie said as she put her arm into Cole's, steering him towards the lounge room.

'Depends … how much is it worth to you?' Cole said.

'You're as bad as her!' Mackenzie said. 'Lauren, you know that it wouldn't be anything bad.'

Mackenzie motioned for Cole to sit on the couch. 'Right, I'll just pop these in some water. Do you want a drink?'

'A beer if you have it,' Cole said.

'I'll do it and I'll bring through the first course. I'm starving,' Lauren said, taking the flowers from Mackenzie and walking away.

'Thanks,' Mackenzie said, sitting down on the couch a little distance from Cole.

'That little cub we rescued, Zulu, is turning out to be quite demanding. We've at last found a puppy, Tala, who's a similar age to him. We introduced them today and they're running about together like lunatics. Zulu still likes to see his humans though, so it's constant around-the-clock play time with him,' Cole said.

'Are you still spending nights in the nursery?' Mackenzie asked.

'No. I'm sharing the shifts with the others. We're taking turns now that he is out of danger. It was touch and go, but he's a fighter that one.'

'Can visitors see him yet?'

'You and Lauren can come and see him with pleasure anytime, but not the general public just yet.'

'Bring me where?' Lauren asked as she walked in with a tray loaded with drinks and starters.

'We're going to see the rescued cub. It's running around now,' Mackenzie said, standing to help.

'Oh yeah! We've been waiting to hear that good news,' Lauren said. 'Right, beer for Cole, wine for Mac. Have you seen Mac's latest sculpture? She took it out of its cast about two days ago. He's stunning.'

Cole looked at Mackenzie. 'Am I allowed to see it? I know how private you are when they are a work-in-progress.'

For a moment Mackenzie hesitated, then she smiled. 'You know what, Lauren has seen them and if she's happy with them why not. Grab one of those fajita things to snack on the way, and come on into the studio.' She led the way through the door, switching on the overhead fluorescent lights as she walked to the work bench. Mackenzie took the canvas off her work-in-progress.

'This is another of my orphans, Jabulani. He doesn't have his patina colour on him yet, but he'll be wearing a blue-striped soccer jersey with darker blue shorts. The soccer ball under his arm is deflated on purpose and his expression is exactly how he looked when I asked him if I could take his photograph. He told me that the photo would steal his soul, but since his ball had already been punctured that day, what else did he have to lose. He's not an easy subject, so I hope I captured that within this bronze.'

'Captured it? He looks almost alive!' Cole said.

'She promised me I could auction this one off in New York,' Lauren said. 'I have a big gala opening night for her new stock and an auction of note to get organised.'

'Auction him off for what?' Cole asked.

'Hopefully about a hundred thousand US dollars. It's in aid of the HIV orphanage in Pietermaritzburg. We're doing a local auction here, too, for Shoebox. Lauren has been working on the campaign while I carried on working on Jabulani and some other things,' Mackenzie said. 'Come, you might as well see them all.'

She walked over to the opposite side where canvases covered all the artworks waiting to be packaged up and shipped. There were wooden crates with lids detached, waiting to be filled, and sacks of bubble wrap that she stepped around. 'Lauren and I will be filling those soon, so some can be shipped, and when she gets back to New York at the end of November, they'll have cleared customs and be ready for the Christmas trade time.' As she spoke she started taking off the covers.

Then she turned to look at Cole. 'This is what I do to pass the time when I'm not racing your beautiful cheetahs.'

She watched as he ran his eyes slowly over each of her 'Little Creatures of Africa Series': the *nagapie*, the bat-eyed fox, the mother vervet monkey pulling fleas out of her baby's hair, the selection of meerkats and the black-footed cat with its spotted and striped fur. He looked past those and walked towards where she had some of her other bigger works, the fat hippopotamus on a bank, a rhinoceros as it charged, and the largest that was completed, a giraffe that had splayed legs while it drank from a waterhole, with bulrushes beside him, their thick brown seeds at the top bursting open. He reached out to touch the bulrush to see if it was soft and velvety like she had made it look.

She couldn't breathe. This was a big step for her, to show him her work was personal. Although Lauren had sort of orchestrated the viewing, she was now nervous. This man was Africa itself. His whole heart was grown in its soil and she was an import, a voyager, creating replicas of the animals he had known all his life and some that he did everything in his power to save. His opinion meant so much to her. It had begun to be important to her as their friendship deepened.

She put her hand on her heart, wondering why she now cared and she smiled, knowing that the attraction they had been fighting all this time was still so new, still so magnetic, and she wanted him to like her work. Needed him to love her work, because it was so much a part of her. She couldn't live without her art, any more than she suspected he could live without his precious cheetahs. She had begun to care for him and she now wanted that spark of proudness from him.

She watched as his fingers ran down the green stem of the bulrush.

'It's deceptive, it's not soft,' he said as if surprised.

'No, it's bronze,' she said, amused.

'These are amazing. I never knew.'

'I kind of kept it to myself. People in Crystalberg know I'm an artist, but no one has ever been in here except my maid, Maria and my gardener, Tsalala. A few deliverymen when they bring in the heavier stuff. Mostly, the sculptures are covered to protect them, so they don't see anything.'

'And you ship these all to the USA? Sell them all there?' he asked.

'No, I sell a lot of my "Little Creatures of Africa Series" in Cape Town, but this consignment is all going overseas,' she said.

'I can see why, your work is incredible.'

'Thank you,' Mackenzie said and she couldn't stop the little thump she felt in her chest knowing that he liked what she created, that he was touched by her art, because if he hadn't liked it, if he had not been someone who appreciated the beauty and emotions within art, she could never have made a future with him.

A future with him? She snorted at herself, wondering where that thought had come from.

'No cheetahs?' he asked, frowning.

'Not yet. I did sketches after you introduced me to Sasha a few weeks ago. I'll be bringing my camera when we come to visit Zulu and will do a cub or two. I've been thinking about it for a long time but just haven't managed to capture the face I want yet in my head. Once I have you can be sure that there'll be some wonderful babies coming out of that furnace.'

'Can I have first option on the cheetahs?' he asked. 'Name the price, it will be worth it.'

Mackenzie looked at Cole. His face was unreadable, just like it had been the day he'd saved her in the taxi incident. He was serious. He liked her work enough to pay for it.

'Sure,' she said. 'We can see when the time comes. Perhaps decide where you're putting it and I'll try to make something for that place.'

'You'd custom-sculpt something for me?'

'Sure, why not?'

'I'll hold you to that,' he said.

'Well, there goes my commission on that piece of work,' Lauren said, and they were all laughing. 'I'm going to reheat the chicken for the fajitas again, while you guys cover everything up.'

Cole helped Mackenzie with her canvases. Placing each one carefully over her pieces once more.

'Thank you for showing me your artworks. They are astonishingly life-like and incredibly beautiful,' he said. 'I'll remember today for a long time.'

She smiled. 'Much the same as the moment I had when you introduced me to your cheetahs, except yours were living, breathing animals.'

'I guess, but these you create. You're very talented.'

'Thanks,' she said. Her heart was still fluttering.

'When is the auction for the orphanage in Pietermaritzburg? I would love to attend and put in a bid on Shoebox,' he said, before he grabbed yet another covering off the floor with her.

'You would?' Mackenzie asked.

'Yes, I would.'

'That would be wonderful, I'd love to have you there,' Mackenzie said as they covered the last statue, her Jabulani.

'You realise that Lauren has organised it as a black-tie event, so you'll have to wear a suit?'

'I own a suit.'

'You do?'

'Sure. It's just impractical to wear to work every day when playing with cheetahs.'

Mackenzie laughed, as did Cole, and together they walked back into the lounge area.

Much later, after dinner was served and after much more laughter, Lauren went to bed early, leaving Mackenzie and Cole sitting on the couch together.

'So.' Cole threaded his fingers through Mackenzie's. 'Have you noticed that we talk about the weather and about everything going on in the world, but we never talk about us? We spent a year avoiding each other and now a month trying to get to know each other better. With your guest and me having another cub to rescue, we are not getting very far very fast, are we? Why did you leave America and come to live here?'

Mackenzie tried to break the contact with him. 'Some things are best just left in the past.'

'Don't pull away,' he said softly, holding on to her, reaching for her other hand to hold, too. 'Just answer one question for me.'

'Depends on the question.' She hesitated, scared he would actually ask her about more than she wanted to reveal about herself.

'Are you in hiding from the law in the USA at all?'

Mackenzie snorted. 'No, I'm not. At first, coming to South Africa was about finding my independence, finding myself, but now it's about staying and putting down my own roots. Finding a place to belong to.'

'Is belonging important to you?'

'I've found peace here.'

'Great.'

'Have you ever been on the wrong side of the law?' she asked, turning the topic quickly off her and back onto him.

'I've never been convicted of an offence.'

Interesting. 'So no criminal record.'

'Hell no!' Cole protested. 'I'm no saint, I've come closer than I thought I ever would, but you don't want to ever go to jail in South Africa.'

'Good to know we're both model citizens, then,' Mackenzie said.

He took both her hands and turned them over, then drew circles inside her palms. 'So tell me about these hands. How is it that they can create such stunning artworks and bring life to metal?'

She grinned. 'I don't know. It's just something that I can do. I've always done it. I think my parents were lost when they had a creative daughter. They did everything they could to discourage me from my art, but somehow I just kept going back to it.'

'How are they about it now?'

'The same. But I hope that distance makes the family function better,' she said.

'So they are both still alive?'

'Yes, I saw them two years ago when I left, they were fine then. My father wasn't happy that I was planning on going away from Texas. I think if he had his way he would come and fetch me back home,' she said.

'But you are an independent woman in your thirties, why would he want to do that?'

'Just because he's my father and he likes things done his way.'

'He's not some religious fanatic, is he?'

'No. Nothing like that, I promise. Now how has Zulu been?' she asked, taking one of her hands out of his and pushing back her hair.

'Okay, I get the picture, I'll stop digging for now. Zulu is active and getting stronger daily. He's taken to Tala so this afternoon Siphiwe and I put them into one of the empty run pens. Who knew that one little cheetah and a puppy could run so fast. They went right to the other end and were rushing about as if it was their first day of freedom. Then Zulu decided he'd pounce on Tala. Tala started howling at the top of his lungs and of course that attracted the cheetah in the next-door area. Tala was trying really hard to get under that fence and away from Zulu. So we took them inside and had them separated. Neither would settle until we put them back together and they promptly fell asleep next to each other.'

'That's sweet!'

'It's good that Zulu still has a hunting instinct and we won't need to teach him that, but I think I should have introduced an older dog as a companion.'

'Why not a puppy so they can grow up together? Actually why a dog at all?'

'We use dogs as company because they protect the cheetah. A dog can be aggressive and confronts trouble while the cheetah is a scaredy cat and it runs away.'

Mackenzie smiled. 'I can't wait to meet them.'

'Anytime you want to come just let me know and I'll tell them to let you in. It'll be great to have you at *nTabaGrequa* again.'

'Thank you, I'll take you up on that.'

Cole's mobile phone rang. 'I need to take this, it's Dumisani, the night watchman.'

He spoke into his phone and for a moment Mackenzie focused on the tone of his voice, not his words.

'I'll be there shortly,' he said and rang off.

'I need to go. Zulu is unwell and Tala is fretting over him, a sure sign that he's sick again.'

'Of course, you just get back and make that little cheetah well,' she said as she stood up and he stood next to her.

'I wish I could have stayed longer,' he said and he leaned in and kissed her lightly on the lips. Then he stepped away.

They walked together in silence, and as Mackenzie opened both the door and the security screen, he stood near her.

'I had a good time tonight, thanks for the invite,' he said. 'Will you come to dinner at my house?'

She was quiet for a few seconds.

'You can bring Lauren,' he added.

'Yes,' she said, 'and the hesitation wasn't because you hadn't included Lauren. It was more that I was just trying to find the right words for you about tonight. "It's been lovely having you" seems inadequate.'

He smiled and walked to his *bakkie*. He climbed in, started his engine and backed out of the drive when she opened the gate. Watching him drive off, she closed the gate again and then locked both the security and the thick wooden front doors. She rested against there for a moment, her fingers touching where he had kissed her. Her lips still tingled.

CHAPTER

8

There was only one thing more certain than death in the world, and that was if maNtuli said she would kill you, it would happen. There would be no witnesses and no one would ever find out who murdered you during the night.

Tobeko Ntuli ruled her empire. From her huge taxi fleet and its domain, to the shebeens with their sex workers, to her chain of night clubs, with its head office inside The Zenith Club in Hillbrow, Johannesburg. MaNtuli was the ultimate boss. Even the Nigerian drug lords, who basically owned the area, were scared of this Swazi woman.

Dominic glanced at her sitting in her office dressed as a prosperous African princess. Despite the warmer September spring weather, she still wore her black power-suit jacket and its long, layered ethnic-print skirt with pantihose, and bright-red stiletto shoes. Her head was wrapped in an elaborately styled headscarf in the same fabric as the skirt. A mix of traditional and modern wrappings for a younger, less well-endowed and curvy lady. He looked away because these days it was her dark-brown eyes that betrayed everything and nothing. She was a black mamba in human skin.

Those eyes showed no emotion except the greed that remained, just a hard, rich businesswoman, determined to succeed, no matter the cost to anyone else. The area around her eyes lacked laughter lines and movement. He had thought more than once lately that perhaps she had gone to too many fancy salons and injected too much Botox there, but then he realised that laughter lines only graced the faces of those who laughed.

MaNtuli never did, and if she smiled it was like a jackal's grin, one to be wary of. She was not someone you ever crossed and lived to talk about it. It had been many, many years since even he had seen a real smile on her face.

But he had to make her understand that what she asked was impossible.

She smiled now in that exact wicked way, despite the news he was trying unsuccessfully to make her understand. One that signalled she was going to come in for the kill once she had all the information and had him where she wanted him. He wouldn't win in a word match with her. He never had. He never would.

'What do you mean the Transnet officer took the cubs?'

'MaNtuli, it wasn't my fault. The e-customs officers changed shifts, and the one on shift doesn't take bribes,' Dominic pleaded.

'Not good enough. The deal was two or more cubs.'

'Ma, I delivered them, they were on the ship for e-three days before they were confiscated! I delivered,' he challenged, scared that if he took the blame, he might never see another member of his family safe ever again. She knew him, she knew who his family was. All of them.

'You lost them before the ship departed. It is your responsibility to deliver more in time for the new ship coming in.'

He could hear the steely determination in her voice. The voice that said – don't fail me again, I will not be so forgiving a second time – without having to say a word.

'But there are no other cheetah cubs in the reserve. Noah can't steal any more, because there are no more to take.' Dominic again tried to reason with the devil.

'That, Dominic Bongwanan, is your problem. I paid you good money for two cheetahs this time. I already told you, my client doesn't care if they are cubs or fully grown, as long as no one can track them. I don't care how you get them, just know that the next ship out is in six weeks, and you are a dead man if you don't deliver at least two live cheetahs to the cook on *Al Ihsaa* when it docks. Do you understand?'

Dominic shook his head. 'Why not tell him that there are no more? Why are you *e*-risking everything just to get these cheetahs?'

MaNtuli crossed over to her large fish tank that was recessed into the wall, its neon light shining blue in her office. Fat orange-and-black oscars swam around, lazily moving in the water in a hypnotic fashion, while a dark-brown plecostomus sucked on the glass, removing any hint of algae, its long whiskers twitching. She lifted the lid and her male Oscar came up for food like it always did, its fat lips pulsating, waiting expectantly.

'See, I feed Oscar, he trusts me. Him and I meet every day. I provide a place for him to exist. He swims in the water I pay for and he eats the food I drop in so he can survive. So he can grow.'

She reached in and pulled the fish out of the water using both hands. 'You see, I raised him from when he was only five centimetres, now he is almost thirty. He has grown so much, my little Oscar.' She kissed the air next to the fish.

'I see that,' Dominic said, his back now ramrod straight, waiting for what she was about to do.

'But I want to show you something, because lately you are thinking that you can argue with me, and you are not completing your side of the bargain. I own you, Dominic. I came and I saved you from a life inside the shacks, living on a little bit of food and perhaps selling your body to those who wanted it. Remember?'

'I always remember, but this time, your order is unreasonable, we need to look further—'

'See Oscar, how he gasps for breath, not knowing that every breath he takes into his lungs is air, not water, and every breath is slowly killing him.'

'I see, I understand—'

'No you don't. You have never understood the need to survive. Even as kids, you thought you could protect me, but you couldn't. It was me in the end who came back and saved you. I made you! I gave you everything, and I can take it away, too. Look at Oscar, and know that if you fail me, I will do this to you.'

She ran her forefinger's acrylic nail over the fish's belly and gutted it. The insides oozed out into her hand. She pulled at them, threading them through her fingers. The fish took its last breath as she pulled its vital organs out of the open cavity.

Dominic shook his head. 'You liked that fish. You nurtured that fish!'

'I like you more, that is why I'm giving you this warning and you're not already dead.'

Dominic stared at her.

She held up her hands. '"Yes, ma". That is all I want to hear.'

'*Hobaneng?*' he asked, looking at the dead fish still held in her hands.

'Because it's business. I earned my reputation as someone who never goes back on a business deal. I said we would deliver one hundred cheetahs, and I keep my word. If you are not helping, you are hindering and I can't have that. I am simply reminding you.'

He stood dead still.

She dropped the dead fish into the wastepaper basket and plopped the guts on top of it, then she washed her hands in her tank. Slowly she withdrew them.

'It's always business, Dominic.'

She stood looking at him, her cold eyes devoid of emotion.

'But, ma—'

'No excuses, Dominic. Just do it. Or there will be severe consequences.'

CHAPTER

9

Mackenzie watched Lauren finish her chocolate milkshake. She sipped right to the bottom, making a slurping noise. 'Come on, slow poke, we're going to be late!'

Lauren put the straw down into the cup, sighed deeply and placed her hand on her stomach. 'What gives? First you influence me to try these delights, then you try to hurry me up while sampling them. I tell you, I'm never leaving, this place makes the best waffles and milkshakes ever! So, what's next?'

'I booked a private CityHop minibus so we can tour Soweto. Drive down Vilakazi Street, and see Madiba's house. It's amazing what a bit of tourism did to lift the living standards in that area. He'll also take us to the Soweto Market. I love the vibrant colours of that place, just hang onto your bag, that's all. It's still an African market and can sometimes have some interesting characters in it.'

'Why don't we just drive ourselves?'

'Ah – no. We're white and both have American accents. We can enter the Soweto Market, but there might not be much of a car left for us to venture out in again, even if we paid a car guard.'

'I guess we're taking the taxi, then,' Lauren said.

'You guessed right,' Mackenzie said.

'What happened to never taking a taxi?'

'This isn't a commuter taxi. The CityHop operates tours. There's a difference. The bus and taxi drivers pay the Soweto gangs to take tourists in and ensure that they'll be safe. I met George, who's one of their drivers, on a tour and he went above expectations, so I started booking him whenever I'm in town. He seems protective of his passengers. I always tip him well because I think he misses out on other jobs by pandering to me. The CityHop service vehicles are all well marked and safe, but I wanted a little bit more one-on-one protection and individual care. Call me paranoid, but that's just how it is.'

'I'm game. So where's he?'

'First we need to pay, then he'll be across the road in the taxi rank.'

Lauren smiled. 'You sound like a tourist guide. You sure have fallen in love with this place.'

'I have.'

'So there's no sign of my friend who likes the smell of New York City, who thrived on the hustle and bustle of people, and who danced on tour nights at concerts around the world with her famous husband? The one who grew up with me and hated anything outdoors? Is she in there anywhere?'

'She is, but I kind of found all this new stuff to do. And I love it. Life is slower, but I like it that way. I'm stopping to smell a lot of *fynbos* along the way now.'

'Seriously, you're even beginning to speak like them … *Fynbos?*'

'Wild flowers of the bush.'

Lauren laughed. 'It suits you, you're so relaxed. Well, let's go do some of this stuff. If this is what makes your art so wonderful, perhaps it can inject something into my agent services and make me sell more at galleries,' Lauren said and she stood up. 'Lead the way to adventure. Beware, South Africa, I'm a tourist, I have my camera, and I'm not afraid to shoot!'

They exited the Milky Way and walked to the taxi rank on the corner, Lauren snapping more pictures as they went.

The red minivan taxi that arrived had the words 'Hop On Hop Off' written in bold letters all over, and there was no mistaking that this was no ordinary commuter taxi but a tour bus. Even the driver was dressed in red, with the same slogan branded across his pressed shirt. His black shorts looked almost dull in comparison. George was tall, he had no facial hair and the hair on his head was teased out in an afro, obviously styled on the yesteryears of the 1970s.

'Miss Mackenzie,' George greeted them and then shook her hand. 'Good to see you again. I was happy to get your telephone call that you were visiting in Johannesburg again.'

'Hi, George,' Mackenzie said. 'So glad you could make it today.'

'For you, Miss Mackenzie, I would make it any day you asked.'

'Thank you,' Mackenzie said. 'This is my friend, Lauren, she was born in Canada.'

'Nice to meet you, Miss Lauren.' George nodded at her. 'You are the second Canadian I have shown my beautiful country to this week.'

'Really?' Lauren asked.

'*Yebo.*' He nodded. 'Yesterday there was a family from outside Calgary. They said it gets so much snow there that sometimes their car is covered and they have to dig it out if they don't put it in the garage at night.'

'That's true,' Lauren said.

'I can never imagine so much snow, but they laughed when I said at least all they have to worry about is some white snow. If I forget to put my car away someone is sure to steal it during the night. Perhaps they did not understand how we live here in South Africa, because they said they don't even have bars on the windows of their house either.' He opened the sliding door of his taxi and the ladies got in.

'No, there is no need in many other countries for bars,' Lauren said.

'*Eish.* I wish for a time when South Africans can live like that, too.' He closed the door and soon was driving through Johannesburg and on the way to Soweto. He gave them a commentary as he drove, pointing out different landmarks and places where things had happened. Like where a friend of his was shot in a drive-by.

'I might have been born Canadian, but I've spent most of my life in America,' Lauren said. 'Mac likes to tease me about being Canadian.'

'You are one of the lucky ones to live in The Land of the Free. *Eish*, lots of South Africans wish they could run away and live there.'

Lauren smiled.

'At the robot coming up, at Empire Road,' George continued, 'there is usually a man who reads books and writes a review on them. If you like his review, you can buy the books from him, too. This is his way of making money for his family, instead of just begging.' He looked around. 'He is not here today, this is sad because Miss Mackenzie often buys his books ...'

'He means the traffic light and I do,' Mackenzie said. 'I think if he can take the time to write a review, I can read a few of his books.'

They continued driving south-west for another half hour until they came into Soweto.

'Do you want a picture with the welcome sign?' George asked.

Lauren was looking out of the window and shook her head. 'You sure this is safe here?'

'Very safe now, this bus, it brings the money into Soweto. The people they look out for it and make it safe,' George explained.

'No, it's okay, thanks but no thanks,' Lauren said.

'Should we do the markets first, Miss Mackenzie?' George asked.

'That'd be great,' Mackenzie said. 'And we want to see Madiba's house afterwards.'

'I hope you can find some bargains,' George said as he stopped in the parking lot. The market was set up in a large red-brick warehouse building and spilled out into the streets around. Vendors could be seen selling their goods to passers-by, people of all nationalities and backgrounds milled around browsing, looking for bargains within the second-hand market and shopping area.

'Do you want me to walk with you today?' George asked.

'Not unless you want to, we should be alright,' Mackenzie said.

George nodded. 'I have some telephone calls to make. I promise I will be here when you are finished.'

'Thank you,' Mackenzie said.

George got out, then came around and opened their door.

The first thing Mackenzie heard when she got out was the music. Loud and distinctively African. Someone beat a drum, someone else played a squash box or a piano accordion, yet somehow the sounds all melded together creating an African melody.

The Soweto Market was vibrant and alive. Street vendors hawked their goods, from fresh piles of rich spices, through to household bric-à-brac, clothes and skins of all sorts were for sale, as were freshly cooked *boerewors* and steak rolls. Peanuts caramelised in a stand next to a sunglasses knock-off shop, next to a material shop that sold silk saris and clothing with bells on it for the Indian population. There was no order to the market, just chaos as hawkers shouted out in all the languages of Africa.

'This is fabulous!' Lauren took yet another photograph of a vendor, this time, an old woman.

Stooped over, the old lady was every bit a traditional nanny. The blanket she had wrapped around her shoulders was a distorted tartan, as if it didn't know if it were an All-Ireland Red Tartan or a Scottish highland pattern. It was a thicker pile with a fringed edge hanging off the bottom in bright maroon. She wore a scarf wrapped around her head and knotted in the front. Her face was lined with years of weathering, and yet she still smiled at them as they approached her table. Her bright skirt fell from waist to mid-calf and was an interesting blend of orange and yellow. Another layer stuck out behind it with a dark-blue bottom. Her feet were covered in blue trainers that looked flat like boat shoes but were not. She stood next to her table, and clapped quietly as she rocked to the music that blasted out all around, while her feet danced to the rhythm. A walking stick lay against the traditional-looking tablecloth. The head seemed gnarled, as if it came directly from an ancient tree and only time and usage had smoothed it. Although there were carvings threading down the stick, the end had a rubber tip on it, as if someone cared that the old woman didn't slip and fall when she relied on the stick to support her weight.

Mackenzie lifted her camera and took photos, changing her settings to take a series of panoramic shots.

Lauren lifted up a glass off a table that held various kitchen utensils, crockery and cutlery. 'Wow,' she said. Leaving her camera hanging around her neck, she dug in her bag and grabbed her torch, and shone it on the glass. The black light made the glass glow a pale lime yellow. 'Oh my God. It's fluorescent!'

Mackenzie asked, 'You telling me you carry around an ultraviolet torch?'

'Hey, I'm an art dealer, you never know when you might need it.' Lauren turned to the vendor, her voice was excited but she tried hard to suppress it. 'Have you got more like this one?'

The old vendor moved behind her table, and nodded her head. '*Robedi.*'

Lauren shook her head and instead held her hands up for six, and the vendor held up eight fingers.

'How much?'

'Two hundred rand each one, special price for you, madam.'

'That's sixteen hundred rand, I don't have that amount on me,' Lauren said.

'Money machine in the wall over there.' The vendor pointed to a part of the market that was covered.

Mackenzie shook her head. 'Don't draw money here, it's not safe.'

Lauren tried the bargaining game. 'I only have one thousand three hundred ...'

'Money machine over there,' the old lady pointed again, not budging on her price.

Lauren turned her back on the woman and dropped her voice. 'I really want those. They're real vintage glass.'

'I'll add to yours and when we get to a safer place, we can draw money,' Mackenzie said. 'If you draw money here, you'll find your account empty.'

Lauren turned to the vendor. 'Okay, I'll take them, one thousand six hundred rand.'

The woman nodded.

Lauren dug in her bag and brought out her wallet, as did Mackenzie, and the vendor began to wrap the glasses in newspaper.

'Wait, I want to check each one,' Lauren said.

The old lady frowned.

Lauren reached for the first of the new ones that the vendor had produced and shone her light, and it also changed colour. As did the next one, but the fourth one glowed purple-pink. She put it aside, and completed the procedure. 'Any more?' she asked.

The vendor shook her head.

'Do you know where these came from?' she asked. 'I'd be interested in finding more like this.'

'I don't remember,' the vendor said.

'Thank you,' Mackenzie interrupted, 'it's alright, she just wanted ten, but we'll take all these, and this one,' she said, adding the one that Lauren had separated from the rest.

'What are you doing?' Lauren said.

'We need to get this and leave. We've attracted unwanted attention and we can do without that. We're being watched by those four men a few tables along. We need to go. Now.'

'Thank you,' Lauren said to the vendor and she quickly paid the money – counting it out.

Mackenzie added hers to make up the total. '*Siyabonga, mma.*' She grabbed the plastic bag with the glasses stacked carefully in it and walked away.

'Mac, you know that one's a fake?' Lauren said.

'I gathered, but your black light has alerted some people and I've learnt to trust my gut here, it's not good. Walk fast, they're following. We need to get to George at the front of the market. If we can get to him before they get to us, we'll be okay.'

They walked quickly, not bumping into anyone. The men still trailing them.

They walked faster, and although they could see that the men had split up, they were still following. The one older man was bald. Mackenzie could see the deep lines in his face. Shorter than the other guard, he stood upright, as if perhaps he'd had military training in his younger days. The taller, darker black man wore a knitted hat pulled down low over his hair, his eyes just peeping out.

'Mackenzie …' Lauren said.

'I know. A few more metres …'

They broke out of the front of the markets, and true to his word, George was waiting near his red minivan. 'George!' Mackenzie called.

He looked up at them, and he ran to assist.

'We're being followed,' Mackenzie said.

He looked over her shoulder, towards the entrance of the markets.

'Get in my taxi, quickly,' he said. 'Lock all the doors.' Then he stood his ground, between the women and the approaching men.

Mackenzie opened the sliding door of the taxi and climbed in, Lauren followed. They shut the door behind them and locked it. Mackenzie reached into the front and made sure the doors there were locked as well.

She turned back and saw that Lauren had her camera out and was snapping off pictures through the back window of George speaking to the men. They were talking, but there was a heap of arm animation happening, and George was shaking his head a lot. Soon two of the men backed away, but two of them remained, who looked like they waited for something.

George walked to his taxi and unlocked the sliding door.

'Miss Mac, what light did your friend have at the market? It made the security there very angry. They said she is the police.'

'Security? They looked like thugs to us. She isn't police. She's an art dealer, she has an ultraviolet torch to test things, see if they are fake or not,' Mackenzie said.

'They didn't like it, they said that lights like that are only used by the police at a crime scene and the old vendor, she didn't need any trouble. She's just selling other people's junk to put some food on her table. She didn't need investigating.'

'No, they have it wrong,' Mackenzie insisted. 'I promise my friend isn't a police officer. We don't care if it was stolen or not, she just likes the glasses and she thinks they're very old. She deals in old art and new art in America.'

'Do you want to see the light?' Lauren asked.

'No! Don't bring it out your bag again,' George said. 'That will make them more angry. Understand?'

'Fine, got it loud and clear,' Lauren said.

George walked away from his taxi and he went back to where two of the guards still stood.

One man was slouched with his feet apart, his hand on his hip, and Mackenzie concentrated on him for a moment. But as she tried to view more of them, the guards turned away from George and walked back into the entrance of the markets, blending into the crowd.

George turned to his taxi, unlocking the driver's door. He got in, then turned around to speak. 'Miss Mac, you are my friend, and many times we have visited this market together. But next time your friend, she must not bring her special light. These security guards, they don't like it.'

'Okay, we won't,' Mackenzie said.

'It's only a black light—' Lauren began to protest, while she was putting her camera away.

'Don't,' Mackenzie said as George started his taxi and pulled into the traffic. 'Things here are not always easy to understand. If he says don't bring it, we don't, Lauren, it's that simple, because next time he might not be able to talk us out of a situation. We could've been in real trouble then. George just saved us, but we don't know at what cost to him.'

'Man, I don't understand Africa,' Lauren said.

CHAPTER
10

Special Agent Hope Anderson stood next to her bed in the NetCare St Anne's Private hospital. Her three weeks in hospital on bed rest were at last over and she was gnashing at the bit to return to active service. What she wanted was being ignored by her bosses, who were insisting that she have a further month's compulsory recovery time, until at least the middle of October. However, they had agreed to her remaining in South Africa and not returning to England.

She'd been lucky. After being Helivaced out of the Ndumo Game Reserve and put into an induced coma for a week, the swelling on her brain had at last reduced sufficiently for the specialists to wake her up. Every single memory had come rushing back. She'd also remembered everything else that had happened afterwards.

Now she just felt anger that she had been forced to miss being in Richards Bay to help save the cubs herself. She'd tipped off the harbour master to the possibility of there being unrecorded live exports on the manifest log and was on her way there when she was shot down.

She couldn't wait to get out and find out what had happened, whether or not they had managed to intercept them. Her boss in London, James Williams, had refused to tell her anything, keeping her in the dark, claiming it was for her own good.

Good would be knowing that her tip had helped.

Good would be knowing that the stolen cubs had been saved.

Not good was being kept out of the loop.

From her work done before the crash, she knew that there was an international mastermind behind the call for cheetahs to be delivered to Bahrain, but she still didn't have the name of the ships involved. She needed to find that mastermind. Infiltrating the underground network of low-lives that ruled the live-animal trade across the world had been her most important undercover assignment to date, and in their recent phone calls James said she had to take extreme care and not trust anyone.

But she did trust one person. The same person who had created one of her best memories, when she had woken up wrapped in the embrace of a warm male body. She had asked the nurses about him at the hospital, and what they said had been interesting because it confirmed everything she already knew and suspected about him. She remembered how her hero had lugged her through the African bush to safety, been a gentleman during the night, and medicated her once she was awake, probably saving her life twice over. The aspirin he'd given her had helped to thin her blood and stop her having an aneurism. She had a lot to thank Mandla Mabuza for, including that he was coming to collect her from the hospital, and giving her a place to stay until she got the all-clear from England. She was looking forward to living in a real home as opposed to her usual hotel stints.

'Hope.' She heard his distinctive voice as he walked through the door.

'Hi,' she said, quickly looking him over. He was just as tall as she remembered.

'Good to see you up and about.'

'It's good to be up and active.'

'Come on, once we grab your bag we can head home.'

Hope was suddenly nervous. 'I can go to a hotel …' She suddenly thought she didn't know her hero that well, other than a few visits to her in hospital, and his thoughtfulness of bringing her clothes, cosmetics and flowers. What if he lived in a hut? What if he was a traditional African who lived in a hut on a farm somewhere? She hadn't thought to ask.

'Come, see my place. If you are uncomfortable when you visit, then we can always take you to a hotel later,' he reassured her, and without even knowing it, settled her nerves totally.

They collected her small hospital discharge bag from the bed. She was so grateful for the clothes he'd brought her to wear as the green linen suit she'd worn on her undercover hunting operation at Thompson's farm was completely ruined.

'I loved the flowers, but I took them into the children's ward earlier so that they could enjoy them now,' she said.

'Great idea. I'm glad you found someone who would continue to appreciate them.'

They walked out of the front doors and to his vehicle in the parking lot. A black BMW X5 blinked at them when he pushed the button on his key ring. He opened the passenger door, waited while she climbed in before he walked around to the driver's side.

'Nice car,' she said.

'I like it. I really don't get to use it as much as I would like. I'm often away from my place, so it sits in the garage a lot.' He smiled at her.

'So, where exactly do you live?' she asked.

'In a gated townhouse in Hilton. That way I don't have to worry about mowing the grass when I'm away, it's done for me, and I can just close the door and leave. It's safe.'

Hope felt a hot blush start at her chest and flutter over her face.

'You thought I was taking you to a traditional mud hut or into an informal settlement, because I'm black and I must live in a shack?'

'We've slept in less before—'

He stammered. Lost for words.

She laughed. 'Got you! But yes, I had a moment of panic just as you arrived. Admitting that before then I hadn't given it a thought.'

'Fair enough, your English world and mine are very different.'

'They are, but they're similar, too. So many things that South Africans do are so very colonial. I guess because you were once part of the British Empire there will always be remnants of a shared history.'

'Never thought of it like that, but yes,' he said.

'Do you have a computer at your house I could borrow? I know it's a lot to ask.'

'It's not too much to ask and of course you can use it. I think we have your phone at the company, we can grab that for you, too.'

'You found my cell phone?'

'After Charl collected you, I went back to your plane. I found it then.'

'Does it still work?'

'It does now. I had to do a few repairs, replace the glass, but I got it working.'

Hope thought hard as to what was on her cell phone and how much he would have seen when he was repairing it. Messages to and from her folks, and her personal notes on her case were on there.

'I didn't read your messages or anything, just got it working again. I respected your privacy. Although your boss asked for copies of your texts and documents, I told him I couldn't access them,' Mandla said.

An eerie feeling washed over Hope as she wondered if Mandla was psychic as he continually anticipated her next move. 'Thank you. I'm not sure why you did that, but thank you.'

'Because it's your phone, not his. Anyway, we didn't know what you had got yourself involved in. When I went back to your plane I had a good look around. You were right, you crashed because you were sabotaged. You were also way off your flight plan, way off. So until we know who you trusted and who you didn't, we were not sharing anything about you with anyone. No matter what they said, not even your boss, and not until you came out of hospital and were one hundred percent okay.'

'Thank you,' Hope said. 'I know I sound like a stuck record, but there isn't much else I can say.'

Mandla smiled. 'So, all your memories are back?'

'I think so,' she said. 'But some things don't make sense.'

'Do you want to talk through anything?' Mandla asked.

'I've been a lone agent for so long. Learning to trust someone else just doesn't come naturally, but it would be great to talk a few things through with someone I know is on the same side of the fight.'

'Like?'

'There's this one memory that's worrying me. I remembered huts and a face of a man talking to me, but I can't quite place a name, and I'm usually so good with names.'

'What can you remember about the huts?'

Hope closed her eyes and concentrated on her breathing. 'Round. Made with mud. Thatch roof. Decorated with some type of tribal pattern in brown. There were other houses, built of corrugated iron and cardboard. And a proper house, made of brick. A group of dogs barked constantly.'

'And the man?'

'Dark honey-brown, missing both his front teeth. Animated when he speaks, with excessive gestures. A bit slow, like he has a slight disability perhaps. He wasn't overly tall, just average, a massive scar up his leg. His clothes were tatty and frayed, and yet there was a TV aerial on their roof. I can't hear his voice, but there was a woman beside him, she was old. Really old, she walked with an ornate walking stick. She wore more traditional dress, a headscarf, an impala skin around her stomach area. And a bright-pink bra with nothing covering it. And she was hitting him with a grass broom on his arm, over and over while we were talking.'

'That's a start. Anything else? Trees? Colour of the ground? Can you smell anything?'

'No trees. There were flies, lots of flies. The ground was swept clean, nothing growing near the house. No maize patch or veggie garden before the next structure. They were really close and I had to walk carefully between them so I didn't get lost. It's like a passage, only the walls are people's homes.'

'And other than dogs, any other animals?'

Hope kept her eyes closed for a moment more, then opened them. 'Nope, but there were transport cages for smaller animals, maybe for cats. I was definitely there on business.'

'Keep your eyes closed, Hope, perhaps you will see more.'

Hope moved her head on her shoulders to ease the tension building there. 'No, that won't help. I'll just wait for more to come to me about why this is haunting me. I know that it's significant, but I don't know why yet.'

'The pieces will fit eventually. Don't stress over it. There is a possibility that you hadn't managed to connect the dots yet before the crash, so now your mind is still working on a problem it was trying to resolve then.'

'Oh I'm not stressing, believe me, you'll know when I stress. I just need to work it out. Perhaps my phone and access to my computer files will help.'

'Your head took quite a knock, and it'll still be a bit tender. You gave us a reality check dropping out the sky. That could have been any of us fighting this war against the illegal animal trade.'

'I know, and I promise to take it slow, not act on anything until I'm certain of it.'

They drove for another twenty minutes in silence, climbing slightly into the hills. A 'Welcome to Hilton' sign came into view, and she saw Mandla smile. He stopped outside a set of huge black iron gates, and a security guard came out of his century box on the inside of the gate, and opened them.

'Thank you, Sam,' Mandla called out.

Sam waved at him and his broad grin spoke of the easy friendship between the men, despite their different stations in life.

Driving around the smart modern complex, Hope began to laugh. 'I'm so sorry for doubting you,' she said as they waited while a double garage door made of what looked suspiciously like oak folded upwards, admitting them into a spacious and neat garage.

'Home,' Mandla said.

'I see that.'

'*Eish.* Come on. I'll give you the grand tour.' He retrieved her bag from the boot and walked into the townhouse.

Decorated in creams and tranquil natural shades, it was as if it was lifted from an interior decorator's magazine.

'Did you decorate?'

'No, it came like this when I bought it off plan, but I did purchase the rug in my bedroom,' he said proudly.

He walked her to his room and opened the door. It was decked out in the same neutral colours, except for the beautiful mat spread over the cream carpet. It was some native design in browns, blues and greens, with a silhouetted bushman walking along in a line. It was stunning.

'I saw it in a curio shop in Mbabane, Swaziland, and I just had to buy it. It's the only thing that ever spoke to me and said, "buy me".'

'It's beautiful!'

'That it is,' he said, when they walked out of his room. 'This is your room here opposite mine. I bought you a few things to wear while you were here. The labels are still on so you can take them back if you don't like them, but I figured you would need some essentials until you got to go shoppings, since your stuff from the plane crash was totalled.'

She looked into the guest room. 'Thank you, that was really nice of you. I'll pay you back, just let me know how much I owe you for all that you've bought and for the clothes in hospital. It would've been embarrassing walking out in a hospital gown. I can't remember ever being so pampered before by a man and we're not even a couple.' Then, realising what she had said, she stopped talking for a moment, and an awkward silence weighed heavily between them. 'Um, you know what I mean—'

Mandla laughed. 'I know and understand. Come, we can eat some lunch on the verandah. You must be starved for real food. That hospital's fancy, but the meals are still hospital catering.'

They walked down the stairs. The ample four-bedroom unit was obviously too large for the bachelor, and he rattled around in it. Walking out onto the patio, the scene took her breath away.

Looking out over the green hills, and to the majestic Drakensberg in the distance, the panoramic view was spectacular. 'Wow,' she said.

Mandla nodded. 'I thought that when I stood here before they built it. It was the reason I bought here, it's like looking at freedom.'

'That it is,' she said, sitting down into the chair he'd pulled out for her. 'And it's so not a hut.'

'A smart *ikhaya*.'

She laughed.

He poured her a glass of fruit cocktail, and unwrapped a seafood platter and placed it on the table between them.

'Did you cook this earlier?' she asked.

'No, my maid, Emily looks after the place, makes sure there is not too much dust around, and feeds me when I'm home. I share her with Charl, but when I told her you were coming, she arranged it all. She had to take her baby to the doctor, or she would be here to meet you.'

'That's sweet, I'll remember to thank her when I meet her.'

'Advanced warning, she is very curious about you, being a British woman with a mixed racial heritage, flying your own plane. She thinks the world of you already.'

'Oh as long as you didn't talk me up to her or anything.'

He grinned. Mandla's cell phone rang. He glanced at the screen. 'I need to get that, excuse me,' Mandla said as he rose from the table and walked into the lounge area.

She could hear his voice muffled in the room, then it rose in volume, and then quietened down again, as if he had got his temper back under control. After a long while Mandla came back out.

'I'm sorry, Hope. I know I was supposed to be on leave, but we have lost contact with another of our GPS trackers, this time in the Kruger National Park. I need to go. You are welcome to stay here, make yourself at home. Or perhaps you might want to go into a hotel, but I have to find this animal.'

'Or I could come with you? I'm a good agent in the field. I know I'm a little unfit from being in hospital but I can cover your back.'

He stared at her as if she was insane.

'I won't break in the bush. I've hiked in Siberia while smashing a tiger poaching ring there. And spent months in the Indian jungles. I'm not going to freak out in South Africa. I might be slow to begin with, but my fitness will come back fast. I need to be active, and getting right back into my life would help me so much.'

'Hope, it's going to be strenuous.'

'I know, and I won't slow you down.'

'What if you get captured, raped? A woman in the bush—'

'You think I can't look after myself, after all these years I've been an agent, that I'm not capable?'

'No, I believe you are. If any woman I have met can hold her own, it's you. But your boss is going to go crazy at us, you are supposed to be on holiday resting.'

'So what? Don't tell him,' she said, then scratched her head. 'Actually, better yet, I'll tell him, because yes he's going to freak out, but he'll see the sense in all this when he sees the link between my work and yours. I can call it interagency cooperation.'

'Only we are both private firms.'

'Let me come with, you could use the help, and I could use the time feeling useful again, knowing I'm doing something useful.'

Mandla looked at her, and for a fraction of a second he hesitated, but then he caved. 'Fine,' he said. 'But you'll have to do as I say, run when I say so. We will be in the middle of the reserve again and God knows there are no animals in the world like the wild African beasts. I don't care what other people say, they are always dangerous. And if you can't keep up, then Charl will come and fetch you in the helicopter, understood?'

'Yes, sir.' She saluted him cheekily.

* * *

Mandla was behind the wheel of his BMW again, driving towards headquarters. He stopped at an army surplus store in Kirk Street, and Hope jumped out. 'I'll only be ten minutes, don't bother parking,' she said.

She checked her watch as she ran into the store. It wasn't the best set out place in town, but it had loads of surplus stock and she quickly found what she was looking for. Paying for the supplies, she checked her watch as she left – ten minutes on the dot.

'You sure you are all set?' he asked, looking at her shopping bags.

'I think so,' she said.

For twenty minutes Hope sat watching the buildings go past, through the town and into the industrial side of Pietermaritzburg, and finally into a gated complex.

'Headquarters,' Mandla said.

The Bushman's Software Company had a large traditional shield and assegai with their BSC logo painted on the front of the building. The actual building itself looked like almost every other building in the complex, grey concrete with a high roof of silver corrugated iron, with lots of windows to let in natural light and whirlybird extractor fans on the roof to remove the heat inside. There was allocated parking in one section and visitors' spaces.

'Nice building, unassuming,' Hope said.

'It's functional,' Mandla said, then pressed a security tag to a reader and the door clicked open. He motioned her in first and then walked inside after her.

Standing around a snooker table were three white and two black men. She knew them all from Mandla's descriptions, but had only met them briefly when they came to see her in hospital, except Charl, who she remembered well from their flight to the hospital. At least up until she had passed out on him when her brain had started swelling again.

Mandla cleared his throat. 'Hope, this is the team.'

Brian walked forward and shook her hand. 'Nice to see you again, Special Agent Anderson.'

Charl stepped up and enveloped her hand in his. '*Ag*, it's so great to see you up and about.'

'Thanks, and thank you again,' Hope said.

'*Ag*, was my pleasure, but I did the easy part, Mandla was the one who did the hard work with saving you.'

Hope smiled.

The other men were introduced as Colin, the Australian code genius, and Moses and Owen, who were rangers who monitored some of the computers tracking the animals.

Mandla said, 'Hope's coming with me into Kruger.'

'Great,' Brian said as if he was expecting it. He turned his back to them and walked into the next room. 'You might want to follow me in here, Hope.'

She walked after him, leaving Mandla with the men.

Brian had a gun safe open. 'I guess you could use this, then.' He passed Hope her Glock.

She pulled the weapon out of the worn leather holster. She knew the scratches on the barrel and remembered how she had run the tip over concrete in Bhutan a year before, accidentally making the distinctive marks, and how angry she had been with herself for spoiling it. 'Thank you.'

'Great,' Mandla said. 'Now I just have to hope you remember how to shoot it so you don't put one in my back.'

'I can assure you that I remember how to shoot,' she said.

'All the same, would be good to have you in the range for a few rounds before we go out there,' Mandla said. 'Just for fifteen minutes, brush up because you have been out of it.'

'Sure.' She smiled.

Brian opened a second wall safe, then he passed her the magazine and ammunition. She checked over her weapon. It was clean, oiled and lint free. Obviously someone had cleaned it regularly, even though it was packed away. The smell of the oil was familiar.

'Right, Mandla,' Brian said, 'other than your .303, what else are you taking this time?'

'I think also a .9mm and two knives.'

'Can I have throwing knives, too, if you have any spare? I bought a simple bush one at the surplus store on the way here, but I'm not sure of the quality.'

Brian shook his head. 'You're amazing. Just three weeks ago you fell out of the sky and here you are looking for a good knife to go back into the combat zone with. Be careful of this one, Mandla, I can see nothing but trouble ahead with her.'

Mandla punched his friend in the arm. Hard.

Brian signed out the weapons and ammunition to Mandla and Hope. He also added two transmitter radios and a portable GPS. A small sat phone briefcase was next, and lastly he added to their pile a laptop computer. 'Go find it,' he said. 'We need an explanation as to what's happening. If it's poachers, we need to pin these bastards to the floor. Your helicopter is waiting at hangar one at the airport.'

Mandla went to another locker and extracted two backpacks and space blankets, four canteen bottles and ration packs for a week.

'Do you eat eggs?' he asked Hope.

'I eat anything,' she said. 'I'm blessed with a cast-iron constitution.'

'Good, makes rationing easier,' he said as he shared out the energy bars between the packs.

Charl came into the room. '*Is jy* ready?'

'We just need a bit of time in the shooting range,' Mandla replied.

'Give me five minutes to change.' Hope took her bag from the army surplus and went into the ladies.

Within five minutes, the professional agent returned, dressed all in camo. She passed a small bag of cosmetics to Mandla to add into her pack.

He stared at her.

Charl pointed to the shooting range in the back. 'Range is that way.'

Mandla entered a security code on a door, then stepped back for Hope to precede him. Inside was an indoor shooting range, as modern as she had seen in the UK and anywhere else she had worked in the world.

Brian arrived and issued out extra ammo, then he put on earmuffs and waited at the back as Charl joined him.

Mandla took the booth on the right and Hope took the one on the left. The red light flashed, indicating that the range was occupied and active. Both put their ear protection on.

The human target dropped down at the back and Mandla emptied his .9mm into it. Hope did the same into hers. They both pushed the retrieve buttons and a string brought them the cardboard cut-outs.

Mandla had a cluster accurate around the heart area. Hope's first bullet had hit high in the shoulder, but then training had taken over and she'd adjusted, and her cluster was as close as Mandla's.

'Guess that answers that one,' Mandla said.

'Nice to know he's going in there with competent backup,' Brian said, resting his hand lightly on Hope's shoulder. 'Makes a change from his lone-wolf missions.'

'Guess we are ready then,' Mandla said as they returned to the main area.

Hope grinned. She shouldered her pack and followed him out to the BMW. Gone was the feminine light swirly skirt she had worn just a few hours ago. Gone, too, was the loose, flowing wild hair, as she had bound it and tucked it up into her cap.

She was a soldier going to war.

CHAPTER
11

Flying in the chopper didn't trigger any nightmare moments for Hope. The only thing that gave her away as being excited was that she couldn't sit still. Finally she was moving again. She was out in the wide-open spaces and doing something to save the beloved wildlife of the world. Her job as an undercover wildlife dealer for Global Wildlife International had its perks. Lots of fresh air, open spaces, but also its downfalls, like having your plane sabotaged.

She took a deep breath.

'You okay?' asked Mandla.

'Yes, I'm good.'

'Perhaps next time you can fly us in to the nearest airstrip with our company plane, save Charl the trip,' he said.

Hope knew that she was a damn good pilot. Having flown solo on her sixteenth birthday, the sky was as much part of her as the wildlife of the world that she chose to protect, but since going down, she now doubted herself.

'I would need a few co-pilot trips again. I hate admitting weakness, but I'm scared to take the controls,' she said.

'I'm happy to take you on those when you get back. If it can get airborne, I fly it,' Charl said. 'You can't have your wings clipped.'

'Thanks, Charl, I'll hold you to that,' she said.

It wasn't that she was scared, was it? Of course not. Why would any girl be scared after crashing because someone had tampered with her plane? She'd survived though, hadn't she?

Hope was lost in her memories as they landed in Nelspruit for fuel and soon continued their journey north-east towards the way-point in the Kruger Park.

'ETA three minutes,' Charl said to them through their headphones.

Soon the familiar pitch of the drone of the engine vibrating through her seat changed and she could feel the helicopter land lightly in a clearing. Two men leant against a green 4x4 waiting for them.

Charl cut the engine, and as soon as the blades had slowed he got out and walked to the other side to remove the luggage he had stowed there.

'Howzit, Martie.' Mandla shook hands with the ranger. 'Meet Peg, my girlfriend.' They had decided to lie to everyone who didn't know Hope already until they had time to fully discuss her case together.

'Mandla, I've known you since our army days and that's the first big whopper yous ever spun me. That's no girlfriend of yours. Special Agent Hope Anderson paid us a visit a few months ago, and I knows yous is *regter*-right, so she wouldn't be investigating anything by yous.'

'Martie Viljoen,' Hope said, nodding. 'And Zonke, nice to see you both again.'

Martie put his hand out and shook hers. 'I heard about your accident, I'm sorry to hear about yous is plane. Man she was sweet, too. Good thing yous is alright anyway. Glad yous is back. I hope yous are working on yous is case and find these bastards that keep stealing my cubs, because I tell yous, they are gonna pay big time if I ever catches them. It will be like a bullet and an *aardvark* hole for thems, no bladdy court case to drag me away from my post while they steal and snare our animals.'

'Thank you,' she said. 'I'm getting back up to speed fast, but I think I was lucky that it was Mandla who found me. He's been a real lifesaver.'

'Hey, Martie,' Charl said as he came around from the other side of the helicopter with their packs.

'*Ja*, Charl.' Martie shook his hand. 'Good to see yous, too. I was just telling Hope here that Mandla saved her, but someone else found her first. We have's seen more children's spoor in our reserve, too, now that Mandla alerted us-es to watch out for them. It seems that the someones is sending kids into the bush alone to check the snare lines and spot the game, and thems are only coming in when they are safe to.'

'Child soldiers with a difference?' Hope asked.

'Hell no, no difference, these kids are well armed, theys will take yous down if you gives them a half a chance. It's organised crime, not local tribal trouble,' Martie said. 'Before, we just didn't realise hows well managed and hows many were in the park.'

'*Eish*,' Mandla said. 'And your patrols, they never noticed children in your park before?'

'No. Always before it's beens the adult footprints we was interested in, so I guess we never focused on the smaller spoor. The park is a unnecessarily dangerous place for anyone's children.'

'I wonder what changed that they decided to send in kids and who the children belong to?' Hope said.

'I don't know, but we haves you and Mandla to thanks for alerting us-es to this,' Martie said.

'I have flown low over here and Hluhluwe recently and I haven't seen anyone from the air,' Charl said.

Martie shook his head. '*Ja*, man, seems a kid can hide easier and perhaps get away if caught, easier than a full-grown man and those bladdy poachers have worked it out.'

'What changed? Why the children?' Mandla asked.

'Would you shoots a kid? Neither would any of my anti-poaching guards. Most of thems is fathers themselves. So even with a increases in the foot patrols and the new mounted patrols, but they only seen thems in person once. And they didn't shoots to kill. They didn't even shoots.'

'A new threat, but at least now we are all aware of it,' Mandla said.

Martie nodded. 'Glad Hope is working with you and isn't still having to hang with that snotty Thompson *oke* from the Limpopo.'

'Me, too,' Mandla said.

'Me three,' said Hope.

'Right, be safe, both of you. I'm off,' Charl said as he reached forward and bumped his knuckles with Mandla. 'Safe, man.' He jogged back to his chopper and they watched him lift off.

Zonke had taken both their packs and stowed them in the back of the green Land Rover. It was old and battered, the windscreen was broken in a spider pattern across the passenger side and there was no roof.

'I thought you guys got new vehicles donated a few months back,' Mandla said, before he opened the back door for Hope to get in.

'We did, but the poachers put sugar in my petrol tank three weeks ago. Then they shots one of my big tuskers. They thought I couldn't chase them, but Zonke had put this old thing in one of the sheds, he was trying to save up enough to pay for it, so we gots it out. This old girl will go anywhere, and her diesel tank, it just keeps going and going. So we chased and we caught the bladdy black bastards, thanks to your tracking devices, we chased thems through the *bundu* and got thems. Pity, the jumbo, he was already dead. We got the signal it was in distress, but by the time we gots to it, *ag*, man – it was a sad sight.'

'Sorry to hear that,' Mandla said.

'*Ja*, thanks hey, but we caught them red-handed with thems tusks. And the bladdy poachers are now in jail awaiting trial, but they wills probably just pay someone and get off with a fine. Burns my ass, I tell yous. One we shot in the bum, just wish it had been in the chest and he was dead. Until they know we ares going to kill them like they do in Zimbabwe, they going to continue to poach in my park.'

Mandla slammed the door. 'Lucky thing this tracking system is as good as it is and it just keeps getting better.'

'*Ja, boet*, but that's why you is here now. My cheetah cubs. Before we get to chip them, they are being stolen and now the mum, her chip went *dood*. Just like those in Hluhluwe a few months back, except we didn't even sees it blink again. And we checks the area, there is human tracks leaving but not cat spoor. No cheetah walks away from that area and we haves no comms with it. It disappeared. Poof.'

'I hear that, it's not good,' Mandla said.

'We're hoping we are wrong and it's just the GPS tracker failing, like the one from Hluhluwe.'

Mandla shook his head. 'We don't think so. We found the Hluhluwe male in Ndumo. Darted it and took it back. It went through two weeks in a quarantine *boma* to get rid of its homing sense, so it doesn't go back again. We put a new chip in it. We are still waiting on the lab to see if there was a faulty chip or what happened there.'

Martie started the vehicle. 'It travelled far, *Ja*?'

'A hundred and thirty-three kilometres.'

'Not as far as that Darlington male in the Cape, hey?'

'He was about 350 kilometres. He took just under a year to travel through the bush. The Hluhluwe cheetah got to Ndumo in a few hours. We think this one had help. We don't think he got out, but was taken. He showed a new animosity towards the people handling him. More aggression than a normal wild cheetah.'

'You think he is taken? And someone is messing with yous' GPS trackers?' Martie asked.

'Yes.'

'*Jusses, boet*. That stinks if they have found a way around yous' system, man, wes rely on it all the time.'

'You and almost every other game reserve, private or government owned,' Hope said.

'So what yous doing to stop the tampering?'

Mandla adjusted his belt. 'Our coders are working on that. Brian has some new whizz-bang teenager who has joined us from

Australia and they are convinced the system isn't compromised. Someone is transporting these cats. Shutting down their trackers. I just have to find the proof and find out how.'

Martie nodded.

Zonke sat in the front seat. 'Good, because I don't want to learn a new computer. I likes this one, it is easy even for me.'

Mandla laughed. 'I hope you don't change or I'll have to find another way to pay the bills and I'm too old to start again.'

Hope put her hand over her mouth to try and cover her laugh, but the two guffawed aloud as they bumped their way over the uneven bush and were soon at the site where the last GPS beep had shown the mother cheetah's tracker.

* * *

'Who else has been here?' Mandla asked.

'No one. We know when we find a problem to radio you guys at headquarters and wait for you to get here. Not to move anything,' Zonke said.

'I drove right here, yesterday,' Martie said. 'I rang yours company when I gots home again, cell phones just don't work this far into the reserve.'

'No towers, that's why the GPSes work on satellite, not cellular,' Mandla commented.

'I'm sure these cellular companies wills bribe some official sooner or laters and we'll get an artificial palm tree sitting somewhere above the acacia trees, too,' Martie said. 'A nice high artificial tree for the *breekoparend* eagles to nest in, now that would looks good in all the photographs for the tourists, wouldn't it?'

Mandla grunted as he put his pack on, then turned to help Hope. Hope smothered a smile as hers was on already.

Mandla began walking in circles around the 4x4, working outwards.

Soon he called to Hope, 'This way. Two sets of prints. The left one weaker than the man on the right. They are transporting something heavy. I suspect they carried the cheetah out in some type of crate. That's why there are no cheetah footprints here,' he said. 'Cheers, Martie, Zonke, see you soon with good news, I hope.'

Like a bloodhound on a scent, he went off in the direction of the thickest bush. Hope followed, jogging at first to catch up, but then finding her stride she fell into step, keeping up with his easy gait.

They tracked the spoor for six hours, only stopping for water and bush-styled breaks. Energy bars were eaten as they walked and there was no speaking as they conserved strength. Too soon the darkness swept over them and Mandla called a halt on his search for a suitable campsite. 'Here's a really good place, this mopani will do well.' He set his pack down underneath a huge tree.

'Tomorrow, we pick up the spoor again. It's a new moon tonight, which means it will be as dark as dark and I don't want to run into anything,' he cautioned.

Hope followed suit. Her back muscles were killing her, being unused to the pack. She didn't complain. She felt alive for the first time since her accident.

'Dinner and bed and we have an early morning. There is bad weather forecast for later this week, and I could lose the spoor, so we'll need to move it tomorrow. How you holding up?' Mandla asked as he took out a billycan and two plates.

'Ah, crystal this time,' Hope commented. 'I'm holding up just fine.'

'Planning. If I'd known I was getting company the last time, I would have gladly provided cutlery and crockery, crystal glasses and some Cape Velvet, too.'

'I could drink a lot of that creamy liqueur if given half the chance. It's smooth-as-smooth.'

'That it is, but sorry, all out this time too, Miss Hope,' Mandla said as he winked.

Sitting across the small fire from each other, they ate dinner in silence and made sweet coffee for afterwards.

Mandla had made their beds while there was dappled light. Not asking her if she wanted to sleep near him, but putting his stretcher against hers. The mosquitoes buzzed insistently, and although Hope sprayed more repellent on her skin, they still seemed to bite her all over. She rolled her head in tiredness, her shoulders tight.

'So you lied to me. You are not holding up so fine. Come on over here and I can rub your back for you,' Mandla offered. She didn't need to be asked twice. She scooted to the other side of the fire and sat in between his athletic legs while he worked magic. He started at the bottom of her back, rubbing gently, then he increased the pressure, then again, as he found where the muscles had knotted because of the excess weight.

'Your pack is too heavy,' he said.

'No, I'm just out of practice. Mandla, Martie mentioned Thompson.'

'I know of him. He's quite a nasty player in the hunting fraternity. He has a big farm near Tzaneen in the Limpopo region, and although nothing has been proved, he's suspected of being involved in canned hunting of lions and other cats on his property.'

'I know, I spent a week there posing as a hunting client. Putting up with his arrogant attitude and his overpowering cologne, trying to collect evidence on him, and I found nothing to suggest that he's doing what he was accused of. I purposely missed every single animal he lined up for me on my really overpriced charter and I eventually left empty-handed, except for what looked like a bank account number I found on his notepad when I rubbed a pencil across the indentations: "Two. Tuesday – Richards Bay!" was written under that number. He's the reason I was flying to Richards Bay. I was on my way to check out the docks, looking for two cheetah cubs that I knew had been taken from the Kruger. I figured they were destined for a ship when I went down. So I couldn't nail Thompson's arse for canned hunting, or for illegal animal trade, not yet, but I'm close. I'm just waiting to see what my boss digs up on that bank account.'

'I had no idea you were after him,' Mandla said.

She nodded. 'I'm after the mastermind, the top player. So I can't take down the smaller fish along the way until I crack the whole chain, but someone with lots of power and deep pockets is arranging for a lot of cheetahs to be taken from the wild and from all over the world. They're amassing cheetahs somewhere. I suspect that at least some CITES officials are involved somehow, but I'm still trying to gather evidence.'

'So you were undercover here in South Africa. How did Martie know who you were? Why did you trust Martie with your real identity?'

'I just trusted him. There's something about him and his passion for the animals, it's real, not put on for the tourist trade.'

Mandla nodded. 'I've known Martie since we were in the army together. He likes to talk, but he would die before knowingly helping a poacher to kill anything in his game reserve. Zonke joined Martie many years ago, when Martie was first starting out in the Parks Board. Zonke was his tracker. He had a shady past, but from what I've seen, he's true to their cause now, and he'd lay down his life before helping a poacher. So your trust was well placed.'

'Do you remember earlier, when I spoke of that memory? The village, the man and the old woman? I know how the man fitted in. I went to see Martie about him. Sometimes he lives on the border of the Kruger National Park in Polokwani, sometimes he's in Alex township. His name is Noah Bongwanan. He's one of the small fish I've found on the way. So far I've traced his "boss" to be his brother, Dominic, who lives in Sandton in a house way above his means. I haven't had a chance to dig further on those two yet, because that was when I was told about Thompson and my boss asked me if I could investigate him further. But I'm still trying to figure out the old woman's part, or if she even has one.'

They sat together, both lost in their own thoughts.

A branch snapped nearby. Mandla was alert immediately, drawing his .9mm. Hope saw his reaction and drew her Glock.

Mandla heard a rumble and more breaking trees. 'Listen. Jumbo.'

'Then why are we just standing here? Shouldn't we be up a tree or something?'

'Depends on the elephant, but that's why we are camped right next to this mopani tree, so we can climb it if need be. It has no thorns, perhaps a few caterpillars from the mopani moth, but we should be good to get from there onto that big boulder behind us, and no elephant's getting on top of that rock.'

A lone elephant bull walked into their campsite, musth marks clearly running from near his ears, and urine leaking down his back legs. The bull was in the height of his sexual arousal and at his most dangerous. He shook his head, his trunk jiggling and he trumpeted.

'Shit, up the tree,' Mandla said.

She climbed quickly into the branches, while Mandla was pushing her, helping her up. Somehow he had grabbed his .303 from its resting place and his backpack and soon they were up high enough to jump onto the boulder.

The elephant used his trunk to smell her pack and avoided the small fire that Mandla had lit in the pit. He lifted a water bottle in his trunk, trying to get into it, as if he could smell the water inside. Hope held her breath.

Somewhere in the distance another elephant trumpeted. The bull lifted his huge head and he trumpeted back.

The hairs on her body stood on end. Hope looked at Mandla. He was seated on a small ledge of the boulder, using it as if it was a giant chair back and he had his computer open.

'Meet Jolo. He's a male, approximately thirty-five years old and a known mischief. He has been caught outside of Kruger more than once and been relocated back into the park. He's a crop raider of the maize in the informal settlements on the border. And he's a lion hater. He's known to attack them when he comes upon them.'

'Wow,' Hope whispered. 'He has quite the honour roll.'

'He usually is in the company of Mlalazi and Mahamba. I wonder where they are tonight?'

'Can't you look for them on your system?'

'I'm doing that as we speak,' Mandla said.

'Ah, there they are, there is a whole herd heading this way. There is a waterhole nearby, they obviously want to browse in the forest here during the night, then will get to water first thing in the morning. Guess we are stuck up on this rock for a little while.'

'Right.' Hope moved herself next to Mandla and dangled her legs over the edge.

Soon another elephant moved into their line of sight and then a third. Carefully, they picked their way around the stretchers and over the now dying fire, not disturbing the camp. The three bulls walked out, not damaging anything and not worried about the humans.

Mandla sighed. 'That was rather well behaved for those three. They must be on their best behaviour because they are close to a herd. Now for the main event, that herd is definitely still ambling this way. It could mean youngsters and youngsters invariably mean trouble.'

'Babies are always sweet though.'

'That they are, no matter if they are human or animal.'

Hope settled back on the rock and looked at Mandla. 'You haven't told me much about you now that I think about it, it's always about me.'

'Not much to tell, really.'

'But you sounded so sad a moment ago when you spoke of babies.'

'I was married once. She – she died.'

'I'm so sorry.'

'You think that you make a choice to spend the rest of your life with someone, but you never know what turn of events life will bring.'

'Can I ask what happened, or is it still too painful?'

'It's been twenty-five years. Some pain cuts your heart so deeply, not even time can repair it.'

'Twenty-five years ago and you never remarried?'

'No. It was in 1987. Someone threw a grenade into my wife's classroom. She died, as did six of her students. No one was ever charged over it.'

'That's so sad. What was her name?'

'Dudu Vanessa Mabuza. We were only married for one year. One happy year. She was five years older than me, but I didn't care. I loved her from the very first second I met her, when she stopped her little car to give me a lift when I was standing in the SADF pick-up zone, in my browns.'

'A pick-up what?'

'In South Africa we used to have an army pick-up zone on most major roads. They were for men moving around who were part of the Defence Force. You could stand there and hitchhike and someone would always pick you up and help you get home, or back to barracks.'

'You serious? The army didn't make sure you got back home, give you transport?'

'There was a war going on, they couldn't afford the cost to taxi us around the country. I spent four years fighting with them to keep out the Soviets, the Chinese and the Cubans. Many black and coloured men fought alongside the white men for the SADF. People forget that while there was apartheid, there was also a national pride of the people within South Africa. We all knew that the apartheid system had to change. But there were other threats to all the people, of being taken over by a foreign government, of having our borders overrun.'

'I didn't know that.'

'Perhaps because people focus so much on the liberation struggle that they forget that in some ways apartheid shaped all the people of South Africa, and while some black people didn't like apartheid ways, they were at least reasonably safe. In the years since the ANC has taken power, the average man on the street has seen a decline in his country. A marked increase in crime, murder, car hijackings and robbery. They can no longer blame the apartheid government, but they refuse to take responsibility themselves. They are too busy lining their own pockets to think of all the people in their country.'

'What made you decide to join the SADF?'

'It was honest pay and it fed you and clothed you. Unlike many of the other men my age who were joining the activists, I could make something of myself. People of colour ranked within the SADF. And as long as you kept to the rules, you were fine.'

'That's reasonable thinking in anyone's books. So were you in the army when Dudu was killed?'

'Yes, I was a volunteer. I got the news of her death when I was in a camp up on the Angolan border with the guys. Brian, Charl, Cole and I, we have been together a long time. We all got compassionate leave, but by the time I came home she was already buried by her family and I never got to see her, only where she was laid to rest. I emptied out our home, gave everything away and vowed to never marry again.'

'Oh, Mandla, that's so sad,' Hope said.

Mandla was quiet, lost deep in thought. 'Here comes the herd.'

They watched as elephant after elephant walked through their small camp. Everyone smelling the presence of humans, but somehow knowing that they were not in any danger.

A young one smelt Hope's backpack and for an instant attempted to pull it with its trunk, but the pack fell over. The baby trumpeted, flapped its ears and ran away.

Hope laughed. Loudly. The elephants below heard. They moved off away from the camp, a little more alert than they had been when they'd sauntered in now they knew that humans were still there. A quietness descended on the area.

'It's so silent now,' Hope said.

'It's as if the bush has finally gone to sleep. Come on, we should be alright to go down and catch some z's now.' He began his descent back onto the tree branch, then down the trunk.

Hope followed. 'That was incredible, such gentle giants. So light on their feet, they didn't even step on our beds.'

'Gentle's the right term. Usually. But I have seen a vehicle after a bull elephant got hold of it in the park. Crumpled like a beer can. It was not a pretty sight.'

'I believe that.' She jumped down the last few feet. 'Well after all the excitement for the day, I guess it's bed, then. I'm so tired.'

'Not surprising. You sleep, I will take the first watch for a few hours, then we can swap while I grab a few myself.'

She took the loo paper from her pack. 'I'm not going far.'

After a while she returned, and setting her cosmetics and water bottle back into her pack, she climbed onto her stretcher. 'Night.'

'Night, Hope.'

'Thank you for bringing me with you, because the more time I have to think about it, the more I believe that the man who sabotaged my plane is going to come after me again, so at least here in the bush, he has no clue where I am.'

'Do you know who it was?'

'I saw a white man walking away from my plane. I suspect it's CITES consultant Paul Joyce.'

'You sure it was him?' Mandla asked.

'Almost a hundred percent. I noticed him at Thompson's farm earlier in the day. I think he recognised me. He was the only one I saw near my plane and one of my chocks had been moved. I should've unpacked and checked my whole plane again. I shouldn't have overruled my gut feeling and been in so much of a hurry to get out of there.'

'So how does he fit into your bigger picture of the cheetah smugglers?'

'I don't know yet.'

CHAPTER
12

Three days later, Mandla and Hope broke from the game trail under the mopani trees onto a dirt road going through the Mozambique side of the Limpopo Transfrontier National Park. The road was dug low into the sandy soil and the ground pushed up on each side.

'According to the GPS, we are now well into Mozambique territory,' Mandla said. 'I'm certain that sooner or later we'll come across some sort of civilisation other than those beautiful nguni cows yesterday.'

'Stunning horns, but still, they were in the National Park!'

'I'm not sure who got a bigger fright, them or their young herder when you took off at him at the top of your voice. Man, I had no idea a lady could make so much noise.'

'Well, he shouldn't have them in the National Park,' she said.

Mandla smiled. 'They live in harmony with the park on this side, it's all different to Kruger.'

'I see that,' Hope said.

'These men we follow, they must have had some destination in mind, other than an island with cocktails and sunning themselves under a beach umbrella.'

Hope laughed at the image. Mandla wasn't a man of many words while walking, but he would make her laugh every time he did open his mouth.

'Our poachers have rested on the road for a bit here. The one walking at the back's leg is dragging more and more. The crate rested here with our cheetah in it. They gave it water. Look, there is a mark of a puddle in the dirt. They are trying to take an easier path. His print is changing as he becomes tired. As they walk up the road,' he said as he stretched his back.

Hope followed him blindly. 'Perfect, my legs could do with a break, too. Easier walking than on the rough game track.'

He swatted flies away from his face with his hand, still concentrating on the road ahead. Checking the spoor.

Mandla veered off the road, back into the mopani forest.

'Dang, I thought we were getting a soft walk for longer,' Hope said. 'Maybe even a free shower from those clouds. They're looking darker and darker as the afternoon progresses.'

Mandla chuckled and looked at the sky. 'It better hold out enough for us to catch them, or we could lose the spoor.'

They walked in silence for a few kilometres more, the green forest humid and oppressive as it converged around them. They saw no game. Then the vegetation began to thin, the trees became more sporadic and the green grasses higher. Mandla's hand motioned a halt position.

'Well just look at that, Hope,' he said. 'It's an unexploded, 82mm Russian mortar.' He pointed to the left side of the clearing.

'Oh crap,' Hope said as she stared at the mortar just lying on top of the ground, the leaf litter level high around it from it resting there for many years, but the fins at the back and the silhouette of the weapon were clearly visible. 'It's really rusty.'

'It's been exposed to the elements for many, many years. Once we are finished here, I'll come back and detonate it so that it doesn't hurt any wildlife. These things can still be found all over the place, a by-product of war years.'

'But I thought that Mozambique cleared its landmine fields?' Hope said.

'They tried and continue trying. They had a setback in 2000 after the worst floods in history. They found that many of the plastic mines had washed out of the ground and gone downstream. They now have mines in riverbeds and settled in new places, previously thought to be cleared. This mortar's in the middle of nowhere and I can blow it easily and safely. But not now, the poachers are still in front of us.'

They walked away from the unexploded mortar, a hazard waiting to maim or kill an unsuspecting animal or human, all these years after peace had been restored. Back onto the game trail.

They hadn't gone far when Mandla signalled to her to remain hidden and she crouched down, trying to make herself as inconspicuous as possible against the thorn tree near her.

This time he sneaked forward, his .303 ready, the thick rubber butt in his shoulder. Then her sight was obstructed by a branch and she held her breath, her ears straining. Listening.

There were no sounds, no birds calling, no crickets, and yet the constant call of the cicadas was shrill.

'Dammit to hell!' Mandla cursed. 'Hope, you can come out, but it's not good news.'

She quickly rose up and walked to where he stood, his .303 now hung from its strap on his shoulder, his hands on his head. She could smell something rotting. In front of him, dropped in the sand was a wooden box. It had poles attached so that it could be carried either at knee height or on both shoulders, as if it came from a different era, when cargo was carried upon black shoulders that glistened with sweat in the African sun. A time of slaves and human trafficking. The lid of the box was off. She put her hand over her nose against the smell and peeked inside.

'Your cheetah?' she said, looking away quickly, the site of the decomposing cat making her stomach churn.

'Been dead for over thirty-six hours to be smelling that ripe already. That's the second cheetah found dead after being taken. However, last time, the body was just dumped in the bushes. Now they left the box, too, obviously they don't plan to use this particular box again. Which is fortunate, because it finally explains how the GPS trackers are going silent. This box has a thin layer of lead nailed to the inside.'

'Oh the poor cheetah never stood a chance!' Hope said.

'No it didn't. The heat inside must have been oppressive. There are holes on the side of the wood for air, but only slits in the lead lining. I'm not so sure that it could breathe so easily either. It would have only just fitted in there. They must have drugged it and boxed it immediately. Then they haven't even given it a water bowl. No wonder it died. Most likely dehydration as its body overheated.'

She watched as he dug in his pack for his sat phone and called his head office. Hope examined the box closely, looking for other clues. She used her own phone to record the box, including a wood marking in the corner of one of the pieces of simple pine.

'The box will go back to BSC's headquarters. You'll have time to study it there.'

'That'd be really helpful. The markings might give us some clue as to the origin of the wood and perhaps we can find who manufactured the box for the poachers.'

The lead lining was thin, almost like a rolled plastic, but it had done its job.

'Charl's flying to this location, but he'll only get here in the morning. We're almost at Massingir. We've been skirting the Massingir Dam the whole way. Whoever came along this route, they know this part of the park well. They avoided going north towards Machampane, where the walking would have been easier. Instead, they have stayed to higher ground. They avoided the *Campismo Aguia Pesqueira* on the shores of the dam. They have been here when it's flooded before. They're scared of being caught in the dongas with the oncoming rain forecast, that's why they've stuck to the higher ground. If we continue to follow their spoor, I bet it ends at a taxi rank at Massingir. From there, they'll have access to road transport all the way to Maputo and that's probably where they were heading originally. To the docks, to ship this cheetah.'

'Something isn't right,' Hope said. 'I've always been on the search for cubs and juveniles. This cat's fully grown.'

'They appear to be taking the cheetah indiscriminately,' Mandla said. 'They may have been looking for a juvenile and when they couldn't find any they started trying to take the adults, and because they are all monitored and tracked they came up with this lead-lined box. Effective, but their planning's really bad. They didn't think to change anything for the size and weight of the adult cheetahs.'

'This might be a piece of the puzzle I've missed. I need to look at other cheetah figures and see who else is missing adult cats.'

'A whole new ball game, but one that's over for them with this cheetah,' Mandla said.

'We're going to lose a lot of time waiting for Charl,' Hope said.

'No, I didn't say we were staying, we're pushing on. He'll retrieve the box. But we need to step up the pace now, they will not be so slow without carrying it.'

'Lead the way,' Hope said as they continued trekking through the bush, but her heart was sore.

There was no happy ending for this cheetah.

CHAPTER
13

Two weeks had passed since their disastrous foray into Mozambique to rendezvous with the *Al Ihsaa* in Maputo, followed by the treacherous drive back into South Africa after recrossing the border through the Ndumo National Park in KwaZulu-Natal, before finally getting home to safety in Sandton. And once again, Dominic was pleading for his life, begging his childhood friend for understanding.

'*Tjhee.* I didn't make *e*-mistake. We tried. We tried—' he begged. 'We did everything you told us, but we couldn't keep it alive.'

'Trying wasn't good enough. Delivering was the only acceptable situation,' maNtuli said.

He shook his head, trying to reaffirm what he was saying. '*Tjhee.* We tried. We carried that box for days. Our arms ached. Our shoulders ached and we could hardly walk anymore. The cheetah died in her lead *e*-box well into Mozambique before we had to leave it. I told you that this was not a good method for us to use again. It has failed before and it didn't work this time either. Lead-lined *e*-boxes are not our answer to transporting the cheetahs with implants. The ones with the implants are too big, too *e*-heavy for those boxes.'

'Then find a way to get the microchips out of the cats before you transport them!'

'There is no way, the game guards are too *e*-modern, they monitor the cheetahs all the time. The implant is inside the cat's stomach. If we put darts in them, they know there is a change in vitals and they come looking in their helicopters. They will find us.'

MaNtuli looked skywards. 'That's your problem. I don't pay you to tell me your problems. I pay you to deliver.'

'But they are dying! I can't deliver *e*-dead cat and there are no more cheetahs in the game reserve without trackers. The game rangers, they are too high-tech.'

'Dominic, have I ever asked anything of you that you couldn't do?'

'But—'

'No buts! I have a very rich, very influential Iranian client who wants one hundred untraceable cheetahs delivered alive in Bahrain. You are my number two. It's your job to ensure that people get them for me. If you want the money for helping get them that's fine, but you have to figure out a way to source them. So stop wasting my time with empty promises.'

'The Iranian will have to take less on his order. We have taken all those that can't be tracked already. The ones that are left will bring unwanted *e*-trouble. They will capture you because of those trackers.'

'Not me.' She shook her head. 'You. They will never trace you to me, except as a friend. They capture anyone, it will be you and your crippled brother, not me. You need to find a way to get rid of the trackers. We are still thirty-five cheetahs short for the delivery. And you know when I promise something, I deliver. No matter what.'

'We have *e*-taken from the KwaZulu-Natal's northern Zululand parks and from the Kruger, from the Cape, there are none now that haven't got those trackers.'

'Then find some, you idiot. There must be other places where there are cheetahs, not just in the wild. People keep them like pets, find them and take them.'

'But—'

'Enough. I knew you would try argue with me.' She walked to her desk and pushed the intercom. 'Send Sizani and my guest in.'

The man who opened the door was not large but he looked as if he could have taken on the Springbok rugby team and won. His squat frame was covered in bulging muscles. Showing off the scarring from many knife fights across his shoulders and down onto his chest as they disappeared behind the cloth of the white vest, his arms rippled as he flexed his fingers. On one side, at his hip, he carried a *panga*. On the other was a *sjambok*.

Behind him, tied in ropes as if in an old-fashioned slave auction, was his brother, Noah.

'That one needs a lesson.' MaNtuli pointed to Dominic. 'Don't kill him and make sure you don't inflict the pain where it will impede his ability to work. His brother needs an incentive to complete a job.'

Sizani stepped forward.

Noah was hobbled and unable to get away. His mouth gagged with a rag that was tightly tied to stop his cries for help being heard.

'*Tjhee. Ema! Ema!*' Dominic rushed to his brother's side. Pleading with maNtuli.

'Step aside, Dominic,' maNtuli instructed, her voice cold.

'You don't need to do this, Tobeko. Don't hurt Noah, already he has suffered so much.'

She looked at him and pointed with her finger. 'Move, or I might have you beaten, too.'

Sizani took out his *sjambok* from where it hung and he raised it high.

Dominic shook his head. He could tell that this was not a plastic replica but a real, traditionally crafted whip. He wondered in a flash if it was made from hippopotamus hide or if Sizani had poached a rhinoceros for the leather. This would cut deep and leave scars.

Acting on instinct, Dominic rushed at Sizani.

MaNtuli nodded once.

The lash that landed across Dominic's face opened up the old scar under his eye and created a new one across his nose. He brought his hands up to his face as the blood ran into his eyes and blurred his vision.

Dominic stopped, still holding his nose.

Sizani adjusted himself fast and turned to Noah. His next blow landed behind Noah's knees and his brother dropped to the ground, shaking in pain and curling into a foetal ball. Sizani hit him again on his side and onto his back as the leather cut deeply through his T-shirt and bit into the flesh. He landed a third lashing before Dominic managed to orientate himself through his own pain, and charged at Sizani again. Knocking him to the left in the unexpected attack. Sizani righted himself quickly and turned towards Dominic, his *sjambok* raised again.

'Enough,' maNtuli said.

Sizani lowered his weapon immediately and Dominic dropped to his knees beside his brother.

'Noah, Noah!' he shouted as he tore off the cloth that held his mouth bound tightly.

'Dominic, I hurt,' Noah said. '*Eina*, I hurt.'

'Shoosh. Don't give him the pleasure. You need to stand, *e*-lean on me,' he said as he took his knife from his pocket and cut the ropes that bound his brother.

When he stood up, Noah clung to his side. Dominic turned on maNtuli. 'You have gone mad, Tobeko. You are no longer the woman I knew as a girl, the one I loved. Sometimes she's there, the person I used to protect. I see her when you sit at your *e*-computer and you tap your pen on the *e*-table next to you. I see her when we go out in public and you walk closer to me than to the kerbside, but I see nothing of her now. *E*-Nothing. What about those times that Noah helped *e*-save you? When he begged as a cripple and we got to share his food that was given to him? You forget too easily. You have him beaten with a *sjambok* like *e*-dog, or like protestor in the old apartheid days? Like *e*-criminal?'

'Don't you tell me what you see and don't see in me. I am who I am! And you work for me.'

'No, Tobeko. Not anymore. My friend is lost to me. My love for you, it is dead. You have killed it. All this e-time, you never want to kill things yourself, but you were e-killing my love.'

MaNtuli just glared at him. 'Dom—'

'No. You are lost in your e-fancy clothes and your money. You have been corrupted now. You rescued a kitten once, remember that? Cleo. You called it Cleopatra because you were learning about the e-Egyptians in the school. It was e-orange and white and you found it, all wet and dirty, you dried it up and you fed it from your own e-food so you could keep her. That cat stayed with you for years, until your mother took you away. Then me and Noah, we looked after it and when it died we took it into the bushes and we buried it for you. We dug e-deep hole in the ground and gave it a proper burial because that's what you would have wanted. Yet you just hurt Noah. Crippled, simple Noah, and for what? To try e-show me that you have no heart anymore?' His chest heaved, his heart raced and all the time he could feel his brother's arms around him, holding him for support.

'Always it has been me who gets bloody for you. I thought that perhaps you couldn't be cruel. I was wrong. How can I be so wrong? I have e-killed for you, to make sure there was no e-blood on your hands. You just beat my brother as if he was e-nothing to you. Like you didn't grow up knowing him in Alex township. You had Sizani beat e-cripple, someone whose mind is simple and who should be protected by you, not beaten. You are no better than the Nigerian drug lords in this area!'

'Dominic, that girl died inside years ago. You know that. If you ever mention her again, I'll do more than have you or your crippled brother beaten. You misunderstand when you think you mean anything to me. There is always someone to take your place as my number two. Someone with ambitions that you are having to beat down. It would be easy to let them just take your place. Like Sizani here.'

'You are wrong. For me it's always been personal. I loved you, it's always been my e-job to see that no law could touch you, that you were safe. *E*-untouchable. To make amends that when your mother *e*-sold you, I couldn't come and save you from Samuel Ntuli. I see now I was *e*-wrong. I mean *e*-nothing to you. All these years, I have waited for you to show me *e*-sign that you loved me, even just a little. But you don't. And you never will.' He stopped as he waited for his words to sink in.

She didn't make a sound. Her face remained devoid of any emotion.

'*Sala hantle*, Tobeko Ntuli. Noah and I, we cannot fill your *e*-ridiculous order this time. I will no longer be here to protect you and when things are going *e*-roughly, like when the men won't listen to their woman *baas*, I will no longer get rid of *e*-bodies you want hidden. We are done. You can have *e*-house back and you can go to hell!' He lifted his brother on his shoulder and began walking away.

'Run away, Dominic and remember when you calm down, you will come crawling back. You always do!' she shouted at him and stamped her foot.

'Don't hold your *e*-breath this time.' He walked from her office, his brother shuffling as much as he could next to him, but he carried the majority of his weight. Only silence and unsettled dust followed the brothers out of the office and into the street in Hillbrow.

CHAPTER

14

The birds were already serenading the bright morning sunshine when Dominic Bongwanan walked into the Kopa shebeen in Sharpville, to buy some breakfast, more from habit than from need after an uncomfortable night spent sleeping in his taxi. So close to home, and yet unable to reach it. His taxi had got a flat in Vereeniging, and while his passengers had all got a lift with another taxi, that stupid excuse for a spare was useless when he attempted to use it, so he had to wait until the morning to buy a new tyre. Once he would have hit the shebeen, in the hope that he would find some food, some good beer and perhaps a woman or two to share a bed with. Instead he'd had dinner, then slept in his taxi alone, making sure no one stole it during the night. Protecting what was his.

Too many years he had travelled around, checking on his friend's business – ex-friend – and being the muscle behind keeping her operation functioning. It wasn't that he was lost now that they had had a fight, it was more that now he had walked away from her, he had found himself.

It had taken him six weeks to complete the break from her. He had saved up all the money from selling everything from his

Sandton house. Everything. Cashed up, he had moved back into Alex township, back to where he had once lived free.

Now he owed nothing to her. He could start again, and this time, he knew what he would do. He had all the experience from working for her and from working his own family business quietly alongside hers. In these last few weeks, he had bought three brand-new taxis. They started on a different route and in a different territory to those that maNtuli's ran on. He wasn't so stupid as to go into competition with her – yet.

He would one day encroach on her routes and her territory, but not now, now he needed to gain a fleet and to do that he needed to make money from his taxis.

He also needed to expand his own family business. His *nkgono*, his mother's mother, she was a wise and crafty old woman. She had been the head of the business for as many years as he could count, but lately she was starting to tire, wanting to step back, and she had hinted that he needed to step up. So he did.

Apart from wanting to break from maNtuli permanently, it was also a business decision. If he could prove to his *nkgono* that he had washed his hands of maNtuli, she would allow him to take the reins of their family business and she could retire properly, perhaps leave him to run the business alone. Play with her grandchildren from his simple brother, while he took over and expanded their arms trading. The hiring out of weapons with the serial numbers filed off for people to use, no questions asked. Making untraceable zippy guns and supplying guns to those who couldn't legitimately acquire them through any other means. His clients were not only those in the townships. Already he had moved the larger cache to a house in Barlow Park, where they were better protected than in the shack they had been in. Now he only had a small selection with him in his Alex home that he rented from his *nkgono*. She had been in her brick house since 1960 and there were five shacks built in her little garden. His whole family lived there together now that he had talked Noah into giving up his house on the border of the Kruger National Park at Polokwani that maNtuli had given him.

He cursed that he had ever accepted the presents, now knowing that big, thick emotional blackmail strings were always attached to anything she gave you. She always had an ulterior motive. It had just taken him all these years to see it clearly.

He had done the right thing to walk away from maNtuli. Her demands had become impossible. She just didn't seem to understand that these days the park was run with the same management plans that private game reserves had. They had game counts and full-time vets and anti-poaching patrols.

Finally, his family were all together again, and full-time business with *nkgono* was going well.

Dominic glanced up at the television that blared behind the bar area. 'Turn that up, *Ke mamela*,' he told the buxom woman serving breakfast from behind the counter. 'I live there.'

She did and she turned to watch.

He felt sick as he watched the news on the television. The camera panned and he saw giant orange flames leap from one shack to another, the residents of yet another burning shack ran out in their pyjamas, with no possessions in their arms, just fleeing for their lives. The fire engulfed their homes, dark black smoke rose from a roof that had a tarpaulin held down with tyres as it began to burn, and the cameraman adjusted his focus again.

He knew that section of Alex. He knew this place. It was close to their family home. He saw a woman he recognised as his own *nkgono* running, crouched over. In her arms she carried a small baby, and a child of about three held tight to her nightdress and ran with her, illuminated by the fire behind. He could clearly see the fear in the child as they ran towards where the fire trucks pumped an inadequate amount of water onto the shacks closest to the engines, but it was not reaching where the main body of the fire raged.

He reached out towards the TV.

'*Tjhee!*' he cried. 'Oh, God, not my family.'

Quickly he looked at his phone, and saw a message.

We are safe. The fire did not get us – Nkgono.

He slumped in the chair.

Someone came behind him and put their hand on his shoulder. A deathly silence fell in the shebeen as people turned their attention to the flat-screen TV on the wall. The woman turned the volume higher.

The cameraman showed men hastily pulling down a line of shacks to try to make a firebreak between the buildings. They had choppers and crowbars, shovels and square fencing posts as weapons as they beat down and trampled shack after shack, trying to clear an area between them that the oncoming flames wouldn't breach.

He saw Noah, his clothes wet with sweat as he put his whole weight behind a corner of a shack, trying to push it over to help stop the fire. He had a T-shirt wrapped around his face, but Dominic would know his brother anywhere. He could see the scar that ran the whole way up Noah's right leg from where a wild pig had gored him and a much younger Dominic had stitched him back together himself. Without his shirt on, he could still see the new scarring from the strikes Noah has received from the *sjambok* at the instruction of maNtuli. Hatred burnt deep in his stomach.

Suddenly, gunshots could be heard and the cameraman's picture wobbled as he hit the ground, trying to get out of the way of danger. They continued for a while, as the cameraman panned around, looking for the area the gunfire was coming from.

Dominic's heart sank further as the cameraman caught a blast in the left-hand side of his lens. He moved to capture the whole image just as another blast rocked them. The cameraman continued to film the scene.

Dominic couldn't pull his eyes away from the TV. Even though he knew they were safe, he couldn't stop watching as the horror unfolded.

He should have been home last night, except he never got there.

This fire had been set for him. He knew it. His *nkgono* knew it. He had walked away from maNtuli and this was the price his family was paying. Six weeks. That's all the time she had taken to come after him.

Another bullet exploded in the intense heat, bringing his eyes back to the square screen.

He knew that it was his family's weapons cache, some that had been under his bed, that had obviously just exploded. And that there were still two more much bigger explosions to happen. He had acquired those limpet mines at the Soweto Market. Those he was holding for a specific customer, but the CITES official, Paul Joyce, had failed to collect the mines he had ordered. His late collection was going to cost him his mines as Dominic knew what was coming. There was no way that with that amount of heat and fire the explosives in the mines wouldn't explode.

He heard the TV reporter talking:

'Disaster teams continue to battle to control the blaze. It is believed that this fire broke out just after two am this morning, but no one seems to know what started it. It could have been a candle or paraffin stove.

'It is believed to be one of the worst in history. It has already destroyed over one thousand five hundred shacks. Most of those who escaped had little time to collect any of their possessions as they ran for their lives. Many have lost everything, their identity papers, their money and their meagre possessions. Some even their lives. There are seven confirmed deaths so far and that number is set to rise by the morning when the fire crews can search the burnt-out shacks.'

Dominic stared at the TV. No one in the shebeen moved, there was an unnatural silence. He focused again on the reporter.

'... because the rate at which the fire is spreading between the informal settlement homes is out of control and the crews on the ground were finding it difficult to reach the hot points of the fire owning to the lack of access room between the shacks, and the strong wind pushing it through this settlement.'

The cameraman caught the exact moment that the mines exploded as he was thrown to the floor. Dominic watched as the flames jumped the containment line and continued to burn. The fire licked out of the windows of the wooden and cardboard house that another cameraman zoomed in on. He showed how the roof quickly collapsed and the fire was already lapping at the corrugated iron on the shack next to it.

A young boy ran out and barrelled towards the camera crew. For a moment, the cameraman focused on the boy, then he withdrew again and the enormity of the fire could be seen as an orange hue glowing brightly over the township.

Dominic's cell phone rang.

He ignored it. It rang out.

A few seconds later it rang again.

He answered, cringing, knowing the caller was maNtuli.

'Are you watching the television?' Her distinctive voice was clear, as if she was standing right next to him.

'You psychopathic bitch!'

'Don't raise your voice at me, Dominic. Or you will not see another sunrise. Do you understand? Did you not learn anything?'

Dominic's fist clenched and his voice dropped as he looked around the shebeen, suddenly aware of where he was again. 'What do you *e*-want?'

'I have a ship arriving. If there are no cats left in the game reserves without GPS trackers implanted, find a place where they are not used. A private place. Just get me a cat. I have to deliver, my client is getting restless. His venture is not happening fast enough.'

'*Tjhee*. I don't *e*-work for you anymore.'

She laughed, but it was stiff and forced. 'No one walks away, Dominic. You know that. Let this fire be your last warning. Your pathetic family has always meant too much to you. It's your biggest weakness. Get back to work and get your good-for-nothing brother back into the reserve. I have a need and you are going to deliver. Next time there will not be time enough for your family to run away from the flames, it will start closer to them.'

Dominic nodded as he ran his fingers over his temples. He was trapped, like one of the cheetahs he'd been catching.

'I already told you, the cats left have *e*-trackers, the game rangers invested *e*-millions into protecting their wildlife, to stop the *e*-poaching and hunting of their wildlife,' he pleaded.

'And *I already told you* to get them from somewhere that doesn't have cats out in the wild. Find a place where they have them like pets and take them from there. Those will not have trackers because they would never expect anyone to try to steal those.' She exhaled loudly when she had completed talking. 'Dominic, do I have to spell it out for you? Are you that stupid? Go raid a cheetah conservation breeding program, where they breed cheetahs for tourists to pet. They have lots of cheetahs at parks like that!'

Dominic scratched his head. He remembered a place that had tame cheetahs, where tourists could go and sit with them inside their cages to pet them. He used to pass it on one of maNtuli's taxi routes when checking on her workers. It was in KwaZulu-Natal, so he'd be able to take them directly to the ship before it left Richards Bay. 'I'll get *e*-cheetahs,' he said, talking quietly into the phone. 'I know *e*-place like that.'

'I knew you would see things my way.'

Dominic hung his head and remained silent.

'So quiet? No fight left in you now? See, you are always my dog, Dominic, I'll always own you. You will do as I say, or I guess that wherever the settlers go, might just burn down, too.'

'No more *e*-fire.'

'I see that your *nkgono* can still run fast when there is a fire behind her!'

'*Ema!* Don't hurt my family anymore. I'll find some.'

'Two weeks to get me my cheetahs. Have them on the ship by the night of the fourth of December. Or it won't just be your possessions you lose.'

The line went dead.

He looked back over his shoulder at the screen.

'... *causing the explosions, it could be that there are Eskom substations blowing up as there was originally electricity in this area. Emergency crews are also experiencing low water pressure. This area was designed for a population of about 70,000. Today close to 750,000 people live here.*'

Dominic had seen enough. He knew now what he had to do. He had been a fool to think that he could walk away, start a new life. He knew that he would have to get her those damn cats, then when he was done, he would put his family into his taxis and drive as far into Namibia as he could and start again so far away from that bitch that she could never find him.

Then he stilled. He knew it was a pipe dream. The only way he would ever get away from her was to kill her and he wasn't sure he could ever do that. To kill a stranger, or even an acquaintance was simple, but killing the one woman who had always held his heart since they were children, that was never going to be easy. Even if he now realised that he meant absolutely nothing to her, that he was just a means to an end.

He turned his back on the TV and his half-eaten meal. He was at the door before he remembered that the only destination he could go was to the tyre shop to wait for it to open at eight o'clock.

CHAPTER
15

Hope looked around Brian's modest CEO office at the Bushman's Software Company. On the walls were huge sepia-toned pictures of white Lipizzaners that danced in different poses across the paper, their proud nature clearly visible within the black-and-white frames. In the last photograph the horses appeared to be bowing low to the lone man in the middle of the theatre, filled to capacity with people standing on their feet, clapping. It was a hauntingly beautiful collection of family history.

Mandla had told her that Brian's father had lived in Vienna and been a stable master of the magnificent horses. He had left there when he was a young man to seek adventure in Africa and find his own destiny. So Brian had grown up surrounded by horses and had trained first-hand with a world-class master. Only his passion for wildlife rivalled his passion for horses. He still kept a few in his own stables on his property in Hilton, further down the same road as where Mandla had bought his townhouse. Sometimes he still trained stallions for clients who didn't want to geld their horses but needed help with their highly strung animals. Yet the pictures were not of him but his heritage. She smiled as they revealed so much about him, his pride, and the fact that he was a collector of 'things'.

People, animals, anything that needed a little help, would find a place with Brian.

His office suited him perfectly. It wasn't a rat-race-style space where one man had pissed on another to claim the corner office, but a place where employees felt comfortable talking to their boss and where people could sit and create solutions to problems. Just as they were doing today.

Mandla and Charl sat in the visitors' chairs behind the desk with Brian so they could all see the screens. On the right monitor was her boss, James Williams in England, and the left, the mostly silent partner in Bushman's Software, Cole Howe from *nTabaGrequa* Wildlife Rescue and Cheetah Conservation Ranch.

'Cole,' Brian said, 'this is Special Agent Hope Anderson from Global Wildlife International.'

Cole's khaki shirt was rolled up to the elbows, which rested on his antique desk. He looked like a man used to people obeying his every command.

Hope waved.

'Nice to meet you finally,' Cole said. 'So glad that you are all mended and back to work.'

'Thanks and good to meet you, too,' Hope said.

'Congratulations on making the connection between your case and the increase in cheetah-cub rescues. It's sure nice to have an explanation for what has been happening over the last eighteen months or so. Apparently you have some news. Care to fill us in on what's going on?'

'I wanted to make sure everyone in a position of authority here was aware of what I've discovered. You already know that I've been working closely with Mandla and this team at Bushman's since I came out of hospital.'

'Yes, but you didn't ask for a conference call because of that. What have you discovered that's going to impact me here on *nTabaGrequa*?'

'I need to get you up to speed with a few things before I ask you a favour. A huge favour that could impact on your cheetah rescue centre.'

Cole was quiet for a while, just looking at Hope through the camera, then he said, 'Must be a doozy if you have brought your boss in and the guys as backup.'

'It is,' Hope said. 'Over the last few months we've discovered that many of the cheetahs from Southern Africa have been exported on the ship *Al Ihsaa*. Apparently, your last rescue cub, Zulu was confiscated off this ship.'

'That it was,' Cole said.

'Transnet National Port Authority got hit really hard as a result of this particular confiscation. A few days after the *Al Ihsaa* departed, having paid its fines, four of their custom officials in Richards Bay were found floating facedown in the harbour. Generally, South African customs officers are passionate about protecting their wildlife, but there're always those who'll either take a bribe or whose families are threatened to ensure he or she cooperates. These dead men were suspected of taking bribes, and when we looked into their financials and lifestyles, they were definitely living beyond their means. We think that your cheetah was a slip-up by one of them.'

'That would make sense. On the morning we rescued Zulu the official mentioned that he had swapped shifts.'

'That's what he told us, too. One of the men found dead was the colleague he'd swapped with, which was no surprise,' Hope said. 'Many of the officers are angry that their fellow officials were involved in smuggling and expressed their concern, but we're sure that not all of those who are taking the bribes were killed. With permission and cooperation from Transnet, we managed to look into the Richards Bay payroll, and because the *Al Ihsaa* docked in Durban, their customs officers as well. There's evidence that there are still a handful of men and women we're aware of who are involved. We believe this isn't over.'

'So why not arrest them?' asked Cole. 'Why are you telling me all this?'

James interrupted. 'She'll be getting there shortly, but I thought you needed all the facts to understand the magnitude of what we're going to ask you. That we aren't taking this lightly.'

Cole nodded.

'Thank you, James,' Hope said, and carried on. 'The *Al Ihsaa* is registered to a cargo company in Bahrain, but as yet we haven't been able to discover who actually owns it. It seems to be a lot of shell companies within trusts and still more holding companies. James and our London office are still working to track down the owners. Bahrain has already been called to "explain" on more than one occasion by CITES for violation of trafficking in trade of endangered animals and everyone knows there's a Middle Eastern problem, but so far we have no proof that anyone from that area is involved. I was able to pull the maritime log for the ship and we've tracked its trade route.'

She held up a map of Africa that had a red line running around it and she followed the ship's route with the tip of her pen. 'Not unusual for a freighter, it follows the same route each time, the furthest it travels in the west is Walvis Bay, then south to Port of Luderitz, around the Cape Horn, then north into Durban and Richards Bay in South Africa, before heading back to Bahrain, stopping at a few ports along the way that we are aware of, Maputo in Mozambique and Majunga in Madagascar being two of its regular stops. I suspect whoever owns that ship is either in cahoots with, or paying the Somali pirates, because travelling closer to Indian waters, adding weeks to each journey, is unlikely since they're carrying live cargo. Suggesting deep pockets behind the wheel of the vessel.

'Next time it docks, I'm ready to try to secure a position on the ship as a deckhand for a trusted informant within my network. If we can get someone onto that ship we might be able to find out where the cheetahs are going after they reach Bahrain. I don't believe that they remain there, it's just the heart of the shipping access, the stepping stone into the Middle Eastern countries. But I believe Iran requires deeper scrutiny. The fact the lawyers who were involved in settling the fine were all Iranian suggests to me that the man who owns that ship resides in Iran.'

'But that's across the Persian Gulf, and Iran still has cheetahs. They are protected and their government is part of the CITES treaty,' Cole said.

'True, but Bahrain is connected by the King Fahd Causeway. Saudi Arabia has no local population of cheetahs, only those that the rich, bored Arabs have to hunt with and keep as pets.'

James interrupted again. 'Our company has an undercover worker already in Bahrain watching to try to find out where the cheetahs that arrive there are going. He has been instructed not to intercept them.'

'Any leads?' Cole asked.

'Not yet, he hasn't observed any making it through between the time we put this information together and now. He's still watching. That's why Hope will try for someone on the ship itself.'

Hope watched Cole nod, then adjust his sleeve. She'd noticed that it seemed to be his 'tell' for when he wasn't happy about something. 'But we do have movement on the South African side. The anonymous telephone line that was set up for rhino-and-elephant-poaching information has yielded some interesting leads in other areas, too. From one of those tips we've received, we've learnt that the people pulling the strings in South Africa have shifted their focus from cubs to acquiring adult cheetahs. They've attempted to steal one or two domesticated pets in the Pretoria region recently. Apparently, they're looking at places that have many, preferably untagged, but will take any they can find now that they have learnt how to silence the trackers until a veterinarian can remove them.'

'The lead box?' Cole said.

Brian shook his head. 'We have beefed up the coding and the signal so the next box they use will have to be considerably thicker than the one retrieved in Mozambique to mask it now. We might still have a problem with some of the older trackers that are due to be replaced. They might still fail if the animals are placed in that box.'

'How many of my cheetahs have the older trackers?' Cole asked.

'Five or six, but the poachers don't have access to information like we do, they'll assume it worked like previously, unaware of the updates,' Brian said.

Hope continued, 'We're expecting them to start carrying out smash-and-grab-style robberies or even a full-scale attack on one of the centres. Exactly where and when is still a mystery, but I believe that every rescue centre should be on full alert just in case.'

Hope watched Cole's face as he frowned.

'That's bad news,' Cole said, 'an attack on a rescue centre would take poaching to a different level.'

Hope nodded. 'Yes it would, and that brings us to the favour. I think this is an ideal opportunity to lay a trap for them. On *nTaba-Grequa*. Let them in easily, but then we close the trap behind them, capturing the poachers alive so we can get information from them.'

'What makes you think that they are going to target me, and not one of the other centres?' Cole asked.

'Logistics. You are in KwaZulu-Natal and are the closest cheetah rescue centre to a port. *Al Ihsaa* docks regularly in Richards Bay. They might change her name and repaint her before she comes back because of the last fiasco, but I believe that she's on her way here, sooner than we hoped.'

Cole shook his head. 'I need more information. This plan's risky to my centre, to my cheetahs. It would be so much easier to simply fortify, keep these bastards out instead. What else have you got?'

James said, 'Cole, I understand your reservations, but I believe that Hope's correct. We perfectly understand that you want to fortify your facility, however, we believe the best course of action is to capture some of these men involved and question them.'

'You realise that you are putting a lot of cheetahs at risk here?' Cole said.

'I know,' Hope said. 'But we'll never get this opportunity again. I've seen what the men in this room can do. You guys have military training and you have the resources that other people don't. James, I've been lucky enough to be around this team at BSC, their dedication is unquestionable. Like I said to you, it's worth the risk. I'll bet my job on that.'

'I'm trusting you on this one, Hope,' her boss said. 'I haven't changed my mind.'

'I'll be on the ground, too. It's not like I would leave them to execute this alone,' Hope said.

'Tell me more,' Cole said.

'We have another reason to believe they're coming for your chee-tahs. A man called Dominic Bongwanan moved into a room in your area two days ago. He and his brother, Noah are on my watch list. I truly believe that he's doing the surveillance and testing on your ranch security, getting to know the everyday details. So the trick will be to make you look like you aren't actually getting ready for the raid. The fact that your team are also friends and regular visitors on the ranch will make it all easier to not raise suspicion with the locals. This way you can fortify, draw them in, and try to capture the poachers rather than kill them, while you protect your cheetahs.

'I've spent almost eighteen months tracking this crime across the continents. I believe that if we can catch these two red-handed, they'll buckle under interrogation. I've spoken to both these men before, they're not capable of hatching this plan alone. I think that there's someone much more well connected and with bigger means than their boss pulling the strings of this operation and I believe she might have told them who. She's just part of the chain. I need the top dog.'

'So who do they work for?' Cole asked.

'We're watching Dominic's friend in Hillbrow, they call her maNtuli. A really nasty but extremely clever and devious woman. The police said they've been observing her for years but have never been able to press charges against her. They suspect her of much, but proving it has so far been as elusive as a pleasant-smelling polecat.'

'I might bring Alan in on this, he's the Member in Charge in our area and one of us, too,' Cole said.

Hope looked at James.

James nodded. 'That's fine, if you're sure that you can trust him.'

'You have pictures of these men and this woman so I can show my guards who to look out for?' Cole said.

'I'll email them right after this meeting,' Hope said.

'So,' Brian said, 'from our side, we can certainly visit *nTaba-Grequa* and set up some new gadgets and things, slip in a few more security lights up poles in your pens, perhaps a few more infra-red cameras onto the perimeter. It's nothing unusual, you always have jobs for us to do and we are always checking on things, so if they have anyone on the inside double-crossing you they won't be tipped off at all. Perhaps Michelle can do an early upgrade on the trackers in your cats that need replacements, just to be safe at the same time.'

'I'd like to believe that none of my staff would be involved in something like that, but you never know what pressure is being applied to anyone externally,' Cole said. 'I'll get onto Michelle.'

'Too true,' James said.

'So, it's not even Christmas yet and we are coming for a visit,' Mandla said. 'Best get Thandi cooking those jam thumb drops and *koeksisters*, because we're going to need the sugar rush to help us keep awake on watch at night.'

'Since when have you needed anything to keep you awake?' Cole said. 'There are owls that couldn't function on as little sleep as you, and you still see better in the dark than they do. I swear, in a former life you were a *nagapie*!'

Mandla laughed. '*Eish*, okay, *bra*, I admit it, I've always been a sucker for anything sweet Thandi cooks, night or day. And just so you know, Hope, I don't pee on my hands.' He was looking at his hands in a disgusted manner.

Cole burst out laughing, as did Brian and Charl.

Hope just looked between the men, shaking her head.

James said. 'Right, I'm glad that you're on board. Thank you. I'll keep up to date with Hope, but know that I sure appreciate what you men are willing to do for those cats and each other.'

Charl asked, 'While we have you here, how's your Mackenzie?'

'Just fine,' Cole said.

'That's great,' Brian said. He pointed at Mandla and Charl, who were grinning, and put his finger over his lips to keep them quiet.

'You know I can see you guys?' Cole said.

Mandla and Charl started laughing again.

James frowned, obviously not in on this joke either.

Hope smiled. It was typical behaviour for this team. The men might have originally bonded because of serving in the armed forces, but it was this easy friendship that kept them together. She brought the conversation back to work. 'Remember, I need some of these men alive when they come for your cheetahs.'

'Do you have any idea if they will have guns and if so what type?' Cole asked.

'They seem to have access to everything they want. Dominic is suspected of being a gun runner, too. Expect the worst,' Hope said.

'Great,' Cole said.

'If we are shot at, we shoot back,' Brian warned.

'Yes, but just wound a few, won't you,' James said, 'not kill them outright. Dead men can't talk or testify in court.'

'We can't promise that,' Brian said, 'but we can try!'

CHAPTER

16

The sun was already sinking behind the mountains, casting long shadows across the valley. Mackenzie took a deep breath and tipped her head back, closing her eyes for a moment, then stole a glance at Cole, who seemed content to relax on the grass as he watched the dog and the cheetah cub play. Tala and Zulu were romping with each other as if they didn't realise that they were different species. Tala, with his perfect black labrador coat, was walking along towards Mackenzie and Zulu caught his tail, grabbing it with both his paws and pinning it to the ground. The pup reacted by turning on Zulu and nipping him, who in turn jumped upwards, his hair all spiked and standing on end, spitting at Tala, who promptly licked Zulu's nose, as if apologising. Zulu rubbed up against Tala in an affectionate all-is-forgiven way, and the two of them tumbled together, playing.

Mackenzie took yet another picture. Knowing that when she did the series of photographs of these two unlikely friends, they would be perfect. She would keep her promise to Cole and give him one, but she'd already decided it would be a gift, to sit in his office.

But her bronze after that would be called: A man in his element. Showcasing his relaxed posture, his easiness with life, as she'd captured him on her camera. It would translate so perfectly into a full-size bronze and she would keep that one for herself, a little bit of Cole to accompany her in the studio while she worked. He constantly reminded her of the slogan he had in the reception area of his rescue centre: *Saving One Animal Won't Change the World, But It Will Change the World for That One Animal.*

Saving Zulu had changed his life; he would have died like his little brother, which Cole had told her about. Now he had a chance, perhaps one out in the wild in a reserve somewhere, running free like he was supposed to in Cole's reintroduction program. She smiled. Zulu and Tala had gone to Cole for some fussing and comfort, before intertwining into each other and sleeping between his legs, as if in a safe harbour. That would be her bronze, where the body of the man, the cheetah and the dog came together. As if they knew that together they could all survive the cruel world outside their fences.

'Can you smell that fresh air? I still can't believe it's so cold and it's November. And there's snow predicted!' Mackenzie said.

Cole nodded. 'Nothing like fresh snow in the summer months to kill the crops and the wildlife. Do you know that my cheetahs love the snow?'

'They do?'

'You should see them. They play in the snow when it first falls, trying to catch the snowflakes. They can't sit still when it's falling on them, they twitch and turn and swipe their paws at it.'

'Just like domestic cats. I've seen them do that in snow when I was skiing in Vermont—' Mackenzie stopped herself and looked down. Being with Cole was dangerous. He made her want to talk about the life she had left behind. About the life she was no longer part of.

'Exactly,' Cole said. 'Eventually, they just accept it as part of their domain. They seem to adapt quickly to it. In the paddocks where they have to catch their own prey when we're getting them ready for release back into the wild, they learn fast that snow makes tracks and the impala can see where they have been, so they walk carefully, trying to avoid making their presence known.'

Mackenzie was relieved that Cole had just carried on talking, as if sensing she was reluctant to talk more about that life. She cleared her throat. 'You kidding me?'

'No. And they have acquired this incredible skill, too. They do what is termed "fence hunting". We have seen it in wild cheetahs that are inside the game reserves. They use the fence to help them corner and catch their game. They stay around the outer edges, using the fence lines. It's incredible. Evolution happening before our eyes.'

'They sound so wonderful. They're so lucky to have you in their court fighting for them.'

'They are,' Cole said. Then he smiled. 'You know, Lauren coming out here with you so often, and then making up excuses to return to your house – she must know by now that we are onto her "date night" tricks, but I sure appreciate the time alone together.'

'She said she was unwell,' Mackenzie automatically defended her friend.

'Have you noticed she always says that? She makes time for you to have dates, without feeling like you're leaving her out. Lauren's a schemer when it comes to you, putting us in the same place, and having us spend more time together. So what do you think about the idea that tonight we make a real date of it? Get dressed a little and have dinner somewhere better than going just to Tannie Essie's in Crystalberg? Maybe reserve a table at the Drakensburg Gardens Hotel? They have a new chef, and it'll only take us about half an hour to drive there from your house.'

'But I love having dinner at Tannie Essie's. It's home-cooked and it's always so tasty.'

'We eat there all the time. I have lost count of the number of dinners we have actually had sitting outside, enjoying that view in the last few weeks. What about something different? A bit more polished. A real date? A really nice restaurant.'

Mackenzie shook her head. 'I've had polished, I don't miss it. Seriously. I've kind of fallen in love with homemade and humble.'

Cole looked at her then he reached across and put his hand on hers as they lay on the ground. Gently, just holding them still.

'Mackenzie, you know that I won't force you into anything, but I feel like I take one step forward with you and we move a millennium further away. I get that you have baggage, we all do. I didn't get to forty-five without any.'

'It's not your baggage I'm afraid of.'

'I know that. I like that we are now friends and friends share things, especially things that kept them totally distracted, like the fact that for the last half hour while these two have slept, you have just sat there. Usually you can't sit still, you move constantly.'

She thought for a minute before she looked at him. 'Okay. Tell me what you think. I don't want you to do that macho male thing and try to fix this. I just want your opinion.'

Cole took a while before saying, 'Okay, shoot. Bring it on.'

'Before we came for the visit this afternoon, something happened. Remember that taxi incident that you and Siphiwe came and saved me from?'

'It's a bit hard to forget, it's etched into my mind.'

'Well, when Lauren and I visited the Soweto Market. She had a black light she uses to see if vintage lead-crystal glasses are authentic or newer imitations. These guards got a bit testy and we fled. We took pictures. Lots of them. When we got home she had a few of her digital photos printed because she's really into this whole scrapbooking thing. Anyhow, we forgot about it until earlier today when we were in Duduzo's Kofi Shop and we saw the man from the market there. It was the driver from the taxi. Lauren saw him and pointed him out, rather loudly, and he hightailed it out of there so fast.'

'You sure it's the same man?' Cole said.

'He's got a very distinctive scar. Even though he has shaved off his spiked hair, I'm sure it's him. Lauren thinks we should tell the police to find out who he is in case he's following us.'

'Following you, not Lauren.' Cole removed his hand from hers and sat back with his arms now crossed.

'I tried to explain to her that the police here have enough trouble keeping up with crime, they can't get involved in some foreigner's petty stalking problem.'

'Did Duduzo see him?' Cole asked, frowning.

'He talked with him before the man ran off.'

'Good, hopefully he'll know his name,' Cole said. 'Do you have the picture of him?'

'The printed one's still in Lauren's handbag. There are digital ones on my computer and on hers. We shared our SD cards so we have copies of each other's pictures. Why?'

'There are a few things happening at *nTabaGrequa*. We are watching for some specific people – one of them has a distinctive scar on his face. Siphiwe and I never got a good look at the taxi driver when he attacked you. I wonder if it's the same man? Too much of a coincidence, I think.'

'The man in Lauren's picture and the man who attacked me are definitely the same person.'

'That's worrying. What type of security alarm do you have at home?'

'I don't, but there are bars on the windows and I have Trellidor on all the external exits,' Mackenzie said. 'The salesman said those were the most reliable security doors available.'

'They are, but perhaps you should consider putting in an alarm.'

'I've thought about it. I even had a rep come in and give me a quote before Lauren came for her visit.'

'And?'

'And that's as far as I got. I was going to call for an installation date when we got home after coffee, but Lauren decided we should come and visit Tala and Zulu again. Then she conveniently felt ill …'

'She means well, your matchmaker friend.'

'Seriously? You letting her off that easily? I think she's being an interfering art agent who should keep her nose out of my personal life!' she said but then she laughed. 'I know she means well. She's always been that friend behind me who pushed me further, made me want more, do better, take a chance when I didn't want to. It was she who suggested I come to South Africa, become my own person in my own time. But this ditching us and rushing off is getting old.'

'I'm not complaining about seeing more of you. Besides, she's awesome and she seems like she's a great friend,' Cole said with a smile.

'She is. And talking of being a great friend, I should get home and check on her to make sure she didn't crash my truck into the garage or anything. It takes a while getting used to driving on the left-hand side of the road.'

Cole nodded. 'So I guess that means that you don't want me to organise a friend to come install an alarm system?'

'No thanks. I'll get it sorted. So do you think I should take his photo to the police?'

'Show me on the way to dinner. If it's the same guy we are watching for then I would say we will go and see them tonight, don't wait any longer.'

'Fine, you talked me into dinner. But just so you know, it doesn't have to be fancy to impress me. I'm happy as long as I'm not cooking the food and washing the dishes.'

He waited for a moment, as if she was supposed to say something else, then he prompted her. 'And the man in the photo?'

'Okay, if it's the same guy then I'll take all the help I can get to protect us. How does that sound?'

'Perfect. But either way I would be happier if you would get your alarm installed soon. With a back-to-base satellite monitoring, make sure that's on the quote. No phone lines, they can cut the lines too easily,' Cole said. 'Come on, let's put these two characters safely away so we can go see this photograph, check on Lauren, then we can get going on our dinner date.'

CHAPTER
17

Mackenzie opened the gate with the spare garage control she carried in her handbag. Cole drove in and parked in front of the garage. He got out and opened her door, like he always did, and waited for her to climb out.

As they walked up the path towards the front door Cole suddenly stopped. The metal security gate's lock was cut from the frame and it lay discarded in the rose garden at the front entrance. The wooden frame around the lock had been hacked out and the door was splintered.

'Get behind me!' Cole hissed, putting himself as a human shield between her and the door as they backed up the path to his *bakkie*.

'But Lauren's in there. Lauren told us she was coming right home!' Mackenzie protested, trying to push past him.

'Mackenzie, look at me. We'll get her help, but whoever has broken in there means business. We'll call the cops to make sure we have backup. You call Lauren, see if perhaps she isn't there, before we rush in ourselves.'

She pulled her phone from her pocket and dialled, listening to the exchanges clicking through. She watched as Cole pulled his cell phone from his pocket and made the call.

His call connected quicker than hers.

'Police station. *Dumelang.*' The lady's voice came out of the phone speaker loudly enough for her to hear.

'It's Cole. Is Sergeant Alan there?'

'I'll transfer you.'

A booming voice broke the metallic clicking. 'Cole?'

Her call went to voicemail as she listened half-heartedly to Lauren's message, the sound of Cole's voice drowning most of it out.

'There's a problem. I'm in the driveway of 5 Botha Street. A break-in is in progress. I'm unarmed and have Mackenzie with me. Her friend, Lauren's in the house.'

'I'll be there in a minute.'

'Thanks.' Cole hung up.

'Lauren, call me. I need to know where you are, it's urgent!'

Cole nodded as he waited for her to finish leaving her message. 'They're on their way. We need to get back inside the car. We're safer there than out here in the dark.' After she was seated she watched him as he ran around and climbed in the driver's seat, and locked both doors.

'Who are you that a policeman will attend to my house so quickly? I know how often these break-ins happen in South Africa and how low on the priority list they are,' Mackenzie said.

Cole cleared his throat. 'You're wrong. If the robbers are still in the house and there's a chance of catching them, the police will jump at it.'

'And the rest?'

'The rest?'

'What pull do you have with the sergeant?' she asked.

'We went to high school together. He went to the police force when I went to university and the army. He's one of the reasons I chose to settle in this area. Alan and Michelle, she's the vet. Two of the best friends anyone could ask for.'

'You're lucky,' Mackenzie said. 'And talking about friends, that's why we have to go in and get Lauren now, just in case she can't answer because she's in the house.' She tried to open the locked door but he kept relocking it on the panel near him.

'You know there's a possibility that she isn't here? That there is no one in your house and that's why they're in there. If we rush in we could get killed and then she would be identifying us resting in the morgue.'

She stilled. She hated that he might have a point.

In the silence of the cab of the *bakkie*, they looked back towards the house, trying to catch a glimpse of what was happening inside.

A white van spun around the corner into Botha Street.

'The police,' Cole said. 'We wait here till it's all over where it's safer for you.'

'No way.'

The police parked behind the *bakkie*, exited their vehicle and barrelled past them into the house, making her statement redundant.

'We'll get through this, Mackenzie. Alan will get those burglars and we'll get Lauren,' Cole said.

Her stomach clenched. If only Lauren hadn't come home early. What might have happened if she'd been there, too? She bit her lip to try to stop her teeth chattering.

The minute they had seen her attacker in town she should have gone straight to the police. Fight or flee, those were her only options. And fleeing seemed so much easier, only now she had her whole studio to pack and move as well, she couldn't leave her artworks behind, or Lauren.

How had she let things get so settled in Crystalberg?

*   *   *

Of the four policemen who had run into the house, only two came out through the front door.

'A man ran out the back. Two of my men are in pursuit,' Alan said, bumping his knuckles to Cole's.

'Alan, this is Mackenzie. The owner of this house.'

He put his hand out and shook hers. 'Good to meet you at last. Sorry it's under these circumstances and not over a beer at Cole's place,' he said to Mackenzie but he looked to Cole and raised an eyebrow.

'Where's Lauren?' Mackenzie asked.

Alan shook his head. 'There was no sign of anyone inside. Are you sure she was home? There's no vehicle in your garage.'

Mackenzie almost collapsed from relief. 'She isn't here. That's great! She isn't hurt! Lauren had a headache so she took my truck and left Cole and me at his cheetah centre.'

Cole quietly said, 'But that was over three hours ago. Where would she have gone?'

'Does Lauren carry a cell phone?' Alan asked.

'Yes, she's attached at the hip to it. I tried her before and it went directly to voice message. Hang on, I'll call her again,' Mackenzie said. She opened her phone and attempted to unlock its screen and push the favourite button for Lauren's number. Only her fingers wouldn't listen to her brain as they shook and she was unable to press the correct combination.

Cole took the phone from her and listened as she gave him her log-in code.

They put it on speaker but it rang out to her message bank again.

'Lauren, it's me again. Call please – it's urgent,' Mackenzie said.

Cole hung up.

'Is her phone also an iPhone?' Alan asked.

'Yes.'

'Good. We can try track it then find her and make sure she's safe and not in any trouble. These mountain roads have steep cliffs and to anyone who isn't local it's easy to go down the side. I'll need to call a friend in Durban and set that up. Can I borrow your phone?'

Mackenzie nodded as Cole handed over her phone.

'Does she have any next-of-kin that we need to contact?' Alan asked.

'No, she was an only child and her parents have both passed on,' Mackenzie said.

Alan nodded then walked away from them back into the house as he spoke into his own cell phone, holding Mackenzie's in his other hand, reading the screen as he walked. A short while later he returned and gave Mackenzie back her phone. 'You can go in now and have a look around. Let us know if anything is missing.'

'Come on,' Cole said. 'At least we know that Lauren wasn't in the house and your *bakkie* isn't in the garage. So for now we can think of her as alive and safe.'

'But where is she?' Mackenzie asked.

'We don't know,' Alan said, 'but we will soon.'

Cole squeezed her hand. 'They have her number, there isn't much more you can do right now. Just let the police do their jobs.'

'But what if she's hurt?' Mackenzie said.

'There's no sign of a struggle, so we have to assume that she hadn't got home yet. Maybe she stopped for coffee on the way, met someone and got talking,' Alan said.

They reached the door and walked inside. Looking at the damage inflicted on her house was maddening. Bile rose in her throat when they walked into the living room. She fought it down.

Cole frowned. 'This isn't normal. Trashing a place is a waste of good stuff that can be sold or used. Can you see if anything has been stolen?' Cole asked as he stepped over the broken plasma TV lying on the floor.

Mackenzie picked her way through her downstairs rooms almost zombie-like, noting each piece of furniture that had been systematically destroyed, each ornament and pot plant smashed. Even the curtains were pulled down and shredded into piles of rags.

She had to clamp her hands together to stop them from shaking.

Eventually, Cole opened the door into her studio. Alan ghosted behind them all the time.

'Oh thank God!' she said. Relief swept through her as she held on to Cole before walking in. Nothing had been touched. Her computer was still on the desk with her camera sitting next to it. Most importantly, none of her work had been destroyed. She ran her fingers lovingly over her sculptures of African animals. Her works-in-progress.

She walked over to her latest African baby elephant sculpture. The bronze was undamaged. She placed her hand over it. It was safe. She looked around, her orphans waiting to come out of their castings were safe, too.

Relief ran through her as she sank to her knees. 'I thought it would all be gone. Seeing the house, I thought that whoever had broken in would have destroyed it all as well.'

'Thank God they didn't. I know nothing about art, but those are stunning,' Alan said.

'I don't know if this is that guy we spoke about, Cole or if it's someone else's way of getting to me. Showing me they know who I really am.'

'What guy?' Alan said.

'Who are you?' Cole asked.

Alan raised his eyebrow.

'My question first,' said Cole, 'then you fire up your computer and show Alan and I that photo, check his identity.'

'It doesn't matter, this is all just stuff, material possessions, I can replace it all, but not Lauren. We need to find Lauren,' Mackenzie said.

'We'll find her, Mackenzie. We will!' Cole drew her to him in a hug and she melted into his body. Needing the human contact and male strength. Letting him share his warmth with her. She picked an imaginary cotton thread off Cole's shirt. Touching him for reassurance that he was real, and she wasn't trapped in a nightmare. Somehow her totally female reaction to the situation, didn't seem too out of place with a man who was as earthy and rugged as Cole. Despite the clean jeans and checked shirt he had changed into in his office, she knew what it covered underneath, and for a few stolen moments, she drew on his masculine strength.

Now she was going to have to trust Cole was man enough to accept her story. She was going to have to tell him about the real

Mackenzie, warts and all. Nothing could change her past, but since coming to South Africa, she realised that she wasn't running anymore. She might have thought that at first, but now she realised that she had simply made a decision and kept to it. Removing herself from a bad situation, and ensuring that she had control over her new life. That wasn't fleeing, that was good decision making.

She'd come to Africa to find herself and liked what she found. She'd come to accept that she was strong and independent. Lauren had recognised it all those years ago, but it had taken her time away from her family for her to realise it, too. Now she had to reveal the truth of her identity to find Lauren.

'Mackenzie, as much as you don't want me involved in your troubles, I already am, so you might as well tell me from the beginning. What's going on?' Cole said.

'I can't help you unless I know the truth, Mackenzie,' Alan said.

'My real name is Nicole Mackenzie Aurette Carter. My father is Robert, Bob, Aurette. He's a US senator from Texas with an ego just as big.'

'You're hiding from your father?' Cole asked.

'No. I left the US to be my own person. My dad's controlling nature was just part of the problem.' Mackenzie took a deep breath and moved her shoulders, as though physically shaking off the demons from the past. It felt good to get the truth out there, so it would no longer darken anything between her and Cole.

Now that Lauren was missing, Mackenzie needed his help. They both did.

She was going to have to come completely clean, no matter what it was to her. Her best friend needed her, and to help Lauren, she would even stand in front of a camera crew and face down the media if she had to.

'My husband was Sebastian Carter. The rock star who was assassinated just over two and a half years ago. A man sat on a rooftop and aimed a gun to his chest as he sang to a sold-out show. Forty-three more people died in the stampede trying to get out of the stadium as the killer continued to randomly fire shots into the crowd. Then he packed up his gun and walked away like it never happened. "The Urban Shooter", the FBI called him.' She took a second to catch her breath, and continued. 'I was there in the back area like always, and even though I rushed onto the stage my husband bled out in my arms and there was nothing I could do about it. I called 911 and told them to hurry, but the FBI wouldn't allow the paramedics in to us until they had verified that it was safe, and they knew that the shooter had gone, that the people coming in wouldn't be shot. By then it was too late. Sebastian was dead.'

'How did you happen to be there?' Alan asked.

Mackenzie replied, 'I was at every concert with him.'

'So why are you in South Africa?'

'They never found or arrested the man who murdered Sebastian and I still don't know why anyone would want to kill him. There was no possible reason to want him dead and all those people attending the concert. The media wouldn't stop hounding me. Wouldn't leave me alone. They were convinced I knew something and wasn't talking. I lost not only my husband and best friend that day, I lost my privacy. They became like a fungus I couldn't get rid of, thinking it was alright to have access into every part of my life. After all, I had grown up in their eyes, the senator's daughter, and I had the fairytale marriage to a rock star when I was barely out of school. Then the tragic ending – just like John Lennon. My life was taken over by the media's speculations and constant attention.'

Alan frowned. 'You must have been scared. Surely your father's office could have protected you?'

She shook her head. 'You don't understand. My father encouraged them. He didn't try to protect me. He used my increased social profile to get himself re-elected and move up on the ladder towards the White House. He never defended me. Even when they made up lies that Sebastian had planned to leave me and that he had a love child, or that I was in rehab for a drug problem. He wouldn't allow me to sue them because it was bad for his reputation.'

Cole snorted, then he reached for her again and hugged her close. 'Sorry, that wasn't at you, it was at your father's treatment of you.'

'It's alright, I would understand if it was for me, because if I had just told you who I was in the beginning, you would've understood why I was keeping my distance from everyone in this town,' Mackenzie said.

'No I wouldn't have,' Cole said, 'and what's in a name anyway?'

Mackenzie pulled away from Cole and smiled weakly.

Alan asked, 'And how does Lauren fit into all this?'

Mackenzie wrung her fingers together. 'Lauren and I were friends from when we were in nursery school. She was born Canadian, but her folks moved to Texas soon after that. We grew up together. She became my art agent during college. Lauren has always been my best friend and stuck by me through everything.'

Cole reached for her hand, as if giving her his strength to lean on while they talked.

'Why exile to South Africa?' Alan continued his questioning.

'Relocate, not exile. The idea was actually Lauren's. Reinvent myself, away from the pressure of the media and my overprotective family.'

'And your parents? Do they know where you are?' Alan asked.

'I called my mom from a phone box when I got to Cape Town and told her I was safe but not where I was. I haven't spoken to my dad since the day I left.' She thought how sad that must sound. Her family was thousands of miles away. One day she would get to sort out her problems, but not today. Today was about Lauren and where she had got to.

'Fair enough,' Cole said. 'Alan, remember the taxi incident? I sort of fudged it a bit. Mackenzie was there and the taxi wasn't just pulled onto the side of the road and shooting at us, the men had attacked Mackenzie on her bike ride. Now I understand why she asked me not to mention her name.'

'I knew there was something weird about your report, the dots didn't join up,' Alan said. 'You can amend it tonight when we get to the station to file the reports for the break-in. I would have kept your secret, Mackenzie, you didn't need to get Cole to lie to me.'

'Sorry,' she said, 'trust doesn't come easily and I didn't know you.'

'Duly noted,' Alan said. 'Now, why South Africa and how did you get here?'

'Two years ago, six months after Sebastian's funeral, I left the US. I was so ready to go away, strike out on my own. If I hadn't I'm sure I would've been in a mental hospital by now, driven there by my folks. I love them, but my parents are old-fashioned and couldn't accept the fact that thirteen years had passed since I was last at home with them. That I'd grown up.'

'You went back to your parents' house after that long?' Cole asked.

'I did. But without Sebastian they thought I was still daddy's little puppet. It felt claustrophobic, as if I'd never escape their smothering tentacles again. The first thing my dad did was encourage me to change my name back to his and that immediately fuelled the media interest. I should've seen what he was doing, but I didn't. My mother had come to help with Sebastian's funeral but was more of a hindrance. She pressured me into a promise that I'd go to the family home for a few weeks and stay with them again.

'So I went home to Texas. I thought it was the right thing to do. It wasn't. It was as if I was a seventeen-year-old again, having my life run by my parents. Suddenly, I wasn't an educated and accomplished sculptor, I was just husbandless and that made me useless in their eyes.' She sniffed, fighting back the tears at the hurtful memory as every emotion she'd locked away so tightly came rushing back. Talking about it was creating fissures in her heart, as if it ripped apart the small Band-Aids that had kept them under control. Even two and a half years later, time had not healed it sufficiently enough to stop the eruption of emotions that threatened to choke her.

Cole put his hand under her chin. 'Look at me. You were hurting having just lost your husband. It's natural to want to go home.'

Mackenzie took a deep breath. Now that she had started talking about it, she just wanted to get it all out. 'I'd packed up my apartment and flown to my parents' house in Dallas. What a mistake I made!'

'We all make mistakes,' Cole said.

'To think I could return home for even a day without them interfering and trying to dominate my life again was stupid.' She paused.

Cole looked at her. 'You don't have to tell us all this if you don't want to.' He reached for her hands and covered them with his own.

'I might as well tell you the rest, something might help find Lauren. Perhaps this way, hearing it first-hand, you won't think too badly of me and I won't look like too much of a spoilt rich man's daughter.'

'You don't look like that at all, Mackenzie,' Cole said.

'No, you don't. You sound like someone who should have spoken about this a while ago, instead of bottling it up,' Alan said.

'Probably,' she said, then smiled weakly. 'And you're right, the emotional stress of keeping my identity hidden here has taken its own toll. At least I was out of the public eye. My father didn't understand, I didn't want to be in the public eye at all!'

'Now that I do understand,' Cole said.

'He accused me of taunting the press, that while I was playing at sculpting in New York when we weren't touring, he'd been waiting patiently for the time to progress to the White House. I begged him to listen, just like I used to when I was a kid but …' She shrugged her shoulders.

Cole's hands continued to stroke hers, calming her nerves, helping her compose herself. The shakes she'd had were at last subsiding.

'Thinking back, I'm not sure what I was angrier about. That they had ignored my own achievements over the past years while I was married to Sebastian, being too busy with their political career to care that I'd actually been growing in the world of sculpting, even though I never did a showing and my photo was never attached to my work, or that he took the media's side!'

'Understandable,' Cole said.

Mackenzie laughed nervously and blew her nose. 'Do you know that my father said I was too "flighty" and didn't live in reality?'

'Are you flighty?' Cole asked.

'I don't think so. By the time we had that argument, I was past caring what my father said anymore. I told them I was leaving.

We said our goodbyes, well my mom and I did, my father refused to speak to me. I knew he would try to find me when I didn't come home, so I'd already cleaned out one of my bank accounts. I'd withdrawn it from different branches over a few days and deposited it into Lauren's business account and kept some cash for my immediate use. Luckily, Sebastian and I hadn't lived on credit, so there were no bills to take care of. I packed a backpack of clothes, a few of my favourite sculpting tools and walked out the door.'

'How did you end up here?' Alan asked. 'I need to know in case there is something along the way that happened, that is, anything in your past that we need to look into.'

'Other than overzealous photographers and news hounds, and having my phone lines bugged, nothing else happened,' she said. 'But as for getting here. Sebastian and I had friends who used to drive the tour equipment trucks, and I had a valid visa to visit South Africa. With their help, I eventually found myself on a cargo freighter bound for Cape Town. The very same men who had been there when the shooting happened, and had been unable to help save Sebastian that horrible night, were there to help me when I asked them to. The merchant ship customs control in Cape Town isn't that strict and wasn't computerised. So my father couldn't use his influence to find out where I was and attempt to fetch me back home.'

'That was a different strategy. These men who stood by you, they seem like men whose hands I need to shake one day,' Cole said.

'They are. You'd like them,' Mackenzie said.

Cole nodded. 'So, then? You got to Cape Town.'

'To tell the truth I was scared without Sebastian. I needed space to heal, to grow and to be myself.'

'Those are not unreasonable things to want in life. How did you land up here in Crystalberg?' Cole asked, running his hand up her arm.

She smiled at the action. It was so natural. It felt right. She was drawing a new type of strength from him, one she hadn't felt for a long time. She was sharing.

'Using cash, I bought a new truck and drove north, stopping here and there for a few weeks at a time, staying in bed and breakfasts or hotels until I got to Crystalberg. It's a small enough town to be a non-person, but big enough to be slightly hostile to outsiders. This house was for sale, and I could see at once that the isolation was perfect. I could work at any hour and it was big enough for all my art paraphernalia. I knew this was where I was going to stay. I contacted a lawyer in Durban and we arranged the purchase. I started sculpting again, generating an income. I'd always used a nom de plume for my work, so I continued using it. Lauren was still my art agent and she knew where I was. She's got a gallery in Cape Town which receives my work and ships it over to her. I'm Monique.'

'Really?' Cole raised his eyebrows. 'So, you are Mackenzie, who's really Nicole Mackenzie Aurette Carter, who's known in the art world as Monique.'

She smiled. 'Monique was the name I chose to use during art school. I was already married to Sebastian and I didn't want to use his fame to get places, so we thought of the name Monique and I went with that. Few people know the person behind the artist's name. As my reputation in the art world was already forged on Monique, I continued selling my work at a reasonable profit and didn't need to start from the bottom again.'

'Couldn't your father or the press have tracked you through your art?' Alan said.

'Unlikely. The Cape Town art gallery manager has been extremely careful with anyone who wanted to know personal details about me, or from where he'd acquired my work. Until tonight, only my lawyer in Durban and Lauren's manager in Cape Town knew my secrets, my location and real name in South Africa. I guess anyone who follows my art would know I'm in Africa somewhere, it's kind of obvious with the change in animals that I've been casting, but Africa is a big place to start looking. It all seems pretty trivial now. Lauren is the most important thing at this moment, and getting her back is more critical to me than spilling all this personal information.'

'You kept those secrets well, but your house was trashed, so it's unlikely that it was the press. There's something else going on here,' Alan said.

'There's the man with the scar,' Mackenzie said. She quickly told Alan about the Soweto Market photographs.

'Even knowing this and putting it together with the information about the taxi shooting and the Soweto Market man who had walked into the café, none of this explains why Lauren has been taken. How does she fit into the wrecking of your house?' Alan said.

'I don't know,' Mackenzie said.

'Let's take a look at these photographs. Perhaps they can shed some light, give me a face to start looking for,' Alan said.

They walked to her workstation, where she brought up the picture of the man. His face filled the huge monitor.

'This is him,' she said.

'Shit,' said Alan and Cole together.

'You both know him?' Mackenzie asked.

'Unfortunately,' Cole said. 'Dominic Bongwanan. He's a bad son of a bitch, but he's not going to harm you on my watch. Come on, let's pack you a bag. You can't sleep here. I'll call the ranch and Siphiwe will bring some workers to board up the doors and windows. He can also send over two game guards to stay here to make sure none of your artwork gets stolen. You can sleep at the ranch.'

Alan shook his head. 'I'll be posting a policeman till morning.'

'The more armed guards here, the better,' Cole said. 'I'm sure Thandi would love to help clean up the mess in the morning. Till then it can just stay where it is.'

Alan said, 'It would probably be best that you wait until we have completed our investigation and dusted for prints. I'll let Thandi know when we are done.'

Mackenzie just stared at Cole and Alan.

Cole cleared his throat. 'I want you to know that I'm not taking over, I'm not trying to fix this, just keep you safe. I know what it's like to need help and have nowhere to turn to get it. I've seen enough senseless violence and killings to last both our lifetimes and would rather you don't become another statistic. Besides, my cheetahs need you for their exercise.' Cole looked at her, and raised his hand, as if to touch her, then dropped it. 'When Lauren comes home, Siphiwe will be here and he can call us and send her out to the ranch.'

'Fine.' Mackenzie said. 'I need to find Farren though.'

'She's probably made herself scarce with intruders in the house,' Cole said.

'Hopefully she's in my bedroom,' Mackenzie said.

'Her cat,' Cole explained.

Alan nodded. 'The cat. Right. Go upstairs. I'll wait down here. Do you mind if I copy a few of these photos?'

'Go ahead, help yourself,' Mackenzie said. 'There are spare flash drives in the left-hand desk drawer if you need one.'

They walked up the stairs and once on the landing just stood there, surveying the room.

'Alan obviously got here before they'd finished their job upstairs. Seems untouched so far.'

'I'm just happy he got here.'

As they entered her bedroom, a fur ball streaked out from under the bed straight for her and ran up her body. Claws biting into her flesh in its haste to get to safety.

'Hey, it's okay, Farren. Nothing's going to hurt you now.' She gathered her cat up to her and held it.

It yowled as if trying to tell her about the terror.

'It's okay, Farren. I'm home and you're safe.'

A talkative meow in answer and a loud purring sound filled the silence.

Cole laughed softly. 'Bring your cat, too. It'll probably take a few days for this to be cleaned up and the furnishings replaced.' He reached out his hand to stroke the cat gently and give it a few moments of his time before he pulled his cell phone from his pocket and walked away, giving instructions to whoever was on the other side.

She could hear Alan downstairs, still talking to his policemen.

Mackenzie was going to stay at Cole's ranch and it had been his decision, not hers. He hadn't asked for her opinion, just assumed that the safest place was going to be with him and she would comply. Mackenzie wasn't that girl anymore who relied on a man to make her decisions, the girl who no longer stood up to authority. She knew why she hadn't argued with him.

This was different. He was different. He hadn't even flinched when he heard her real name. Either he didn't know who she was, or he simply didn't care.

She smiled at the realisation that in the last few weeks, she probably had got to know him well enough to say that if he had realised who she was, he wouldn't have changed his behaviour towards her at all, because he wasn't the type to be starstruck and hung up on anyone associated with fame. She knew it was never her who was famous, just her now dead husband and her political powerhouse father, but for a time in her life, when the press wouldn't leave her alone, it had seemed like hers was the face that was slashed across every magazine and newspaper around. She knew she wasn't like Paris Hilton, where everyone would recognise her instantly, and she silently thanked the universe for that, but in America she still would get recognised far more often than she would have liked. More like Chelsea Clinton, people knew of her but she had managed to mostly stay out of the limelight.

Shaking her head, she returned to the here and now. She chewed her lip as she realised that it wasn't that Cole was simply making the decisions, he'd also made the calls to secure her home, to bring his game guards to her house to protect her artwork. He was considering her the whole time, even if he never gave her the chance to say, *Yes, thank you, Cole, I'd love to hide behind your fence and rest. Regroup while we make sure that Lauren is okay!*

Cole was not imposing his decisions on Mackenzie, he was merely doing what he'd said before. *He knew what it was like to need help and have nowhere to turn to get it.* His world wasn't as perfect as she'd thought. He was helping her.

Mackenzie turned towards the wardrobe, took out a flight case and began packing, her mind reeling. They had basically ruled out the press coming after her, she was yesterday's news, and she hoped they would never react in such a horrendous way again. So, the likelihood of it being that Dominic-what's-his-name was the most probable one now. But why the hell was he after her and Lauren? Because of a photograph in a market?

She chewed her lip some more. At least she had a plan for tonight. No way was she staying in her trashed house when the ranch had an eight-foot electrified security game fence around it to keep whoever was after her away. She could spend a night in safety, and when Lauren did show her face she was going to murder her because if she had just stayed at Cole's ranch with them she wouldn't be missing!

CHAPTER
18

'FUCK!' Dominic stubbed out the joint he'd been smoking and picked up a bottle still covered in brown paper. He popped four white pills into his mouth and downed the remnants of the alcohol in one huge gulp.

He spoke into his cell phone. '*Lumela, Koko.*'

He listened for a moment then replied. 'No, Nkgono, I tell you. It was *e*-luck that I went into Duduzo's Kofi Shop in Crystalberg, and there was this fat white woman telling everyone at the top of her voice that she had a *e*-photo of me in the Soweto Market, she was *e*-sitting with the cycling woman who Shaggie wanted to have some *e*-fun with, but was too much of a *e*-wildcat, months ago. I remember them both. The one I *e*-got, she was the nosy one with her *e*-light and *e*-camera, who said she wasn't *e*-policewoman. Now, she is *e*-unnecessary complication.'

'It's always complication after complication with you,' Nkgono said.

He took the phone away from his ear as she reprimanded him like only a matriarch could. Making a grown man feel like a small boy again. Bringing back every single feeling of inadequacy that he had known when he was growing up. Making him feel once again like that lost boy in the Alexandra township, when she was the only one who had looked after him after his *tata* had been killed fighting for freedom and his *mma* had been murdered by the security forces for trying to find her husband's body. He had been young then, very young. Now he was a grown man and yet his *nkgono* still treated him like a piccaninny.

'I can't *e*-calm down. Understand, maNtuli is going to kill our family. You all only just got away in the last *e*-shack fire; she means to kill us if I don't deliver these cats this time. Now there is a *e*-photograph of me in the market, the day I bought those limpet mines. And of you, Nkgono. If the police get their hands on that *e*-picture, they are going to know exactly what exploded in the shack fire. What if maNtuli finds out about our family business? That we hush-hush carry on the business without her knowing all these years, without giving her any of the profits like those around us had to. What will happen if the *e*-truth comes out that I was running guns with you, beginning our business of hiring our guns out? If she finds out that all this time, I didn't only serve her *e*-needs but my own, too. We are dead. No second chance on that one.'

'Stop talking, boy. Do you have the photos?'

'*Ee*, I have one of them. I had to beat her to get her to tell me, but she said it's a digital print and it's already in the cloud, whatever that is, and even though we have the printed copy there can be more and more made.'

'*Eish*. You need to get her computer. Go back to the house and get her computer.'

'*Tjhee*. I already tried to go back. There are anti-poaching guards there now and they are armed with .303s, and *e*-police car. The police almost caught me there already. I had to run fast!'

'So? You have access to our weapons. Take a R1 or a R5, take an AK-47 rifle. Those guards won't stand a chance. Are you sure you looked everywhere?'

'I can't go in there and *e*-shoot everyone. The policemen here are not like in *Jozi*, they can't be bought. I have *e*-tried before with a detective. It didn't end well for him then. The police in this area, they work on *e*-old-fashioned honour system. But it doesn't matter. I have her. We only have five days left to get those cheetahs now, then we can get away from Tobeko Ntuli for good! I looked everywhere, *ee*!'

'You made her your enemy. You might never get away from her, did you think of that?'

'I know. It's all I have been thinking about since the fire. But right now, I have the *e*-white woman and she can put our whole *e*-operation in Mozambique in jeopardy, and those guns. They were what was going to give us *e*-space and money to go somewhere far away!'

'Kill her and throw her down a ravine! There are plenty there that are steep enough. No one will find her.'

He turned to the window and looked out.

The view was crap. The weather had become unseasonably cold and there was snow threatening. The locals had all been joking that the only month it hadn't snowed in Crystalberg was January, otherwise cold weather could come any time.

The mountain outside the window towered over the town, casting its shadow just as maNtuli's shadow now darkened his life. Once, when she had come back to the shacks as a smart and successful woman, he had believed that she could love him, want him as a man, but she had spurned him.

He wondered if it was Sizani who had set the fire for her, and made a mental note that when he finished this job he would return and kill him anyway. First for hurting Noah and for the new scar across his face, but also to make sure that he never started another fire near his family again.

He rubbed his temples as the Panado began to help his headache.

'So are you going to get rid of her?' Nkgono asked loudly.

'*Tjhee*. I don't have *e*-computer password yet to get the picture out the cloud! And I can't kill anyone in front of Noah, you know how he gets.'

'*Ee*. I was going to surprise you with a visit anyways. You take your brother and leave him at the shebeen for a while and meet me back at the farm. I'll take care of this one and get the information from her. An animal or a woman, black or white, they all die the same to me.'

'*Tsamaya hantle*,' Dominic said and hung up the phone. He sat on the end of the bed.

He had sunk lower than he had ever thought possible. Having his *nkgono* come to help him finish off this job was admitting weakness. It had been many years since Dominic had needed help from anyone.

It was all her fault. That bitch maNtuli had him by his short and curlies and was crushing his nuts in a vice. When this was over, he was going to go after her and ensure she knew that she could no longer touch his family.

CHAPTER
19

Farren meowed loudly on the seat between them. Tucked inside the pet carrier, the cat was making it known that it was unhappy with the move and the late hour in which she was being transported to Cole's farm. Completing the police report had taken far longer than Mackenzie thought it would. It was almost midnight and the blackness of the mountains pressed inwards.

Mackenzie looked in the rear-view mirror. There was nothing following them, no lights other than theirs on the open road. That didn't stop the jittery nerves and the flutter of fear in her stomach.

Someone out there might have Lauren.

She had learnt early in her new adventure that big girls don't cry, so instead she laid back and attempted to clear her mind. She closed her eyes. Trying desperately to make her heart beat at a normal rate because from the shortest hair on her head, right down to her toes, she was terrified something had happened to Lauren.

'Almost there,' Cole said, wrenching her from her deep thoughts. He turned the *bakkie* right. Mackenzie scanned the rusted old nameplate above the entrance, *'nTabaGrequa* – Wildlife Rescue and Cheetah Conservation Ranch', under the yellowish lights that illuminated it. She waved to the old game guard who she recognised from her many rides past on her bike as he opened and closed the double entrance gates that were manned 24/7.

Instinctively, her eyes were drawn to the cheetah cage but it was in darkness. She imagined Sasha in there now. Sitting on her anthill waiting, looking sad with the black tear-like streaks down her face. Sasha wouldn't know that Mackenzie was also a captive behind the same fence that protected her. Hopefully, that electric fence would keep out the predators who threatened her and the beautiful cats. Providing them all with protection.

Exactly what were the few things happening at the farm that Cole had mentioned that he had been looking out for Dominic already?

Was she jumping into more trouble sheltering with him?

They passed the information centre attached to the huge cat enclosures and continued down the road. Until now, she and Lauren had always remained at the visitors' centre when they popped in. A sharp bend concealed the house, and as they rounded it Mackenzie saw the homestead drenched in light with floodlit gardens. It was a typical African-style, sprawling farmhouse. A majestic single-storey home dominated by large verandahs with a high-pitched green tin roof and a few chimneys. She couldn't see if it was in need of a coat of paint but she could make out that there wasn't much garden, just an immaculately cut lawn across the front yard. The house nestled into a hill at the back and seemed to preside over the surrounding area.

They stopped at the steps. 'Give me a second,' Cole said, then hopped out and went around the *bakkie* to open the passenger door to help her down. He put a hand on her back, a welcome touch. She needed the human contact.

'This way,' he said, lifting her cat carrier and bringing Farren along with them.

A small elderly black woman dressed in a khaki uniform walked briskly down the steps to meet them, as if it wasn't past midnight. '*Ubasie*, Cole,' she greeted him, bifocals screening her eyes from close scrutiny. Her face, although wrinkled, held a vitality that her voice only hinted at.

'Mackenzie,' Cole said. 'This is my housekeeper and long-time friend, Thandi.'

With her hands outstretched, Thandi took both Mackenzie's hands into hers. '*Ngiyajabula ukukwazi*. Welcome, Miss Mackenzie. *Oww*, Cole and she's so pretty, too. *Ubuhle bami*. My goodness.' Still holding Mackenzie's hands, she opened the younger woman's arms wide and examined her.

The assessment was friendly, and not at all hostile. An easiness rippled through Mackenzie, as if she'd known Thandi for a long time.

'Welcome to *nTabaGrequa*, Miss Mackenzie,' Thandi said. 'Come inside. First I take you to your room. Then I'll serve drinks, now-now.' Thandi motioned for Mackenzie to follow her.

'Go with Thandi, I'll settle Farren in the kitchen,' Cole said.

Mackenzie looked quickly at the front of the house. It wasn't spot-lit like the visitors' centre had been when they had passed there, but warm, yellow lights beckoned inside. She looked out across the *vlei* to the dark mountains that surrounded the ranch and shivered.

Mackenzie nodded to Cole and she followed Thandi. 'It's so late. I'm so sorry to have got you out of—' she began, but Thandi waved the words away.

'If you need anything I've left a little bell by your bed. It may seem colonial but I won't hear you if you call. This is a big house. It's good to have another woman around,' she said, bustling off and leaving a bewildered Mackenzie behind.

Her mind kept flashing back to images of her trashed house, but more frightening was the thought that it could be Dominic who had Lauren.

She looked down at the clothes she still wore from the visit to the centre that same afternoon. Her jeans were crinkled beyond the point she knew that they could crease and her track suit top hung limply. Opening her case, she unpacked her few belongings into the walk-in wardrobe. Leaving the case on the bed, she crossed slowly over to the antique dressing table and dainty tapestry seat that accompanied it. It was almost a sin to put her toiletries and brush on the smooth wood with its distinct lemony smell of newly applied polish. The smell of a home where people took care of their furniture. And people took care of other people.

But where was Lauren?

Lauren had always taken care of her, and vice versa. Growing up, they had become more like sisters than friends. Even when she had been married to Sebastian and had found herself in some foreign country, she would call Lauren and it was as if home was never far away. Something about the house reminded her of that, and her stomach clenched at the dread that something bad had happened to Lauren.

Cole knocking softly on the door brought her back to the present. 'You okay?'

'Yes, thank you. Did you get Farren to settle?'

'She's in the kitchen with Thandi. There are no other domestic cats here. She'll be fine. She had butter on her paws and was sitting in front of the big stove cleaning when I left. Let me pop that case up onto the top shelf of the cupboard,' he said and as she stretched to pass him the case he took it off the bed. Unbalanced, she swayed slightly forward, brushing against him.

She stilled, and she felt him do the same.

'Thank you for everything,' she said.

She watched as he ran his hand through his hair.

'Don't mention it,' he said, but she could hear that his voice was hoarse and thick with emotion. He strode over to the walk-in and swung the case up onto the shelf.

'Bathroom is down the passage, first on your left,' he said as he ducked out of the door.

Mackenzie stared at the empty space where he'd been standing. With just one look from him her whole being had been taken to paradise and then rudely dumped back down on earth.

Man-oh-man if she was having this reaction from just one look then she was in a mess. To be honest, despite their fragile friendship that had formed recently, there was an undeniable chemistry surging between them.

Lauren's voice crept into her subconscious. *Why don't you let him make that decision.*

She smiled. Lauren always knew how to see through her and she was right this time, too. From her first crush on Richard Duke in junior school, to when she had met Sebastian at a charity function, Lauren had known the men who meant something to her. She'd picked up on Cole, also, doing her best to try to help their relationship along, despite being there for a holiday with her friend. She hadn't monopolised her time but had rather tried to steer her towards Cole, as if it was important to her to have her friend happy, so when she went home to New York she knew that Mackenzie would be with Cole and not be alone again.

She couldn't even begin to understand how the attraction she felt for him had been ignited when she thought she had it under control, but her traitorous body was letting her down big time. They had crossed over so many barriers recently. She thought that the attraction was just as strong from his side, but then it had always been there, smouldering, even that very first day they had met. Then he'd saved her from the taxi driver and she had excused the butterfly heart as hero worship. After that their relationship had at last progressed, and they had become such firm friends since August. He seemed to recognise that she was skittish and she was thankful for the breathing space he gave her.

Now they were under the same roof.

Her heart beat a little faster at the thought, and she held her hand to her stomach to still the butterflies there. She had to acknowledge and admit that they were more than just friends, and she was ready for the next step in their relationship. However, being forced into that step by the invasion into her home wasn't quite how she ever imagined it happening. She didn't want to intrude on his space. Her head throbbed with a tension headache. Crossing back to the bed, she kicked off her shoes onto the wooden floor with a hollow thwack.

Soon, she sat numbly on the side of the deluxe spa bath, fully clothed, idly playing with the water as it ran from the faucet in the middle of the decadent tub. 'Where are you, Lauren?' she mumbled. 'Please be okay.'

She watched the bubbles rise higher on the side. Slowly, her chin came up as determination won over the defeated feeling she had been experiencing.

If it was Dominic who had Lauren and was threatening her, that was a whole new ball game. One that she was happy to have Cole and Alan around to fight with her. She still didn't know exactly what she had got into, but from his rap sheet, Dominic sounded like a dangerous man. One she didn't want to meet alone ever again.

*　　*　　*

Tired but unable to sleep, Mackenzie was wrapped up in a tracksuit to keep off the chill. 'Thanks,' she said as Cole threw a soft blanket over her legs to cover her feet as she sat cross-legged on a lounge. She took a sip of her coffee from a mug, her hands enfolding the pottery to warm them.

A nightjar sang in the distance and wild animal noises echoed off the walls of the valley. There was a cough of a zebra close by and the distant call of a jackal. She looked out from the verandah across the inky-blue sky towards where she knew the majestic black mountains stood, then upwards at the stars. It was so bright up there and yet so peaceful. She listened to the night noises, so different to her city-girl upbringing.

Something sounded almost like a baby crying in the distance. A bug made a noise nearby, at least she hoped it was just a bug, and there were definitely other animal grunts and groans she simply couldn't identify.

The conversation had turned to the ranch's workings, including the security that Cole already had in place inside his electric game fence to protect his cheetahs and other game from being stolen. Neither mentioned that Lauren was still missing and Siphiwe hadn't called to say she had got home, but it was like a huge elephant in the room as she thought of it constantly.

Cole took a sip from his coffee, his eyes looking out into the dark night. 'While I appreciate that you don't want me so involved in your life right now, I am. I brought you here to *nTabaGrequa* to keep you safe.'

'You have it wrong. I do want you in my life. It's just I had to work through the gaining-my-own-independence-and-finding-myself thing,' she admitted. 'Then I didn't know how to reapproach the subject with you.'

'I can understand that. And now?' Cole asked.

'Well, this living under your roof has happened quicker than I ever thought it would.'

'So the reason you kept your distance was because you didn't want to lose your independence? Not because you were not attracted to me?'

'Oh, the attraction is there, but I needed space to work things out on my own, then—'

She saw him smile, and his dimples showed even in the low light.

'So, no more secrets? Anything else you want to tell me?' he asked.

'Not that I know of. You have basically got my whole sordid history in one night.' She sighed.

'I get that with your experience with your father in the past, you might think someone else might try to exploit you again, but I want you to know that it will never knowingly be me.'

She nodded. 'Thanks. That means a lot. I was so worried that my true identity would freak you out, and you'd run a million miles in the opposite direction if you knew my background.'

'You were wrong. We don't get the privilege of living to our ages without some history behind us. It's just part of life. You haven't let what happened to you define who you are, so why would I have needed to think badly of it.'

'How do you know that? You don't know me well enough.'

'I know you better than you think. The local people talk about you and it's with kindness and respect. The white community here might think you a bit of a recluse, but the black community judges you because of your actions towards people. You can't hide what type of caring person you really are, even if you try hide behind sculpting all the time.'

'How so?' she asked.

'Your garden boy, Tsalala, he now goes to the local school and he has new uniforms, the books he needs and all his tuition is paid. His father is a drunk and his mother is a hard worker but doesn't earn enough money to have paid for that. You will only let him work on a Saturday and you garden with him, not to show him which plants to pull or not, but so that he doesn't do all the heavy work alone. You also feed him three meals in that time.'

'How do you know all this? He's a proud kid, he'd never tell anyone that I do that.'

'He didn't. The bush telegraph did. You might have tried to keep quiet about who you really are, but it didn't matter because the caring person who ensures that those in her employment are looked after, that defines you in the eyes of the bigger community. That is the woman I know. So I was never going to run, knowing your name.'

'Bush telegraph?'

'The people talk. Although families are separated by distance because of jobs and circumstances, somehow they always communicate. With the increase in mobile-phone service, it's got even better.'

'Right.'

'Believe me, if I had thought anything less of you, I wouldn't have continued trying to be your friend all this time.'

Mackenzie nodded. 'Thank you for understanding, and also, thank you for inviting me into your home.'

'I wish we had sorted out that part about your independence sooner. We've wasted so much time dancing around each other when we could have been together. Just know that I'll never suffocate your newly acquired independence.'

'Thank you for that, too, it means a lot to me.'

He reached out and took her hand in his. His was so warm, despite the coolness around. She shivered.

He cupped her face with his other hand, running it to her jaw-line and leaving it there. 'I learnt to stand on my own two feet far too early in life. For some people, it takes a little longer.'

'I guess I'm one of those who just took a while. Even Lauren said I should tell you, give you the choice—'

The telephone rang.

'Hold that thought,' he said.

'Lauren,' she said as they both jumped up from their chairs and ran into the study to answer it, Cole leading the way with Macken-zie close behind him.

CHAPTER

20

Dominic watched the white woman as she tried to cough and the gag in her mouth made her almost vomit. He watched her stomach heave, but nothing got past the rag he'd forced into her to shut her up. He saw that the pathetic foreigner was shivering as she attempted to focus her one undamaged eye on her surroundings. They were in a farm shed. There was no concrete on the floor, just sand. Further away, there were tools attached to the aging corrugated iron on the left side, pitch forks, *budzas* and shovels that cast shadows in the dim yellow light from the single bulb that swung above.

He watched as she attempted to sit up but found that she couldn't. Her legs and hands were tied together behind her back, forcing her stomach and breasts onto the ground. She turned her head the other way, away from him, to the large tractor parked nearby, its black tyres towering over her and its green metalwork clearly said 'John Deer' in bright yellow on the side. The woman's *bakkie* stood next to it. It was hidden inside away from any prying eyes that happened to pass.

She moved her head back towards him, looking right at him. He suspected she couldn't see much out of her right eye after the last punch he'd delivered to her face. He rubbed his knuckles, thinking about the feel of the woman's flesh crushing under his fist. He hated to admit that it was his *nkgono*'s stick that had ensured she lost sight and it was then that the woman called Lauren had almost given up her code. After his *nkgono* had beaten her, dark blood had oozed down into her mouth and stained the gag.

He looked down at her in satisfaction. Her left eye could barely open to a slit. Her nose was broken. The blood from that had dried like a moustache around her mouth so she looked like Yosemite Sam from the *Looney Tunes* cartoon he used to watch on TV when he was a kid.

Her time was running out and he supposed she knew it, too.

He rocked back on his stool. Who would have known that one woman shopping in the Soweto Market would cause him and his grandmother so much worry? He should have known that day with her black light that she was trouble.

Had she suspected no retribution after yelling at the top of her voice that he was in the *kofi* shop, bringing unnecessary and unwanted attention to him? When he had pointed the gun at her head after she had driven up to the artist's garage, she had looked like a kudu in the headlights. Stupid bitch didn't appreciate what a small community she was visiting, of course he would find out where she lived quickly so he could deal with her. She hadn't even noticed him until she had driven through the gates and inside, and it was only when she'd reached for the control to close the garage behind her that he'd opened her door and shoved his black gun against her white temple.

He hadn't killed a white woman before. He liked the contrast between his gun and her skin, like a zebra.

He smiled as he remembered putting the gag on her right there in the garage. She had tried to wriggle free as he had tied her up tightly and put her on the floor in the passenger's side before he drove out. He'd closed the garage and the electric gates after leaving, making it look as if they were never there.

This was where the foreign woman was going to die. In the middle of the bush in some farm shed. Far away from her beautiful life in the USA.

He got up and his stool fell over into the dirt. He walked over to her and put his knee into her back as he removed the gag from her mouth. 'One last time. This is your final chance,' Dominic said. 'How do I get *e*-pictures out of the cloud and destroyed?'

She shook her head then rested her chin in the dirt.

'Talk, bitch!'

She lifted her head up. Then she moved it from side to side. He heard a loud popping sound, like when people clicked their knuckles. For a moment she stared at him. 'I can't access it because you threw my bag into the river and you drowned my phone. The only way I could get into my account was with my phone. It's all gone, everything, please let me go. Just let me go,' she begged.

He kicked her once in her kidney area and heard her gasp for breath.

Nkgono got up from her stool and walked towards him. She stopped about a step away and hit him on his head with her walking stick.

'Dominic, you stupid. You didn't think again before you acted. You threw her bag away. Everything a woman has is always in her handbag. *Eish!* I raised two simple grandchildren, not one.' She shook her head. 'And you left evidence for the police to find. A woman and her bag are never parted. Her bag should be with her when she drives off a cliff, not in a river somewhere. *Eish.*'

'Nkgono, that's *e*-unfair that you say these things to me. How was I supposed to know that the *e*-iPhone could get us into her pictures in the cloud?'

'Because you should have talked to her first. Looked through her purse.'

'I did, I got *e*-printed pictures, all of those *e*-printed photographs,' Dominic said.

'But you were too fast to throw away her handbag. This, my grandchild, is why I have run our business for so long and you have worked for maNtuli, because you are still hot-headed. You still need someone to do your thinking for you.'

'I have changed, Nkgono, and after this I will *e*-sort her out. You were right, all these years. You were right. She was *e*-using me and she never loved me. Never.'

'See, I told you. You think too much with your cock, not your brain.' She pointed to her own head. 'That Tobeko, she played you all these years and now this one played you, too. This white whore. It is time she went for a long drive off a steep cliff.' Nkgono walked towards the woman lying on the floor, her steps slow but deliberate. He noticed for the first time that she walked with a bit of a hunch, as if age had begun eating at her spine.

She prodded with the end of the stick at Lauren's neck. 'My grandson asked you a question.'

'I told him. I can't. I can't get it out. They're all gone. Please let me go. Please don't throw me off a cliff.'

'But the police can? They can make copies?' Nkgono said.

'No, they have to have my code to get into my account and they don't have that. You've destroyed the only copy of the photo, there are no more copies. Please let me go. Let me go. Please don't kill me.'

Nkgono hit the woman on the head with her stick, still holding onto the knob at the end.

'Are you *e*-sure, Nkgono?' Dominic asked.

Nkgono humphed. 'My grandson thinks I am a bully. That you have no more information for us and yet I keep hurting you.'

'I've told you everything. There are no more copies, only those in the cloud, and they can't be accessed,' Lauren said.

'Tell me your code!' Nkgono demanded.

'Five-six-zero-one, but it's no use, it would only work on the phone. Please, please stop. Please stop hurting me,' Lauren pleaded.

'Do you think I am a bully?' Nkgono asked.

'Yes.' Lauren lifted her head and looked at the old lady. 'You are a bully!' she shouted.

Dominic shook his head. It was as if she knew that now they had her code, they would end her suffering. As if she knew that her time was up.

Dominic watched as his *nkgono* took her walking stick, turned it around and she held it like a golf club, so that the woman could clearly see the carvings – snakes that intertwined on the stick. They started at the tip of the wood and the heads created the ball at the end. It was the kiss of death from the snakes when the walking stick was used as a true weapon.

He watched in silence as his grandmother swung her stick and it landed right on the woman's temple. The woman didn't even try to move or deflect the club. It was as if she was welcoming death.

Nkgono raised the stick again as if to give her another blow, but Dominic held her arm and stopped her. He bent down to the woman and felt for a pulse in her neck.

'Nkgono, she is *e*-dead now,' Dominic said.

'We were finished with her. You take her and put her in the *bakkie* before I fetch Noah from the shebeen. Get rid of the body. You know how he gets when he sees dead things. Drive her in her *bakkie* up the Sani Pass. About halfway, do a U-turn, put her in the driver's seat and make sure her car is in gear to drive it off the side. It must look like an accident. Like she didn't take the corner. Noah and I will meet you when it is done and you are walking alone down the empty road. No witnesses. Understand?'

'*Ee*, Nkgono,' he said as he began cutting the ropes from Lauren's hands.

His *nkgono* had always been the backbone of their family. Even now she had refused to run away with them when he was planning the move to Namibia, despite being threatened by maNtuli. She had dug her heels in and declared she wasn't going.

Her original brick house, although it had been damaged in the fire, still stood tall, and she kept telling Dominic that she had survived maNtuli's wrath, that soon it would be maNtuli's turn to *matha* from her.

Dominic was well aware that his grandmother knew him very well. And she had taken this opportune moment to point out that maNtuli had pushed him too far this time. When this job was finished, he would kill her. But right at this time he needed to think about other things. Like getting the woman off the cliff and out of their way.

He continued to remove the ropes. He needed to get her out of here so that Noah could return to their hiding place and have a good night's sleep. Right now he needed Noah to be as calm as he could be, to walk into the pens and get the cheetahs. The wild cats would never hurt a spastic man. Having a corpse around always made Noah uneasy and an uneasy Noah was an unpredictable and uncontrollable simpleton. Calm, no death around, that was what Noah liked.

It had been Noah's idea to go into *nTabaGrequa* as tourists, and going on the tour of the facility had been a good plan. They had met the ambassador cheetahs and seen them on their leashes. They had learnt that the cheetahs were tame, like dogs. So they could be treated like dogs. They had bought steak to feed them and had it in the freezer, ready and waiting.

Time was running out. He only had four days left to get the cheetahs for maNtuli and get them to Richards Bay, before she came after his family and him again. But he had a plan. A good plan. Tomorrow his most trusted would gather together. Those who were still on maNtuli's payroll but were not happy about it. Those men who, like him, did not agree with her treatment of her male workers, who she controlled like a pack of dogs, without ever giving any one of them credit for what they achieved.

There was discord inside her business structure. He had known it was there before he'd attempted to walk away and he had warned her about it. She hadn't listened. So now he would use it to his advantage.

Those that were loyal to him would complete this job with him, take up arms that his family supplied and steal the cheetahs necessary to cancel out his debt with her, but then they would continue to work for him once he killed her. He had earned their respect long ago by being her number two, but now he would be number-one-what-counts. The *baas*. And they would work for him.

He tingled all over at the thought and realised this might just be what winning the lottery felt like.

CHAPTER

21

Cole's home office was large, dominated by a masculine desk of dark oak with impressive drawers on each side. The walls were lined with books. The rug on the floor was of African rock art printed in burnt oranges and gentle tones of yellow. In between an overstuffed bulky sofa and chairs sat a wooden table, its intricately carved legs the shape of elephant trunks. Like the rest of the house, the room smelt of lemon polish, declaring Thandi's presence. On the wall opposite to the desk hung a huge painting of a cheetah running across grassland in full stride, all four feet off the ground, which transformed the room into an oasis where one would come to contemplate.

Mackenzie hung her head. She knew in her heart what was about to happen. 'Lauren's dead. That's why Alan has come here to tell us in person, despite it being almost two in the morning,' Mackenzie said.

'Not necessarily,' Cole said, taking her arm in his hand.

The fact that Alan was driving up the road towards her supposed sanctuary had to mean her friend was gone for good.

Deep fear paralysed her, and despite seeing the familiar white police *bakkie* and Alan emerge from it, she couldn't move. Sweat broke out on her palms, and she began to tremble silently. Cole gave her hand a little tug and they walked out together to greet Alan. Her heart continued to hammer loudly in her chest, sounding as if it was an elephant trumpeting into a teacup. It echoed around her, vibrating into the shakes.

She stood her ground next to Cole.

Alan walked up the steps and met them at the top. He put his hand out to his friend. 'Cole, sorry about the lateness – well earliness – of the visit.'

'Come in.' Cole motioned with his hand towards the verandah.

'We were sitting out here, but we can move inside if you prefer?' Cole said.

'Wherever you were is fine with me. It's kind of refreshing having this cold snap now, but I bet it will heat up again real quick by Christmas,' Alan said.

'It always does,' Cole said.

Alan sat down in a chair opposite Mackenzie, as she wrapped herself in the blanket again. Cole sat next to her and reached for her hand, as if this was exactly where it should be at this time. She held on tightly to it.

Alan looked over at Mackenzie. 'My deepest condolences, Lauren has been located, but she was already deceased.'

'I'm so sorry, Mackenzie,' Cole said.

Mackenzie took in a breath and a small sound came from her, not quite a word, not quite a wail. Cole pulled her into his lap, blanket and all. Cradling her in his arms, patting her back and hugging her. He placed his chin on the top of her head as huge sobs racked her body.

'I'm so sorry you were right,' he said.

Mackenzie clung to him. The cold from the unseasonal weather was nothing compared to the chill that was rising inside of her. Alan passed Cole a tissue box that was on the table and Cole took a tissue and gave it to her.

Slowly the sobs subsided. Now she just wanted answers. Lauren was gone and she wanted to know why. She blew her nose and shifted a little in Cole's lap so that she could see Alan. 'Where was she found?'

'Your *bakkie* was located sitting on the bottom of the *krans*, on one of the bends on Sani Pass, but the injuries Lauren sustained to her body didn't happen there. She was murdered before and it was made to look like an accident.'

'You found the *bakkie* in the dark?' Cole asked. 'That was really lucky.'

'A motorist coming down the pass noticed an unusual light shining up the side of the bend and called the traffic police when they realised the barrier on the side was taken out and they thought it might be a crash. The sergeant there knows me well and was already on the lookout for Lauren and your *bakkie*. I had sent him one of your holiday pictures of Lauren and your registration number.'

'Can I see her?' Mackenzie asked, clutching Cole's hand tighter.

'Not tonight. The police still need to process her. The ambulance paramedics said that even under the emergency lighting of the crash site, it was obvious that she had been beaten, and it wasn't just crash injuries they were looking at, and unfortunately they see enough bodies to know the difference. I'm so sorry.'

A strange quietness came over her, not one of sorrow, but of anger. Anger for the loss of a friend, a young life taken too soon. Hatred boiled inside her for the unknown killer.

'Do you know who did this?' Mackenzie asked.

'Not at this stage, there will be a full investigation into her murder before we will release any more of the details,' Alan said. 'Do you know if she belonged to any specific religion that we need to take into consideration with the treatment of her body?'

'No. Not that I know of. We never talked about dying,' Mackenzie said, as she began to sob again, new tears welling into her eyes, she buried her head into Cole's broad chest. His hand smoothed the back of her hair and he held her tightly once again.

'I know this has been a difficult night, first your house, Lauren going missing, and now us finding her body, but I need you to answer a few questions and I thought here was better than calling you into the police station.'

Mackenzie looked up. 'I'll answer whatever I can.'

Alan nodded. 'You and Lauren seem to have stumbled into something, and until we know exactly what it is, I need to keep you protected, and I would like you to let me help you.'

Mackenzie sniffed and Cole passed her another tissue, and she blew her nose.

Alan leant back in his chair. 'The trashing of your home was not an ordinary burglary. It's obviously personal, and I believe that Lauren's murder is directly related.'

Icy-cold chills ran through Mackenzie. She knew the danger was still there but being confronted with it again was not easy.

Cole looked at her. 'You are safe here, they have to get through me first.'

'And past Cole's game guards and the South African Police force,' added Alan.

'I can see Alan has already made up his mind that you're staying here for a while,' Cole said. 'If you need to be kept safe, there is no safer place within a few hundred kilometres than right here at *nTabaGrequa*. But the decision to stay here until this is sorted out is all yours, not mine and not Alan's.'

They were offering solutions but they wanted her to make the decision. They were giving her the final choice.

Fear gripped her heart, and questions about how they would protect her swam around her head. Guilt that Lauren hadn't been offered this same protection and that it was too late for her friend swarmed over her. As did questions about what she would have to do now that she'd involved them in her fight and about how Cole would keep his beautiful cheetahs safe against the monsters who had killed Lauren. Acid churned in her stomach and a dull thud that began at the base of her skull snaked through to her temples.

'So, what do we do now?' Her voice sounded shaky. Her caged heart still beat erratically.

Alan said, 'If you choose to stay, not just tonight, but until we catch the murderer, then we decide who else we need to involve, if I should bring in the city detective squad to help.'

'I'm happy to stay here with Cole and to do whatever it takes to help find Lauren's killer,' Mackenzie said.

Alan continued, 'Cole, you had best fill Mackenzie in with what's happening here before Brian and the crew arrive. Let her know more about what she's stepping into. We don't know if the incidents are linked and especially not now that she's on your farm when you're getting ready to go to war with those bastard poachers.'

CHAPTER
22

After a day of making calls to the US, emailing, faxing and generally sorting out Lauren's affairs from within Cole's home-office sanctuary, Mackenzie slumped into a recliner on the wide verandah. She had showered and now wore blue jeans with a simple T-shirt and sweater to ward off the chill in the air. Her favourite pink boots covered her feet as she settled in to watch the last minutes of the working farm ahead of her, as the panoramic view of the ranch faded fast behind dim lighting that danced across the valley. The shadow from the mountains closed in around her.

She saw Cole return from a horse ride, acknowledged his wave with one of her own and admired him in his natural surroundings. This man rode as one with his horse. When he nimbly jumped down and led the majestic animal into the barn, he walked as if he was a caged predator, gliding over the ground in an effortless dance, exactly like one of his cheetahs.

He came out of the barn and looked towards the road when the sound of a powerful diesel vehicle caught his attention. She watched him check the white 4x4's progress towards the homestead. Eventually it stopped.

Four people climbed out. Three men were dressed in camo pants, with tight-fitting khaki shirts, and they stretched, as if recovering from a long journey. Two were Caucasian. One blonde, the other with hair as black as volcanic sand. The third was a black man who was as dark as his companion's hair. A woman climbed out too, dressed all in black from her head to the black trainers on her feet.

Cole dropped the steel bucket he was carrying and wiped his hands on his pants. He sprang easily over the fence separating them and greeted each one with a handshake and a manly hug. He seemed to be introduced to the woman, who shook his hand.

She watched as they all strolled up the pathway and mounted the stairs, and she stood up.

'Mackenzie, I want you to meet my friends,' Cole said.

'Hello,' she said and waved to them all.

'This is Brian, Charl and Mandla. They head up one of the best hi-tech stock-management and anti-poaching companies in Southern Africa. And this is Hope, she's a Global International agent, and attached to Mandla at the hip at the moment with an investigation into the stock theft of cheetahs across the world.'

Hope stepped forward and shook her hand. 'Hi, nice to meet you and sorry about the loss of your friend.'

Her English heritage was strangely not at odds with her obviously mixed African roots. 'You're English?' Mackenzie said.

'Guilty as charged,' Hope replied, 'but please don't hold that against me.'

Mackenzie grinned. 'I won't. It's a pleasure to meet you.'

The shortest of the men, even shorter than Mackenzie, stepped forward to shake her hand. 'I'm Brian, pleased to meet you, Sunshine. So sorry to hear about your friend. If there's anything we can do to help, just let us know. Now, sit, sit, little lady. We heard you were in need of a few knights in a shiny white new 4x4.'

She chuckled aloud at Brian's fatherly attitude, wondering just how much of her story Cole had passed onto this group. She liked Brian immediately, and what Brian lacked in height against the others in the group, he made up for in personality.

Mandla stepped up and shook her hand, smiling. 'Don't mind Brian. He's the best man with a horse in the world but can't keep his mouth shut in front of the ladies,' he said, his voice warm and soft and full of affection. Brian *klapped* him a sharp smack, flat-handed across the back of the head for his trouble. 'I, too, am sorry to hear about Lauren,' Mandla added, rubbing his head.

Lastly, Charl shook her hand. 'Nice to meet you and condolences for your friend,' he said, but Mackenzie could see his smile didn't reach his eyes. It was just an automated reaction. She wondered what had happened to this man to remove the light from his spirit. The look made her feel uneasy about Charl. He was a dark horse among the group, one she would be wary of.

'Nice to meet you all,' she said and lowered herself in her chair. 'And thank you for your kind words.'

Cole sat down next to her and threaded his warm fingers through her cold hand. The heat spread from him, up her arm.

Warmth. Rightness. Home.

'We men served in the forces together. You can trust them with your life,' Cole said.

She looked into his eyes and saw the total honesty there, and also something that not only gave her the shivers but made her scared. She briefly saw lust, the same attraction that she tried so desperately to keep out of hers. Then it was gone, and he had his feelings back under control. She knew that this was not the time nor the place to let her battered emotions rule her life.

'Well then, it's a lucky thing you have such good friends,' she said.

Alan walked out of the house and onto the verandah.

'Ah, Alan,' Charl said, standing up. 'We're all here for the party now.' He shook hands, as did the others.

Thandi appeared and the visitors all crowded around her, shaking her hand and giving her hugs. Obviously the reunion with Thandi was a cherished moment with the men and she was eagerly introduced to Hope.

'Boys, enough,' she chastised, as she made sure her glasses were on straight. 'Welcome home. What can I get you to drink?' she asked.

All the men grinned, clearly at ease in their surroundings.

Mackenzie suddenly felt like an intruder. She was the one visiting, the rest were all already home.

'A Castle lager please,' said Cole. 'Mackenzie?'

'Just a diet soda for me, thank you.'

'Same as Mackenzie,' Alan replied, as he sat down across the table from her.

'And for me,' Hope said and sat next to Mandla.

Thandi brought the drinks out on a tray. Cole handed Mackenzie hers first, then opened his beer and drank thirstily from the bottle. Mackenzie admired how his Adam's apple bobbed under his five-o'clock shadow as he swallowed. She had to make a conscious effort to remember to drink her soda.

'It's been too long since our last visit here,' Mandla said, opening his beer and breaking the comfortable silence that had followed the excitement of their arrival.

'How you holding up?' Hope asked Mackenzie quietly. 'This is quite a gathering, could be intimidating with all this testosterone settling into the homestead.'

'No, I know they are here to sort things out, so I'm fine with you all arriving now. And as for holding on, well, I guess it's still one hour at a time, and getting through each day for a while. What's the saying? "Put one foot in front of the other and just walk", or something like that.' She smiled at Hope, touched that she was making an effort at conversation with her.

Hope nodded. 'Never easy losing anyone, but know that these guys, they'll put things right. They can't bring Lauren back, but they can sure help find out who killed her, and bring you closure. I have only been with the group a little while, but I have seen what they can do. This is a lethal mixture of men sitting here. Sharp. Driven. And what's best for you is they are emotionally connected to each other like brothers, so when one hurts, they all join in the fray to protect. Close ranks.'

'Dinner will be served when you are ready,' Thandi said breaking into their conversation, before she went back into the house.

'Thanks, Thandi,' Brian called.

Cole hollered out to her, 'Give us a few minutes and we'll be through.'

Mackenzie looked around. She didn't doubt for a moment that these men and Hope would raise holy hell when necessary. 'Thank you, Hope,' she said.

'Cole, how's Liza doing?' Brian asked in a quiet tone.

'Still hasn't spoken, but we live in hope,' Cole said. 'Shoosh now, Charl will hear you.'

Charl looked out across the pasture and Mackenzie could have sworn she saw his jaw clench and anger flutter over his face, before he ran his hands over it, almost wiping it clean of any emotion. She wondered who Liza was.

Cole followed Mackenzie as they adjourned into the formal lounge after dinner. The room carried through the African theme, only a little more formally. Huge cement elephant tusks framed a large fireplace that now crackled with a lit fire and threw warmth across the room. Dark leather couches with bright leopard-print cushions invited people to sit down. During the day the breathtaking view through the glass wall of the lounge didn't need any trimmings, as nature showed off the grey craggy mountains and the clouds descending like cotton balls rushing to cover them. Emerald grass pastures met the darker trim of the tree line in an explosion of contrasting colours. At night it framed the stars and the majestic beauty of the skies. Of all the rooms in his home, this one most pictured serenity and peacefulness.

They were all seated around the coffee table when Alan began handing out pink folders. 'I have copies of two files for you all to look over. This one is on Mackenzie and Lauren and the other one,' Alan handed everyone a manila folder, 'Lauren and Mackenzie took photographs in the Soweto Market of a man in possession of limpet mines. I haven't managed to connect all the dots yet on how acquiring the ammo, the taxi wars and the stock theft fit together, but we know it's coming back to the same group of people. We are looking at Dominic Bongwanan. His photo is in there, and his known accomplices, his brother, Noah and his boss, Tobeko Ntuli, known as maNtuli. Cole's told me that you guys know about him from his poaching activities.'

'Not much use knowing all this information did, if he was the one who killed Lauren right under our noses,' Hope said.

'Agreed,' Alan said. 'So, right now Mackenzie's safety is top of our priority list.' He looked at her. 'I'm sorry that I have to put this information out there, but everyone has been reminded of their duty of being policemen and not selling this information. Lauren's murder changed the playing field. For now, we can keep her death quiet, but soon it will be in the news and because of who you are this could potentially catapult into the international news arena. The chances of having the press descend on Crystalberg are extremely high.'

Mackenzie nodded. 'I understand. I'll do anything to bring Lauren's killer to justice, and if that means dealing with the media again then so be it.'

'Everyone, meet Nicole Mackenzie Aurette Carter – widow of the late singer Sebastian Carter,' Alan said matter-of-fact-like, with no emotion in his voice.

'I knew you looked familiar,' Hope said. 'Of course, you were all over the papers and the magazines after his death. So sorry for that, it must've been hard to be hounded like that for months afterwards by the media, saying what they did about you.'

Mackenzie smiled weakly. 'That's good, it means I've been out of the news for a while and people are forgetting.'

'Dream on,' Brian said. 'People will always have a morbid interest in anyone's life who has been in the spotlight for whatever reason.'

The telephone rang despite the late hour. The answering machine picked it up.

Cole said, 'I'll divert the phone to my cell later, so it doesn't disturb anyone.'

'No, don't do that, I'll turn down the volume a bit now, but we can all help by answering it if need be,' Mandla said, and he got up from his chair and strode out of the room.

The phone rang again.

Brian closed his file and tossed it on the coffee table.

Charl did the same and asked, 'So what now? We already have our jobs to do to boost the security around the place and to lay the ambush for the poachers. It makes it easier if they are the same group. If you think that they are responsible for Lauren's murder, why aren't we finding them and bringing them in?'

'We don't have any positive intel as to them having murdered Lauren,' Alan said. 'Whoever put her in the car attempted to cover up the murder by making this look like an accident. We have no proof of what happened beforehand. We have, however, found out where "our group of interest" are staying, so we are observing them while they are in the area. I have a policeman watching, and he'll report in as soon as he has more news. Hope, have you had any news from your informant who told us about Bongwanan?'

'Nothing yet, he'll contact me when it's safe for him to. I didn't tell him to watch for car crashes and the murder of a woman, just that I wanted information on all of Dominic's movements to here and any other place where cheetahs are, so he could have seen something and not said anything, thinking it wasn't worth it for him. I'll be sure to question him when he contacts me.'

'Right,' Brian said. 'So we concentrate our energy on the ranch as planned and leave Lauren's murder to Alan and his police force.'

Everyone nodded.

'What's the plan for Mackenzie?' Charl asked.

'I have a plan and it includes Mackenzie *not* going anywhere,' Cole said.

Mackenzie could have hugged him and kissed him right there.

Sitting next to her, holding onto her hand as if his life depended on it, was a man who knew next to nothing about her but was prepared to fight for her, believing she was good, no matter what.

She'd found an old-fashioned champion.

How could she have been so lucky to find a man like this, not once, but now twice in her lifetime? Sebastian had once stood between her and her father. Between her and intimidation. Now Cole stood in the face of danger, only this time, she wasn't a college student with no life experience, this time she would stand next to this man and fight for her freedom by his side.

Mackenzie listened as they discussed a plan to secure her home and to make security changes at *nTabaGrequa*: put in more lights, boost electrical current, install infra-red cameras on fence lines. Soon she lost track of who was responsible for what. All she knew was that as long as she remained inside the cheetah conservation ranch she felt safe.

Not one demented taxi driver would be able to get to her.

She'd relived the last few days in her head over and over and over. And she questioned herself constantly as to if she could have done something different. Not gone out for coffee? Been with Lauren that afternoon? Perhaps she might have somehow prevented the abduction? And yet she knew that nothing would ever change. She still couldn't believe that something like the fortifying of the cheetah rescue centre was happening because she was now sheltering behind its fence too. And now she knew that the cheetahs were also threatened. It was all so tragic. Lauren was dead. As she thought about her best friend being gone, the tears welled in her eyes.

Cole passed her another tissue and squeezed her hand. She'd noticed that Cole liked holding onto her, whether they were alone or when they were with other people. He seemed to like the contact with her, and if she was being honest, she enjoyed the fact that he liked touching her, too.

Cole was protecting and providing sanctuary. She smiled a little thinking of the showdown that would potentially happen when he met her father. Her father. Well, she'd cross that bridge when he arrived. Because he would arrive once she let them know about Lauren's death and where she was living. Losing Lauren had highlighted how quickly lives could be taken away, and she knew it was time for her to reach out and bring her family together again. She would have to broach the subject with Cole, who was already helping so much. More rewarding than all his help were Cole's words to the group assembled, *I have a plan and it includes Mackenzie not going anywhere.* The conviction with which he'd said it amazed her.

It was as if he was telling her that he believed in her and she was worth protecting.

She realised that was her father's problem. Once it had mattered to her that her father didn't believe in her or her artistic abilities. He didn't imagine that her art could support her and he didn't respect her views or opinions. Deep down it was the fact that she knew that he hadn't taken her side, choosing not to correct the media in their lies about love-children, emotional collapses and all the other untrue conspiracy theories they had printed after Sebastian's death. But living in South Africa had shown her that she wasn't the weak woman her father assumed her to be. She didn't need his style of protecting.

Over the last two years she'd realised that she felt sorry for her father. He had his priorities wrong. It was his own misjudgement of the value of the press that he needed to come to terms with, not the fact that Mackenzie had become a widow so early in her life. She acknowledged that more than anything, accepting the help offered by Cole and his friends was a giant step backwards in her hard-earned independence. But it was a huge leap forward in her journey towards reclaiming her life.

Just then there was a knock on the sliding door of the lounge that jerked Mackenzie back from her own thoughts. Siphiwe was standing outside, his face pressed to the glass, a cell phone on his ear, and on a piece of rope threaded around its neck was one of the cheetahs. It sat next to him as if it was used to being walked on a leash.

'Excuse me,' said Cole as he quickly got up and went to the door.

The next instant, he was letting in Siphiwe and the cheetah. He took the rope off the cheetah's neck and the cheetah padded towards the fire and arranged itself on the carpet there, as if it had been there and done that many times before.

'Someone just attempted to steal Sasha,' Cole said.

'Shit!' Charl said aloud.

'Already?' Brian said.

Mandla came back into the room. 'Cole, your guards need you – oh, hiya, Siphiwe.'

Siphiwe smiled and raised his hand in a salute to Mandla.

Cole nodded. 'I know. Thank God her tracker went nuts, sending Siphiwe SMS messages to the monitoring phone. He pushed the alert button and rushed to her enclosure, and other guards followed within a few minutes. Sasha was already out of her cage and ran to him. Siphiwe said that there is a large hole cut in her fence and the rope was around her neck. The guards are tracking back now to find the person who cut the fence. Hopefully we mobilised fast enough. Siphiwe thought the walk up the road might help calm Sasha while he tried to call me,' Cole said. 'I need to go check the CCTV to see how they got into the farm and up to the cages to cut a hole in the side.'

'We can be ready in five minutes,' Brian said. 'We have everything we need with us. When you called for help we came prepared. We never expected it to come so soon, but we should have.'

'Perhaps a perimeter check tonight would be a good plan. I fear that you will be fighting someone sooner than what we thought. Clearly something didn't work with their plan because Sasha got away from them,' Cole said.

Sasha was not sitting on the mat anymore, she had made her way towards the couch where Mandla had sat down next to Hope again. Hope reached out a hand towards the cat. Her fingers shook as she put her hand on her head and Sasha began to purr. Sasha closed her mouth, swallowed and then her mouth opened again as she panted. She just stayed where she was, Hope's hand resting on her head.

Hope said, 'For all the work I do with these cats, I can never quite get my head around the fact that some are domesticated and like to spend their time in human company and not in the wild. That we might be the last generation to have this sort of interaction with these beautiful creatures, because we can't stop the poaching and looting.'

'That's a sad thought,' Mackenzie said.

'But unfortunately true,' Cole said. 'Right, time to get moving. Mackenzie, I'll leave Sasha here with you while I go down to the visitors' centre and view the footage. She'll probably try to sleep on the couch, but don't let her, she chews the cushions. Thandi is in her quarters if you need her. Hope, are you staying at the house?'

'I'll go with Mandla wherever he goes. I'm not getting stuck inside when the fun's going to be outside,' Hope said.

Cole smiled. 'Fine. Brian?'

'I think perhaps after we talk to your guards and Siphiwe some more, we'll go find the tracks and do our thing,' Brian said. 'Everyone, be ready and meet in the kitchen in five minutes.'

Mandla, Charl and Hope stood up.

'Bye,' Hope said, 'stay safe here, Mackenzie and keep Sasha safe, too.'

Mackenzie smiled. 'I'll try my best.'

*   *   *

Cole returned in the early hours of the next morning. He made his way in the dark to the lounge where he could see a small table light was still blazing.

Mackenzie was snoozing on the couch and Sasha was lying with her. Obviously, Sasha had started at Mackenzie's feet but then sneaked further up, pushing Mackenzie further into the couch until she was up to Mackenzie's stomach. Her hand rested on Sasha's neck, as natural as if she had lived with big cats all her life. Sasha opened her golden eyes, saw he was there and closed them again; content to stay where it was warm against her newest friend.

He stood watching them sleep for a while, then he walked to Mackenzie and crouched down. He ran his hand lightly over her shoulder. 'Mackenzie, wake up. I'm home,' he said.

She half opened her eyes. 'Hi.' She went to sit up and found Sasha tucked into her and smiled. 'I didn't let her on here, she was on the floor next to me when I fell asleep. Honest!'

'It's okay,' he said as he reached for Sasha, who was now purring, despite having her sleep interrupted. 'I need to check on the horses and do a walk around the cheetah pens, take Sasha here and put her in a different enclosure. She can't start sleeping in my house again, that was a bad habit she and I got into when she was younger. Everyone's back and have now gone to their rooms for what's left of the night.'

'Your friends and Hope seem nice,' Mackenzie said, but she made no effort to move.

'They are. We've all been together for many years,' he sat down on his haunches, leaving his hand on her shoulder. 'You look really comfortable on the couch, but you should go to your own bed.'

'Why? Sasha and I are comfy here, although Farren will begin to think I've abandoned her. She came to investigate earlier and ran out like a puff-up fish, a fur ball deluxe. Sasha was so good, she didn't even try to chase her.'

Cole laughed. 'Mac,' he said sobering, 'You know you have had to reveal so many things about yourself in the last three days. You've never mentioned before to me in all the time we have known each other that you were once married. I didn't know that was why you needed space.'

She opened her eyes and looked at him.

'Losing Sebastian was so hard. I lost my rock in life. Now I've lost Lauren and all that hurt is back, just when I thought it was all under control, when I thought I couldn't hurt more, I do.'

He watched as tears glistened in her eyes. 'I know what it's like to lose those closest to you.'

'You do?'

'It happened a long time ago, but the pain cuts deep for many years.'

Cole now understood that they had both suffered. Both had lost people who should still be with them but weren't. Both of them were broken, holding onto ghosts from their pasts. He shook his head, trying to dislodge the sadness that he felt.

Mackenzie pulled her legs free of Sasha and sat up. Then she leant forward and put her hands on either side of Cole's face, looking at him.

'I'm not going to let myself die along with Sebastian and Lauren, without reaching for everything in life first.' She leant forward and placed her lips softly against his.

Her lips tested his, brushing lightly.

He took over the kiss as she opened her mouth, granting him access. He explored the soft outside, simply enjoying the sensations and the knowledge that she was at last, after all this time, in his arms, revelling in a kiss. He nibbled at her bottom lip and stroked her hair, threading his fingers through the silky strands. The smell of Mackenzie so near pushed him closer and closer to the edge. When she deepened the kiss, he was lost.

He felt the pressure of her hands run through his hair as she caressed the back of his head and he couldn't suppress a smile.

He felt her pull away slightly and the kiss ended. They stared at each other for some time, neither saying anything. Her expression was suddenly wary, the deep frown lines evident on her forehead, confusion clearly visible in her eyes.

She touched her forehead gently to his. 'You said you needed to take Sasha back to the centre. Go. I'm beat and ready to turn in. It's really late, well really early. Goodnight. And Cole, thanks for everything.'

He held her closely for a second longer, then he removed her hands from his face but continued to hold them. He stood and pulled her upwards until they were standing toe-to-toe and nose-to-nose.

He could hear that his own breath was laboured, echoing hers, yet neither had exerted themselves. 'Goodnight,' he said eventually, then he touched her briefly on the cheek with his hand before he forced himself to turn from her, called Sasha to his side and walked out of the door, into the cold black night towards the stables, his torch flashing in front of him, checking for night adders and *rinkhals* – spitting cobras.

* * *

At the visitors' centre, Sasha walked calmly into one of the pens used for holding newly rescued cheetahs and settled in just fine. Cole lingered near her, thinking how lucky he had been that her tracker had worked and how lucky he was that his friends used his animals as guinea pigs for all their new gadgets. He was the finance behind BSC, the silent partner. From the beginning, he'd believed in the men starting the stock-management company as he could appreciate keeping abreast of technology in the farming sector. He would be the first one to admit that the cost of running the rescue centre was high enough, without the additional cost of now having to add in new-age stock-management electronics to his bill. Yet those electronics had saved his cheetah tonight. They were worth investing in. And he knew that many farmers saw that advantage, too, including the game reserves, who now used the very same technology he did.

Seth and Siphiwe walked the second lockdown with him in the early hours of the morning, as they all chatted to the cheetahs and rechecked that each pen was secured. Eventually, he said goodnight to Siphiwe, and ensured that extra guards were on duty to see them through the rest of the night.

Cole walked up to his stables, where he gave some horse pellets to Catherine the zebra and her new, as yet unnamed, foal. He relaxed in their company as she rubbed her head against his and snorted when the food was finished. He patted her thick neck and inhaled the distinctly wild zebra smell that even being stabled couldn't mask.

Soon Catherine would be out there on the farm again. The birth, which had taken place sometime yesterday morning, had been a quiet and dignified occasion, performed by nature, not a vet, thank goodness. Mum and foal were progressing beautifully.

He wished he'd asked Mackenzie to accompany him on his rounds, to see her now and share the moment with her, instead of insisting she go to bed.

Cole took pleasure in the habitual lockdown of the ranch, confirming all his charges were safe.

It was his duty, his job, his life.

CHAPTER
23

Vervet monkeys sounded the natural alarm clock alongside the rooster from the workers' compound. The copper sun crept over the horizon, quickly warming the surrounding bush. Cole awoke to tangled sheets as if he'd actually spent the whole night making love to Mackenzie instead of just in his head. He hadn't had a reaction to any woman like this since he was in his teens, since Melissa.

He shook his head, trying to fasten the lid on the memories, on the hurt. Melissa had been taken away from him permanently, and he'd switched off the part of his heart that controlled desire and commitment. He never thought he would feel a want like this ever again. He shouldn't feel this now. He had controlled his life and emotions all these years. Yet he wasn't able to blot out Mackenzie.

His need was so intense. It wasn't as if he could go into town, find a one-night stand and appease 'the itch' either, it had to be her. No substitute. And this after only a kiss – an amazing kiss.

He was prepared to wait and work for it though. Time. She still needed more time. And he had that time to spend with her.

He walked into the en suite with Mackenzie still on his mind. 'Get over it, Cole!' He stepped into an icy-cold shower. Thoughts of Melissa burst through his barrier. Even after all these years, the memory of that time hurt too much. Her falling pregnant in their first year of university wasn't planned, but when he'd put a diamond on her finger he'd meant every word: he would have supported her and their child and stood by them always.

But always was not forever. Fate had intervened and taken both of them from him in a car crash before they'd even got married. He had failed to protect them.

Now, he simply didn't do love. Cole wasn't put on this earth to love, because everything he'd ever loved had been taken away from him. He hadn't allowed himself to love another. But that didn't stop him wanting the fairytale with Mackenzie.

*   *   *

Waking up to a laden tea tray being brought into her room was a luxury Mackenzie hadn't grown up with. Sure they'd had a maid and cleaning and catering services for hosting parties, but they hadn't had this twenty-four-hour care that she now received in Cole's house.

'Good morning, Miss Mackenzie,' Thandi said as she put the tray on the bed. 'I brought you some hot chocolate and a rusk. Breakfast is ready when you are and is set in the dining room. Be careful if you go eat on the verandah. The monkeys are visiting this morning. I had to chase them out of my kitchen with a broom.'

Mackenzie blinked. Today Thandi wore a black uniform, trimmed with white broderie anglaise. It was almost a French-maid outfit, except for its demure length to below the knee and its buttons respectably to the neck. Once again, it was immaculately pressed and a matching scarf was wrapped around her head.

'Wow, thank you. Is Cole around?'

'No, he left early this morning with Mandla. But he said if you are up that you are welcome to explore if you want to. He'll be back after lunchtime. He suggested if you are feeling up to it, we could go into town and tidy your place after morning tea. Alan says it's okay now to go inside, the police are finished with it. The hardware shop will come and fix your windows and doors today. Oh yes and Cole said to tell you that once it's fixed up, Mandla and Charl would swing by and fit your new alarm system to your house for you, so you didn't have to worry about that.'

'Mandla and Charl will fit my alarm system?' Mackenzie asked as she stroked Farren, who had gone from being curled up on the end of the bed to nosing the tray, and she redirected the inquisitive animal off the bed.

Thandi scooped her up before the cat reached the floor and cuddled the feline to her chest, as if she belonged there. Farren's tractor-purr started up loudly. 'Yes, Mandla and Charl will do a good job on your alarm to keep you safe. They have always been good with electronics.'

* * *

Breakfast was a lazy affair in the dining room, the black-and-white zebra design used on the fabric of the chairs and carried through into the furniture seemed a natural fit in the modern room. It made Mackenzie feel calmer, more at ease than she had been. With only Thandi and Farren for company, she relaxed as she finished her toast at the large glass table. Today she felt flat and needed the rest after the emotional day before. She still thought of Lauren constantly, but now instead of tearing up, she just got angry at the wait to find the killer. 'I think I'll check emails in the office and then go outside, explore a little,' she said.

'Good idea, get some sunshine on your face. You will feel better being outdoors, in nature,' Thandi said.

Mackenzie smiled. Thandi was an enigma, sometimes so old-fashioned, like when she met her that first night, and yet sometimes she overstepped the boundaries of a maid, like now, telling her to go outside. She was more like a resident granny and Mackenzie loved that.

An hour later, Mackenzie walked through the kitchen door and onto the verandah. It was time to explore outside in the sunlight.

It was nice not to be alone at this time, but the people around her here acted so differently as to when Sebastian had died. At home she had been treated like spun glass. Everyone had been quiet and no one had mentioned Sebastian, and when they did, they would apologise to her. Here the house was filled to the brim with people, everyone talked and gave their opinion about Lauren's murder, and although now and again they would ask her 'how she was holding up,' they went about their business, leaving her to hers, but still somehow keeping her company and not letting her drown in her own sorrow.

Thandi placed a wide-brimmed leather hat on Mackenzie's head as she headed out. 'Stay close to the house, Miss Mackenzie,' she instructed. 'Cole said to please not go near the visitors' centre just yet without someone with you. He knows you might want to see Zulu and Tala, but he'll take you there later.'

'Okay, I won't,' Mackenzie said, as she adjusted the hat. It was too big but at least it would protect her from the harsh African sun that was already dancing heatwaves across the tin roof of the two vehicles parked outside. Contrary to the cold wind that blew and still threatened snow, the sun was hot.

Mackenzie explored the buildings near the side of the house. The stables were well maintained, neat and orderly. She dipped her hand into the container in the feed room and bribed the mare in the second stall into receiving a pat on her silver head and a rub down her neck, while being fed the pellets. The smell of the horses filled the air, strong in her nose but familiar.

It made her think of happier times, times when her daddy was her hero, when she'd ridden in the annual barrel-racing competitions before he made it to senator, before he became so domineering. Before she was a teenager. She shook her head, trying to shake free of the memory.

She looked in wonder at the tiny zebra foal in the stall, standing with her fat mother, who bared her teeth and pinned back her ears at Mackenzie as soon as she approached the door. She chose not to feed the zebra and wandered outside instead.

Between the stables and the house, it looked as if there had once been a garden. A sad-looking, broken paved path wound between the two buildings then continued as a smaller, well-worn winding path into a grove of trees. The invading plants had been neatly cut back away from it, allowing easy access. Curious, she followed the path.

At the end was a miniature white-washed fence surrounding a small marble cross. The names Melissa & Marco, and no date, but the words 'You are loved always' were engraved in black on the plaque at the bottom.

She looked around, the grass was neatly clipped and an arrangement of dried, pink protea flowers rested against the cross. Emotion lodged in her throat at the thought that this was obviously some sort of memorial and it had deep meaning to Cole. This was the hurt that he had spoken of last night, Mackenzie thought.

It was silent here, as if even nature felt the pain from the loss of this loved one and dared not call, or peep in any way. Mackenzie felt as if she was trespassing on sacred ground. She turned away from the grotto and ambled back to the stables. The only flowers she could see in the garden belonged to a huge red bougainvillea, the most dominant plant still living in the area. It splashed vibrant colour over the side of the barn. The artist in Mackenzie wanted to capture the scene of ordered chaos. She burnt it into her memory. Later she could sculpt it, use bronze and steel, perhaps add some copper-leaf effect.

She felt really safe for the first time in ages being here. So much had been sorted out. She was enjoying not having to look over her shoulder now that everyone knew who she really was, and it didn't seem to have made much of a difference to the way Cole treated her. She loved that she was able to talk to anyone. It was almost like freedom, but the freedom was an illusion, only possible because there was an eight-foot electrical fence creating it.

She stepped up to the verandah that wrapped around the house, its black concrete shining marble-like in the sun. Cool and inviting. Dry, empty plant containers hung from hooks here. Mackenzie could already picture them, filled with red geraniums to match the bougainvillea and fragrant white alyssum, adding a hint of perfume to the African night air; the filigree ironwork, freshly painted federation green and white. She smiled and touched her lips, remembering their kiss the night before and knowing it was why she felt so differently today. She'd put her own emotional life on ice over the past two years, and now having someone to share that empty space with made her relax a little.

*   *   *

After morning tea, Mackenzie and Thandi drove into Crystalberg in one of the ranch's 4x4s. Thandi changed gears as she chatted. 'Cole taught me to drive when I came to work for him. He was only a young man. Already he was before his time. The men on the ranch laughed at him for taking the time to teach an older black woman to drive.'

'But you drive well,' Mackenzie said.

'That's because Cole didn't give up on me. I was just his maid, but he said I needed to be a housekeeper and I needed to be able to do everything if I was to stay, as he was never having a wife. So I tried hard and I learnt. I was forty and already had three grandchildren to look after when he bought *nTabaGrequa*. I owe him my life and that of my children's children. He's a good man. Good heart.'

Never having a wife? That was an extreme thing for a man to say. She wondered about the reasoning behind such a statement. Her dream of a husband and a family were strong, that one day she would settle and have them again, but to say *never* – that puzzled her.

'Why no wife?' Mackenzie asked, curiosity getting the better of good manners, suspecting that Thandi had dropped the hint on purpose.

'He didn't tell me, but the first week he was at the ranch, he built the little grotto.'

The grotto. Now she had confirmation that it did belong to Cole! Melissa and Marco had been those who had died, and who still caused him anguish so many years later.

Having had Sebastian taken from her, she knew how hard it was to lose someone you loved. Now with Lauren passing, it was bringing all the hurt back to the surface. She fought against the lump forming in her throat and the tears threatening her eyes.

Thandi carried on watching the road, and talking. 'He's never been married. He was nineteen when he purchased this ranch. Just a boy at university in Pietermaritzburg, then he went to the army. Before that, he lived in Johannesburg with an old aunt. His parents were killed when he was eleven.'

If it were possible, she felt even more compassion for Cole. 'So many losses and he was so young. That's so sad. Turn here,' Mackenzie said, and as Thandi parked in the driveway, Mackenzie sat looking at what had been her home for almost a year and a half.

Her heart ached for the young boy on the verge of manhood. He'd lost his family and she'd chosen to walk away from hers. What a depressing pair they made.

The red-face brick cottage with its white trimmings appeared neat and tidy. The automatic gates sat open, showing a lovely lawn area set in just two acres of trees. The distance from her neighbours had been what attracted her to this mountain house, but that distance had nearly been her downfall. She saw the hedge of yesterday-today-and-tomorrow bushes in full bloom and smelt their sweet fragrance heavy on the air.

'Come on, Mackenzie. We need to go inside and make your home liveable again.' Thandi grabbed the large garbage bags and extra cleaning equipment from the back.

A slim black girl sat on the front doorstep in front of a burly game guard. At the sight of the *bakkie*, she jumped up and smoothed out the creases of her faded maid's uniform. It was slightly too tight for her figure, but immaculately pressed.

'My granddaughter, Liza. *Sawubona*, Themba,' Thandi said to the man standing by her broken door, and her granddaughter waved quickly.

'*Sawubona*, Thandiwe,' Themba said and his face broke into a smile. 'Madam.' He nodded in respect as he unblocked the doorway.

'*Sawubona*, Lisa, Themba,' Mackenzie said.

The three women trooped inside, as Themba remained guarding the door.

'What a mess!' Thandi said as she surveyed the lounge area.

'They did a good job.' Mackenzie took a garbage bag from Thandi and started to pick up broken bits and pieces. She stood holding half a photograph that had been on the table of her and Lauren at the game reserve, ready to go into Lauren's scrapbook. Her heart broke. Never again would she see her friend sitting cross-legged on her couch, gluing photos and mementos into her book and writing next to the pictures.

Never again would she hear Lauren laugh as she teased her about something. Lauren had been in her life for so long and now she had been robbed of her friendship.

Tears blurred her vision as slowly she put the bit of cardboard into her rubbish bag. She had a copy of the photo on her laptop so the physical photograph didn't matter. She moved along to the next piece of her home that had been trashed and cleared that away, too. Slowly, through the tears, she could see the carpet begin to emerge. The task of cleaning and tidying had a cathartic effect of relaxing her, keeping her hands occupied and her mind just slightly engaged, so that she stopped thinking sad thoughts and just concentrated on tidying up the mess. For a moment, the pressure cooker that had become her eyes settled down, only simmering gently and not letting out any emotional steam.

Soon both the dining room and lounge were clean and only the ruined carpet remained, which would need to be pulled up and replaced. A few tiles in the dining-room floor had been broken, but there wasn't much they could do about those today, except remove the loose pieces.

The second game guard, Anton, had joined in as well, always remaining in a separate room to the women, clearing out the larger items into the *bakkie*, then collecting the full bags from the doorways. Anton drove the *bakkie* repeatedly to the rubbish dump just outside the town. Themba remained at the door on guard. Thandi stayed almost always by Mackenzie's side, along with silent Liza, quietly working together with her gran.

'Everyone break. It's lunchtime,' Thandi said, and began unpacking drinks and food from the cooler box for all of them to share.

'Oh thank goodness,' Mackenzie said, just as her stomach gave off a loud groan, telling the whole room that it was hungry.

Everyone laughed as they headed out to the pool area to eat.

After eating two beef-and-pickle sandwiches with garnish and a small packet of Nik Nak chips, Mackenzie patted her stomach. 'Thanks, Thandi, that hit the spot.'

Thandi smiled. 'Liza and I can do the bathroom and the rest of the kitchen, Miss Mackenzie. You can take a break away from the cleaning, we are basically finished.'

'But—'

'You have done enough. Sit. Rest,' Thandi insisted, just as the representative from the hardware store arrived, with his apprentice. Thandi took control, speaking in her native Zulu and gesturing wildly with her hands. Mackenzie, not understanding any of it, wandered through the house.

'Hello, studio,' she said into the bright room as she walked in, as if greeting an old friend, and she closed the door. She'd been lucky that they hadn't got to destroy this part of the house when she had arrived home with Cole and interrupted them. With Alan's quick response, he'd most likely saved her studio. The house furniture was easily replaced – it was just furniture and held no sentimental value – but her artworks were different. If they had been demolished it might have destroyed her.

Situated at the back of the house, her studio was at least the size of a triple garage. It had easy access for deliveries and loads of natural light. The previous owner had housed his antique car collection there, so she hadn't needed to change a thing to use it as a studio.

At first she tried to tidy her tools but was soon distracted, her mind reeling, so she started sculpting in her clay block instead. Immediately she was at peace, absorbed in her own world. She scraped away slowly at the clay, the image in her head clearly visible, another one of the orphans. She had the picture on the wall but she didn't need it for reference. Not yet. Her fingers stroked the clay and she changed the angle on the contour of the sculpture slightly. She smiled at the emergence. Gradually it took shape, with a thick cut here, a scrape with a thinner file there. The child's beautiful face appeared.

The smell of her studio was familiar and soothing. The noises of her house washed over her, the sound of a *piet-my-vrou* in the trees somewhere near. The game guard and hardware men sang an African song together as they worked, a hypnotic road-gang tune so unique, low in tone, almost morbid but beautiful. She knew the melody would haunt her forever.

She let out a sigh of contentment. She was happy here in Crystalberg. At peace with herself and glad that this was the place she'd chosen to stop. Her search for a home was over because she wanted to stay. She *needed* to stay.

Thandi laid her hand on Mackenzie's shoulder. 'Time to go home to *nTabaGrequa*.'

Mackenzie jumped at the intrusion and raised her hand to her heart.

'Sorry, I didn't mean to startle you,' Thandi said.

'That's okay, I was absorbed in my work, that's all. Strange how this was my home until—' She stopped, not wanting to say what was obvious. 'Isn't it funny how quickly things change.'

Thandi took off her glasses and cleaned them on her apron. 'We all have to move on with life, it's too short to stay crying for a long time. You need to live it to the fullest, take every second you have because it passes too fast and you don't want to be the one running and running to catch up,' Thandi said but she smiled.

Mackenzie saw the shine on her old wrinkled face and her dark eyes so filled with laughter, as they crinkled up at the outer edges.

'Can I take a photo of you just like you are?' Mackenzie asked her, already turning around and looking for the digital camera she kept in her studio.

'Of me? With no glasses on? I'm an old black woman, why?' Thandi started.

'I have an idea, but I'll need your picture, would you mind?' she asked, already with the camera focused on Thandi.

'Okay.'

Mackenzie shot a couple of pictures and was taking more when Liza walked in.

'Come on, Liza, come and stand by your grandmother,' Mackenzie said and flapped her arm in a 'join in' motion.

Liza shook her head and looked down at her feet.

'That's alright, you don't have to if it makes you uncomfortable. Look at these great shots I snapped of your gran,' Mackenzie said as she began flicking back on the screen to view the photos she'd just taken. Liza strained forward and peered at the pictures. Thandi looked back at them in various poses, all beautiful. Liza smiled at her gran, nodding.

'She likes them,' Thandi said, then she frowned as Liza gestured towards the camera. 'No, I don't think so,' she told Liza.

'What is it?' asked Mackenzie. 'What does she want?'

Thandi looked at Liza before glancing at Mackenzie. 'To take your picture.'

'Sure.' Mackenzie grinned and she held the camera out towards Liza. 'You push this button when you're ready and you put me inside this frame.' She showed her the basic working of the camera.

Liza stood as still as one of Mackenzie's bronze works. It was as if a light had been lit inside her and she began taking photos of Mackenzie, who moved and put her arm around Thandi. Liza took more photos, the flash working overtime while she snapped one after another in fast repetition, despite the bright natural light.

'Let's see what they look like.' Mackenzie put her hand out for the camera. Liza handed it back and bobbed a curtsey.

'She said thank you,' Thandi informed her.

Together they looked at the photos.

'Wow, Liza, these are good. Do you like taking photos?' Mackenzie asked, seeing natural raw talent right away.

Liza nodded.

'Perhaps one of these days you can take my camera and bring me back some interesting photos of other people?'

'No, she can't take your expensive camera,' Thandi began, but Mackenzie hushed her.

'Liza, let me quickly download these onto my computer and then you can take it till the weekend, but you need to return it. Okay?'

Another curtsey, but this time Liza smiled at Mackenzie instead of dipping her eyes. *Progress*, thought Mackenzie.

'Thank you,' Thandi said and Mackenzie saw tears in her eyes. 'Bless you for your kind heart.'

*   *   *

Going to Tannie Essie's for a takeaway meal took them across town, but owing to Thandi cleaning almost all day at Mackenzie's house, and Cole's home being filled with hungry men, the stop was a necessity. The darkness of night pressed in as they drove towards the rescue centre with two buckets of fried chicken for the main house, and a smaller box for Liza, who disappeared within moments of parking the *bakkie* in the shed, the camera safely in its carry case and slung over her shoulder. Mackenzie wondered at the silence of Liza, if she could speak and why she didn't.

'She doesn't talk much,' she said to Thandi.

'That little one's had big troubles. Cole always says she'll talk when she's ready, but I worry that she'll always be haunted. Not every man in this country is good like Cole,' Thandi said.

'What happened?' Mackenzie asked, her curiosity getting the better of her.

'It's very, very difficult. Six years ago, just after her mother died, she was set upon and those men they raped my granddaughter. There were three girls attacked that same day. Cole paid the big city lawyers lots of money and the men responsible were jailed. Liza, she hasn't talked since.'

'Oh Thandi.'

'But my grandchild, she works hard and loves the cheetahs and the other animals here with Cole, and she is safe. She just can't be near men who she doesn't know and trust. That's why Anton stayed mostly in a different room to her. She'd have been uncomfortable with him working one by one, even though he has been here at *nTabaGrequa* for maybe a year. She doesn't trust easily. Themba, he has been around for many years. Cole and Charl, they are the only ones she ever relaxes nearby.'

'Charl?' Mackenzie asked.

'Yes. He is another big man with a kind heart. That day, her baby brother was in the room next door when it happened and it was him that called the ranch for help. Charl was here visiting Cole and together they rescued her.'

'That is so sad.' Mackenzie swallowed hard, now knowing why there was no light in Charl's eyes. He had seen things that no one should have to.

'Afterwards, when the police said they couldn't do anything, Cole, Charl and the rest of the unit went after the men involved. Each rapist they brought to the police station, alive, but only enough to be arrested. After the last one was brought in, the police chief tried to put the friends in jail for assault.'

'That's not right!'

'No, it was not. Cole's attorney was too clever for them and he went to the paper. The trial had big publicity. Those rapists were sentenced and the police chief in the area was fired for corruption and obstruction of justice. Then Alan, he took over as being in charge of the police station and he's like Cole. He has a good heart, that man.'

'Why is it so hard for people to get justice?' Mackenzie said.

'That's life in South Africa. It's not always easy or fair, to either black or white people,' Thandi said as they climbed out of the *bakkie*.

CHAPTER
24

It was early Saturday morning. Mackenzie's breath caught as she spotted Cole sitting alone at the breakfast table in the kitchen. His cotton shirt was open in the front. *Nice.* There was no hair on that expansive chest.

He shifted in the chair and glanced at her. 'Come on in, sit, we might as well figure out a routine while we get to stop this madness.' He stood and pulled out a chair for her. She walked into the room and slumped down into it. He gave her shoulder a little squeeze and ran his fingers lightly over her back.

She rolled her head. 'Thanks,' she replied sleepily, not quite ready to give up all the sensations from her dream, enhanced by his touch.

'Breakfast, what do you want?'

'Just coffee for now,' she said. He put a mug in front of her and poured her a black coffee.

'Thank you.'

He pushed his chair in, and leaving his own cup there, he walked over to the fridge and began digging in it.

She reached in front of her and started folding the napkins from the middle of the table into shapes. She made a giraffe, then set it aside, reaching for another one. She made that one into an elephant, its trunk not working out as long as she wanted, so she pulled the napkin flat again and started over. Her mind was whirling with thoughts of her dream.

'So what made you want to be a sculptor?' Cole asked, placing bacon and eggs on the table.

She snorted, pulled back to the real world from the one she'd been in, where feeling ruled her body and nothing else mattered.

'I always was. At kindergarten I made a doll out of playdough; I made it look like me. I dried it and took it home. My mother threw 'the filthy bit of stuff' away. Later, in high school, when I modelled two puppets and won first prize at the art fair, my parents didn't even glance at them. Everyone else who saw them remarked what close resemblance they bore to my parents.'

'That must have been hard,' he said as he continued to gather his cooking utensils together.

'I survived,' she said after a small pause.

Cole smiled. 'Being independent is obviously important to you.'

'You have no idea.'

He frowned. 'Oh I do. Believe me, I know what it is like to be independent, to be your own man. Sometimes the price seems too high to pay, but that sweet taste of success and knowing you did it on your own, there is nothing like that achievement, the satisfaction that it brings.'

'You don't look like you do too badly.' She took a sip of her coffee and signalled around the kitchen, the farmhouse, the ranch. He had done so well in life.

'I survive.'

She smiled at him. 'Such modesty. I'm laying it all on the line and you give me two words.'

'You were telling me how you became a sculptor,' he said, waving a spatula around as he resumed cooking.

She looked at the elephant napkin in her hands, now perfectly formed, and set it next to the tall-necked giraffe. 'My art teacher told me that my art would support me one day and that I must keep at it. My father told me art wouldn't feed me, but it does. I never realised how important it was to me that I prove to him how wrong he was. Only he doesn't even know. Ironic, isn't it? That being away from my family is what made me realise I could only rely on myself and make my art pay its way. My poor art teacher was such a bohemian at heart. He looked at the world through a different lens to me back then. He was also a hopeless romantic who believed that there was a soul mate out there for everyone and karma would always bite the offender in the butt later in life.' She laughed at the thought.

'You find that funny?' he asked.

'No, my art teacher. He believes in divine destiny and karma. I was just hoping one of your cheetahs got a chance to bite my father in the butt – that would be karma!'

Cole laughed in his deep, sexy way.

She could do this every day, have him near her in the mornings, laughing, his bedroom eyes crinkling at the sides, sparkling at her.

Cole stopped laughing. 'Eat some breakfast, you need more than coffee to get you through the day or you won't get to play with Zulu and Tala in that *divine future.*'

'A future, now there's something I've not given much thought to in the last two years. Sort of been living day by day,' commented Mackenzie.

She paused for a while as he put some bacon and eggs with toast in front of her. Picking up a fork she looked at him. Although early in the morning, his face was clean-shaven, but he had deep shadows around his eyes. Obviously he hadn't slept much in the last few days. His expression was serious.

Cole sat down in his chair, a plate of food in front of him. 'Time to stop doing that, I think.' He rolled his head on his neck. The motion was obviously meant to relieve a tension build-up, but all Mackenzie could think of was how supple he was and what an intimate moment it was watching him do it. Her hands itched to rub his shoulders.

She pushed her plate away, barely touched. It was too early for her to eat.

Cole pushed it back. Then he reached over and took her hand in his.

'It's okay, Mackenzie, no one can get to you here, not now.'

She smiled weakly. 'They nearly got Sasha—'

'But they didn't. The alarm systems worked, they ran away when the lights came on and the guards rushed to check on her. Today the fences will be fixed and believe me, now the team is here, my ranch's in for some serious upgrades. Looks like both of us will be inside my fence defending what's here. Now eat, you need your strength. Today's going to be long.'

She picked up her fork again.

Thandi walked into the room, followed closely by Mandla, Brian and Charl.

'Morning all,' Cole said and his friends grunted back and sat down around the table.

Mandla said, 'I've let Hope sleep. She was on the phone last night to her boss in the UK until the early hours of this morning. We can catch up with her later.'

Brian nodded. 'So what were you two talking about so seriously already?'

'Plans for the day,' Cole said.

Mandla said, 'Charl and I put some more equipment into your office last night, Cole. We'll clear it out today and install it here and into the visitors' centre on all your lines. We have also decided that you need another satellite dish on your roof. We have time on a new satellite coming online any day now, so you will be the tester. Might as well do that while we are here.'

'Okay,' Cole said.

Mackenzie looked down at the congealed eggs on her plate.

'Thanks, Thandi,' Charl acknowledged as she placed a coffee mug in front of him.

The phone rang and Cole dashed out to pick up the call. When he returned, his face was unreadable and a little stern.

'Siphiwe just called in to report a different hole in the outer fence line at the bottom of the ranch. Dumisani noticed it when he was doing his patrol. I'll need to go fix it this morning. And I'm supposed to be participating in the district *blesbok* count today.'

He looked around the table at everyone.

Charl studied his mug of coffee and said, 'Sorry, don't look at me for help. Counting buck has always been boring. I'll be hanging near the visitors' centre, seeing if Liza needs anything done.'

'Perhaps you'd like to check on how she's doing with my camera? She took fantastic pictures yesterday and I promised her that she could have it until the weekend. I'm just happy if you touch base with her, make sure she knows how to change the batteries if she had flattened them already,' Mackenzie said.

'That's real nice of you, I'll do that, thanks, Mackenzie,' Charl said and he smiled. Knowing what she did about the man, she noticed that while his eyes didn't light up the world they did hold appreciation and something else. Worry.

'Couldn't you rearrange that game count, Cole? The poaching issue is more serious. With Mackenzie, Hope and your cheetahs to protect, you have to realise that we are up against a bit more than some local Sothos trying to poach a few buck,' Brian said.

'Of course I know. I would put it off, but it's been arranged for months. I can start it later, once we've sorted the hole. The neighbours will understand the delay, but no one can skip it. It has to be done today or we could alert those poachers to a change in routine. Besides, it won't take long. I have them already assembled in two areas, so looking over them will be quick,' Cole said, running his hand through his hair.

'I can ride with you and help with the fences this morning. I already said last night that I was happy to count a few deer, that's why I'm up at this ungodly hour anyway,' Mackenzie offered.

Cole looked at her. 'Thanks, not quite a deer, but the idea was to take you with us. Okay,' he said, 'great. Brian, if you can run the new face-recognition software you installed yesterday, see if you have footage of the new breach while you are at the visitors' centre this morning, it would sure help me.'

'I'll be there to help him,' Charl said.

'Thanks. I think we all realise that things are going to have to be implemented quicker than initially thought. The idea of the trap was good, but I can't have them cutting into my fences all the time!' Cole said.

'Agreed,' Mandla said.

Brian said, 'Charl and Mandla were planning on working on increasing the electricity supply to your fences this morning and the new lighting was installed yesterday. Charl'll start on the extra security in the visitors' centre and in the cheetah pens. Mandla will do the boost last. He can work with Hope when she wakes up. I'll be putting in those new cameras and testing that update I implemented on your computer software. Later on I'll make a few surprises for them should they try to get through your fence again, just small deterrents, don't want to kill them before Alan gets to question them. We're all in radio contact if Hope has anything else to report from her call last night that will impact us.'

'Great, but I probably need to finish mending them first, not only for the cheetahs, but also to stop my game getting into the forestry area,' Cole said. 'Mackenzie and I'll ride perimeter fences. We should be done by morning-tea time, then we can take the *bakkie* and be a little more comfortable for the *blesbok* count while we do the ones at the back of the farm. We will be checking for any activity while we're there. Being the day of the count, it won't look odd that I'm driving into all my land areas to ensure no one is squatting in the old hunting lodge.'

'I'll enjoy the fresh morning air and the chance to look at your spread,' Mackenzie said.

Mandla said, 'Hey, Charl you know what will happen if Cole doesn't get that fence fixed, right? The moment we put that extra current through it, it shorts out. I reckon I'm riding fences, too, you watch Hope for me. I just have to make sure Cole does a good job.' He looked at Cole. 'No offence, but the last time I trusted you with wiring I ended up with a scar on my hand to prove it didn't go well.'

'Geez, Mandla, that was over ten years ago and you're still going on about it like an old woman!' Cole said.

'I don't know how to fix fences either. I was kind of hoping that Cole was going to show me, but ...' Mackenzie said, getting into the spirit of teasing Cole.

Everyone laughed.

Cole looked at Mackenzie, offering her an out. 'You don't have to actually help fix the fence or count the *blesbok*. You can stay with Thandi if you want to now that Mandla changed his plans and is coming with me.'

'I think I'll still ride along. I'm just a little worried about what Thandi can do if someone does come at me. No offence, but—' Mackenzie began.

'None taken,' Thandi interrupted as she reached across the table to clear Brian's empty plate.

Cole laughed then said, 'I'm glad you are still going to be with me, but just so you know, by twenty-one Thandi was already known as one of the best freedom fighters South Africa ever had and she can still shoot the shit out of any target better than most men in the armed forces today, oh and probably disarm most of them if they came at her with a knife, too.'

Mackenzie looked up at Thandi, and saw her face glowing with pride. 'No kidding, way to go, Thandi,' she said and high-fived the old housekeeper as she passed.

*   *   *

Cole was quietly going nuts. He was strung as tight as the wire in his fences, and even the gentle green rolling expanse of his ranch wasn't having its usual relaxing effect. Mackenzie had lagged behind again and Mandla was asking him too many personal questions that he didn't know how to answer.

His feelings were in turmoil. He had made a promise all those years before to not let any woman into his life, and for the first time ever, he was now thinking about the future – with someone in it, other than his cheetahs.

'So, you dropped us her name, told us a little, then backed off with no more details,' Mandla persisted.

Cole rolled his eyes skywards. He moved his gelding towards the fence. 'Mandla, I told you, the relationship is changing and it's more, but so far there isn't much to tell.'

'Yeah, but you didn't tell us how much you like her. It's so obvious when you two are together.'

'You didn't tell me about your Hope either,' Cole pointed out.

'Hope isn't mine. You know I said I wasn't ever getting married again.'

'She seems interesting.'

'Nice dodge, we were talking about you and Mackenzie.'

Cole shifted in the saddle to try to loosen his denims.

Mandla grinned. 'All these years and now I can't believe it's happened to you. You're sunk, man! I mention her name and you are a goner.'

Cole didn't dignify the statement with a response.

Mandla continued, 'So are you thinking of long-term here, because you have never been so cagey about anyone before.'

'Yes. No. I don't know. She's rich. Really rich. She might think I'm after her money.'

'That's ridiculous.'

Cole said, 'And her home's in the USA.'

'She lives here now and you could make her want to stay.'

'And how do you propose I do that?' Cole asked, still uncomfortable with the conversation.

'Tell her you've fallen for her.'

'That's the stupidest thing you've ever said, Mandla.'

'Hey, if it's so stupid why are you bothering to protest so much, why haven't you just dismissed it?'

Cole stayed silent. He couldn't answer Mandla. They had taken it slow, secrets had been revealed and all the while his feelings for Mackenzie hadn't changed. He could see their future together, picture her sitting next to him on the jetty fishing for trout in their dam, grey-haired and as beautiful as ever. He could see them having a family, a little child with blue eyes, just like her mother. He wanted to re-create every one of his dreams with her.

Like one of his cheetahs after a long sprint, he'd needed time to recover from the deaths of Melissa and his son. Now with Mackenzie, he was beginning to think perhaps there was a chance of some happiness in his life. He had to tread carefully though, Mackenzie had been hurt and had guarded her heart. He didn't want her spooked into running.

Mandla nodded his head slowly. 'Because you know she's special, your actions around her are different. It's almost like watching Charl and Liza dance around each other. Charl with his staunch Afrikaners upbringing falling for a black girl, even all these years later now that she's in her twenties, and the age gap doesn't matter at all, they still can't move on. So, are you going to waste more time, or are you going to do something about it?'

'When did you become so interested in affairs of the heart?'

'Maybe when this wonderful person literally dropped out of the sky, and the hardest thing I had to do after a few hours together was let her go. I thought I had lost something precious, that she would never return, but she did. She fought hard and she lived. I always believed that there was no second chance for me, but I was wrong. Hope is bringing out the younger man still hiding in this old body and she's constantly reminding me that I'm not so old.'

Cole laughed.

'When you lost Melissa and Marco years ago, you put everything of yourself into this land, into your cheetahs, into everything except yourself. It's time to stop running. If Mackenzie is what your heart wants, tell her. You need to give it a chance. Don't screw it up because of emotional constipation.'

'I'm not going to screw it up!'

'You are. But that's alright, she'll get to understand that, too, pretty soon.'

Cole protested with a loud exhale of breath through his lips, just as Mackenzie moved her mount into a trot and caught up.

'You enjoying the ride?' Mandla asked her.

'I am. I haven't been on a horse in forever, but I guess it's true, you never forget how to ride.' She leant forward and gave her mare a pat on the neck. 'She's so gentle and responsive.'

Cole smiled. 'That she is. *Ntetuetu* in Xhosa means "we talk". We just call her Tet. When she was a foal, she was so vocal you could hear her every time anyone walked into the stable. She would greet them and let the world know they were there.'

'Unlike her owner,' Mandla murmured.

Cole could have smacked his friend over the head.

'Pardon?' Mackenzie asked.

'Nothing,' Mandla said, 'glad you are enjoying Tet, she's one of my favourites on the ranch. Talkative.'

Cole sent Mandla a death stare.

Mandla just smirked.

Cole broke into a trot and the other two horses followed his lead. Together the three rode towards the outer fence. Past the dam and the construction site of the latest tourist lodge, where cabins made with wooden logs were set high into the trees, blending into the environment and almost camouflaged, just the way the architect had said they would be. The trout fishing resort would bring in more money for his ranch and help finance his cheetah conservation project further. It was always good to see more money coming into your bank account than departing.

Cole grinned with satisfaction. Everything on the ranch was progressing well, except for the new threat of poachers.

Cole was conscious of Mackenzie watching him as she held the reins of the horses, while he and Mandla mended the fence. He kept glancing over to see what she was doing.

'Concentrate,' Mandla said.

'It's a bit hard.'

'You're going to slice your hand off if you don't.'

He tried to, but every breath of wind brought her scent to his nose. 'Keep close, Mackenzie,' Cole warned.

'Will do.'

He saw her pull the horses closer and move inside a perimeter he was happier with, where they could still react to a situation if need be. She was still in danger and so were his cheetahs. The threat to Hope was real as well. Someone had caused her plane to crash, and although the unit was pursuing angles on that, no arrests had been made, so her perpetrator was still out there. Everyone relied on the integrity of his fences now and he felt responsible.

Before mid-morning the fence was done, all the damage repaired and the electrical current running again.

'Good job, right up to an electrical standard,' Mandla called to Cole as he shorted a non-insulated screwdriver and made an impressive spark. The smell of burnt plastic immediately filled the country air.

'You idiot,' Cole said, but smiled at his friend.

For now, his wildlife was safe. Mackenzie was safe.

Mackenzie wandered back with the horses and passed the reins to the men.

Mandla mounted his and said, 'I'm going to ride in the opposite direction because I suspect that whoever these poachers are that cut this hole, they're still here judging by those tracks. More than likely they're working on another part of the fence, testing us.'

Cole swore. 'It's been over ten years since you guys sorted out the last bunch of Sothos who were rustling my game. The educational program for everyone around the ranch is running well. The people in this area are better off now than ever before. Why would the locals even think of helping an incoming poaching ring? It makes no sense.'

'That's what I'm going to find out,' Mandla said as he rode off at a brisk trot along the fence towards the mountains.

'Be careful!' Cole shouted at Mandla's departing back.

Mandla gave him the middle finger.

*   *   *

Rubbing down her horse next to Cole, Mackenzie admired the man he was. At seventeen, Sebastian had swept her off her feet. He was so handsome in his Yves Saint Laurent suits, his Armani sports shirts and the Calvin Klein tailored pants. That was the circle she'd lived in, everything designer-labelled and packaged.

Cole wasn't anything like Sebastian. He was all male, sun-browned, not solarium-tanned. His athletic body came from manual labour on his ranch, not hours in the gym. He wore denim jeans that had already today seen many hours in a saddle. Cole was the most beautiful specimen of man she'd ever had the pleasure of knowing.

She gave both horses one last carrot as they turned them loose into the field.

'How're you doing? Did you enjoy the ride?' His voice was soft as he reached for a stray piece of hair and tucked it behind her ear.

She smiled that he'd played with her hair again. 'Loved it. Can't wait to get in your 4x4 and go *blesbok* counting.'

He brought his hand back to his side. 'I was thinking, you expressed a need to call your folks. You should call them today. Don't put it off any longer. Let them know about Lauren and what your arrangements are for her to rest in the cemetery here. Perhaps invite them to come visit, attend the funeral. That way, as you said, you are setting the rules first up and calling the shots.'

'Are you serious? Invite them here while all this is going on? With everyone after your cheetahs and after Hope and without us knowing yet who murdered Lauren?'

'It's intense at the moment, but there's never going to be a perfect time. If your dad knows where you are, wouldn't you rather he comes on your terms than on his? It's a proactive move on your part.'

She was still for a moment, then she said, 'You know what, it's not such a crazy idea. I'm actually really looking forward to talking to my mom again. I've missed her. The news is going to be hard on her. She loved Lauren like a second daughter, and despite everything with my dad, I do want to know that he's okay, too.'

'Let's go call them, before you change your mind.' He tucked her arm into his. 'The sooner we get all this over with the better.'

'Okay.' She was silent, as if contemplating her next words. 'I've been thinking about how much I've told you. All my laundry is being aired and I'm not learning anything about you,' she said, glancing up at him.

He pulled her to him. 'Just so you know, whatever happens I'm on your side.' He increased the pressure slightly, bringing her into a casual hug, his hands running down her back and pulling her body into his.

'Me, too,' Mackenzie replied. 'Where were you during my first years in South Africa?'

'Keeping my distance on your orders, remember?'

How typically chivalrous of Cole. That was another thing she really liked about him, his honesty and his ability to control his actions.

They walked away from the stables and into the house, still arm in arm. Mackenzie liked that Cole stood back for her to enter the doorway first and added that to his growing list of mannerisms that she had to ensure she never took for granted. As she led the way to the home study she grinned briefly, but she could feel it slip from her face as they entered the room and she was confronted with the phone.

The reality of facing the moment.

'You'll feel better after talking to them. Besides, as you said, they knew Lauren, so it would be good for them to have closure for her as well,' Cole said, giving her a little nudge with his shoulder towards the phone.

Mackenzie looked at him. 'I guess in the bigger scheme of things, our family fallout is nothing.'

'Remember, when you invite him, he'll be coming on your terms. You're setting the ground rules for him.'

She smiled at him in a forced manner. 'I know it needs to be done, but that doesn't make it easier!'

'Come on, you're strong,' he told her.

'I know. I know.' She sighed. 'It's time I squared off with them.'

'Stop overthinking it. Just call them.'

Cole reached for the phone and pushed it towards her.

Mackenzie looked up, her eyes blazing. 'Helping me face my fears and insecurities is one thing …'

'Call them,' Cole said quietly.

She reached for the phone and slowly dialled the number, placing the phone on speaker as she stood quite still, her hands on the desk as the other end picked up.

'Hello.'

'Hello, Dad.'

A small silence then, 'Nicole. Nicole, it's you.' The distinguished baritone voice on the other end cracked with emotion. 'Hang on, I'm putting you on speaker, your mom is right next to me.'

A sweeter, almost hysterical voice said, 'Nicole, it's Mom. Please don't hang up on us; your father needs a minute to compose himself. Are you still there?'

'I'm here.'

'We've been wondering how you were doing,' her father began again. 'Where are you?'

'I'm in a town called Crystalberg in South Africa, staying with my friend on his safari rescue centre.'

'Are you in trouble?' her mother asked.

'No, Mom but I have some sad news. Lauren was visiting and she's been murdered.'

'Oh my God,' her mother said. 'Bob, did you hear that?'

'I did,' her father said. 'I'm so sorry. We'll charter a plane out of Dallas as soon as possible. You shouldn't be alone, you should have family around you for support.'

Mackenzie looked at Cole, surprised at the response from her father.

'Dad, I'm fine,' replied Mackenzie. 'I wanted to let you know in case you wanted to attend Lauren's funeral. It probably won't be for another two weeks or so because they still haven't released the body to me. We're waiting on a legal courier from the US with a copy of her will, giving me full authority as the executor of her estate.'

Cole reached out and squeezed her hand, mouthing, 'You okay?'

Mackenzie clutched back and gave a sharp nod, but she didn't let go of his hand.

'It's good to hear your voice,' her father said. 'Even if it's with such terrible news. How do I let you know what time our charter will arrive?'

Cole wrote his number on a pad and gave it to her. She read it out to her parents.

'Dad, you can come on a commercial flight, you don't have to charter one to get here. I'll meet you in Pietermaritzburg.'

'We'll let you know the flight details,' her father said.

She lifted her eyes skywards. She should have known that he would just do his own thing.

'I have so many questions, Nicole, so many,' her mother said.

'I know,' Mackenzie said.

'Honey,' her mother said, 'is there anything you need that we can bring with us?' Her voice sounded strained, tired.

'No. I have everything I need here,' she said and looked directly at Cole. Mackenzie rubbed her forehead to try to relieve some of the stress building there.

'Anything we can do from this side?' her father asked, his rich voice travelling over the miles between them.

'We can't broadcast her death yet because of the investigation. So no newspapers, no media.'

'They won't hear from us, Nicole. No media. You were right about them last time,' her father said.

There was a long pause and silence as no one spoke for a while, then Mackenzie broke it.

'That means a lot, Dad. It really does.'

'Yes, well. We'll see you soon and talk more face to face. I'm looking forward to seeing you.'

'Me, too. See your soon. Bye, Mom. Bye, Dad.' And she reached over and hung up, then she stood there, looking totally lost.

Cole tugged her hand as he sat down in his office chair, and Mackenzie sank into his lap. Cole hugged her

'They're coming,' she announced unnecessarily.

Cole nodded. 'You did great!'

'Wow, not so sure why I put that off for so long now that it's done,' Mackenzie said.

'So it wasn't so bad was it?' he said.

Mackenzie tried to stand but Cole placed his hands firmly on her hips.

'Not yet,' he said as he explored her neck, raining tiny kisses onto it. 'Stay here with me a while. We have a few minutes.'

Mackenzie smiled. She tightened her butt in his lap and took pleasure in the way his pupils dilated. He closed the few millimetres' distance between them and captured her lips in his. Instantly, she was lost. But just as suddenly, he pulled away from her, breaking the kiss, and touched his forehead to hers. 'Oh my God, her timing sucks,' Cole said and dragged a hand though his hair, disbelief colouring his face as he set her away from him.

Confused about the abrupt departure of the seducer and the re-emergence of the intensely controlled man, she blinked, speechless. She didn't want him to stop.

'Thandi's about to burst through the door any moment, I heard her calling us.' His chest heaved under the restraint of regaining control of his body.

'Oh man, if she finds us like this …' she murmured, before touching her head to his again. 'This isn't finished, not by a long shot.'

'I know, but come on, we need to go and count *blesbok* and I can show you my farm. I have something special to share with you once the count's over.' He rose up and put her on her own feet as Thandi knocked softly and opened the door.

CHAPTER
25

'Look at that. It's amazing!' Mackenzie said as she took in the sight before her. A herd of *blesbok* grouped together, their black-and-deep-red coats glossy in the sun. The white blazes on their faces crowned with ringed horns gave them an intelligent look. The wild animals ignored the humans as they drove past, content with eating the sweet summer grass.

'They're used to people so us coming into the herd isn't stressful to them. I don't allow any hunting here so they have no fear of humans. I'm fortunate enough to have GPS trackers in all of them, so doing the count is more to see if anyone else's have mixed in with mine than about my numbers. The guys love calving season, Mandla and Charl especially. They come and we herd the buck into the *kraal* and we implant the GPS trackers into the calves as soon as we can so if they get stolen or they're poached we can track them and get them back.'

'I'm glad you don't allow shooting. It's sad to kill such a beautiful animal,' she said, looking at them grazing on the side of the mountain, their lips delicately nipping off the green shoots at the ground level, not pulling up a single root so the grass would regenerate itself quickly.

'Fifty-three in this group,' Cole said, 'do you agree?'

'I lost count – again.'

'It's an acquired skill.' He smiled at her. 'Come, we have one last game enclosure to complete. It's extra-special to me and we should check that no *blesbok* have found a way in.'

'How can they with all these huge fences?'

'Breaks in the fence lines, holes under the fences, anything. I swear, *blesbok* are the Houdinis of the game world. Fences mean as little to them as to elephants.'

They travelled into another high-fenced enclosure and Cole shut the gate.

'So no lions or tigers or bears in this one,' she teased him as he walked back to the vehicle.

'Single gate so no cats. Giraffe, zebra, wildebeest, perhaps some kudu, eland and, hopefully, my nyala. They're usually found in dense bush and this is the bushiest enclosure on the ranch. The land belonged to a neighbour before I bought him out and expanded a few years back. I left the land fallow to rejuvenate and the bush quickly returned. I realised I'd created the perfect hideaway safari spot for the luxury traveller. The house was a one-hundred-year-old stone cottage located near a small dam. I recycled the stone and built the safari lodge and increased the dam size considerably, but there's no one there today,' Cole said as they broke out of the thick trees and into a clearing.

The waterhole before her was magnificent, as was the stone lodge surrounded by a wooden deck that sat on the edge of the water. The whole building appeared to float like a boat.

'Wow! That's awesome,' she said.

'Wait till you see inside,' he said as he climbed out of the *bakkie* and walked around to the passenger side to open her door.

Tumbling out of the vehicle and directly into his arms seemed so natural. 'You know, I could get used to all this attention you're throwing at me.'

'I could get used to giving it if you would stay here,' he replied.

Mackenzie frowned. 'What does that mean?'

'It means stay after the madness is over. Once we have taken care of the threat against my cheetahs and we're sure there is no longer anyone after you, stay here with me?'

Her heart hammered in her chest and she couldn't breathe. He was asking her for a relationship, but he was the one who had also said he wasn't in the market. Neither had she been, but she felt this connection to him now, the attraction that threatened to explode all the time, and she knew that she was lost.

He brought his head down to hers and kissed her. His mouth fused to hers and their tongues duelled, giving, taking from each other. Cole lifted her up and carried her onto the large deck of the lodge.

Collapsing together onto the huge couch overlooking the water, Mackenzie hardly noticed the scenery.

He ran his fingertips up her spine and under her hair. She shivered.

'Cold?'

'No.'

He moved his lips up her neck, nipping and suckling gently as he went.

Batting his hand away at the feeling he was creating on her neck, Mackenzie murmured in approval as he changed to caressing instead. 'I liked that. That was good. Ticklish but good.'

'I want to make love to you but I hadn't planned this. I don't have any protection with me. A pistol and ammo, sure, but a condom – out of luck. There is no way I can do this without any protection. We have spoken about your mistakes, this was one of mine. I was young, I trusted someone, and then we got pregnant. I was going to marry her, but I lost her and my unborn son in a car accident. I learnt a valuable but hard lesson then to take responsibility in the creation of another life. I'm sorry.'

She frowned. 'Thank you for telling me, and my heart breaks for your loss.'

They were silent for a heartbeat, together but each lost in their own thoughts.

Mackenzie said, 'I want you to know that despite losing Lauren and despite the fact that we're waiting for an attack on your farm, this is the most alive I've felt in the last two years.'

'Me, too,' he said and he kissed her gently. He lifted his head. 'Look, a kudu coming to drink.' He pointed and she looked excitedly over to the water's edge.

The huge grey antelope, with its towering spiral horns, drank deeply from the cold mountain water, its legs splayed apart, its head dipping majestically. A dove cooed in the trees somewhere and a second kudu joined the first.

'Beautiful,' she said.

'You are,' he replied and hugged her, 'and those kudu bulls aren't so bad either.'

They sat in comfortable silence for a while, watching as a warthog followed the kudu out of the trees and to the water, its tail a comical aerial behind it. Cole had one arm draped over her shoulders, the other held her hand, massaging her wrist and arm.

She forgot all about conversation as he captured her lips with his again and drank heavily. Soon, Mackenzie was drowning in emotion.

He caressed down her side. Desire gripped her low in her belly when Cole drew his fingers lightly over her breasts, over her dirty T-shirt.

'Do you know that keeping my hands off you is proving harder and harder.' His voice trembled when he spoke.

She looked back at his face, where the lines around his eyes were etched deep by the harsh African sun. His hair flip-flopped as if her hands had run passionately through it. His sensual lips were full, the side of his face throbbing, as if he was struggling to keep himself in check.

Taking a deep breath she said, 'I know and I feel the same. But like you said, now is not the time.' She snuggled into him again.

'I know.' Cole rubbed her back, looking over her head at the waterhole. 'Finally, a nyala,' he whispered, as the shy creature stepped out of the bush and tiptoed to the water, constantly checking around.

Its shaggy coat was grey, distinctly different to the earlier kudu with its striped legs and with more elongated horns, a perfect match for the bushlands it lived in.

'I wonder where the female is,' Cole said.

On cue she timidly emerged from the bush. Her red-and-white-striped sleek coat contrasted deeply with the rich black of the soil around the dam.

'She's so different to him,' Mackenzie said as she watched the nyala's big ears pitch forward like giant satellite dishes, twitching this way and that, as if listening to her talk.

'She can probably hear us, they have good hearing.'

The female nyala dug her front hooves deep into the mud, balked backwards and bolted into the bush. The male galloped after her.

'Damn, she spooked,' Cole swore, then he held onto Mackenzie really tightly.

And as Mackenzie looked at the deserted waterhole, she wondered if Cole was trying to tell her he was worried that she would do the same thing, because now he had told her a little about his past.

CHAPTER
26

Cole shook his head. Since arriving home near afternoon-tea time, after showing the old hunting lodge to Mackenzie, he hadn't been able to radio in the count numbers to the coordinator.

Mandla had located another hole deliberately cut in *nTaba-Grequa's* boundary fence. It was obviously done by someone with electrical experience who had come prepared and cut where there were no security cameras. The current had been effectively diverted through a buried wire. Twelve eland had escaped onto National Park land. His workers had already spent three hours recovering nine of those so far and the others appeared to have taken a long walk over the mountain and were on the other side. Dumisani had gone with Siphiwe in a *bakkie* to herd them home with the help of the dogs, but the darkness of night was coming on fast. If they took much longer they would be walking them in guided by torch lights.

Cole's anti-poaching team had been out since three, tracking the stock and recovering them from the mountains. None of their stock's GPS trackers had signalled stress, and after riding home, Cole had loaded his *bakkie* and headed out to rejoin them with more supplies. After leaving the men at the fence, he had headed home to check on Mackenzie.

Brian waved Cole down. 'I'll be in the horse shed,' he said. 'I've picked up some good stuff to make a few explosives, I'm going to play.'

'No way. You go and make noise in the workshop, not in my horse barn. Catherine and her baby will go ballistic if you start blowing things up in there,' Cole said.

Set apart from the visitors' centre, the vehicle sheds were the working hub of his farm. It was where the farming equipment and the salt for the trout and winter licks for the wild game were stored. It was where the workshops with the welding machines, which sprayed blue arc light over everything, created gates and cages for the cheetahs. It was also where the strong room for the ammunition for the ranch was kept, as well as the bigger gun safes of the anti-poaching guards. It was the centre of the game guards' universe, where they learnt their skills, so there was a built-in boxing ring, training area, and because Brian had insisted on building it, an indoor range for the men to practise in so that they didn't have to alert the neighbourhood every time they came home and needed to let off steam, and it had morphed into the practice range for the game guards.

Cole felt an enormous amount of pride in the fact that they had built it on the same spot where the original owner of the farm had stored his hunting traps and utilised a hunting tree, where many animals had died. That ground was now used to save animals, not slaughter them.

'I see your point. Your zebra has a nasty temper. Okay, I'll be in the workshop nowhere near your precious stables or your visitors' centre,' Brian said and clapped Cole on the back. 'Let's get this show on the road.'

'Not a moment too soon,' Cole said. 'Nothing like a real threat to whip us into shape, is there?'

'Still not so sure everything is not linked. Seems a bit suspicious with the timing to me,' Brian said. 'Mackenzie's taxi attack, Hope's sabotaged plane, Lauren's death and the poachers' coming to the ranch.'

'I agree, but either way we need to stop all of them.' He knew his forehead showed frown lines to match those that creased Brian's. If the guys from the BSC were worried that was never a good sign. It meant that they were either on a case they knew was a lost cause, or perhaps they knew there might be fatalities within the farm's own defence personnel itself, and no one wanted those.

'It's always harder on us when it's someone close, and you are as close as a brother,' Brian said. 'The stakes are higher, but we'll protect your cheetahs, Cole. When have we ever let you down?'

'Never.'

'See, there's hope yet. Hang in there,' Brian said.

'Talking about Hope, where is she?'

'Last I saw she was with Alan in your study.'

Cole nodded. 'I'll catch up with them there, then. Later.'

He watched Brian head in the direction of the workshop. They'd been friends since their army days, and although Brian was the 'old man' of the group, his friendship was unwavering. Brian had been his weapons instructor, but a friendship had formed. They'd watched each other's backs. Ensuring the welfare of the other during a dark time. Even though it was an age when it was compulsory for every man to fight for a government that believed in apartheid, the men in their defence forces lived the opposite existence. Where black and white men served together, saved each other's lives, became as close as men could become.

When they went home to civilian lives, they were expected to integrate back into a separated society. A society that dictated where you fitted into their tiers of hierarchy by the colour of your skin, not by the type of person you were.

Now, with a new government in place and the 'rainbow nation' healing slowly, they were once more fighting together against an unseen foe. Only this time it threatened Cole's ranch. The place they all escaped to and had called home at some time.

There was never any doubt that they would be there for Cole. Mandla, Charl, Brian and Alan. They were as good as any family he could've had. Better, as they had chosen each other. They each knew that the brotherhood was stronger than any blood relative. He had men on his farm who fitted into the same bracket. Siphiwe had been with him since he was just twenty years old. He was the one who had first started clearing the overgrown wattles from the land, to make pasture lands for Cole to farm *blesbok* and impala to feed his cheetahs, and it was Siphiwe who had held the farming side together for Cole while he was in the army. Dumisani had been a game guard in the Hluhluwe Game Park, and had left his job there about fifteen years ago to be with Cole when Cole had gone to collect a cheetah cub that had been mauled by a lion. The rangers hadn't given it good odds, but Michelle and Cole had pulled it through, and it had been returned to the wild a year later.

Dumisani had packed up and travelled with them to *nTaba-Grequa* because he wanted to make a difference and work with saving the cheetahs, and Seth had been a young boy begging for a job. He'd been orphaned and alone, and Cole had taken him in, ensured he was housed on the farm, fed by Thandi and that he completed his schooling. After he had completed a bookkeeping course, he had come back to the farm to do office work. But Seth loved the interaction with the cats so much he had taken on extra duties, and had continued to study. Now he was a qualified game ranger and tracker. He refused to acquire a hunting licence because he wouldn't shoot an elephant as required by the final test, but he had fulfilled every other part of the qualification. Cole was so proud as he'd watched the boy become a man and make good decisions.

He checked his cell phone. A text message from Michelle read:

I'm at the nursery. Lady Bess is in labour. Come as soon as you can.

He smiled, just typical that one of his cheetahs would go into labour when the whole farm was in overload.

He continued in the direction of the house to see if Hope had any progress to report from her side of the investigation, and to find Mackenzie. Knowing that she'd not grown up in the African environment, he wanted to warn her that Brian would be testing a few explosives. He didn't want her to think she might be under attack, and she needed to see the cubs being born. He wanted to share the moment with her.

*   *   *

Mackenzie was sketching with a pencil on the couch in the study. Thandi's news about Cole fixing the new hole in the fence wasn't sitting easy in her stomach. Worrying about another person was new and slightly alien after the years she'd spent alone, and yet she couldn't suppress the happiness that bubbled up inside her.

Hope and Alan were deep in conversation at Cole's desk, talking about some farmer named Thompson in the Limpopo area, but she had zoned out long ago.

She shaded the picture on the pad she'd borrowed from Cole's study and looked at it critically. Cole's face stared back at her from astride his horse, man and beast in perfect union as they cantered across a field of grass. She wanted to go to her house and begin the clay moulding for the bronze of this sketch.

'Every time I see your work, I'm still amazed and in awe. You are really talented,' Cole said.

Mackenzie jumped in fright at the intrusion. Her pencil went flying in one direction and her notebook in another. She held her hand to her racing heart. 'You scared me!'

'Nice you could join us.' Alan looked up from the desk.

'Hiya,' said Hope, waving her fingers at him.

'Hi, guys,' Cole said. Then he turned his attention back to Mackenzie, bending to retrieve the notebook. 'May I?'

She nodded.

He opened it.

'Wow,' he said as he went through them. 'And these took you how long?'

'They're just roughs.'

'From someone who can't even draw a stick figure, these don't look like roughs. I think they're wonderful.'

'Thank you,' she said, taking back the pad. 'I hope you don't mind me scratching around on your desk to borrow your notebook. I put the only used page under your desk calendar so it didn't blow away.'

'Glad there was something in the house that you could use. Perhaps we should go into your place and collect some supplies. I never thought of that when I hurried you out of there.'

'I would love that. I'll keep it to things that don't make a mess.'

'You can make as much mess as you need. We can clear you a room in the stables if you want, or you can use the kitchen or the verandah. You're going to be here for a while, so if you need your artist paraphernalia, then we should go get it. Perhaps tomorrow morning, while everything's still quiet?'

Mackenzie smiled. 'Thanks, Cole, for this and for everything.'

'Don't thank me,' he said. 'I have an ulterior motive. If you feel happy and safe here …' He stopped as if realising that they weren't alone.

She looked at him. This was the second time he was asking her to give them a chance, give them a future.

He raised his voice and asked Alan and Hope, 'You guys still good there? Nothing to share with us yet?'

'Still mapping out some things with Hope,' Alan said. 'Perhaps after dinner there might be a few things we can shed light on.'

'Great. Charl is just going to drop off some more wire and lighting at the fence. Mandla's supervising that. Things around here might get a bit noisy. Brian's mixing explosives to set into the new anti-poaching traps, but not for long because Mackenzie and I are going to help Lady Bess. She has gone into labour, so he won't get more than one or two bangs in before he has to stop as it will upset her.'

'Your cheetah's having babies, oh that's exciting.' Mackenzie stood up, retrieving her pencil and tucking her pad against her chest.

Hope said, 'Wow, what an experience. Hopefully, we'll be done here in about half an hour and I'll go join Brian if he hasn't finished already.'

'Enjoy that. I need to check in at the police station and follow up on a lead my guys were following up on Lauren,' Alan said. 'It might take a bit of time, but we will catch her killer.'

Mackenzie said, 'Thanks, Alan.'

'See you guys later, once the birthing is over,' Cole said as he put his hand into the small of Mackenzie's back and all but pushed her from the room.

CHAPTER
27

Walking into yet another corridor in the *nTabaGrequa* centre, Mackenzie realised that it was made up of several large buildings that were so close together they looked like one, as if they were added when needed, not planned. But they all fitted together really well.

'This way,' Cole said, stepping into the room.

She followed eagerly.

Behind a large glass-viewing window was Lady Bess, pacing, panting, her painted face alert as she moved backwards and forwards.

A woman with mousy-brown hair haphazardly piled on top of her head sat inside the enclosure with the cheetah, but the animal ignored her. There was an array of equipment within the area, a small stainless-steel table with a scale, a stethoscope and a pile of towels. A veterinarian's black bag and a big, comfy-looking pillow that the woman was perched on completed the human paraphernalia in the room.

Cole unlocked a small gate and bent down to enter the enclosure. 'Stay close,' he said as he guided her through. The door closed automatically behind them.

The cat chirped at him when he entered. 'Yes, Lady, I'm here, of course I wouldn't miss this, my beautiful.' She came to him and head-butted his leg. Cole stroked her, ran his hand down her back and patted her.

Mackenzie couldn't move. She was riveted to the spot. The cat stood just below her hip height, but she eyed Mackenzie closely. She sniffed the air with her black nose and then abandoned Cole and focused her attention on Mackenzie.

'Get down to her level,' Cole said. 'She doesn't know you yet, but she wants to.'

Mackenzie dropped to her knees on the soft straw, and held out her hand for the cat to sniff. It licked her fingers and up her arm. The cheetah smelt her all over. The sandpaper effect made Mackenzie laugh. When the cheetah reached the point where Mackenzie's sleeves covered her skin, she stopped, chirped a rapid chorus and then sat down next to her. Purring. Her swollen baby-filled belly clearly visible.

'She likes you,' Cole said. His smile was infectious and Mackenzie grinned back at him in delight.

'She likes most females,' the other woman in the enclosure said. 'Hi, you have to be Mackenzie, I'm Michelle. Pleased to meet you at last.'

Mackenzie nodded at Michelle. 'You, too.'

'I'm so sorry to hear about your friend, my condolences. So sad that that happened. I know that Alan will catch the bastard who murdered her, he has to.'

'Thank you,' Mackenzie said.

'Michelle and I are old friends. We both share the passion of wildlife and open spaces. She's married to my next-door neighbour, Koos Oosthuizen. He'll probably drop in later. He hardly ever misses the birth of the cubs, no matter how many we have born in the centre.'

Lady got up and continued her pacing, up and down in front of the glass.

'Move over here. It'll be more comfortable,' Cole said as he shifted against the wall, next to Michelle. When Mackenzie stood up and sat with him, he encircled her with his legs and tugged her back against him.

Mackenzie put her pad and pencil next to her. 'She's gorgeous! And so tame.'

Michelle grunted. 'Just wait till she gives birth. She won't be half as agreeable as she is now. Lady'll turn into an aggressive, protective mama.'

Mackenzie relaxed against Cole. She rotated her neck, trying to relieve the tension there.

'Here, let me,' Cole said as he began to massage her shoulders, moving gradually upwards. Mackenzie closed her eyes and enjoyed the sensations.

The soft click of the door closing woke her from her relaxed position in the confines of Cole's legs. Opening her eyes, she saw the biggest man she'd ever seen. A gasp escaped before she registered Cole's lack of concern at his presence.

Michelle moved to open the inner door, and Mackenzie watched in wonder as his hard, chiselled face softened when he reached for Michelle and kissed her soundly. It had to be Koos.

'Cole,' Koos said as he pumped his neighbour's hand.

'This is Mackenzie,' Cole said.

'Pleased to meet you,' Mackenzie said politely.

'Any friend of Cole's is mine, too,' he said, his voice as thick as wild honey with his Afrikaans accent, and he drew her up off her feet into a huge bear hug. 'And I shall greet you like one.'

'Um, thanks,' Mackenzie said when she was eventually released.

'I hope you enjoy your first time seeing one of the miracles that Cole performs here at *nTabaGrequa*,' Koos said.

'I'm sure I'll love it,' Mackenzie said, quickly sitting down again.

'Here's hoping it won't be your last.' He took the camera and then the backpack off his shoulder and sat down in the hay next to Michelle. He poured coffee into the three cups, his hands surprisingly nimble for their size.

'Sorry, didn't know there were more of us this time, but I'll remember in future.' He laughed and passed a cup to Michelle. 'We can share, *liefie*.' Then one to Mackenzie and Cole.

'Thanks,' Mackenzie said.

Both sat down again to drink their coffee.

Lady paced up and down, ignoring the humans. Her breathing sounded a little laboured but she didn't look distressed.

After a while, Mackenzie asked, 'Won't we all be in her way?'

Cole shook his head. 'No, she's a seasoned mum, but because she's having so many this time we want to be on hand, just in case. If it was one of the first-timers, we wouldn't encroach on her space, but Lady doesn't mind. She's used to us. I've had her since she was a tiny cub herself.'

Her curiosity now piqued, Mackenzie enquired, 'How many cubs do they normally have?'

'Three or four,' Michelle said. 'Lady here is having eight.'

Mackenzie asked, 'Is that bad?'

'Good that we'll have so many,' said Cole. 'Scary, because we haven't had that many delivered at the same time here before. DeWildt um Ann van Dyk Cheetah Centre up north has though. It should be alright.'

Mackenzie heard the slight hitch in his voice. He was anxious, the joy, the emotion he felt for his cheetahs in his every word.

She sketched one picture of the expectant mother, then another, but soon she, too, sat in silence, watching Lady pace back and forth. Eventually, warmed by Cole's body heat, Mackenzie's eyes closed.

'Wake up, sleepyhead. It's happening.' Cole kissed her temple area.

Her eyes snapped open. He was squatted in front of her. She hadn't even noticed he'd moved away while she slept and that she was reclining flat in the hay, Cole's jacket under her head. *How long had she been asleep?*

Lady lay on her side against the glass. She'd moved the grass around herself and was panting heavily, her tongue lolled out of her mouth slightly.

'Is she okay?' Mackenzie whispered.

'Yeah, she's doing perfectly,' Cole said.

Michelle had her stethoscope on Lady's stomach and as they watched, she said, 'Here comes the first one.'

Koos stepped behind his tripod and began taking pictures.

Mackenzie didn't bother picking up her sketch pad, as she wanted to experience every moment of the birthing process.

'Come on, girl, you are doing great,' Cole encouraged.

Sure enough out popped a tiny, wet, grey body, followed closely by another. Lady, with all dignity, chirped and reached back for her babies. While she cleaned the first two with her rough tongue, out slid the third and fourth.

Mackenzie smiled. She watched in wonder as the next four slipped silently into the world, with Michelle's gentle hands waiting, and were passed to Lady to smell. Cole had a towel and was helping dry off the little cubs.

'*Siestog*, isn't that the sweetest wonder in the world you've ever seen,' Koos said.

'It sure is,' Mackenzie replied, as she saw the tiny bodies blindly seek out their mother's teats, helped by Cole and Michelle.

Michelle weighed each one in turn. 'Two hundred and ten grams, a good weight since there were eight of them.'

Koos put down his camera and got busy with a notepad taken from inside the black bag, recording the vital information. Mackenzie watched the three of them together. The ease in which they worked spoke volumes about the number of times this event had happened previously.

'Come on over here,' Cole said and held out his hand to her, beckoning. Cradled in his other hand was a small cub.

'She's the runt of the litter, but it looks like she's a fighter,' he told Mackenzie as he placed the small body into her open palms. Razor-sharp claws gripped into her fingers as the cub tried to stabilise herself. She raised the fur ball up to her eyes and stared. The grey fur stuck up at all angles. Her tiny eyes were closed, but already the defining black tear marks were clearly visible on either side of her button nose. A soft, mewing sound came from her mouth.

'Hello, little one,' she said.

'She needs a name,' Cole said. 'Do you have one in mind?'

'Me? You're asking me to name your cheetah cub?'

'Yes.'

Mackenzie looked into his green eyes, the gentle eyes of a man trusting her to name one of his babies.

'Jewels. Because she's precious,' Mackenzie said with a small nod of her head.

'Nice name,' Cole said.

'Agreed,' Koos and Michelle said together. Then Michelle poked her husband in the ribs. 'We've been married too long. We think too much alike!'

'Never too long,' Koos said and kissed the tip of her nose.

Mackenzie couldn't stop smiling. It was so good to hear the banter between the obviously happy couple. She wanted that, too.

'Jewels needs her mum for a while. You going to put her down with the others?' Cole asked.

'Sure.' She bent down immediately, but couldn't resist kissing the tiny cheetah on the top of her head before putting her near a teat to feed.

Mackenzie felt Cole's arm slip around her waist when she stood again to watch the mother and babies.

'This part never gets old,' he said.

'No, never,' Koos and Michelle said together again and Michelle smiled.

Koos swatted her backside. 'Come on then, Mrs Oosthuizen, your job here is done for the night. Let's go home.'

They packed up their supplies and the camera, said their goodbyes and soon Mackenzie and Cole were left alone.

They slid back down to the floor, content with sitting simply watching the family before them.

'Will they be alright?' Mackenzie said.

'They'll get extra hand-fed supplements from tomorrow morning. Michelle will be back early to check on them and she'll decide what extra vitamins they each need.'

'Michelle is so great,' she said.

'That she is, but Michelle is not you,' he said quietly, his voice suddenly very serious. 'You're everything I've ever wanted and more.'

Slowly, his words sank in.

'Really?' she asked, turning around to face him.

'Yes.'

He leant forward, taking her face gently in both hands, then lowered his head. He kissed her tenderly, seeking out a response.

'Mackenzie,' he murmured, taking possession of her mouth with his.

The assault left her wanting more. She lost all ability to think. All she could do was feel. Heat radiated from his body. She swayed forward, into him, pushed her face into his neck and inhaled deeply. His distinct smell cocooned her. The faint tinge of fresh hay reminded her of where they were.

'Someone can see us,' she murmured as she nipped his neck.

'Everyone's gone. It's us and the cats.' He dragged her mouth back up to his and drank deeply. Eventually he lifted his head. 'Thank you for sharing this with me.'

'Are you kidding? It was sensational and wonderful, thank you for asking me to share it,' she kissed him again, 'with you,' she murmured into his mouth, knowing it was nothing less than the truth.

Mackenzie felt the change in Cole's body as if it was an extension of her own. His shoulders relaxed and lowered. His back curved into a comfortable position, the cords of stress around his neck disappeared. She ran her hand over the smooth skin. His hands reached down and adjusted their hips to fit more comfortably.

They were as close as two people with clothes on could get.

Cole tugged up on her tracksuit top and removed it. 'God, Mackenzie, if I'd known you'd no bra on ...' He cursed as his hands roamed her breasts freely, stroking, caressing. He laid her slightly backwards to gain access to them and dipped his head, taking one taut nipple in his mouth.

Heat seared and sweat formed on her upper lip as desire burnt. A desire so strong that she knew this time nothing would keep her from having Cole inside her.

She drew his lips to hers again and impatiently ran her hands down his back, then she dragged her hands to the front and undid the buttons on his shirt. She moved herself away from him slightly so she could better access the front of his body with her mouth. As each button either snapped open or went flying in her haste, she kissed his chest, ran her tongue around his pebbled nipples and then pushed his shirt off his shoulders and ventured lower.

'Wait, Mackenzie,' he said breathlessly as he retrieved his shirt and placed it over the hay. 'For comfort,' he explained. 'Straw isn't so soft when it's directly below your skin.' Then he lay down on it so that Mackenzie could straddle him.

She licked the soft skin just above his waistline and reached for the button on his fly. Slowly it slipped open. She heard his intake of breath and smiled at the raspy sound.

Pausing a moment, she returned to kiss his lips, lingered for a while, enjoying the sensations rippling through her body. Mackenzie couldn't breathe. His hands were touching her all over, the rough pads of his fingers drawing erotic circles down her back and into her tracksuit pants. Heat pooled and there was only one solution.

She wrenched herself away from Cole and stood up.

'What?' he asked.

She kicked off her trainers. 'Too many clothes.' Next she pushed her trackpants down and shimmied out of them and her socks all in one movement, then wrapped her arms around his neck.

'Look what I made sure we had.' He flashed a strip of condoms he'd retrieved from his pants pocket.

Mackenzie grinned. Longing and need flashed through her. She was floating. Raw emotions flooded her body as his lips touched hers. She shuddered as the molten heat surged from the junction of her legs upwards, across her stomach, and burnt its way to her breasts, where his body, hard as an ironbark tree, held hers tightly.

His lips held hers as his tongue flicked over her mouth. She was his willing captive slave. Unable to move, unable to do anything except feel.

She felt alive!

Her nipples hardened against him and her knees weakened. She kissed him. Hungrily. Without warning, she felt the beginnings of a small climax ripple through her. Cole groaned low in his throat. She swore she felt the vibration deep in his chest.

She gasped as Cole's mouth found one nipple and suckled harder than he had before. The sensation of him pulling the tight nub into his mouth drove her nearer to the edge of ecstasy. Moisture gathered between her legs. Fighting total meltdown, she tugged at his belt and managed to undo that, only to find his pants had buttons, too.

They wouldn't budge when she tugged at them. She panted. 'Take them off.' Her nails raked down his chest and across his six-pack.

'Yes, Ma'am,' he said, as he followed her order.

He undid the barrier holding him prisoner. She watched one button pop at a time.

Removing his hand from his buttons, he shook his head. 'No. Not yet.' But he continued to stroke her breasts. 'Come for me, then you can have more.'

'Help me, Cole. I can't do this alone.'

He laughed softly and bit her on the neck. 'Anytime, Mac. Anytime. You only needed to ask.'

Cole ravished her neck with his mouth, nipping, licking and kissing in the hollow behind her ear where she was so sensitive to his touch. One hand slipped to her breast. He stroked it from base to nipple, circling the hard nub with his callused finger. Slowly, he moved to the next one, pinching it lightly. Tugging her until she felt a response in her core. His other hand ran up her thigh, and she parted her legs, willingly granting him access. Instead of zeroing in on her womanhood, he stroked the soft folds and ran the tip of his finger up and down, spreading the moisture already there.

She shivered.

He flicked her with his forefinger. The small pain was a comfort in the heat that threatened to spill over. She groaned as she bucked upwards towards him.

His mouth recaptured hers. She pulled away and looked at him. A faint five-o'clock shadow covered his face and neck, and she watched closely as he swallowed and his Adam's apple bobbed in his throat.

'I don't want to come alone, come with me,' she whispered.

He pulled his pants down, and the last remaining button slipped free. They dropped, complete with his soft cotton jocks inside, crumpling onto his *veldskoens*. He quickly ripped open the condom packet with his teeth and sheathed himself. Then in one smooth motion, he pushed into her.

'My Mackenzie,' he said almost breathlessly. She saw that he barely held on as cords of muscles bunched in his neck, and sweat on his upper lip was testament that he strove to control the passion ripping through him. He began to withdraw, and then plunged back. She looked down at where their bodies joined, to the erotic glide of him travelling in and out of her.

Her muscles spasmed.

Holding her butt with both hands, he pulled her closer, at the same time plunging deeper.

God he felt amazing. The wet slide of male hardness. A slick sheen of desire on his shoulders. His urgent assault on her mouth as he held her captive. He increased their rhythm. Faster. Harder.

She adored the hardness that was Cole. Owing to the heat that was consuming her, she didn't know the moment he left her mouth to gasp a breath. The tingling sensation radiated circles outwards, down her thighs and into her stomach.

She let go.

He recaptured her lips and she screamed her release into his mouth. Catching her climax within his, he rocked with her, absorbing her noise, pushing her further towards the edge.

Slamming into her twice more, she felt his shudder as he fought for control over his own body. She flexed her inside muscles, her hands clutching at his chest. Finding a rigid male nipple, she rolled it in between her thumb and forefinger, the small nub as precious as a diamond in her hand.

She felt him move again, hard. He withdrew until only his tip remained inside and thrust home one last time. He palmed both breasts, then paid homage to her nipples with his fingers, pulling, twirling them within his large hands. Mackenzie closed her eyes as stars exploded, as he pushed her over into the abyss.

Silently she floated back into the real world. Gently he cradled her in his arms. Lying stretched out over him, she could feel the rhythm of his heart and the exaggerated beat, and she knew hers mirrored his.

She closed her eyes.

CHAPTER
28

Cole and Mackenzie walked holding hands into the already well-lit kitchen. It appeared everyone on the farm was up well before sunrise as they sat around the huge kitchen table. Hope was on the far side fully clothed in black, her working wardrobe. Mandla sat beside her and Thandi stood at the stove making breakfast.

Brian was seated at the far end and he had yesterday's newspaper in front of him. Charl had stolen the comic section from it and sat one chair up so that there was space for the papers not to overlap. Mandla and Hope looked like they were awake in spirit only, still sluggish and in need of rest. Sunday morning didn't appear to be a sleep-in time at all.

'Lady Bess had eight healthy babies last night,' Cole announced.

'*Agt?*' Charl asked.

'Yes, eight. And she is doing well. We just left her and they were all feeding,' Cole said, the pride evident in his voice.

'Good, so I can continue with those explosives? I need to do a few more bangs, then I'll be done,' Brian said.

'That's fine. So what's been happening? What have you guys rigged up?' Cole asked.

'Would you like some breakfast?' Thandi asked Cole and Mackenzie.

'Ahh, would love a coffee and full breakfast thanks, Thandi.' Cole pulled out Mackenzie's chair next to the head of the table on the right-hand side.

'I'll just have a black coffee and muesli thanks, Thandi,' Mackenzie said as she sat down in the offered chair. Farren ran from her cat basket near the stove and jumped on her lap, purring, demanding a fuss as retribution for not being with her during the night. Her vocal greeting made Mackenzie smile.

Brian's head didn't lift from the newspaper, but Mandla smirked at Cole.

The telephone began ringing.

'I'll get it,' Cole said just as he was about to sit, and he left the room.

Thandi put the hot coffee in front of Mackenzie and she wrapped her left hand around the mug. Her right still scratched the cat beneath the chin as it curled up on her lap.

'So you watched the birth of the kitty-cats. It's quite something, hey?' Charl said.

Mackenzie looked at him. This was the most she had heard him utter. 'Yes it was, they were beautiful!'

'You staying then at *nTabaGrequa* for good, because Cole, he doesn't let just anyone go in there for the babies' birthing, it's always a private affair.'

'Pardon?' Mackenzie asked, not sure she had heard right.

'Well, if you are going to go back to your house, Cole is sure going to miss you. He seems taken by you,' Charl said.

'Charl!' Mandla warned. 'That's for him to say, not you.'

'*Ja*, but he won't. So I likes Mackenzie and how Cole is with her around. Calmer. I'm just getting in here first and saying I'm glad she'll be sticking around in the future. Cole needs some happiness.'

'Thank you but—' Mackenzie began.

'Hell, we all know he's sweet on her, but you don't need to embarrass the girl,' Brian said.

Mackenzie opened her mouth to protest, but no sound came out.

Hope said, 'Don't mind them, they gave me a completely different grilling when we came back from Mozambique. They're just like brothers watching out for each other. They don't get the whole other man's territory thing, that you're dating Cole and not all of them. They say inappropriate stuff but mean well. Besides, they're all jealous as hell that you got to watch the birth. Every one of them wanted to be there with their friend, like they usually are if they're on the farm, but they kept their distance, knowing you two needed some time alone. So it's all kind of sweet that these little macho boys care.'

Mackenzie just smiled in reply.

'Good to know you are staying then, Miss Mackenzie. Can I move your case into Cole's room?' Thandi asked.

'Thandi!' Mackenzie said.

'It's just less work washing one set of sheets rather than two if you are going to be pretending you are sleeping in them,' Thandi said.

Everyone laughed as Mackenzie felt herself blush.

Cole came back into the room and sat down. 'So what were you all laughing about?'

'Bad defence strategies, and if we have enough body armour and ammunition to take on the poachers,' Brian said.

Charl snorted, and Mandla laughed again.

'Liars.' He looked around. 'Tell me you're not harassing Mackenzie.'

'Not at all,' Mackenzie said, but she looked at her coffee and not at Cole.

'You lying to me now, too? *Eish*, I leave you alone with this lot for one quick phone call and you're siding with them?' Cole said as Thandi placed his breakfast in front of him.

'In all seriousness, we need to order more body armour,' Brian said. 'I'm not sure we have enough for everyone on the ranch.'

'Fine, I'll get Seth onto it. You mentioned you need more rounds? You always travel like your own private army, why do you think we'll be short?'

'I don't, I'm hoping not to use too many,' Brian said.

'*Ja*, but you might need more when this is over. I have had a few of your anti-poaching guards practising in the range because if they are going to be in the field with me, then I'm not getting shot in the back by accident,' Charl said.

'Understandable. How were their scores?'

'Man, you have some sharp shooters in your squad. I wish more farmers trained their guards as well as you do,' Charl said.

Mackenzie listened to the exchange going on around the table. They sounded like a family. They argued but in a nice way, and they sorted through all their problems together, one way or another.

That was just what she was hoping would happen when her folks arrived the next day. She wanted her family back together. Sure they were probably a little more dysfunctional than most, but at least they were a real family, and they were being given another chance.

CHAPTER
29

The morning sun shone brightly as the private Learjet 45 touched down on the tarmac with a sharp jolt at Pietermaritzburg Airport. Mackenzie paced while she waited. Cole automatically took both her hands in his and pulled her to him. He knew her well enough already to know that distraction was the best method to help her through this time.

'Relax, it's going to be okay,' he whispered to her. She hugged him back tightly. He could feel her anxiety radiating through her body, its normally fluid movements stiff and unnatural.

'Oh my! Look at you,' a shrill voice carried over the small crowd in the lobby, breaking Cole's thoughts.

'Mom!' Mackenzie said, stepping away from Cole. He felt her withdraw into herself as she took that step back, as if she didn't belong in his arms. Her parents were still a direct influence and he wished she had the newfound strength to stand up to them in person now as much as she'd done on the phone.

'You're so thin,' her mother said.

'I—I'm fine,' Mackenzie answered automatically.

'Typical women, talking about appearances instead of embracing each other,' said a smooth baritone voice beside her.

'Dad.'

Cole saw Mackenzie breathe deeply, hesitate to take a step forward and then it didn't matter, as the whole family was hugging each other. Mackenzie swallowed hard. Her mother cried giant tears but didn't reach for a tissue.

To an outsider, this would look like a normal family reunion. But Cole knew better.

The emotional turmoil Mackenzie had been put through by her father was astounding. He could still almost feel the sobs that had racked her body as he'd held her when she'd spoken about him letting her down. His father had died when he was just a boy but he knew that his family would never have acted so badly. He remembered his family unit always being supportive – until they were taken too early from him. He acknowledged that his family and hers lived in different worlds and that he might take a lifetime to understand hers.

'We're here now, dear.' The senator produced a pressed initialled hankerchief from his pocket and passed it to his wife. 'I'll sort everything out. We can do anything you need us to do for Lauren.'

'Dad, there's nothing to sort out,' Mackenzie said, sniffing, but quite firmly. 'I'll finish organising Lauren's affairs when I can. Until then, just enjoy the visit with me. It's great to see you guys.'

Cole winked at her, letting her know he'd heard her stand up to her dad. He stepped up to the family. 'Cole Howe, Mackenzie's friend,' he said and shook hands with the senator. 'Nice to meet you, Senator.' The senator's handshake was firm but not overpowering. It didn't signal a man trying to be in charge to Cole.

'Please just call me Bob,' the man insisted. 'And my lovely wife, Lilly.'

Cole shook Lilly's hand and felt the smoothness of her skin, but also the cold clamminess of someone who was stressed. Someone who was obviously nervous.

Cole smiled. If Mackenzie's parents were nervous and cautious, that meant they weren't so sure of their place in her life now that she was in South Africa, and that meant that Mackenzie had won this round. She was on the right road towards them accepting her independence from them.

He couldn't wait to tell her.

* * *

The black stretch limousine outside could only be there for someone famous or official and her parents were already climbing in the back. Mackenzie hesitated. She was torn between not wanting to spend the next hour and a half closed up with her parents and wishing to catch up on every detail of their lives. Butterflies fluttered in her stomach as she flip-flopped uncertainly.

Lifting her chin, Mackenzie pushed down the feeling. 'I'm going to travel with Cole,' she told them. 'We'll have plenty of time to chatter when we get to *nTabaGrequa*. You might want to snooze on the way, it's a bit of a journey there.'

She turned towards Cole and the *bakkie*, her decision made. He reached out and captured her waist in his warm hand and, with a gentle tug towards him, he clasped the small of her back and tenderly held her with him as he walked.

She watched her parents' limo as he helped her strap into his vehicle. The chauffeur closed their door and climbed into the driver's seat.

Cole started out of the parking lot. She saw him look in the rearview mirror to ensure the limo was following them.

Mackenzie was shaking her head. 'I can't believe it, even here in the middle of the African bush my family managed to find a limo!'

Cole laughed aloud.

Mackenzie turned around to glance out of the back window.

'That's probably just who they are. Overall, that didn't go too badly,' Cole said. 'Your mum and dad seem happy and genuinely glad to see you.'

Mackenzie started to smile.

'I see it. It's a smile, Mackenzie. You smiled,' teased Cole as he ran his hand along the back of the seat and squeezed her shoulder.

Cole looked at her. 'They are not as sure of themselves as you think they are. Your mum especially. She was nervous.'

'She was?'

'You couldn't tell?'

'No, it's all sort of a blur.'

'Understandable. Your dad wasn't attempting to be an alpha male either. He was a little unsure of where he stood.'

'You think so?'

'I know so. Your parents might not be as much of a force as you remember them to be. It's possible that you leaving them has had an effect on them that you never counted on.'

'I'm sure it's only temporary. My daddy is the strongest, most stubborn man I know.'

'Well, that man might not have survived so well being knocked off the high pedestal he thought you used to hold him on. Give them time when we get to the ranch, see if you notice the changes.'

'I'll watch for that.'

'Right, we have this all down pat for when we get back to the ranch? Remember, despite this, it's still your territory. Your rules.'

'Sure.' She could see his wide grin and the way his eyes crinkled slightly at the corners.

Giving her a another sexy wink, he looked ahead to concentrate on the long drive home.

*　*　*

At the homestead Thandi stood proudly in her best black-and-white uniform on the steps. Just as she had for Mackenzie's first visit, only this time, she was not so friendly. She was very formal, keeping the usually fine line between maid and paid employee open like a steep chasm. Cole introduced Thandi and she showed Bob and Lilly Aurette to their room.

Despite laughing about sleeping in clean sheets, in the end Mackenzie had to move in with Cole to fit her parents in a room with their own bathroom, because she'd known that no hotel in town would have been good enough for her very fussy folks. She just hoped her mother would behave and not criticise anything. Not that there was much to criticise in Cole's house. Thandi ran it perfectly. As proof, the lunch she had laid out for everyone to meet and welcome Mackenzie's parents was a full-on buffet. An array of home-cooked breads, including mixed seed bread, shaved mustard ham, piles of sliced cold beef, plus fresh Cape crayfish salad, potato salad and a wonderful fresh baby spinach salad, graced the table, which Thandi proudly served out on the large verandah surrounding the homestead.

Siphiwe arrived a little late, having brought the zebra herd in for inoculations and then housing them in the large holding yard.

When the meal was over and while the workers returned out to the ranch for their duties, Cole, Mackenzie and her family retired to the loungers in the coolness of the verandah. Mackenzie was hanging on so tight to Cole's hand she thought perhaps the blood could have stopped flowing, but she simply couldn't let go.

'So, Nicole, you live here now?' Lilly asked.

'It feels like it lately, but I own a house in town. I've been here since the night that Lauren disappeared and they trashed my house. Alan, the police sergeant, was happy with the additional security that Cole's ranch provided.' The lump that formed in her throat every time she thought of her friend threatened to suffocate her.

'Don't you have any female friends who could've helped?' Lilly asked.

'No, Mom—'

Cole interrupted. 'Lilly, I sort of insisted as I was with Mackenzie when we interrupted the man who was destroying the contents of her home. The least I could do was to keep her safe. Alan's in total agreement that I can protect her better here, inside my extra-high-voltage security fence, rather than at her house in Crystalberg.'

'So you two are friends?' Bob asked. The tone was more of a statement than a question and the way he emphasised *friends* hit home.

'No. Yes.' Mackenzie didn't know how to describe them. She shifted uncomfortably on her chair.

'Good,' Bob said, looking at Cole. 'Nicole needs a strong man in her life, taking charge.'

'Bob!' Lilly exclaimed. 'You promised.' Her distress at the comment was evident to anyone listening, as she slammed both hands down on the chair. Mackenzie saw her dad's eyes widen in surprise.

'Sorry, ladies, Cole,' Bob said immediately. 'My apologies for the lapse. That's not what I meant at all, Nicole. What I mean is that it's nice that there's someone looking after you, not taking charge of you. I just want my little girl to be happy, I don't want anything bad to happen to you.'

'I appreciate that,' Cole said. 'Neither do I. That's why she's here.' She felt his hand squeeze hers again, then he surprised Mackenzie when he bent his head and kissed her mouth. Her knees went weak, her head spun and she had the most wonderful flying feeling. Cole was really kissing her, in front of her parents.

A discreet cough brought her back to reality. She felt the hot blush start at her chest and flush upwards. She grinned.

'So *friends* it is, Nicole,' her father said.

'Dad, everyone calls me Mackenzie now.'

'Aren't you going to go back to being called Nicole now that they know who you are?' he asked.

'No. I like being just Mackenzie.'

Her father's lips thinned, and he opened his mouth as if he was going to say something, then changed his mind.

'I'm happy for you, Nic—Mackenzie,' her mother said. 'It's nice that even though you were away from your family, you found people who care to surround yourself with. And that you could rely on, even after Lauren was taken from you.'

'I wouldn't want to be anywhere else,' she said and meant every word. 'And Lauren liked Cole, so knowing that brings a little comfort, too.'

Just being around her parents again was hard work. They brought up every insecurity deep inside her. She swallowed. She knew she needed to keep guard to ensure that they were not going to railroad her ever again, but so far, they had been more than nice. They were being pleasant, supportive, and she wondered if over time her views had grown out of proportion to the reality.

'Tomorrow you'll meet the anti-poaching unit that's here to protect Cole's cheetahs. Brian, Charl, Mandla and Hope. They're friends with Cole and have set all these fancy gadgets all over for surveillance, to add to the security,' Mackenzie said. 'They wanted to be here, but unfortunately had some manoeuvre to do this afternoon, so I had to tell you they say hi.'

'Was that added security necessary?' Bob asked, a crease of concern showing between his eyes. 'The double fence looks intimidating enough.'

'It usually is, but we've had some strange goings-on, breaches in security that we're not happy about,' Cole said.

'That's good news that you could call on extra support,' Bob said.

'I've been so spoilt here, Dad and thoroughly looked after,' Mackenzie said, then knowing her mother's heart had not been in the discussion she added, 'Mom, you must have a drink with me at this quaint Duduzo's Kofi Shop in town. They serve these hot chocolates to die for.'

'From the map, Crystalberg doesn't look like much of a town. Maybe a village.'

Mackenzie looked at her mother. Lilly was trying to not be a snob. 'It's a town. Do you know, I was here for over three months before I discovered what half their words meant? They all speak a lingo of Afrikaans, mixed in with Xhosa or Zulu and Sotho in this area. Quite strange.'

'We have a lot to learn about your travels,' Bob said.

'It's mostly been good. I've spent about eighteen months here in the mountains. Fresh air and lots of time for my art.'

Her father just smiled and an awkward silence followed.

Cole saved them. 'And she races my cheetahs, exercises them. It's quite a sight.'

'Now that I have to see,' Bob said. 'When she was a teenager we had to force her to attend martial arts. She was never one to like physical exercise.'

'Really?' Cole squeezed her hand and Mackenzie felt her heart overflow with how he was not alarming her parents about the attack, and how she'd had to fight then.

It was true that she had originally been forced into her classes, but once she began them, she had tried hard to succeed. Gain a new belt. Be the best. Anything to get her busy folks to notice she was doing something that they liked. She'd been so young and had just wanted their approval. Since leaving the States, she'd changed a lot, and although now she knew she no longer needed that approval, she thought it would be nice to at least have peace with her parents.

Bob looked at Mackenzie. 'What did you end up as, a yellow belt or something in Judo?'

'No, Dad, a brown belt in Taekwondo.'

'You have a brown belt in Taekwondo and that isn't mentioned in your folder from Alan?' Cole said, his forehead creased.

'I guess it didn't seem important,' Mackenzie said.

Cole said, 'Would you mind spending a little time with Charl to assess your skills? He's the martial expert in the team.'

'That would be interesting, they're a bit rusty,' Mackenzie said, 'but in case you didn't notice, Charl is rather large.'

Bob spluttered. 'Are you crazy? You're going to let Nic—Mackenzie do Taekwondo with one of your guards? She could get hurt.'

Cole looked at Mackenzie. She rolled her eyes, signalling him she'd had enough, then looked away. He cleared his throat. 'I don't own Mackenzie, she does what she wants, and doesn't need my permission to do anything. It's her choice and I have no right to "let" her do anything. But know that she wouldn't get hurt, not purposely,' Cole said. 'And in the light that Lauren was murdered, if Mackenzie had to land in that position of being captured, I would want her to fight with everything she had to get out alive.'

'I see. Guess that is a different way to look at the situation, then. Mackenzie must do what she feels is right,' Bob said.

Mackenzie looked at her dad. 'Believe me, I'll be getting on the mat to spar with Charl because I need to know for myself that I'm capable of fighting to my best ability if the need arises.'

'Yes, poor Lauren,' Lilly said. 'So tragic. I pray you never get into that situation.'

'Me too, Mom,' Mackenzie said, thinking of Lauren. Alan had told her that afternoon that she had now been transferred from the police morgue into a private facility, awaiting the funeral. Mackenzie hated the thought of her friend all alone. It wasn't a thought she wanted to keep close, instead she wanted to remember Lauren laughing, having a good time. Sharing in the wonders of her South Africa.

She thought back to the taxi incident. Cole had seen her fight for her life then, but afterwards when he had saved her, he'd continued protecting her, and she hadn't thought to remind him she could hold her own in a fight.

They still had so much to learn about each other and no matter how much time they had together, it was not going to ever be enough. Losing Lauren had proven that.

Too soon, the sun began to dip behind the magnificent Drakensberg mountains and dusk was imminent. The splashes of colour in the sky darkened into a deep inky blue when suddenly the air above boiled.

'What on earth?' asked Lilly, looking at the sky that had rippled with movement. She got up to stand by the railing.

'Birds, Mom. Thousands of them. They're called Indian mynas,' explained Mackenzie, joining her there. 'They're like a private army of small noisy aircraft!'

Bob stood on the other side of Lilly and for a moment the Aurette family stood together. Staring up at the sky until the flock of birds had dwindled, gone to roost, and the first evening stars began to sparkle in the night.

Lilly broke the silence. 'It's not that late, but I'm jet-lagged. I think if that's alright with you, we might have a little nap before dinner. Maybe join you later for a night cap if you're still awake?'

'Wonderful idea, dear,' Bob said, but to Mackenzie he seemed subdued.

'Sounds great,' Mackenzie said and looked at Cole. To Mackenzie's delight, he brought her hand up to his mouth and brushed a kiss along her knuckles.

'That it does,' he said. 'If we are not up, please make yourselves at home.'

'We will and thank you again, Cole, for everything.' Bob shook Cole's hand.

'Goodnight, Mackenzie,' he said and pulled her into a hug. He held onto her a bit tighter than he used to and rubbed his hands over her back. 'Thank you for calling us. I'm so relieved you're safe.'

'Oh, Dad,' Mackenzie said, tears welling in her eyes.

He stepped away and held out his hand for Lilly's.

Mackenzie watched her parents walk out of the room hand in hand. They were the same people as two years ago, but they were so much older now. There were subtle changes in them, like the fact that they moved together, where before her mother would have been slightly behind her father.

Cole had been right when he'd said to watch them for differences. She knew she'd changed in the years apart from her parents.

Could something have changed her parents, too, when she hadn't been around?

CHAPTER
30

It was almost eleven as Mackenzie sat in the lounge, sketching pictures of the birth of the cubs that she would use later for the frieze she was planning on doing. She swallowed a yawn just as she was interrupted by a small knock on the open door.

'Hey, Mom. Come on in,' Mackenzie said as she put down her pencil and pad. 'Take a seat. Can I get you a coffee, wine or something to nibble on?'

Her mother sat on the couch near her. Farren looked up as if wanting to know what was interrupting her sleep, then noticing that there was someone else to give her a fuss, she stretched out and attempted to climb onto Lilly's lap. Mackenzie saw her mother scratch Farren behind the ear.

'Nothing at the moment. Honey, I just wanted to say I'm sorry I didn't notice just how much you were living the life we chose and not your own,' said her mother quietly. 'I never realised that I was smothering you.'

'You didn't smother me,' said Mackenzie, immediately falling into passive mode, from years of knowing she was the one who had to give to keep the peace.

'But I didn't exactly let you fly free either.'

'No, you didn't,' replied Mackenzie truthfully, blowing out her breath through pinched lips.

'So, I just wanted you to know we've had lots of counselling together after you went away. After we parted on such bad terms.'

'We? Dad went to a counsellor?'

'Dad and I.' She nodded. 'Yes, him in therapy,' she said. 'Losing trust in one another was a big thing. Therapy was a *huge* step but it was necessary. We nearly fell apart. In trying to come to grips with the fact that you had been forced to turn away from us to protect yourself, because we wouldn't listen to you. We discovered a lot about ourselves we didn't know. I'm sorry.'

'Mom—'

'I promised your dad we'd do this together, so we'll chat more. We know now that we were so busy wanting you to be the perfect paper-doll daughter that we nearly lost you, pushed you away. When you tried to warn us that our perfect world was imploding, we didn't listen. When you left, your father and I were devastated. We nearly got divorced. I never thought that would ever happen to us. Ours was a political marriage, but we were also head-over-heels in love with one another. A true rarity in our circles.'

'You were in therapy? How awful. Causing you pain was never my intention.'

'You can't take all the credit,' she said weakly. 'Things had been wrong for a while, but we had just let them slide. It was easier. But when you went away, it all just came to a head, had to be dealt with.'

'Mom, you guys were only part of the reason. I left for me. I needed to learn to be independent. I knew you guys always wanted the best for me. It was just that we wanted different things. Are you guys still going to continue therapy or—'

'It's alright, honey, we worked it out. That's all that matters. We want you to know that when the time comes and you come home, we'll let those reporters know to respect your privacy. As a family.'

'Thanks, Mom, for treating me as an adult. I do appreciate it.'

Her mother smiled at her and reached for her hand. Mackenzie had missed her.

She swallowed the lump forming in her throat. 'Now, I'm going to have a cold glass of wine. Would you like some?'

'Splendid idea,' Lilly said and all the discomfort from their meeting vanished.

Mackenzie sipped her wine. Cole had indeed shown good taste when he'd introduced her to Graham Beck wines, and she remembered laughing at one of their dinners at Tannie Essie's when Cole had spilt a glass, and the waitress had mocked him about wasting great wine.

Her mother was still sitting near her when her father joined them in the lounge. He paced like a caged jackal. Up and down, almost wearing a path in the flooring.

'Dad, come and sit,' Mackenzie said. 'Have some wine.'

'I'm worried if I sit down, I may not get up again.' He turned towards her and she could see tears gathered in his eyes, unshed but present.

'Dad?' He walked towards her and sat down next to his wife, who made room for him without a word. He reached for Lilly's hand, as if needing her strength to reply.

'I thought I'd lost you forever,' he stated simply. 'My princess taken from me, but here you are. Independent and self-supporting, because I know you haven't been taking anything out of your accounts. I watch those.'

'Dad!'

'Hear me out. You're in a strange country, in a home of your own and living your life, but as far away as you could get from me. I never knew what a tyrant I was being. I worry that I lost you emotionally long before your physical disappearance, as our therapist suggested I might have.' A single tear rolled down his cheek.

Mackenzie realised she'd never seen her father cry.

She saw how tightly her mother held his hand, and looking at the two of them together made Mackenzie sad, too. Their hands were no longer those she remembered. They belonged to old people, veins showing, wrinkled and bony. Her mother's hair was streaked with grey, testament to the trauma they had gone through the last two years. Her dad, always upright and proud, now sat with hunched shoulders, his posture echoing the turmoil.

'Dad,' she said. 'Where do we start and finish without hurting each other more?'

'Again. We start again. That's what the therapist said. We can talk through the past, but we need to start afresh, distance ourselves from it, or we could land up in the same hellhole again and I couldn't stand that.'

Mackenzie thought about his words. In her mind she'd replayed how she expected this scenario to go and not once had her rehearsals gone like this.

He was asking her to forgive and forget. She wanted to, but it wasn't going to be easy. She'd known that even before she'd called them and invited them back into her life.

He interrupted her thoughts. 'I broke your trust. I'm so sorry.'

It was a step in the right direction. Sitting forward on the lounge, her wine abandoned on the floor, she took a deep breath. 'Okay, then we start over. I'd like that. I'm not sure how we'll do this, but I'm willing to try.'

'Me neither, my girl, but it's better than not knowing where you are every day. And if the media hounds come after you again for whatever reason, somehow we'll get them to leave you alone, together. Like we should have from the beginning. Family, that's what's most important.'

'Oh, Dad,' Mackenzie said and she leant over and hugged him. Her heart was filled with great sadness, but also brimming over with joy. He was trying to reach out and understand and she loved him for it. She'd always loved him, but she'd never understood how much he truly loved her, until now. She'd got through to him. Her self-exile to another country had achieved something bigger than she'd ever imagined.

Her family was at peace with each other.

'Look at us,' sniffed Lilly. 'Anyone who saw us would think that someone had died. This is supposed to be a happy reunion.'

'Mom!'

'Lilly,' Bob said.

'Oh, I know poor Lauren did, but that comment just backfired,' Lilly stammered.

And then all three were laughing, her mother wiping her eyes and everyone sitting close.

'You know what Lauren dying taught me?' Mackenzie said quietly. 'It taught me that you need to live your life to the fullest, not hold back, because you never know when you'll reach the end of your time here on earth. I miss her so much.' Her voice choked up on emotion and was barely audible on her last word.

'Oh, Mackenzie, that wasn't a slight on Lauren,' her mother said.

'I know, Mom. But she was murdered. She came here to see me and someone killed her. Alan said he was looking for a suspect, but until they catch him, it's hard not to think of her killer still being free out there, while we hide here, safe behind Cole's fence. It seems unreal. Everything was just going so well. Cole and I were dating, getting to know each other, Lauren visiting, and believe me, she loved it here, and my artworks were shipping to New York, then suddenly everything has gone crazy. The moment I let people back into my life again, it all went haywire.'

'No, don't think like that. We are where we should be, beside you. I know that you don't need looking after anymore. Your mom and I both know that now. Life sometimes takes a strange turn. Lauren was happy here visiting you before she died and you need to hold onto that, not the sadness of her death. You've experienced enough sadness in your life, Mackenzie. Remember her in happier times or you let her killer win, because he'll destroy you, too.'

'When did you get such insight, Dad?' Mackenzie asked as she smiled at him through her tears.

'You know that counsellor your mom took me to, well we talked about lots more than just you.'

Mackenzie grinned.

'So, onto a subject that isn't sad. Mackenzie, tell me about your artistic career and sending artwork to New York,' Bob said.

'Ask, Bob, asking, not instructing, remember,' prompted Lilly.

Bob nodded. 'One and a half years of therapy versus sixty-five years of habit. I'm still working on that one, Lilly.' But there was no malice in his voice after her small reprimand.

Mackenzie stared. This was a side to her parents she'd never seen and she liked it. 'Where do you want me to start? The part where I can tell you my art supports me financially? Or the part that I tell you that I still love being an artist and sculpting? I need it to keep me sane. It helped so much during the last two years. My art filled my days and nights. I've found so many creatures here in Africa that my fingers tingle at the thought of sculpting them. I'm simply dying to do another real-life-size bronze.'

'Your father bought a piece last year. It's called *Bewildered*,' Lilly said, her voice excited, as if sharing something precious and magical with them.

'You bought *Bewildered*?' Mackenzie asked.

'Yes, it's in my office. I bought it from a gallery to remind me you were somewhere out there. It haunts me actually. It reminds me of you when I look at it from one angle and your mom, when she was younger, somehow. I couldn't be sure. It's beautiful. You're so talented, Mackenzie and I'm sorry I didn't see it earlier.'

'Wait here,' she said, then jumped up and went to collect her laptop. Opening it, she quickly navigated to where she wanted them to see and turned it around to share the contents of the screen with them. The process of making *Bewildered*.

'But this clay figure has a face,' commented Bob.

'It did originally. Look closely, Dad, it was my face. I wiped it clean when I did the bronze, that's when *Solitude* became *Bewildered*. I realised I had erased my own identity along with it. I wasn't that girl anymore. That was my last life-size bronze. Until recently, I hadn't started work on another.'

'There's something about that statue, Mackenzie. I was wrong. All those years, I was so wrong.'

'Yes, Dad you were, but it's over. Call it … misguided, instead.'

'That, too. What's your new work?'

'It's just a drawing so far, no clay work done yet. I've been doing a few smaller bronzes. African animals that I can't make fast enough for the gallery to keep on their podiums. They practically walk out by themselves. I'm working on a series of children in a HIV orphanage in Pietermaritzburg. Lauren and I had just completed putting together a marketing campaign to target the American audience as a fundraiser as well. When she saw the first one of a little girl called Shoebox, she was so keen. We had a fundraiser planned for a week before Christmas to auction Shoebox off on the same day in South Africa that we were going to auction off Jabulani at her gallery in New York. Dual auctions for the same cause. Nadia, her assistant, will still run the auction in New York, but I'm not sure I can face the one here. I might postpone it a bit.'

'She was always the one who was smiling, the one who was laughing, coaxing you into doing things you never would have,' Lilly said.

Bob reached over and patted her arm. 'You grieve for your friend, honey and when the police catch the person responsible, you'll have closure.'

'Thanks, guys,' Mackenzie said.

Bob coughed as if clearing emotion from his throat. 'So, back to your art, my child. It has that quality, it seems real. When you touch it, you almost expect to feel warmness and a heartbeat inside.'

'That's a high compliment, Dad!'

'I bet there's a huge price tag attached to each one,' he said.

'Naturally!' She laughed and it felt good.

She and her father were actually having a conversation about art. *Who in the world would ever have imagined that?* She reached over and hugged him again.

She felt her mother squeeze her shoulder. 'That's nice. We're happy for you and proud. So proud, Mackenzie.'

A thought occurred to Mackenzie. She pulled away from her parents. 'Dad, how did you get hold of *Bewildered*?'

'I was contacted by an art dealer from New York who thought I might be interested in it.'

'Why you? You're not a collector.' Mackenzie asked.

'I asked our local gallery if they had seen anything of yours lately and then I got the call, was emailed a photo, saw it and bought it. Why do you ask?'

'Cole and I wondered if my art is being tracked by someone within the media, keeping tabs on where I am.'

'I never said anything to him about Monique being my daughter, not that I remember. In fact, now that I think about it, he was on and on about the mystique behind the artist, that you don't do personal appearances and haven't had a full art showing for years, but your work when it was available always sold really well.'

'It's okay, Dad, we just wondered, that's all,' Mackenzie said as she shut down her computer. 'So, what's new in the senator's office?'

'Nothing,' he replied.

'Oh come on, how can nothing be happening there? You're always doing everything, helping everyone, fighting for the green cause, some piece of dirt in threat of deforestation somewhere, a threatened species. Being the senator.'

'I was. Then once you were gone I found I didn't like the man who greeted me each day in the mirror. I began delegating a lot of my duties to younger staff members, those with real passion and determination to help the earth, not further themselves in politics. Although I'm still a senator, my term in office will be up next year and I'm not going to run for re-election. I've done enough for the people of Texas. Now I need to do things for my family and me. Once you're safe, I want to take your mom away on a long-overdue second honeymoon, perhaps make time for grandchildren—'

'Dad!'

CHAPTER
31

'Shit!' cursed Cole as he sat bolt upright in bed. 'Did you hear that?'

'What is it?' Mackenzie asked, still sleepy but aware that something was wrong.

'Gunfire. Get dressed and don't put the lights on. It's close. No one in the area reported they had any night shooting planned, so I'm suspecting it's our poachers.'

The sound of a small explosion had Cole jumping out of bed.

'Definitely our poaching friends. That was one of Brian's presents going off. We need to wake your folks up, get them to safety and then I'm going out to help Mandla, Charl and Brian.'

'Hope'll be in the thick of it, too, knowing her,' Mackenzie said, pulling on her trainers.

Hurrying, he led her out of their room.

They didn't even get to her parents' door before they saw Siphiwe barrel down the corridor, a semi-automatic weapon on his hip. 'Six shots. Four .9mm, two AK-47s. Explosion in the front fence area. Three different groups on the surveillance cameras. Brian said to come quick.'

Cole nodded. 'Come on, Mackenzie, let's get you all to safety, then I can deal with this.'

Knocking loudly on the door, Cole woke up Bob and Lilly, who although groggy, did exactly as Cole asked, crouching low as they headed for the study.

Fear ripped through her body, sweat beaded and ran down her back. She followed Cole step for step through the house and down the passage, her mom and dad close behind her, Siphiwe at the rear. They entered his study and Cole moved the coffee table. He flipped the mat up and wrenched open a hidden trapdoor in the floor. Siphiwe stood guard.

'Inside, quick,' Cole ordered. 'When you get to the bottom, there's a switch on the ladder, it's the light.'

Bob went first followed by Lilly.

As Mackenzie reached for the wooden ladder attached to the square hole in the floor she hesitated. 'What about you?'

'I want to stay with you but I need to help my team.' He traced the curve of her face with his hand. 'There are some old weapons on the shelf down there if you feel you need to arm yourself. Thandi'll be up here, watching the house. Be safe,' he said and kissed her deeply. 'Now go.'

Despite the logical part of her brain knowing it was best, she selfishly wanted him with her. Not outside being shot at.

'You can help me by staying safe. I can't take the chance you'll be hurt,' Cole said, guessing her thoughts again.

She looked at him then turned and made her way below. Bob had already found the light switch and neon light flooded the room.

'Time to go,' Siphiwe said to Cole.

'Mackenzie,' Cole called. 'I'll be back when it's over. Until then, stay down there. Stay out of sight,' he instructed. 'Lock the door after I close it.'

Mackenzie nodded. She climbed back up the ladder, and when the door thunked closed she fiddled with the latch and locked them in. She could hear the men's feet running on the floorboards above her as they left.

A sick fear churned in the pit of her stomach. It had all happened so fast. One moment she was with Cole, the next he'd chased her down this hole and hidden her. She knew he was protecting her, but who was protecting him?

The fluorescent lighting illuminated the square room. A few deck chairs were set up in the space. Wine-laden shelves surrounded them on three sides. On the last wall were a few shelves. Mackenzie was drawn to the weapons Cole had told her about. A collection of different swords and spears, neatly arranged. Some looked extremely old and exotic. A plaque beneath one spear bore the title: 'Battle of Blood River: 16 December 1838'.

Various other knives, swords and bayonets were all stacked neatly together, but three walking sticks lying on the bottom shelf caught her eye. If one hadn't been open, she wouldn't have known it concealed a dagger. She ran her finger over the shiny wood. No dust. She sniffed the air. Lemon scent lingered. Of course Thandi would also clean in the cellar, that was so typically her. She smiled at the comfort it gave her, knowing that this wasn't some forgotten space within the house, but loved as much as the rest of it.

She examined the other two sticks and saw that one was a gun of some sort, with a trigger in the handle. She could make out the metallic hollow tip at the end. The third stick appeared to be a normal walking aid, nothing menacing. A modern crossbow and a quiver of arrows were propped up in the corner.

'You okay, Mackenzie?' her father asked.

She was shaken but fine. 'Amazingly yes. Mom, you okay?'

'Why did you have to come to South Africa of all places?' Lilly said. 'It's bad enough we hear about the crime, now we're living it.'

Mackenzie said, 'Mom, it's not always like this, there are more good days than bad, I promise. Cole said that this is the poaching attack, the one we've all been waiting for.'

Mackenzie sat on a chair next to her folks. Her legs bounced up and down with tension. Her back was clammy with sweat. She got up and paced the room.

She wanted to be with Cole. She wanted to protect him, make sure no harm came to him. Mostly, she wanted to be sure that he'd be there for her tomorrow and the next day and all the days after that. She wanted to spend those days with him. She *desperately* wanted to, with all her heart. She wanted to spend the rest of her life near him, here on his ranch. With his cats, his zebras, the wildebeest and gentle giraffe. She wanted to hear the workers sing and the jackal cry in the distance. This was his world and she wanted to be part of it.

She was seriously in love with Cole. Just when it had happened she had no idea. Probably when he'd first invited her into his 4x4 to shelter from the storm in his driveway.

Where was he? Was he in danger?

She couldn't see the outline of the entrance in the floor, then she remembered that Cole had a large carpet over it. The light that would show through the outer hinges was most likely smothered by it. She wondered why Cole had a panic room under his house; this was no normal poky cellar.

She glanced at her watch just as it blinked: 3:45 am.

She looked at the ladder again. Just thinking of the danger Cole was in was making her feel queasy. She needed to be up there, too. She was capable of fighting by his side if needed. Sure she couldn't use a gun, but it couldn't be that hard, surely?

What if he died and she hadn't had a chance to tell him she loved him?

She flopped into the spare chair near her parents again. It creaked at the abuse.

Minutes ticked by as if in slow motion. She couldn't stay down here like a pampered princess. She needed to be topside. She needed to prove she could look out for Cole, just as much as he looked out for her.

'I can't do this, I can't stay here and do nothing!' she said, standing up again.

'Of course you can, down here you're safe,' Lilly said.

'What about Cole? How do I know he's safe? What if I could make a difference up there?' Mackenzie said.

'You don't. But that's what soldiers do, they protect you, Mackenzie,' Bob said. 'Your Cole and his team know what they're doing. You'd probably be more in his way than helping.'

'Dad!'

'No, Mackenzie, it's true. He knows what he's doing, he's done everything to protect you so far, to keep you safe. He's done a better job of it that I ever did, so let him do this for you.'

'I want to go up there and help Cole. I need to make sure nothing happens to those baby cheetahs. If anything happened to Jewels I couldn't take it that I was stuffed safely underground and they were hurt because I did nothing. And Zulu and Tala must be scared with all the noise going on. I can't stay here. I have to go above.'

Her dad's shoulders were slumped. Her mother sniffed.

'I don't want to cause you even more pain, but I need to do this,' she told them.

She began to arm herself, one large and one small knife and a third small dagger into her pocket. She looked longingly at the antique gun but she knew she didn't know how to load it. Damn.

'You should take the crossbow,' her father said as he retrieved it from the corner. 'I remember you used one of these at a school camp.'

'You remember that?'

'I remember more than you give me credit for, but that one stands out because I was livid that they'd let you learn to shoot the darn things. It was dangerous! Now I'm thankful that when you go up there, you have some skills that you can use in your defence. As much as I hate it, I can't talk you out of going. You go up there and be with Cole if that's what you have to do.'

'Thanks, Dad,' she said.

'Just promise me that you won't do anything stupid, that you'll try not to get hurt and that you'll take care!' Lilly said.

'I promise, Mom.'

Bob handed Mackenzie the crossbow and a quiver of arrows.

'Thanks, Dad,' she said, slipping them over her shoulder. 'You sure you want to stay in here?'

'Definitely, it's a war zone out there. Besides, Cole asked us to stay here. You might get away with going to him, but we would just be in his way,' Bob said.

She nodded, then turned towards the ladder. 'Lock it behind me when I'm gone,' she said as she climbed up towards the trapdoor and attempted to push the lid against the heavy carpet on top.

'I can't move it alone. Will you help me, Dad?'

'Of course I will if this is what you really want.' Bob began to climb up the ladder and carefully squeezed in next to his daughter.

'I do, Dad. I want him. One, two, three, push,' Mackenzie said as she put every muscle she possessed into pushing the trapdoor open, her father by her side.

CHAPTER
32

She slithered out of the trapdoor and her dad closed it quietly, relocking it behind her. Rolling out from under the carpet, she pulled the crossbow to her and lifted herself into a crouching position, keeping low, and made her way to the window to peer out. She couldn't see anything. It was too dark. But she knew that she should have been seeing the lights of the visitors' centre. Either they had load shedding at a really bad time or the electricity must have been switched off.

Following the outside of the room, she made her way to the door and out of the lounge, down the hall and opened the front door.

No one so far.

Still crouched, she stepped off the verandah.

'*Eish*, Miss Mackenzie,' Thandi said quietly beside her. 'I thought you were in the cellar room, safe.'

Mackenzie jumped. Turning, she answered, 'I can't stay there, I need to be near Cole, make sure he's safe.'

Thandi nodded. 'I think he knew you would do something like this. He asked me to patrol the house. Come on, he's at the vehicle sheds getting ready to go investigate the shootings. Alan just arrived, too. I'll take you there but you must leave that crossbow behind if you don't know how to use it properly. It will hurt you more than help you and some of the knives, too, unless you have knife training along with your martial arts.'

'I thought it would be better that I have something, rather than nothing. I can use a crossbow, but it's been many years—'

'Might come in handy, then. Keep that dagger, it's the best of the three,' Thandi said.

Mackenzie unloaded the rest of her arsenal on the nearby table and followed Thandi. They climbed into one of the ranch vehicles, and without lights drove to the shed where Brian had been concocting his explosives. She saw Cole loading boxes of ammo onto the back of the vehicle, surrounded by his game guards.

*   *   *

He saw Thandi's *bakkie* arrive in the pre-dawn light and knew that Mackenzie was out of hiding. His instincts had been right, he'd known that she wouldn't stay put. She was too strong-willed and stubborn to listen to him. Yet those were the exact qualities that would help her through this attack. He loved her even more for it.

He placed a large box into the tray and walked towards the ladies. 'So, Mackenzie, you didn't remain in the cellar like I asked?' He opened his arms and hugged her as she threw herself into his embrace. She felt perfect there, fitted into him like she was part of a puzzle in his life.

'I couldn't stay in there, knowing you're out here,' Mackenzie said.

Cole blew out a breath. 'What did I ever do to deserve this?' He kissed the top of her head and looked at her. 'I should be furious. I could be putting you at risk having you with me.'

'I know, but I wanted to tell you—'

He put his finger on her lips. 'Mackenzie, don't say anything now, we can talk afterwards, once you are safe, once the ranch is safe. If you are going to stay with me, that's fine, just stick to my side like glue, understood? Don't do anything, just stay by me. This is real danger, are you sure you want to do this?'

'Yes,' she said, 'I'm more than sure.'

'Right,' he said. 'We are almost ready to rock and roll. Thandi, bring Mackenzie some camo cream and a camo overall from the game guards' storeroom. Let's get her ready to go.'

* * *

'Where's Siphiwe?' Mackenzie asked.

'Guarding Hope. Mandla was already out doing perimeter patrol when the poachers hit,' Cole said as he drove with the lights off, her in the passenger seat, Alan standing on the back holding onto the roll bar, the large hunting light he held in his hand off at the moment. Four other game guards and three more policemen sat on the edge of the tray, loaded down with their R4s and extra packs of ammunition.

Alan and Cole both wore camouflage cream and Thandi had smeared some on Mackenzie's face, too. It smelt foul, almost like a mixture of paint and boot polish, and it felt as if her face had been covered with Vaseline. Her dagger was tucked into one of the large pockets on the pants of her overalls and her bulletproof vest was tightened underneath.

Cole had left her crossbow behind in the shed, and instead had placed a rifle between her legs in the car and showed her where the safety was. 'Not expecting you to need it, but just point and shoot if you have to. If it's your life or theirs …'

Taking a deep breath, she scanned the inner and outer fences in front of them for any sign that they had been breached, not that she knew what to look for, as every shadow looked menacing to her.

'Where are the others?' she whispered to Cole. 'Brian and Charl?'

'They already left by foot and have gone to where the fence was cut. They move like cats so they won't be detected easily. They specialise in anti-poaching and this is very much their territory. Hope is with Siphiwe and Dumisani. Their job is to guard the cheetahs and the cubs from within the centre. That's another reason why I didn't insist you return to the house with Thandi, as she'll join them there now. It's been a few years since I had any trouble here, but they seem to have come as an organised bunch this morning.

'Last night Hope found some additional information about her case and she'd passed it to Alan. Dominic and his boss-lady, maNtuli have had a major fallout, and she's out for his blood if he doesn't deliver her something she already paid him for. Our cheetahs. So he's throwing everything he can at this raid. Alan's police spotter also had some interesting intelligence when he made contact. Apparently, three people became eighteen this afternoon, and they came armed to the hilt, complete with a stolen game-capture vehicle. So Alan had his police vehicles already waiting, hidden just around the corner, even before the first shot was fired. He's got ground troops on the ranch already, and they will rendezvous with Mandla, Charl and Brian at the other end of the farm. Everyone was just waiting for the poachers to enter *nTaba-Grequa*, then they began to close the net behind them in the trap as planned.'

He slowed to take a corner and one of the policemen jumped off to open the small internal gate. 'It could still be something that whoever killed Lauren is influencing, so you have to listen to what I say at all times,' Cole said.

She said, 'There are things I need to tell you.'

'Me, too, but they'll have to wait for now. Just know that whatever happens this morning, I believe in you and your abilities or you wouldn't be here with me. I would have insisted that Thandi lock you down in the cellar again.' He paused as he negotiated around a small darker area, then continued. 'We'll go up behind the cheetah cages. That's where the infra-red camera tracked them entering. We'll see if they're there still and if they are, we'll cut them off from leaving again. We need to talk to a few of them, find out some things for Hope. If we can find them and get them in the spotlights then Alan can do his police thing.'

'Okay,' she said, her voice a little unsteady. Coming out to help him had been a great idea in theory, but being in an actual combat zone was scary and surreal.

Suddenly from the back of the *bakkie*, Alan switched the flashlight on, illuminating five figures running on the inside of the outer fence, but not inside the actual cheetah enclosure. On the inside the cheetahs ran together unusually as a pack. Spooked and stressed.

All hell broke loose.

* * *

Everything seemed to happen in slow motion. She watched as Cole reached over and pushed her down towards the floor of the *bakkie* and gunfire exploded around them. The windows shattered, causing glass fragments to rain down on her.

She could feel the difference in the vehicle as the men exited off the back and began scrambling behind it for cover. Cole dragged her out of the vehicle with him through the driver's side and pushed her flat on the ground, shielding her with his body on the opposite side to the poachers.

Cole's urgent voice could be heard above the din. 'Don't shoot into my cheetah pen. Don't shoot the cheetahs. The cheetahs are loose.'

Alan was calling instructions in Zulu to his policemen while bullets rained over the top of them, ricocheting against the metal of the *bakkie*. Someone shot the spotlight out and the area was plunged into darkness.

'Advance,' Alan instructed.

'Shit!' Cole said.

He reached into the cab and grabbed the CB radio from the dash. 'Base One. Base One, this is Mobile One. Come in.'

'Base One,' Hope's distinctive voice answered.

'Be careful. The cheetahs are all out of their pens!'

'Copy, Mobile One.'

'Mobile One out.' He dropped the radio microphone on the seat.

'Come, we need to help the others.' Cole held her hand and motioned for her to get into the back of the *bakkie*. 'Lie flat. Alan and his men have gone after this lot, they have to go close range with the cheetahs out.' While he spoke he was digging in the black ammo box on the back and he pulled out a second hunting lamp. He attached it to the battery pack, which the other light had been attached to.

'Stay down,' he said. Standing up on the back of the *bakkie*, he switched on the lamp and shone it just in front of where the poachers had been when they last saw them.

Three of the poachers were once again in the spotlight, and the policemen were almost on them. There was lots of shouting going on, and soon the men surrendered, putting their hands in the air and dropping to their knees without any further shots being fired. The policemen handcuffed them and started checking for concealed weapons. The other two poachers were missing.

In the silence she strained to hear anything. Then a single shot rang out, breaking the silence. She listened as it echoed within the valley.

'They are shooting at us!' Cole said. 'Get down!'

She tried to stay as flat as she could.

Another shot, louder this time, and there was no echo.

'Shit, I'm hit!' Cole groaned as he dropped onto the floor of the tray of the *bakkie*. Mackenzie watched in horror as the light fell over the side. It hit the ground and now shone upwards. Still attached to the battery pack, the light was creating a column of light in the dark sky. She ignored it and turned her attention to Cole.

'Cole,' Mackenzie whispered as she began a slow but deliberate search over his body in the dark. 'Where were you shot?' She could feel that he was clenching his teeth together, and sweat began to drip from his forehead.

'It's just my leg. I'll be fine. Just the initial shock of being shot, then the adrenaline will kick in and it won't be as bad.'

She felt him attempt to wipe his face on his shirt, and as her hands found his, she realised that he was applying direct pressure with both of his hands to his leg.

'I'm getting the light to see how bad it is.'

'No!' he said. 'If you do that, it'll illuminate us. There's already a chance that that sniper will take us both out. Who knows what type of scope he has, he could even have night vision.'

'So if I point it at him, I could blind him?' she asked. 'Night vision goggles don't like light. Even I know that.'

'Yes, but, you could make us targets—'

The gunfire began again and she scrambled over Cole. She found the light's cord, and pulled it up into the *bakkie*. Grabbing the handle, she pointed it towards where she had heard the shots come from. And showed a man about halfway up an electrical pole. He had his rifle at his side and was spraying bullets at where the poachers had last been seen on their knees.

With the spotlight now on him, he raised his gun to shoot in the general direction of the light.

'Oh my God,' Mackenzie said as she watched him point his gun directly at her.

Suddenly, there was a shot and the man dropped off the pole backwards.

Mackenzie held the light in both hands, still shining at the now bare pole, too stunned to move.

Silence followed.

Mackenzie drew in a ragged breath.

Cole's voice broke into the silence. 'There's still one missing. Sweep the area to help Alan see where he is. That was lucky he never got a shot at us.'

Mackenzie turned the light onto the back of the truck and onto Cole. 'How bad is your leg?' she asked.

There was blood splattered in the back, but it wasn't spraying from Cole's leg.

'I don't know, I'm applying as much pressure as I can just in case, and being honest it hurts like a bitch.' He breathed hard but deeply, trying desperately to control the pain.

She looked at his hands. 'There doesn't seem to be any blood seeping out between your fingers,' she said. 'Do you have a first-aid kit in this vehicle?'

'We can't do this now. You need to sweep the light and help Alan find that last poacher, he's still out there. You are making us a target with the light in the *bakkie*. Just do it, Mackenzie, before we lose him or he finds us and kills us.'

She lifted the light and swung it to where Alan had been when she had last seen him, but there was no one there, so she moved it further, travelling along the cheetah enclosure.

'There's nothing there,' she said.

'Try the other direction.'

She quickly returned the light to its original place, then turned it right, looking down the length of the enclosure. As she got to almost the end of the 180-degree sweep, she saw a person running towards them. She frowned. She didn't know a lot of the people who were helping tonight, but there was something about the man running towards her, fully clothed in camo and his gun pointed at them.

'Someone's coming,' she began to tell Cole but never finished, as a shot rang out. It zinged above her and she ducked.

'Shit,' Cole said as he let go of his leg and grabbed his .9mm from his belt. Pulling her under him protectively, he stabbed the light switch and turned it off, plunging them into darkness.

A different-sounding shot followed. A louder, closer shot, followed by a dull, sickening thud that she knew now meant a bullet had hit flesh. For a moment, all she could hear was their harsh breathing in the stillness of the night. Cole was still alright. The shot had hit the runner.

'Someone got him,' said Cole, but he didn't move. 'We should be okay now. That's all five here taken care of. Now to go save my cheetahs.'

'Cole, how's your leg?' she asked.

'Hurts like crazy, it's bleeding now that I took my hands off, so I've got to keep applying pressure or I would be hugging you.'

'Don't die on me, Cole!' she said. 'I can't have you die, too!'

'I don't plan to,' he said. 'It's only a leg wound.'

'Where do you keep your first-aid kit?' she said.

'In the front behind the seat.'

She jumped down, and finding the box, quickly climbed back into the tray of the *bakkie* and sat next to him.

She smiled then, because despite the fact that she was sitting in the back of a truck that had been shot up by poachers, Cole's actions had been to protect her.

Tears swam in her eyes as she used the scissors to cut away his camo pants from his leg, and expose the hole in his flesh.

CHAPTER
33

Hope already knew they were in deep trouble, so when the radio warning from Cole came through, she didn't allow the elevation of her fear to show.

When they had divvied up the responsibilities and sections for the response to the attack, Brian had split her and Mandla. She hadn't thought about it, knowing that she was a soldier and had to do her job. But now that she was facing cheetahs on the loose, she wished that he was closer to her.

At least he knew the cheetahs by name. They didn't know her at all …

But they knew both Dumisani and Siphiwe and both of them knew the centre as if it was their own home, so at least she had reliable, informed backup.

The original plan had gone to pot when Cole had radioed that the cheetahs were loose. Now instead of using the offices and walls as cover to hide from the poachers, they had taken to the roof space, because if the cheetahs had got inside and were threatened, there was a chance they could attack them in the heat of the moment. Tame or not. Both Siphiwe and Dumisani had been very clear on that point.

Now they were into Plan B. Many of the same preparations would work for the execution of this plan, too, so they would still be able to capture the poachers for interrogation.

They continued to shimmy through, above the office section, over the concrete walls, keeping single file on the interior structure and not putting any weight on the white boards that created the ceiling where they had been fitted. She had almost put her foot through it once already.

It was hot and she wasn't convinced that they wouldn't come across at least a *boomslang* or a fat python in the roof chasing mice while they moved around in it like reptiles themselves.

Siphiwe, on his stomach in front of her, put his hand up in a stop position.

They could hear someone talking below them in Afrikaans, but the voices were arguing. Mutiny among the thieves. The poachers were definitely already in the main building. She couldn't understand everything they said, but Siphiwe was listening intently.

They continued their path, silently passing over the passage area. Leaving the poachers behind. When they were in an office on the side nearest to the cages, Siphiwe opened the trapdoor and dropped noiselessly onto a desk in the office. One of the many preparations for getting the centre ready for the poachers' trap had been for Dumisani to rearrange all the office desks into strategic places. This would ensure they had access to and from the ceilings and roof-cavity areas in as many rooms as possible.

She followed, as did Dumisani behind her, after hanging as low as he could from the manhole before touching his feet to the desk.

Siphiwe drew his .9mm from its holster and stood by the door. Hope nodded, and he turned the handle. Slowly the door opened, making no noise at all.

They could still hear the voices but not as loudly, as they had walked away from their position. Hope patted her lower back with her left hand, checking that her two knives were safe, flat against her. Her Glock was in her right hand.

Dumisani walked soundlessly behind her as she followed Siphiwe down the passage, to a closed door that said, 'Private Do Not Enter'.

The voices were muffled now and they had switched to mostly English, but they were directly behind the door. Siphiwe made a sign with his hands that once again he would open the door and Hope would cover as he walked through first.

Siphiwe reached for the door handle, but it opened from the inside.

The man was looking into the room over his shoulder at his comrade, arguing with the person still inside, and his attention was not focused outwards.

'She's here and we'll find her. I will kill her, or you don't get another cent of your inflated paycheque,' he said. '*Verstaan jy?*'

Hope froze. She knew that voice. Thompson, the canned hunting farmer. She would never forget it. Despite being dressed in camo, she also recognised the crocodile-skin boots he wore constantly. That he spoke of her was obvious.

He was here to kill her.

Thompson still stood holding the door open. 'She thinks she can deceive me into believing that she was a hunting client? She's going to pay for the trickery. She was just lucky that Mandla found her in her plane wreck and not the hyenas or jackals like what should have happened. That bloody Paul Joyce should've done worse to her plane when he saw her at my farm. He should have blown it to bits and made sure she was dead.'

'I already told you, we couldn't confirm she is here, only the *e*-white American artist lady,' the other man spoke, his accent of no distinctive African origin.

'*Jy dom kaffir,* of course she's here, she's fucking Mandla now, and he's here. Why do you think I paid that old black bitch of a grandmother of yours so much money for such good weapons? To hunt measly cheetahs?' He laughed. '*Siestog.* I have to kill her before she returns to the UK. I tell you that's what the receptionist at her headquarters said, she will be going home soon. That or she works out in her silly half-caste head what is going on, and tries to arrest us all. I have to stop her today because I can't get this type of weapons as easily there in Britain and they'll cost more on her English soil.'

'Don't move,' Siphiwe commanded as he put the barrel of his .9mm into Thompson's stomach. Thompson reacted immediately and with surprising speed, despite his size. He barrelled into Siphiwe, knocking his gun out of his hand.

'Die, *kaffir*,' he shouted as he took Siphiwe down onto the floor with him, no weapon in his hand, just full-body-contact fighting.

Hope took a deep breath. Now she was sure who it was, she was enormously grateful that Siphiwe had taken point on the doors. Thompson was a bigger and stronger man than Siphiwe, but Hope had to believe that Siphiwe had the right training to put the man down. As she glanced up, Dumisani gave a shout to take cover as a shot splintered the doorframe from the other man inside the room.

Ignoring the grunts and groans, she slipped past Siphiwe and Thompson grappling on the floor and into the room. She dodged right immediately, looking for cover. There was none in the immediate vicinity, but a desk was situated further along at the end of the wall area.

Her eyes flicked around the room. It was an observation room for a birthing suite. Behind the glass was Cole's Lady Bess and her eight brand-new babies. The mother cheetah had retreated to the furthest corner and was hissing at the intrusion. Her face screwed up in anger, defending her babies against the threat that was too close.

Hope was relieved to see the poachers hadn't yet got their hands on her, or her precious cubs.

She dived forward towards the desk, knowing the cover was inadequate, but it could at least slow the bullets down as they came through the wood first. A shot hit the wall above her.

Dumisani was behind her and she heard him grunt at the sound of flesh being hit by a close contact bullet, but she knew that with the cheetah so close, she couldn't open fire. They couldn't risk the cheetahs.

Her assailant had the advantage. By keeping the glass at his back, he knew that they wouldn't attack, knowing that the cheetahs' mother could be potentially killed.

Hope hid herself behind the set of drawers in the desk, hoping that it had a kick panel in it to hide some of her as she feared she was too big for the small amount of cover. Dumisani had dived there, too, lying at her feet, using the only bit of cover they had, knowing it was weak. But it was better than nothing and they had to have something, at least until the poacher needed to change his magazine, when she could rush him.

The poacher, dressed all in camo and wearing a bottle-green balaclava, shot a few more rounds at them. They ripped through the wood, just as she lay flat on the floor next to Dumisani, her hands covering her head. All the time counting his shots.

Whatever he was using to shoot at them, it wasn't that accurate, as the bullets were all over the place. Even at close range he was the most inaccurate shot she had come across in a long time. That or his weapon was really badly maintained. Either way, she thanked her lucky stars.

She reached behind her and grabbed one of her throwing knives, listening as a few more shots rang out, then the telltale deadly silence of a click. A gun's trigger, connecting with a firing pin, but no ammunition in the chamber.

She raised herself to her knees, and with precision, threw her first knife at the assailant's throat. Her hand was already on her back, ready to throw the second if need be.

He dropped his weapon and clutched at his neck. As he pulled the small knife from where it was lodged, the blood that sprayed out in waves was enough to tell her that he would bleed out in no time.

She'd hit her mark. The carotid artery was closer to the surface than the more famous jugular vein and the bleed-out and immobilisation of a person was faster.

She turned to ensure that they were right in their calculation, in that only two people had been present.

Siphiwe no longer fought his assailant either. The bigger man lay dead on the floor, his neck at an unusual angle. Siphiwe was on his knees next to him, breathing hard from the exertion.

She turned to check Dumisani, who was on the floor behind the desk. Her backup. He had stayed behind her as arranged, watching her back, ensuring no one would get through to her from that side, just as Siphiwe had watched her front.

She called to him. 'Dumisani, you okay?'

No answer.

She walked over to him and could see where one of the bullets that had penetrated the desk had hit him in the cheek, another in his temple as he had crouched alongside her.

'You okay, Siphiwe?' she asked.

'I'm okay. Dumisani?'

'I'm sorry. He's dead. We need to flush out any others that may be inside.'

Siphiwe nodded and got to his feet. He picked up his fallen .9mm and checked his weapon. 'You taking your knife back?'

'Not on your life. I'm not touching his blood. I don't want HIV,' she said, before walking out of the room.

Siphiwe nodded and then followed.

They crept down the passage and together swept the whole of the inside of the visitors' centre. Methodically checking each room, making sure no one else was inside.

They came across Seth and Joel lying on the floor outside the light ammunitions room within the centre. Siphiwe checked their pulse in the neck, but both were dead. He shook his head to Hope. Leaving them where they lay, they ventured further towards the cheetah pens.

'Cole said someone let the cheetahs out of their cages, so someone could still be out there,' Hope said.

'I agree, but surely after all this time, with the shooting going on outside and no communication from the inside of the centre, they would have given up and run?' Siphiwe said.

'We can only hope, but I think we are in for another one. Is there any way we can switch on the lights out there?' Hope asked.

'We can, Mandla made it so we can always use lights when he put them up years ago. But be more than ready because when we flash on those lights, the poacher is either going to run or he's going to start shooting.'

'How far away is the switch?' Hope asked. 'How long till I have backup from you?'

'In the control room.' He indicated the way with his hand. 'Through that door, down a long passage, then it's the room. I will take about a minute to get back to you.'

She looked at the glass door leading out to the cheetah pens. 'Okay, but there is no cover here, I'll need to be off to the side.' She took her Glock out of the holster and loaded it. 'Right, any other lock on the doors and into the cages that I need to know about?'

'They have broken that one in the door and the chains are not there, so no, you will have a clear run out from here. They have probably broken the lock to the main fence of the cheetahs, too, but here is a key in case they have gone through the fence.' He took a bunch of tightly bound keys from his pocket and separated them. Chose one then passed it over. 'Be careful inside the cheetah pens. With them stressed and panicking, they might attack you. If they run at you, climb up the fence as high as you can!'

She nodded, taking the key and tucking it into her top pocket.

'Good luck and don't shoot me when I come to back you up,' Siphiwe said, walking away.

Hope smiled weakly, then she took some deep breaths to prepare herself while she moved to the side so she wasn't visible along with the cages when the lights were turned on again.

Her head was in turmoil. Thompson! Thompson had been there and Siphiwe had taken him down. Thompson had risked everything in being part of a poaching party attacking a cheetah ranch. To the world he was a successful farmer. A game farmer who was only suspected of canned lion hunting, not poaching or animal trapping. His vindictiveness against her meant that she had found something important that day, that she had something on him and he knew it. He had been there to shut her up. Permanently.

He had to have known about the bank account number that she had lifted from his study. She had pressed her boss for more information on it just two days ago and had given Alan the number, hoping that perhaps he would have more luck than their London office. Now her suspicions that they had someone in their office who was talking more than they should were confirmed. She filed the information in her head for use later, to sort out with James.

First the attack on her plane and now Thompson coming to the ranch. Clearly there must be a price on her head. She had obviously come closer to the mastermind than she realised and now she was a real risk for them. Her plan at the cheetah ranch had been to entrap the poachers, but at this moment it was she who felt trapped.

She was a walking target until they found the mastermind.

The lights flicked on, illuminating the whole cheetah pens outside. The area was larger than four soccer stadiums together and yet the lights shone as brightly as daylight.

She heard a diesel generator kick on, its engine loud as she scanned the pens. She saw no movement within the pens closest to the centre, no cheetahs streaking past to get out, no men running for cover from the lights. Nothing.

She looked again. Slower this time, ensuring that she searched in circles from closest to furthest away and back again, sweeping the whole area.

Then she saw them. Some of the cheetahs were there still, not stolen, and until they did a count, they wouldn't know for sure, but she could hear them chirping clearly.

She looked into the furthest enclosure. She could see them bunched together, mostly still.

Unsure if she should break the cover at the side of the centre and go outside, she waited for Siphiwe. She followed protocol and waited for her planned backup.

Before long, he joined her. He was breathing hard, testament that he had sprinted from the control room. Mandla was right, Siphiwe was a man who kept his word and would not let her down.

'I can't see anything, just the cheetahs,' she said.

He double-checked the area. 'Me neither. Come on, let's go out and make sure.'

Siphiwe walked out of the door first, his gun ready. She followed a few steps behind.

They found the cheetah enclosures gate lock broken and the gate open. Siphiwe shut it with the latch behind them and they walked into the first enclosure.

'Old man Nama should be in this enclosure.' Siphiwe whistled and one of the cheetahs broke away from a bunch in the middle pen. He walked towards them. Then he turned and went back into the group, reluctant to leave them.

'Come on, we need to go to them to see what they have. That's not normal behaviour for him,' Siphiwe said as he strode towards the next enclosure where all the cheetahs had congregated.

They approached cautiously. Siphiwe talked to them the whole time, calling each of them. As he got closer, he stopped suddenly, raised his weapon and shouted out.

'Put your hands in the air! Are you armed?'

'*Tjhee. Ema! Ema!* Don't shoot me,' the man called back, his hands going up in the air then going back down and up again.

They walked closer to the cats. Hope couldn't help laughing. The cats had cornered a human in their cage, but instead of mauling him to death, they were all over him.

'Come on, Nama, move.' Siphiwe pushed at one of the cheetahs. 'Sasha come on, stop licking him. He's not your friend.'

'They all want an extra fuss,' Hope said, laughing some more.

Siphiwe pushed them away and got the man to his feet. He patted him down only to find that he didn't have a weapon on him.

'*Lengau*, they likes me, they purr,' he said. 'Noah won't hurt *lengau*.'

Hope looked at Siphiwe and shook her head in disbelief. 'Noah Bongwanan, what did you think you were doing?'

'Madam,' Noah said. 'I see you again. You want some cats this time?'

Siphiwe smiled as he put cable ties around Noah's wrists. 'Man, you are so lucky. They don't realise you are a *skabenga*. Cole is going to love this!'

He began walking Noah out and the cheetahs all followed, chirping, as if knowing that their interaction time was done. 'Come on, guys, fun's over.'

Just then Thandi came into the enclosure with multiple leashes. A few others who worked with the cats hung back, still in the cover of the building.

'Is it safe?' Thandi called.

'You can retrieve the cheetahs and put them all into the quarantine cages inside, but the anti-poaching guards will need to scour the whole cheetah-pen areas for any weapons he might have dropped and for fence holes. I don't see a cage so I am not sure how they planned to remove the cheetahs. But I bet this Noah man will tell us all.'

'Nice cats,' Noah said, 'they are my friends. I fed them steak. Nice steak.'

Siphiwe pulled his phone from his pocket and dialled. 'Michelle, hi. The attack happened, yes … can you come and check the cheetahs for poisoning, just in case … No, one of the poachers claims he fed them steak. See you soon.' He hung up.

Thandi nodded. Then she motioned to the centre workers. A few came out of the shadows and walked into the enclosure with Thandi. Soon all the cheetahs had their own leashes on and were being taken into the visitors' centre to be put into the smaller quarantine cages inside.

Thandi then turned to Siphiwe and Hope. 'You are both needed outside.'

CHAPTER
34

Fear raced through Mackenzie as she drove Cole's *bakkie* towards the visitors' centre. Cole was hurt. He needed medical attention. She turned into the main parking lot and saw the mayhem in front of her and her fear became dread.

She shook her head when she saw how many people had descended onto the farm. It looked like a scene from a movie. The whole visitors' centre was brightly lit, the pens, the buildings, the parking lot. The sheds and the stables, all the other buildings around the enclosures, everywhere looked like daylight, and yet the sun was barely lightening the clouds on the mountains.

There were police vehicles all over the lawn. A helicopter sat in the middle of the parking lot next to the visitors' centre and three large personnel carriers in camouflage colours flanked it. People in various uniforms were gathered around. The helicopter medical personnel in tangerine-orange suits walked purposefully, as if they at least knew what was going on.

She relived the last half hour over and over in her head, especially the part where Alan had arrived at the truck, in no time, and he had to have been the one who shot the final poacher, saving her and Cole.

Alan had taken control of the situation, shouting orders to the men around them, while administering first aid to Cole. He had asked her to drive the *bakkie* to the centre, all the while assuring her that Cole would be okay.

A police van had passed them in the veld before she had got to the gate and Alan had instructed that the dead poachers be placed inside and driven towards the centre somewhere behind her. It seemed that he had been on the police radio constantly since the attack.

As she pulled up into the parking lot, Mandla walked towards her. He was a mess. Camouflage clothes, a floppy hat that now looked like a bird's nest of twigs had been dumped on his head, and his weapon was slung over his shoulder, carried on his back with its barrel pointing down. Opening her door, he reached for her hand as she climbed out of the driver's side. As her feet touched terra firma, her legs collapsed beneath her, refusing to hold her weight. He held her up and against him, her legs still shaking.

'You did good. Put your weight back on your legs slowly. You are strong. We need to get Cole to an ambulance,' Mandla said. 'Come on, be brave. He needs you now. He isn't dead. You did great out there.'

Slowly, he released her and she regained control of her legs.

'Take deep, slow breaths,' he instructed.

She did and she found it helped, but it did nothing to still her racing heart. She watched as the paramedics rushed to Cole's side. She could hear Alan shouting orders to the policemen who'd gathered around his vehicle and gave her a thumbs-up when he looked at her. She did the same to him, letting him know she was alright.

'I need to be with Cole,' Mackenzie said, attempting to stand next to the paramedics who were talking quietly, focused on him.

'Give them some space to do their job,' Mandla said.

She backed off a little but not far and looked around, knowing that Cole was in safe hands.

She scanned the ranch around her. A *piet-my-vrou* serenaded the morning, incongruous after the shooting and violence the ranch had just experienced.

Mandla broke into the fog in her head. 'Your folks are on their way down and will be here shortly. Thandi went to fetch them in one of the *bakkies*.'

'Thank you,' Mackenzie said, keeping an eye on where they were taking Cole. She saw someone signal to Mandla with his hands and point to the ambulance heading towards a helicopter.

Mandla tugged on her arm. 'Come, he's going this way.'

'Is everyone else okay? Are all the cheetahs okay? The babies? Zulu and Tala?'

'The cheetahs are all fine. But we have lost good men,' Mandla said as they walked side by side to the ambulances.

'I'm so sorry,' she said, but Mackenzie only had eyes for the man lying on the stretcher in front of her. The medical team had set up an IV. His trouser leg had been cut up to his crotch and his thigh was already swathed in bandages.

'Hey, Mackenzie. You okay?' Cole asked, his concern for her clear on his face. 'You did so good, I'm so proud of you.'

She studied him anxiously. He was a mess. There was blood splattered on his other pants leg and a fly buzzed around. As she gazed at his chest and into his face she became confused. His face, which was still covered in camo cream, had streaks where he'd attempted to rub sweat off it and the rivulets had left their mark. His green eyes sparkled like a five-year-old caught having fun. He was smiling. When he'd just been shot, had put her through the wringer wondering if he was going to be alright, he had the audacity to smile at her!

'No. Actually, I'm not,' she said as she stood beside him. He took her hand in his and it shook uncontrollably. 'I don't think that I'm as brave as I should be, because when I see you hurting, injured, then no, I'm not okay with that,' she admitted.

'Come here, you.' He pulled her to him. 'It's going to be okay. It's just the rush of danger and now the down afterwards.' He rubbed her arms.

'You got shot!' she said. 'I thought you were going to die too!'

'It's nothing. The hospital will have me up and out of there within a few hours, I'm sure.'

She shook her head. 'I was there, remember? I think it's more than a graze,' Mackenzie argued.

'I'm sure it's just a flesh wound, the bullet's passed right through, damaging nothing important. Seriously, Mackenzie, I'm going to be fine.'

He looked at his friend. 'Mandla, what about Hope, where's she?'

Mandla said, 'Hope is doing good, she'll be out here in a moment. She just went back inside to help put your cheetahs into the quarantine cages with Siphiwe and the other workers. They had an interesting time in there while you were getting shot, but she's good.'

'You going to marry her after this?' Cole asked.

'If she will have an old man like me,' Mandla admitted.

'Good,' Cole said.

'But I'm asking her, so don't go saying anything.'

'My lips are zipped tight,' Cole said.

Mackenzie listened to the exchange. Amazed that at a time like this, they could still be talking about relationships and marriage proposals ...

'Bad news is that Charl is injured. He's bad. He's going to be medevaced out to Durban. Sambo is also shot and will go with you to Crystalberg hospital. Seth, Joel and Dumisani didn't make it.'

'Dammit,' Cole said. 'So many! Tell me we at least got the people for Hope and Alan to question. Tell me we are closer to her mastermind and that their lives were not wasted.'

'They got more to question than we killed,' Mandla admitted.

'I'm so sorry, Cole, so sorry about your men,' Mackenzie said.

He pulled her close again and held her tightly. Looking over her head at Mandla, he asked, 'Any of my cheetahs dead?'

'No, Siphiwe said they're all accounted for. He called Michelle in to check them over, make sure they're all fine, not too stressed.'

'Please tell him thanks, Mandla.'

'There is one more thing. Your cheetahs, instead of mauling an intruder, they made friends with a simpleton named Noah Bongwanan. Hope identified him immediately, he was on the watch list. Apparently he was sent to put ropes around their necks. The guards found them thrown over the fence, but he hadn't got as far as tying them up when your cheetahs mobbed him with kindness.'

'Good, it's always a worry with large cats that they will kill someone. But to show kindness and friendship to an intruder, that also shows just how far some of the reintroduction work still has to go so that the cats know to avoid humans.'

'Guess your work is never done, then,' Mandla said.

Mackenzie stood up. The rising sun was brightening the morning as it began to burn the shadows of night into submission. She was distracted by a white van with black-clothed workers who were loading a closed plastic bag onto a trolley. Nine black bags were neatly lined up next to their vehicle.

'Are Seth, Joel and Dumisani in those bags?' Mackenzie asked Mandla quietly.

'Yes,' he whispered.

'Go safely, my friends, may the way to heaven be bright,' Cole said.

They looked at the morgue van as it loaded each man carefully onto a stretcher and then racked them inside. Their movements slow, deliberate and with the utmost respect in their handling of the corpses.

Tears ran down Mackenzie's face as she thought of the first day she'd been at the ranch and seen Joel. He'd been working with the horses in the paddock, and while Cole was a born horseman, Joel was a natural groom. He'd talked to the horses soothingly, had everything in his tack room spotless and neat. You could almost eat off the floor in his stables, they were so clean. And now he was dead.

Dumisani had been a constant since the day she got there, too, always shadowing Siphiwe and Cole when they locked down at night, always in the office and at the front desk, smiling broadly to the visitors at the centre.

She'd only known Seth briefly, when he'd come to the welcome dinner for her folks, but she could still see his broad nose and infectious smile in her mind. She knew that one day she would make bronze statues of each of them. She would talk to Cole about the idea later, a tribute to the fallen in their honour.

Cole remained silent for a moment, then he said, 'Who are the others in the bags?'

Mandla shook his head. 'Gun runners and poachers who were after the animals. They had split into three groups. The group you got were the poachers after your cheetahs. Their plan appeared to be to get the simpleton, Noah Bongwanan, to put leashes on them and then they would cut a hole in the fence and walk them to two taxis waiting on the side of the road. We got the one taxi, but the other one got away. We don't hold out much hope of getting it. It didn't have any distinctive markings so it will just look like any other minibus and probably had a false numberplate, but Alan has put the call out anyway. Noah's the one in custody. The group that we caught on the far side where we were patrolling were attempting to load your *blesbok* into a game truck. They were more organised than those you took on, seemed more mercenary, well trained. But we brought in a few still for Hope and Alan, we didn't kill them all.'

'Sure they appreciate that. We need information now,' Cole said.

'The odd ball out was a white guy that Hope, Siphiwe and Dumisani encountered inside the centre. Thompson, he was from the Limpopo region. Siphiwe put him down. You have a good man there in Siphiwe.'

'I know, that's why I said he needed to protect your woman in battle. Mind her back when you and I couldn't.'

'Much appreciated, *bra*. Then there was Dominic Bongwanan, who was with Thompson inside the centre. Siphiwe and Hope said that they were looking for her to silence her. Guess that backfired. But that part gives me the willies. That perhaps this isn't over yet. Alan is going to talk with her about them later. It appears there is more to this than just your cheetahs and Hope appears to be in the thick of it.'

Brian appeared next to Mandla as Cole was waiting to be placed in the ambulance. 'You dead and dying or will you pull through?'

'I'll be home by this afternoon, count on it,' Cole said.

'That's my boy!' Brian shook Cole's hand. 'You know most of those poachers aren't locals. We suspect some came in from near the Zimbabwe–Mozambique borders and Alan thinks he recognises some as mercenaries and a few thugs from the Johannesburg area, from the police database. I'm certain that we haven't heard the last of them. Apparently, they were promised big money to come on this cheetah capture. They were taking the *blesbok* for bush meat to sell in the markets. I very much doubt the mastermind behind the operation is here with them, or they would never have tried something like that. Whoever paid them is not in control of this ragtag lot, and the mastermind behind the actual targeting of the cheetahs is obviously somewhere else. Guess a few dead men don't matter much to him.'

Mackenzie squeezed Cole's hand. 'That could have been you,' she said quietly. 'It could have been you who died today.'

'Yes. And it could have been you, too. But it isn't,' Cole said. 'Don't dwell on what could have been, just focus on what is. We're okay.' He turned back to Brian. 'Did you see how Charl was doing?'

'He's stable,' Brian said. 'Doc said the medevac is about to lift off, then your ambulance can get moving. Liza is going with Charl. She just told us so in no uncertain terms.'

'Liza spoke?' Cole asked.

'Oh yes, guess something was at last worth talking about and broke through into her stubborn mind,' Brian said.

'That's the best news today,' Cole said.

'See you when you get back in a few hours,' Brian said. 'You travel safe. Mandla and I'll stay here for the debrief and fill you in when you get home.'

'Thanks, guys,' Cole said. 'Hopefully I won't be long.'

'I'll hold you to that,' Brian said as the paramedics loaded Cole into the ambulance. Other than a faint *beep-beep* sound from a heart monitor that Cole was hooked up to, there was silence inside the vehicle compared to the noise outside.

Seating Mackenzie near him, they closed the doors.

Cole closed his eyes for a second, as the ambulance officer checked his wound. Slowly he opened them again. 'Seth and Joel did the lockup without me last night because your folks had arrived.'

The words *I was with you* were not spoken, but she could hear the guilt in his voice that his men had died. Guilt weighed heavily on her own shoulders. Then relief.

Having her parents here had probably saved his life. She would forever feel relief that he hadn't done his normal lockup for the night, because they had been together after her parents went to bed, but she wouldn't regret it for a moment.

Cole was still alive.

'Apparently the poachers had jumped them and beat them badly. They must have been there for some time before Seth surfaced and dragged himself to the ammunitions room. He'd already unlocked the safe and loaded his weapon when the poachers made a second attempt on him. He killed two attackers. That was the initial shooting that we heard and then everything went to hell when the other poachers tried to come to their aid. We were lucky there weren't more deaths today.'

Mackenzie shuddered. 'You are one amazing man, do you know that?'

'This is my ranch and I protect what's mine.'

She saw a frown creep onto his forehead. He was holding back on her, not telling her everything. She hated that he was treating her like that. So far he had done everything to bolster her courage and her independence, why was he now keeping secrets? How badly would they affect her in the future?

'What, what was the rest you were going to say?' she asked.

'I was going to say I always have and I always will, but I wasn't able to protect Melissa and Marco all those years ago.'

'You can't think like that. You can't protect everyone from everything.'

'I asked her not to drive in that storm. But she did, and because of that they died, and there was nothing I could do.'

'No, because you're not a god. But I'm sure she knew, even with her last breath, how much you loved her and your son. She knew love while she was alive. You need to stop beating yourself up over something that you had no control over. Give yourself some credit for being a decent human being. You can't wrap everyone around you in cotton wool and have them live a half-life. You need to let go of the guilt you've been living with. You did the best you could at the time, and she knew you loved her.'

Cole smiled and kissed her hand. 'Thank you, Mackenzie.'

He rested his eyes and then he opened them quickly and looked at the paramedic. 'Any news on the medevac carrying Charl?'

The paramedic checked over the radio and came back to him. 'He's still stable and travelling well.'

'Hang in there, *boet*,' Cole said.

CHAPTER

35

Bob held the door of the *bakkie* open while Cole arranged his crutches and slipped out, the black rubber bottom gripping on the dirt driveway.

'Thanks,' Cole said.

'My pleasure, take care going up with those,' Bob said as he pointed to Cole's front steps. 'Glad to see you home almost in one piece.'

'Okay,' he said, but he took extra care nonetheless.

Mackenzie got out of the *bakkie* and hugged her mother. 'It's good to be back. I know I was only gone for a few hours, but I never got to talk to you after the attack, make sure you guys were okay.'

'We're both fine. Thandi called us out of that interesting room right after everything settled down,' Lilly said. 'Thanks to Cole putting us down there, we weren't in anyone's way and we were safe.'

Mackenzie smiled. 'Good to know, Mom, and so glad you feel that way. Not having to worry about you sure helped me, as well.'

'We worried about you, and everyone,' Bob said. 'We're eternally grateful that you were unharmed.' He hugged her to his chest and held her close.

Cole watched and couldn't help but think how hard it must be for a father to see his daughter grow up and go into a combat zone, and not try to keep her safe himself, but trust in another to do that. Cole shook his head at the family, now so at ease with each other. He stood in awe of Mackenzie that she had managed to take such deep hurt and put it aside, start again with her folks on a more mature level.

'I'm pleased about that, too.' Mackenzie walked up the steps to where he stood.

He looked around, the police cars had all dispersed and the only evidence Cole could see that they had been there earlier were deep tyre tracks in his lawn. He smelt the air. It was good to be home, even if he'd only been gone a few hours.

Most importantly, it was fantastic to have Mackenzie by his side as he walked onto the verandah. She belonged here with him. It had been the most natural thing to have her with him in the emergency ward, holding his hand. Her touch, above everything, calmed him and brought peace to his world.

'About time, lazybones. Just because you got shot doesn't mean you can waste the whole day away at the hospital. We have tracks to follow, more poachers to catch, new traps to set.' Brian clapped Cole on the back. 'You look well enough. Flesh wound or worse?'

'Flesh. A few painkillers and I'm good to go.'

'That's my *seuntjie*.' Brian nodded his encouragement.

'The doctor said rest, at least three days with your leg up,' Mackenzie reminded him.

'Bah, by tomorrow I'll be able to ditch the crutches and just walk with a small limp,' Cole said, but he reached over and squeezed her shoulder. 'Any news on how Charl's doing?'

'They re-inflated his lung. And they inserted a chest drain. The bullet made a bit of a mess but they have fixed it all up. He's in ICU but he's stable,' Brian said.

'Good to hear,' Cole said, getting ready to lower himself into the chair that Mackenzie was leading him to. He handed her the crutches.

'Darn thing went right through his vest,' Brian said. 'Guess we need to look around for a better type of bulletproof vest, because none of us will trust that make again. We are waiting on Alan to get us samples of the bullets those bastards were using. We think somehow they might have got their hands on some new equipment coming out of the States that's designed to penetrate vests, and if that is the case, we are all in trouble.'

'I'm with you on that. When you find a new supplier, don't forget me and Thandi and I'll order a few for all the guards here on the ranch, too. I think there will be a few protocol changes to lockup at night.' He sat down. 'A cup of tea, shower and then everything will be good.'

He watched Mackenzie drag the table around slightly and leant forward to help.

'I can do it,' she said, batting his hands away. Once she had it where it was wanted, she lifted his leg to rest on it. Mackenzie sat in the chair next to him. He reached over and pulled her hand into his lap and threaded his fingers through her softer ones. Her spicy oriental scent wafted up and he inhaled deeply.

Thandi came out and put a cup of tea on the table next to him, while shaking her head. 'I told you you'd get shot one day,' she said. 'You've got a nice home here, nice woman. I told you to leave chasing *tsotsies* to the others and now look at you.'

'I'm going to be fine. Thanks for your concern anyway,' Cole said.

'Concern? I should smack you on the head with a frying pan for causing Mackenzie and me to worry. Shame on you,' Thandi said, then stalked back into the house.

'We love you too, Thandi,' Brian called.

Cole picked up his tea.

'No offence, Cole, but your maid is mad,' Bob said as he and Lilly joined them.

'Who? Thandi? No. She's family,' Cole said to Mackenzie's parents, who were sitting together. They looked relaxed enough, for having been trapped in the cellar while a war raged.

'The first day I walked into this house after buying the ranch, I was just nineteen and in my second year at university. I'd looked around at other places, but when I saw this chunk of dirt, I knew it was home. The house had been abandoned years before and was a rats' haven. Thandi came to the door while I was looking about. She said something like, "*Baas*, you are so skinny, you are going to need a good maid to take care of you." I took her on that same day.'

Brian chuckled. 'That tough old bird took pity on Charl and me from the first time we visited. There was only one bed in the house for Cole, but she plaited traditional sleeping mats for us to camp on. And when Mandla came along, she told him he had to sleep in the *ikhaya* outside, the mud hut with the thatched roof, because he was black and this was a white man's house, because although she fought for equality, that was just how it was, and she couldn't have people talking horrible about her *baas*. The house has always been her domain.'

'That's just dreadful,' Lilly said, the expression on her face one of horror.

Cole shook his head. 'No, you have to understand, it was before apartheid was disbanded. At that time, it was the norm, except that the four of us were always together in the SADF, so we just ignored her anyway and did our own thing.'

Brian added, 'And times changed soon enough after that, so it didn't seem to matter at the time. I've seen Thandi take down a spitting cobra with a shotgun at about fifteen metres. She's very sane, that old bird. Courageous, strong-willed, opinionated, but not mad.'

Cole watched Mackenzie hide a smile behind her hand. He suspected it was because two grown men had jumped to the defence of an old woman, but he wasn't sure. It might have just been because neither of them thought twice before letting the senator know their opinions, that here her father wasn't treated like a pampered politician, but just her father.

'That she is, and I think she's lovely,' Lilly said. 'It's a totally different life from ours in the States.'

'You can say that again,' Bob said. 'At our press conference earlier there was chaos. Thank goodness we had been briefed about the goings-on here so we were able to swing the focus onto cheetah conservation and illegal smuggling of endangered animals. Not that I know a lot about that, but we sure put light onto the work Global Wildlife International are doing to track the mastermind behind this attack, like Alan asked us to.'

'Alan filled us in about that at the hospital. Thank you. That was quick thinking on your part. No amount of advertising can buy that type of exposure, the cheetahs and I owe you one,' Cole said.

'No, you don't. We're more than even. Not only did you keep Mackenzie safe, I don't believe that the media are a threat to my daughter's life anymore. She can live as she chooses now. She proved beyond a doubt that she's a grown woman and has chosen friends around her who are able to help protect her.'

'We had a little help, but we'll take the credit, thanks, Bob,' Cole said.

'Cole, you've made my daughter happy and I thank you for that,' Bob said.

'Thank you, Dad.' Mackenzie got up and hugged him.

Cole watched the closeness of the family and felt isolated. The same uneasy feeling he'd always had after his mother and father had died in the road accident, the same one he'd felt when he'd lost Melissa and Marco. As if he was on the outside of a glass house, looking in. A feeling of dread crept around his heart.

That was what it would be like if Mackenzie wasn't there anymore. He would feel like that again – every day. He shook his head to clear the image away.

'Bob and I had a quick look in your visitors' centre earlier. It's wonderful, not at all like a zoo,' Lilly said, her voice slicing through his thoughts.

'Thanks,' Cole said. 'We've worked hard to make it more of a natural habitat. I'll take you down once I've had a shower. We can show you the new cubs that were born a few nights ago,' Cole said. 'I want to check on them and my cheetahs myself anyway.'

*   *   *

It had taken three vehicles to transport everyone down to the visitors' centre once Cole had showered. Brian, Hope, and Mandla, all still heavily armed, drove the front car, Thandi driving with Bob sitting shotgun and Lilly in the back were in the middle and finally Mackenzie and Cole at the rear. Although Mackenzie had wanted him to rest and have a sleep, he had laughed at the notion and continued with his day as if he hadn't just been shot.

On entering the centre Mackenzie immediately recognised the difference in the atmosphere. It felt closed and sombre. Everyone felt the effects from the attack on the small community and they were all solemn, guarded and dealing with the loss of their men in their own way.

Cole stopped outside the nursery door, which looked a little beaten up and would need some work to restore it. Mackenzie pushed it open for him.

'Hey, good to see you up and about,' Michelle said to Cole as they entered the cheetah nursery. 'Heard you got shot.'

'Yeah but I'm good. Thanks to both of you for coming and for being here.' Cole shook Koos's hand in greeting.

'*Ja*, you should have told me what was going down, I could have been in on the action,' Koos said.

'Thanks for not telling him, I don't want him shot, too,' Michelle said.

Cole smiled. 'You've met Mackenzie's parents already, I believe?'

'I had the pleasure this morning.' Michelle nodded her head in their direction as a greeting and Koos grinned and waved. 'The babies are doing well. I spoke to the vet up at DeWildt today, remember Vernon? He wanted to come and see them for his research. I told him I would clear it with you first, given all that's been going on.'

'That's fine. He's welcome, but can he stay in a hotel this time around? My house is already kind of overflowing.'

'He can stay at our place,' Koos said. 'He and Michelle can talk shop together because man can they chatter when they get together.'

'Koos!' Michelle said, laughing, and she slapped him gently in the stomach.

Cole nodded. 'Thanks.'

'Do you want my help?' she asked, as she finished packing up some equipment into a black bag.

'We'll be fine. Thanks anyway,' Cole said.

'Lady Bess is still a little stressed after the noise and upset this morning. Take care.' Then she waved at the room. 'Bye, all.'

Cole waved and Koos and Michelle left the nursery. 'I think for now, Mackenzie and I go in and talk to Lady and her cubs. We can show you through the glass. Then we can go into one of the male groups. They're always up for a fuss.'

'That'd be nice,' Lilly said.

Mackenzie noticed that her parents were again holding hands.

Cole opened the door and climbed inside, leaving his crutches outside, then he helped Mackenzie in. Lady immediately chirped at him. He limped over to her and sank to the ground, a little awkwardly. 'Hello, girl. How's mum holding up?' Mackenzie watched as he stroked the cat from her head, down her slinky body to her back legs, then he patted her. She could hear Lady purring from where she stood near the door.

'Come on in closer, Mackenzie,' he called to her.

She walked over and sat down with him. Lady extended her nose to Mackenzie, then licked her outstretched hand. 'Where are the cubs?'

'They're inside that bamboo box in the corner. Michelle would have opened it this morning and helped Lady move her cubs. I'll go in and pass them out to you.'

He stood up with a small struggle and, dragging his leg, went into the hide at the side of the nursery enclosure.

'Here's Jewels,' he said as he passed a tiny grey body out and Mackenzie got up quickly to take the cub.

'How do you know it's Jewels?' she asked. 'Don't they all look alike?'

'Similar. It'll be a few days at least till we notice their individuality. Jewels is the smallest in the litter, so she's easier to spot.'

Mackenzie grinned as she held Jewels up for her mother to see. Lady came over, purring, and gave the cub a lick while Mackenzie still held her. Then plucking the cub neatly out of Mackenzie's hand with her mouth, she trotted back into the hide.

Cole chuckled. 'You old fusspot,' he said to Lady as he gave her another pat.

'Looks as if she wants to be left alone at present,' he said. 'Come on, I want to check on the others.'

He paused before he hobbled towards the door.

'Are you overdoing it?' Mackenzie asked.

'Probably, but now it's just Siphiwe and me to lock up tonight. With Joel, Seth and Dumisani's passing today, I have to do this. I want to make sure they're all settled. I'm their dad.' His voice broke and she saw him swallow.

Mackenzie could see he was fighting back tears. 'Your cheetahs are safe now, you're still here to protect them. The others, they gave their lives to save them, you need to feel proud of them, not sorry for them.' Tears pricked at Mackenzie's eyes as she could hear the level of emotion he held back in his voice.

He nodded. 'They were my family. We have all spent many years together, and now suddenly they are gone.'

She hugged him. 'It's going to be okay, Cole. You're still here to look after your cats, and there are other men and women who'll help you.'

He smiled at her weakly, but his smile didn't reach his eyes.

'Come,' he said, sniffing. 'Out you go.' He put his hand on her head, guiding her to ensure she didn't hit it on the doorway.

'They're so beautiful,' Hope said as they came out from behind the glass, 'and she's such a good mother.'

'Thank you for protecting her, Hope,' Cole said.

Hope nodded. 'I'd die for her before I saw them take her. I might not own any of these beautiful cats, but my life's work is to save them, to stop them becoming rugs or getting put on a leash like a dog in some suburban home somewhere. I'm leaving first thing in the morning. But know that being here today, helping save these cheetahs, it's been a highlight of my life.'

'I suspected you would go soon. I hope you nab the mastermind. I hope you get every person all the way up the chain,' Cole said. 'Nail them for me.'

Hope pulled away slightly and nodded. 'I'm counting on it. But I might still need more of your help there.'

'What else?' Cole asked.

'Later,' Hope said.

Cole slowly moved the group through to the cage area.

'Your cubs are beautiful,' Lilly said. 'Mackenzie, you're so fortunate to have witnessed the birth.'

'Koos took photos,' Mackenzie said, almost bubbling with excitement. 'He said he'd email me copies so now I can do a bronze of Lady and the newborn cubs. All eight.'

'So, you're going to continue sculpting African animals?' Bob asked.

'Of course, what else would I do?' Mackenzie said. She knew she was frowning but couldn't help it.

'Just making sure you weren't throwing such a talent away. I waited too long to enjoy it, but if your wildlife sculptures are anything like *Bewildered* then I'm sure you'll sell them all. I'd like to come to your next gallery showing, wherever in the world it is,' Bob said.

'I'd like that. I can give you a sneak peek at my house tomorrow if you want.'

'I'd love that,' Bob said.

Mackenzie reached for Cole's arm and squeezed it as he laboured along with his crutches. There was a flash of a smile that told her he'd been listening.

They stopped outside a large enclosure. 'You can follow me in,' Cole said as he opened the first gate, with its new locks. Four cheetahs immediately started chirping at him. He closed the gate behind the group, locked it and opened the inner one.

'Come,' he said, as Bob and Lilly walked in. Thandi, Brian, Mandla and Hope followed. Mackenzie stood next to Cole, then held his crutches as he got down to their level.

'I just love the interaction with these cats,' Brian said.

They all came to greet Cole, as if he was one of them.

'Cheetahs are mostly loners, but if they do form a group it's usually of brothers, or a mother and cubs,' Cole explained. 'Brothers from the same litter stick together, but the females go off and have families of their own. Crouch down on your haunches for them, like Thandi's doing.'

Bob and Lilly bent down. The cheetahs, having said their hellos to Cole, wandered around them, sniffing and licking. One male stopped next to Lilly and rubbed up against her back, then sat down next to her, purring.

'That's Naka, it means "trouble" in Zulu. Stroke him and then give him a pat, like a dog. Just mind his tummy,' Cole instructed. 'He has a ticklish spot.'

Lilly was grinning. Mackenzie was laughing at her mother.

Bob had his camera out and was taking photos of his wife with the cheetah. He turned the camera onto Mackenzie, who sat next to Cole on the floor, a cheetah lying on her lap.

'This pest here is Imbali. It means "flower". An undignified name for a male, but Michelle and Koos named him because of the huge mantle he was born with. They said he looked like a sunflower.'

Imbali purred and rolled over on her lap and fell off her legs.

Mackenzie looked over at Brian and Thandi. They looked comfortable enough with a cheetah that had settled near Thandi.

Cole said, 'That one over there is Wohloka, it means fall, because he arrived at our centre during the autumn when the leaves were falling from the trees.'

Brian looked up at Mackenzie as Cole was taking, and she beamed happily at him.

Mandla had the last remaining cheetah in the enclosure and it was sitting a way off, on its haunches, staring at him. Suddenly it bounded at him, almost bowling him over, and licked him.

'Typical,' he said as he wiped the back of his hand over his face. 'Cheetah kisses is all I get these days.'

Hope was laughing.

'Vodka thinks Mandla wants to play,' Cole explained to Bob and Lilly. 'Licking his face signifies him as part of their group and he's decided it's playtime.'

Mandla played for a while, obviously a seasoned animal handler, too, but soon Vodka lost interest and sat down next to him.

After a long while, Cole said, 'As nice as this is, I need to settle the rest of the cats down for the night and it's been a really long day. Siphiwe's waiting for me, so I'll get you out of here and back to the cars.'

They left in relative silence. When they were about to load into the cars, Mandla and Brian appeared next to Cole.

Mackenzie said, 'Should I wait for you?'

'No, you need to go with Thandi and your folks. I'll finish up here soon and then Brian will drive me up to the house. We'll need to be vigilant tonight in case we didn't stamp out the whole raiding party. It's safer for you up at the house.' He leant forward and kissed her softly, almost a ghost of a kiss.

'See you,' he said.

'Bye.' Mackenzie climbed into the *bakkie* after Thandi and watched him walk back into the visitors' centre, relying heavily on his crutches, with Mandla and Brian beside him.

She smiled knowing he was safe with his friends around.

CHAPTER
36

Later that night, Hope closed the video program on her computer after replaying the senator's speech that had been on CNN and turned to the men sitting in Cole's study. James was on the monitor attached to Cole's computer so that he could listen in. 'This newscast went viral today. Social media groups picked up on it and Twitter and Facebook have gone mad with people expressing outrage that a rescue centre was attacked. I think this is what prompted an interesting email to me,' she said. 'I worked with a man in Namibia. He'll remain anonymous for now. At the time I was looking for information about canned lion hunting there and if there was substance to the claim. I spoke to that contact today. He's working for this man – Sheik Mufti Ali Kamara,' she said as she brought a picture up on her screen.

'Meet the mastermind behind the cheetah market at the moment.'

'You one hundred percent sure?' James asked.

Hope nodded. 'They're being stolen from Africa and everywhere else in the world and they're being stabled in Iran. I thought that because there's been a marked resurrection of traditional hunting, now with a modern twist in Iran, that they were being collected to hunt against each other and the owners were using the cheetahs as status symbols. Today I got confirmation that it's worse than that. Sheik Mufti Ali Kamara has amassed almost a thousand cheetahs and has created a breeding centre. He has also captured about fifty of the last remaining Iranian cheetahs and is cross-breeding them with the African cheetahs, in the hope to release them into the wild in Iran and save their wild cheetah population from extinction.'

'That's absurd!' Cole said. 'Why decimate African cheetahs to save Iranian ones?'

'A similar scheme was proposed by India a few years back and has been in international debate for so many years, but they basically lost their chance as the numbers of their natural cheetahs dropped below sustainable and are now beyond the point of no return,' Hope said.

'So this sheik had just gone ahead without anyone's approval? What about CITES? Where were they?' Cole asked.

'Glad you mention them,' Hope said. She flashed another photo on the screen. 'Meet Paul Joyce. He was a consultant for CITES until he was found dead in what looked like a carjacking gone wrong in Johannesburg. Alan doesn't think it was. He said it looked more like an execution when he viewed the file. I agree with him. Alan also at last got into that bank account number that I found on the pad at Thompson's, and it belonged to none other than: Paul Joyce. There's over three million US dollars in the account. This was the man who recognised me when I was at Thompson's, and when Thompson and Dominic were talking during the attack, he confirmed that it was Paul Joyce who sabotaged my plane. I suspected he was dirty, but I needed to push further than him, look higher up the food chain.'

'Thanks for getting that, Alan,' James said, 'I was being stonewalled constantly in Johannesburg by the police department there.'

Alan said, 'Hate to admit this, but I think we have a problem with corruption there, too.'

Hope nodded, then said, 'Now knowing what I do, I'm going after Sheik Mufti Ali Kamara.'

Cole shook his head. 'What a mess. I have to admire him, his methods are wrong but the concept is good. Really good.'

'I agree, there were so many more ways he could have done this more diplomatically,' James said.

'Hope, how do you know your informant told you the truth?' Mandla asked.

'The man who gave it to me is dying of prostate cancer. When he saw that the rescue centre had been attacked, he became worried for his soul. All his life he'd dedicated himself to the preservation of wildlife, and then his company terminated his employment when they found he was ill. Too expensive to keep on medical cover, so when he was approached by Thompson to go work as an expat in Iran, he took the job for the money, to set his family up after he'd gone. He knew he was on his way out, so he wouldn't be prosecuted if anything went wrong. He's carrying around a heavy guilty conscience for what's happening to his mother continent, and his time to make peace with his maker is coming to an end.'

'So it's a case of theft. Can't the police go in there and arrest this sheik?' Brian asked.

'No, there's a better way,' Hope said, and she smiled.

Mandla laughed. 'Here it comes, I have seen that smile. You don't want to be on the receiving end of it. What is your plan exactly?'

'He got them to Iran, now he can pay to relocate them back to Africa,' Hope said.

CHAPTER
37

MaNtuli stood up from behind her desk and walked forward to greet the police officer, her hand outstretched.

'Thank you for seeing us, maNtuli,' Officer Brandt said. 'This is Member in Charge of the Crystalberg Area, Alan Reid.'

Alan shook her hand.

'Sit, gentlemen, can I get you anything to drink?' maNtuli asked.

Alan raised his hand. 'No thank you. This is an official visit.'

She walked back behind her desk and sat down. 'So why do I have the pleasure of an official visit?'

Alan put a folder on her desk and opened it. A picture of Dominic Bongwanan lying on a steel table was at the forefront.

'I believe you were acquainted with Dominic?'

'Aw,' she said, before she covered her mouth with her hand. 'He was my friend. He is dead?'

'He was killed during a stock-theft raid that went wrong,' Alan said, all the time watching maNtuli for expressions. His Hillbrow counterpart, Johannes Brandt, had warned him that they wouldn't get anything out of maNtuli, that she was a hyena in street clothes. He had also made it abundantly clear that in their area, they thought that knowing the evil on the street was better than the one you didn't know about, who would shoot you in the back. So they tolerated her as she was keeping the Nigerians from moving in, creating street gangs and running drugs.

'Aw no, I am so sorry that he was there. My friend, he had gone a little bit off the tracks recently. He moved out of the house I bought him and he was living back in the shacks in Alexandra.'

Alan said, 'I assume you know his shack in his grandmother's yard was burnt down recently.'

'Really? This is a sad tragedy,' maNtuli said. 'I did not know that. Shame. Shack fires are bad. Very bad. Lots of reasons for shack fires.'

Alan continued, 'Do you know his brother, Noah?'

'I do. Noah is a little slow, but not so much that he couldn't still be a functioning citizen in society. He has a wife and children.'

'Did Dominic work for you?' Alan asked.

'No. Dominic and I were friends, that was all. We grew up together until I was thirteen. Then when I came into money, I bought him a proper house to live in. I gave him an out when he needed it from the shack life.'

'So do you have any idea who he worked for?'

'He was a businessman working for himself. He had some taxis.'

Alan passed her a second photograph.

'This is a picture of Dominic in the Soweto Market a few months ago. I believe you have a few stalls at the Soweto Market and you pay people to guard the place against undesirable characters.'

'That is correct, but Dominic can go where he wants to. He is my friend not my dog that I keep on a leash.'

Alan put another photo on the table. 'Can you identify that this is in fact one of your tables that you hire and you sell fresh fruit from and second-hand clothes?'

She looked at it. 'Yes, I hire lots of different people to sell the fruit and those second-hand clothes. I have multiple tables and many, many wares to sell. Many people sell second-hand goods, one person's junk—'

'We know the saying. Is there good profit in the market wares, maNtuli?' Alan asked.

'Yes.'

'But there is better profit in weapons and explosives?' Alan asked.

'I don't understand,' maNtuli said.

'This is the other side of the table. I believe those are limpet mines.' Alan passed her another photograph.

'These are not mine, I am not a gun runner,' maNtuli said.

'No, but Dominic is – ah – was.' Alan passed her another picture. This time, the limpet mines were being placed into a backpack by Dominic.

'No. Dominic wasn't a gun runner. Perhaps he was a little on the wild side, but why would he be buying mines?' she said.

'We hoped you could tell us,' Alan said.

'Oh my poor friend,' she said as she lifted up Dominic's photo again. 'What were you doing? Why would you do this?'

Alan passed her one more photo. 'Do you know this woman?'

'I saw this picture on the news. That is the American lady who was killed in KwaZulu-Natal. Sad news.'

'Had you seen her before that?' Alan asked.

'No. She is a stranger to me.'

'Thank you for your time and for answering our questions, maNtuli.' Alan began to gather all the photographs off the desk and closed them into the file again.

'Always happy to talk with the police.' MaNtuli rose from behind her desk again.

Alan noted that when her hands smoothed down her modern linen white skirt, they were no longer calm but clearly shaking. Something in the file had been bad news to her and it wasn't the death of Dominic, because he was quite convinced that she already knew about that.

They said their goodbyes and walked onto the street below.

Officer Brandt turned to Alan. 'You didn't accuse her of anything. You didn't manage to confirm anything either.'

'Don't be so sure of that,' Alan said. 'Officer Brandt, I suggest that you put a detail onto what remains of the Bongwanan family, because I suspect that they are your gun runners into Hillbrow, not maNtuli, and she wasn't too pleased to hear that they are running a business under her nose on her time, and I also suspect that she will try to take care of it.'

CHAPTER
38

Ten days had passed since Cole had been shot. He was now able to walk without his crutches and there'd been no other poacher activities on *nTabaGrequa*. Lauren's funeral was over, having been held in the quaint little pink church on the outer rim of Crystalberg. Her ashes had been laid to rest in the grotto on *nTabaGrequa*, alongside Melissa and Marco. The funerals of the men who'd died were still being arranged, and they were going to be held the following week.

Although it was only just after lunch, Mackenzie was sitting on a chair in Cole's study, stroking Farren, who was curled in her lap. Cole sat next to her, also in an office chair.

Brian's face showed clearly on the screen monitor. 'I heard from Mandla today, he's with Hope in Dubai.'

Mackenzie frowned. 'Dubai? Why on earth are they there?'

'She has convinced CITES to adhere to Article VIII of their convention,' Brian said.

'What's that?' Mackenzie asked.

'They have legislation in place that allows them to confiscate the illegally imported animals and go after the dealers and corrupt officials with the full weight of the law. And wherever they can, the animals will be taken back to where they were from, so in our case, all over Africa.'

She grinned. 'So Africa will have its cheetahs brought home after all this?'

'Hope is working on a solution that can help the cheetahs, both the African and Iranian ones. They are a long way off it being finalised but it's a good start.'

'That's great,' Cole said.

'Yeah, according to Mandla, she's optimistic because she has managed to find more concrete proof that Thompson and Paul Joyce were responsible for sabotaging her plane. With her proving that Paul Joyce was a corrupt CITES representative, any permits he issued were based on false information provided to CITES, and they have a law that will cancel them all. She's confident that the cheetahs will come home to Africa.'

'That's fantastic news.'

'So will they need my rescue centre for any coming home?' Cole asked.

'No details yet, but apparently Hope has already volunteered it.'

Cole nodded. 'Pass on my thanks.'

'Will do,' Brian said.

'Actually,' Cole said, 'it's kind of sad. Kamara was so determined that Iran's cheetahs wouldn't suffer the same fate as India's that he took everything into his own hands, a desperate attempt to save a species, but done the wrong way.'

'You sound like you feel sorry for him,' Mackenzie said.

'I do in a way. He could see that Iran's cheetahs were in trouble and were dying out, that they were being removed from the wild, domesticated by the men of the land and trained to hunt for sport in the desert dunes.'

'The cheetahs hunt for the men?' Mackenzie asked.

'Sure, they launch their cheetahs from their pick-ups and chase down antelope, then once the buck is dead, the owners call them back and collect the prey. It had become a sport where bored young men competed as to whose cheetah could kill the fastest and many wagers worth millions run in the betting circles on whose cheetahs were the ultimate Iranian predators. I have watched them on You-Tube videos.'

'That's sad, no cheetah should have to live like that.'

'I agree. But Kamara believed he had a solution. Not only would it give these young men a constant supply of cheetahs for their sport, so they didn't have to reap from the wild stock. He attempted to create a successful breeding program in Iran without government funding. Just like the Abu Dhabi Falcon Hospital, it has saved so many birds and ultimately the falconry of the whole Middle East, Kamara believed that his centre would breed and reintroduce the cheetahs back into the Bafq Protected Area of Iran. Their precious cats would be brought back from the brink of extinction. They would avoid the fate of their endangered status and quickly claw their way back into a healthy population. Soon every sheik who kept a cheetah for personal hunting would bring them to his property for veterinary checks and they would find a way to artificially inseminate the females and harvest semen from the males as donors towards the cause. They would progress faster than any other centres around the world, make positive progress.'

'Poor man was not so delusional either, according to Hope,' Brian said. 'Already he had cheetah babies, strong and growing, learning from their mothers, who were in large, spacious areas because he'd invested in professionals who had the knowhow and were prepared to work. Apparently, he was as close as six months away from when he was going to begin a reintroduction program with the juveniles from his first litters. Hope said that when they visited his farm, he had pens of chinkara, goitered gazelle and wild goats to ensure that there was sufficient food to sustain the new cheetah population as well as feeding his hungry cheetahs while they increased in number. He had planned it really well, and with not having to worry about cash at all, his dream almost became a reality. By simply smuggling in cheetahs and not getting bogged down in bureaucratic red tape, he truly believed that Iran would not lose its cheetahs.'

'And now he has to send them all back to Africa?' Mackenzie said.

Both Brian and Cole nodded.

Cole said, 'It's going to be a legal nightmare. With DNA samples, they will see where each of the cheetahs came from.'

'And send them back at his expense,' Brian said.

'He'll get to keep some, I bet,' Mackenzie said.

'There will be grey areas for the cubs he had managed to breed. I don't envy Hope's job of having to sort through all this with her boss and CITES at all,' Cole said.

'Dubai has great shopping, she'll enjoy it there,' Mackenzie said.

Cole laughed. 'I don't think she's into shopping.'

'Don't underestimate any girl and shopping, Cole.'

'I'll take your word for it. Hey, Brian, I chatted to Alan this afternoon. He's still in Johannesburg. Apparently, he set up some sting operation, but he said to tell you hi.'

'Any news from him on following up on why Dominic attacked me in the first place?' Mackenzie asked.

'He's convinced you were just in the wrong place at the wrong time for that taxi attack, that Dominic was driving past on one of maNtuli's routes, checking things, and he was just allowing one of his passengers to have a bit of fun. Oh, and Alan said he would be at the auction of Shoebox at the New Year's Eve ball you are throwing.'

'So the ball is on again?' Brian asked.

'Yes, so all you big-time spenders had best shake the moths from your suits, you'll be needing them after all,' Mackenzie said. 'Now that I've put my name behind the auction, we're getting even more enquiries and people registering, so it looks like it'll be an amazing event, and raise loads of much-needed money.'

Cole reached for her hand and lifted it to his lips. He kissed the top of her finger. 'Good to know.'

'Guys, keep it for your bedroom where I don't need to see,' Brian complained.

'You are just jealous,' Cole said, continuing to hold Mackenzie's hand.

Mackenzie smiled. 'And Charl?'

'Still fighting. He was shot up badly. I went in to see him and got an earful from Liza. It's amazing and wonderful, she's talking more and more. I'm telling you, I couldn't have pried her from his side even physically. She's been his champion the whole time, and even though he's awake now, he didn't seem to be minding her attention.'

'That's sweet,' Mackenzie said. 'When you next go in to visit, please send them our love.'

'It is, but those two have huge demons to slay before they can get their relationship on track,' Cole said.

'Give them time, and space, they'll manage fine without any of you boys interfering!' Mackenzie said.

Brian smiled. 'So, have your folks set a date to go home yet or are they still with you?'

'My parents and I have been discussing the idea of them travelling around South Africa while they're here, seeing some of the game parks, and places I've been to. So tomorrow they're taking a trip to Londolozi, then on to Madikwe and Cape Town. They asked me if we wanted to go on a Christmas holiday with them.'

'And are you going?' Brian asked.

'Yeah, that's also why we called,' Cole said. 'We decided we would go with them, but that depends whether you will come and back up Siphiwe with the farm for the time.'

'We'll be in constant contact because of the auction and everything, but we thought—' Mackenzie started and stopped. 'It's really special, and—'

Cole laughed.

'Look,' Cole said and he lifted Mackenzie's left hand for Brian to see the diamond-and-sapphire ring that glistened on her finger. 'We are going as an engagement present to each other!'

'Oh man, what's in the water? You guys are getting married! Mandla's with Hope. Dang, I had best not sit on your chair,' Brian said, then laughed. 'That's brilliant news. Congratulations.'

'Thank you,' they said together.

CHAPTER
39

MaNtuli stood back to one side at the graveside ceremony at Four-ways Memorial Park as it was conducted for Dominic Bongwanan. She watched as the traditional sangoma did her blessing over the coffin, wishing the man an easy crossing-over.

When she was finished, the priest took up a feeble rendition of 'Amazing Grace', where the women wailed louder and the small children present put their hands over their ears.

MaNtuli wished she, too, could do that, because all the noise was giving her a headache. No one cared that Dominic was dead. In life he had been her second-in-command, done her dirty work and that made him an unpopular man in their society. Despite her paying for his fancy funeral that only the best money could buy to show that she looked after her people, she was seething inside. Most of the people present were only there to show her respect, not to mourn the loss of a man they couldn't stand. Those that were here for his grandmother were all business associates, and they were the second reason she was attending.

Her hands shook.

All this time, it was Dominic who had been double-cross-ing her. He was part of a gun-smuggling ring and he had never offered her a cut. He had been working on his own business while taking her wages. She hadn't known him as well as she thought she had because she'd never suspected he had a brain that could orchestrate an operation like this behind her back. Even when the police had shown her their evidence, she had not believed. But Sizani had brought her the evidence easily enough after he had hired two AK-47s with filed off serial numbers from the house in Barlow Park. It didn't take much digging to find out that the house was rented in Noah's name. Business continued even when a family member died.

She bunched her hands together and flexed them to stop the shaking as the anger threatened to ooze outwards as she searched the crowd again for the familiar face.

So far she had been unable to find him, but what better place to lure him out than his own brother's funeral. Noah was the loose end that needed to be tied up and she hadn't found him yet. Noah was one of Dominic's two weak links left behind. He wasn't even in the police system being held anywhere. And she would know, because she had paid the policeman in Johannesburg enough to supply her with that information, or in this case, lack of information.

Her contacts in the police force had said he had been captured, but it was unconfirmed. She scanned the crowd again. No Noah, but Nkgono Bongwanan was there, as expected, and she was giving her the evil eye.

MaNtuli smiled at her. Dominic's grandmother had never liked her. Even when she was just a child, she had a vivid memory of the woman smacking her hand as she'd reached for a rusk in her shack. Of Nkgono telling Tobeko to get food from her own mother, and lecturing on how hard it was to bring up two grandsons alone on her own.

The song came to an end and the mourners began throwing handfuls of sand into the grave over the expensive coffin, as maNtuli turned her back on the scene and walked under her black umbrella towards the wake, under an expensive *lapa* area at the cemetery that she had catered. Like the recreational hall of a church, only better, custom-designed for funeral refreshments. There were no little sandwiches stuffed with egg, but there were salmon-and-cream-cheese crepes, dainty shrimp vol-au-vent cases, beef fillet with red pepper kebabs, dainty chocolate-drizzled meringues, *koeksisters* and tiny scones with fresh Chantilly cream with homemade strawberry jam. Tall glass jugs filled with Coke stood dripping with condensation onto the once pristine white tablecloths, and glasses waited on ice in galvanised basins.

Sizani was dressed as a waiter. The white collar strained at his thick neck, the black waistcoat pulled over his broad chest. He didn't acknowledge that he knew her, but quickly removed the white linen serviette off the top of the jug that stopped the flies entering the sweet liquid and poured her a drink into a cold glass.

'*Siyabonga*,' maNtuli said as she took the beverage and drank deeply, draining the glass.

A walking stick slammed down on the table next to her, smashing into a platter of food. Sizani grabbed at the jug he held, trying hard not to spill it onto the floor inside the fancy *lapa*.

MaNtuli looked at the stick in disgust. The twin snakes that ran upwards to the large intertwined heads at the top were familiar – she had been on the other end of a beating from it all those years ago.

'Tobeko, why are you here? Come to gloat at my grandson's death?'

'No, Nkgono.' She used the term of endearment for the grandmother almost in a sickly sweet manner. 'I have come to pay my respects. Dominic and I were friends.'

'You were never his friend. You made him think he could achieve things above his station in life. That's what you were to him, you made him into a dreamer. Wanting things. Always wanting more, more, more.'

'No, that was just his nature, but you can believe what you like. Today is for Dominic. I just came to see that he was buried right and people who came to his funeral had a good feed, that he will be celebrated, and he will pass over with dignity.'

'You are not welcome,' Nkgono said.

'You think that? How fast you forget – it was me who has paid for this funeral. It was me who provided this feast and hired this beautiful *lapa* area. I paid for the traditional bull for you waiting at your shack to bleed for your part in the funeral. His coffin, it was grand, with its silver decoration all over the shiny oak wood, was it not? I paid for that, too, not his family. Not you. But you say I am not welcome.'

'He wouldn't be dead if it wasn't for you and your meddling.'

'My meddling? It was not me who was trading in illegal weapons now was it? Limpet mines at the Soweto Market? Seriously, you traded in the open where any tourist could catch a photo of your wares?' She shook her head. 'Another Coke, waiter.'

Sizani poured a drink into the glass she held out to him. She downed that, too, in the heat. 'Make that two, one for the old lady also. She could do with sweetening up.'

Sizani put a new, already cold glass on the table, and filled it with the Coke from the same jug, the ice tinkling against the side.

MaNtuli watched as Nkgono took the glass offered and drank from it.

'Only because it's hot and you went to so much trouble to give my poor Dominic a good party. But know, Tobeko, you do not frighten me.'

'Oh, Nkgono, you have it wrong. I wasn't here to frighten you, just for your clients to see us together, those that have taken the time to come and show their respects to you by attending your grandson's funeral. So that they know that I am not their enemy when I take over your business. All this time, you and Dominic were plotting behind my back, thinking I was stupid for not know-ing what you were doing? No, you started a good business for me to now run. I wanted to thank you.'

'You won't take my business, Tobeko.'

'Oh, Nkgono, all these years and you still don't really know me. You never liked me, you were always like a cobra. Wanting me close then striking me down when you could when I was a girl. You were the one who gave my mother the money so we could go to the Umhlanga Festival and she could sell me to Samuel Ntuli because you didn't want Dominic to be with me. Did you know that I found my mother again? She was living in Umtata in the Transkei. She told me then what happened, and I made peace with my mother when she was dying, but did you ever get a moment to make peace with your Dominic? You wanted your grandson for yourself, but it wasn't because he was your grandson, it was because he was just another cheap worker to you. Another man to take the heat from the law if needed, instead of you.'

'You never suspected a thing, girl,' Nkgono hissed.

MaNtuli laughed. 'All the time you thought I didn't know? I admired Dominic for being a proud male and for running your business, taking more control of it as you got older and older, ensuring its survival in these new times. It was Dominic who moved your weapons cache out of Alex, expanding the business, making zippies now. Your arrogance got Dominic killed, not mine.' She crossed her fingers in a childish gesture behind her back for the lies.

'He was after your cheetahs!' Nkgono said.

'What cheetahs? I don't know anything about any cheetahs, that must have been part of Dominic and Noah's business,' maNtuli said. 'Goodbye, Nkgono. I probably won't see you again; there will be no need now that Dominic is dead. Enjoy the party. Dominic was at least worthy of a decent burial in a nice place, not a farm plot somewhere in the dirt of the Transkei. Believe me, I won't be paying for yours.' She turned and began walking away.

'That's right, leave this place,' Nkgono said to her back. 'Let Dominic rest in peace because he never had any with you around.'

MaNtuli just smiled and carried on walking. Nkgono had always been such a spiteful old woman and she had known that today would be no different. That was why her instructions to Sizani had been clear: nothing in the old woman's first drink, but one small tablet of witchdoctor's aloe per glass thereafter. She wouldn't taste it, but she would by the end of the wake have consumed more than twenty grams, and she would get thirstier when she was drinking as the diuretic effect began. Nkgono would be dead within twenty-four hours.

Sizani would ensure her glass was never found. Her new second-in-command was eager to please her. And maNtuli would take over another enterprise.

EPILOGUE

One year later.

'Ready? On my mark, put the crate down. One, two, three…' Cole instructed.

He bent his knees and lowered his corner of the heavy wooden release crate, letting out a breath as he felt it touch the dry ground at the same time as the other corners.

'Hang in there, Naka,' he said as he looked into the crate at the cheetah staring back at him, his amber eyes alive with interest, panting to regulate his temperature, despite it only being six o'clock in the morning. Every last minute of the interaction with his cat was bitter sweet. He smiled, and Naka chirped at him, as if trying to reassure Cole that he understood what was happening. That he was about to become a wild cheetah.

Tears welled in Coles eyes. Blinking them away, he stood up and looked to where the *bakkies* were all parked together with their tail-gates down. Of the five vehicles, only one still had a crate waiting to be unloaded. He shouted so that he could be heard above the noise being made by the people inside the soft release site set up inside the Kruger National Park. 'You almost ready, Siphiwe?'

'Almost,' Siphiwe called back as the last crate was removed. Soon it was placed carefully into a line alongside the others.

'It's so exciting that this day is here at last,' Mackenzie said, her nose still behind her video camera, as she filmed the release.

'It's been a long time coming,' Martie said. 'I's just happy to see somes young cheetahs back in my park. New blood, new life.'

Cole smiled. He looked at the crates. It was hard to comprehend that the future of the cheetahs in this part of the Kruger National Park had arrived. They had loaded the cheetahs the evening before and driven through the night so that the cheetahs were less stressed, their convoy had made great time, and the dawn release was going well.

Slowly he walked to each crate, and he said a personal farewell word to each cat. Imabali, Vodka and their brother Naka, Wohloka and *nTabaGrequa's* newest rescue who was re-releasing with the male group, Bushman. While each of the cheetahs who had been more captive chirped, and interacted with him, Bushman hissed. It was a great sign that the cat would help the group to settle into the *bundu*, his wild instincts were not affected by his human interaction after being gored badly by a warthog and having to receive treatment from them. His scar was healed up and the x-ray had shown that the pin Michelle had put into his shoulder had mended. It was the ideal release time.

Cole looked to the left where the media stood to one side, huddled in a group, their huge lenses aimed at the crates as they set up waiting for the release. A park ranger stood with them, just in case the cheetahs sprinted in their direction on release, to wave his arms and redirect them away, to protect the cats from any unwanted contact.

Cole would rather not have had them present, but the public outcry of sympathy and interest from the general population had not waned, and in consultation with Hope and Martie, they had decided to capitalise on it, and use the release as part of raising the awareness campaign for the cheetahs.

'Ready?' Mackenzie asked him as she slipped her hand into his.

'I'm never ready to let them go, but it's for their benefit,' he said. He tucked a stray hair behind her ear, then bent his head and kissed her.

Mackenzie said, 'Let's do this, the sooner they're out, the sooner their two weeks in this *boma* begins, then they can be set free and wild.'

He smiled, squeezed her and then said. 'Right, I'm ready. You?'

She nodded.

He lifted her up, and placed her on top of Imbali's crate.

'Everyone up, those not releasing, stand clear!' He shouted.

Hope didn't wait for Mandla to lift her, but easily climbed up onto Wohloka's crate. Mandla stood on top of Vodka's cage, and Martie was the handler on top of Bushman's crate. 'Only fair I should put you backs here boy,' he said, 'after me and Zonke hads to carry you out of here half dead. That's why we chose here to erected this five acre soft release spot, just for you. You will's know where yous are when yous gets out in two weeks. This is yous' territory boy. Its *reg*-right that we welcome yous home again.'

A quietness descended onto the group, and the cats as if knowing their moment was coming were silent. There was no sound from the press group either as everyone held their breath.

'Unlock your latches!' Cole shouted, and hands reached onto the cages and released the locking mechanism.

'Hands inside handles.' He shouted, 'Cole ready.'

'Mackenzie ready.'

'Hope ready.'

'Mandla ready.'

'Martie ready.'

Cole nodded so that the media could see they were about to release. 'On my mark, one, two, three …'

He lifted the wooden panel of the release cage, and for a nanosecond Naka remained in his cage, then he shot out at full speed. But Bushman was the fastest out the crate and streaked away towards the small bushes in front of them, Naka hard on his heels. Imbali came out of his cage and turned sharp right and disappeared that way while Wohloka ran towards the media. The game ranger stationed there lifted his arms and flapped them around. Wohloka changed trajectory, veered right and dashed in that direction. A cheer went up from the media.

The cats had scattered in all directions.

'They will get back together, give them time to settle down, realise they are free, then they will regroup,' Cole said.

'*Ja*, and when they finds the shade and the water here, theys will be good. In two weeks, we can dismantle this soft release site and theys will be wild. Free to explores the whole park, and to hunts whatever game theys want to,' Martie said.

'But there are lions, leopards and hyenas here, they don't know about those ...' Mackenzie said.

'They'll learn,' Hope said, 'they have a good chance because they are already a male coalition, and they will become better at hunting in a pack and have a good chance.' She signed loudly. 'This is what makes my job worthwhile, I get to release a cheetah back into the wild, not one that I had helped save, but it's good enough for now.'

'Those will happen soon enough, when the cheetahs have been retrained for release, and you had best be on hand to help release those too,' Cole said.

'I don't have plans to leave Africa again,' Hope said. 'Mandla is stuck with me.'

Martie jumped down. 'Wells before I gets stuck talking to the press, Zonke and I is going into the bush to tracks those five, make sure theys regroup and makes a kill today. Ready, Zonke?'

'Of course, *Baas*,' Zonke said and he was standing near them, his green pack already on his back, his computer open. 'Already three are together, if we listen perhaps you can hear them chirping, calling to each other ...'

Cole shook Martie's hand, 'Best you go do your part of the job then. *nTabaGrequa* has done its bit, now, how they live the rest of their lives in the wild is up to you and your game rangers. Good luck!'

Mackenzie stood next to Cole as they watched the two rangers walk into the bush, the tawny grass brushing at their legs as they made their way towards the cheetahs in the *boma*.

'This is only the beginning,' he said quietly, 'there is still so much more work to do to save these cats.'

'There is, but together, we'll just take one day at a time.'

FACT VS FICTION

Fact: People inhabiting South African informal settlements live with the threat of fire daily. In 2005, the shack fire in the Joe Slovo settlement, Langa, Cape Town, burnt down 3200 shacks and displaced 11,000–12,000 people. Up to 20,000 people were believed to live in the informal settlement at that time.

Fiction: My shack fire in Alexandra township is fictional.

Fact: CITES (the Convention on International Trade in Endangered Species of Wild Fauna and Flora, also known as the Washington Convention) is real. As are the laws on the trade of wild animals.

Fiction: Global Wildlife International is fictional, and while there are companies out there who do an amazing job looking after and protecting the wildlife around the world, I chose not to represent a specific one.

Fact: Bahrain, Kuwait, Oman, Qatar, Saudi Arabia and the United Arab Emirates are party to CITES and prohibit wild cheetah imports (except for non-commercial purposes in accordance with Article III of the Convention).

Fiction: I have used 'writer's licence' in saying that Bahrain has not signed the CITES treaty.

Fact: Bahrain, Kuwait, Oman, Qatar, Saudi Arabia and the UAE are identified by CITES as consumer markets for illegally imported live wild cheetahs.

Fact: *Acinonyx jubatus* – cheetah – are listed as Vulnerable on the IUCN (International Union for Conservation of Nature and Natural Resources) Red List, with a declining population of fewer than 10,000 (2014). However, despite this, in 1992 the following annotation was added: 'Annual export quotas for live specimens and hunting trophies are granted as follows: Botswana: 5; Namibia: 150; Zimbabwe: 50.' This has not been amended.

Fact: Asian cheetahs are known to exist only in Iran, where the subspecies *A.j. venaticus* numbers are estimated at 60–100 (Hunter et al. 2007) and are listed as Critically Endangered.

Fact: The plants I have named in this book are used as traditional muti – and they are indeed natural poisons. A number of deaths occur each year in Africa because of the incorrect use of traditional medicines, or due to plants being misidentified. For example, the tubers of poisonous plants are mistaken as sweet potatoes.

Fact: Some wild animal stock is now tracked with GPS monitoring, and capsules in herbivores' stomachs are used for full stock vitals monitoring.

Fiction: The GPS satellite monitoring in cheetahs and elephants is not as advanced as I have claimed in my book (but it's getting close).

Fiction: The town of Crystalberg does not exist in South Africa, although I have placed it just outside Underberg, KwaZulu-Natal. Neither does *nTabaGrequa* Wildlife Rescue and Cheetah Conservation Ranch.

GLOSSARY

aardvark – *(Orycteropus afer)* Also called ant bear or ant eater, nocturnal, medium sized burrowing mammal. (Afrikaans)

ag – 'oh' (Afrikaans)

baas – 'boss' (Afrikaans)

bakkie – a South African word for a pick-up truck, a ute in Australian English. (Afrikaans)

bladdy – a swear word often used to emphasise, to replace 'really' alongside 'good', 'fantastic', 'great' – can also be used in derogatory terms, like 'that bladdy so and so', meaning 'that no good/good for nothing'. (South African slang)

blesbok – *(Damaliscus pygargus phillipsi)* A medium size antelope with a white blaze on its face.

blue *duiker* – *(Philantomba monticola)* A really small antelope. Listed as Rare in the SA Red Data Book, and also appears on Appendix II of CITES as Protected Game.

boerewors – a traditional Afrikaans spicy sausage, made in a coil. (Afrikaans)

boet – brother. Also refers to a close friend. *(Afrikaans) boma* – a fenced area used to keep animals enclosed. Also can refer to an area used for outdoor meals and parties. (Swahili, used generally in Africa)

Bonnox – a type of wire mesh fencing used to keep animals inside.

bra – male friend, similar to 'dude'. (Afrikaans)

breekoparend eagles – (*Polemaetus bellicosus*) Martial eagles. They are the largest eagle in Africa. Martial eagles are now listed as Vulnerable in the IUCN Red Data Book. (Afrikaans)

budza – a hoe to scrape weeds from the fields. Sharp gardening tool. (Used generally across Southern Africa)

bundu – the wild bush. (South African slang)

dood – 'dead' (Afrikaans)

dumelang – 'hello' (plural) also used: *lumela* and *dumela* (singular) (Sesotho)

Dumisani – 'Praise God', a Zulu name (Zulu)

ee – 'yes' (Sesotho)

eish – 'wow!' Can also be 'what'. Often used as an expression of surprise or disbelief. (Of Bantu origin)

eland – (*Taurotragus oryx*) Second largest antelope in the world, has straight horns with a twist in them.

ema – 'stop' (Sesotho)

fynbos – wild flowers in South Africa are generally called this, even though these are scientifically only the flowers of the Cape region.

hambani kahle (pl.) – 'goodbye' or 'people leaving' (Zulu)

hobaneng – 'why' (Sesotho)

ikhaya – 'hut/house' (Zulu)

Indian myna – (*Acridotheres tristis*) Introduced to South Africa in about 1900 and native to southern and south-eastern Asia, it is considered an alien invader species within South Africa.

ingulule – 'cheetah' (Zulu)

Jusses – Jesus (Afrikaans)

jy dom kaffir – You dumb *kaffir* – you dumb black. *(Afrikaans) kaffir* – The word *kaffir* has now evolved into an offensive term for black people. But it was previously a neutral term for black southern African people. Also was used as a term for non-believer – referring to the black people not being of Christian upbringing.

ke a leboha – 'thank you' (Sesotho)

Ke mamela – 'I am listening' (Sesotho)

klap – 'smack/strike' (Afrikaans)

koeksisters – Plated deep fried doughnut, dipped in a sugary syrup when hot to absorb the liquid. An Afrikaans sweet 'cookie' from the Dutch descendants, but could be adapted from the Malay heritage too.

kofi – 'coffee' (Sesotho)

koko – 'grandmother', age greeting (Northern Sotho)

kraal – An area where animals are kept, usually found inside an African village/settlement, and usually circular with barricades to keep the stock inside. Can also refer to an African cluster of huts. (Afrikaans, but commonly used in South Africa by all)

krans – 'a sheer rock face' (Afrikaans)

kubili – 'two' (Zulu)

kudu – (*Tragelaphus strepsiceros*) A large grey spiral horned antelope in Southern Africa, can jump high.

lapa – a structure of a dry grass roof, supported by wooden poles. Similar to a gazebo. (South African)

lengau – 'cheetah' (Sotho)

lobola – An African tradition of an arranged payment between a groom and the bride's family, in exchange for their daughter. Can be paid in cattle or cash, and the higher the *lobola*, the greater value the bride is held in the groom's eyes. This payment is the groom's way of thanking the parents for raising a good daughter. It is still applicable to many South African traditional weddings. (Zulu)

Mandla – 'power/strength', an Ndebele name (Ndebele)

matha – 'run' (Southern Sesotho)

mma – 'mother' for a woman greeting (Northern Sotho)

muti – Traditional medicine in Southern Africa. It is used in South Africa as a slang word for medicine in general. Also spelt '*umuthi*' (Zulu, general slang)

nagapie – also called galago, or bush baby. A small nocturnal African primate. (Meaning 'little night monkey') (Afrikaans)

ngiyajabula ukukwazi – 'pleased to meet you' (Sesotho)

nkgono – 'grandmother' (Sesotho)

nyala – *(Nyala angasii* or *Tragelaphus angasii)* Spiral horned medium sized antelope, can be shy in behaviour.

o a bua Sesotho – 'do you speak Sesotho?' (Sesotho)

oke – used in South Africa for a person or a man, and generally used for a man you don't know. (South African slang)

Panado – Paracetamol medication used for headaches and fever.

panga – a large bush knife (like a machete), once used generally to cut sugarcane, these became commonly used as weapons. (Swahili, but used generally in Southern Africa)

piccaninny – also spelt *pickaninny*. A young black child. At one time the word may have been used as a term of affection, but it is now considered derogatory. In this story this word is used with affection. (English)

sala hantle – used to say 'goodbye' to a person staying (Sesotho)

sawubona – 'hello' (Zulu)

seuntjie – a small boy, baby boy. Son. (Afrikaans)

shebeen – a tavern with a prominently black patronage – not always legal in its activities.

shoosh – used to tell someone to keep quiet. Sounds like 'bush'. (South African slang)

siestog – 'ah, that's a shame'. (South African slang)

siphahluka – *(Boophone disticha)* A poisonous flower. Also known as Fan-leaved Boophone, Poison Bulb, Sore-eye Flower, Tumblehead. (Swazi)

Siphiwe – 'we are given', a Zulu name. (Zulu)

siyabonga – 'thank you' (Zulu and Swazi)

Sizani – 'you all help', a Zulu name. (Zulu)

sjambok – a leather whip, it used to be made from rhino or hippopotamus hide, but is now made from plastic. Used as fighting weapons in South Africa. (Afrikaans)

skabenga – 'rascal', 'scallywag' (general South African term)

skinner – (Originally *skinder* in Afrikaans) to talk about, gossip behind someone's back or tell someone the latest news. (South African slang)

spoor – tracks, usually left by animals (Afrikaans)

tannie – 'Aunty' (Afrikaans)

tata – 'father' or a man greeting (Northern Sotho)

Thandiwe – 'loved', a Zulu name, 'Thandi' for short (Zulu)

Themba – 'trust', 'hope', 'faith', a Zulu name (Zulu)

Tjhee – 'no' (South African Sotho)

tsamaya hantle – 'goodbye' said to the person leaving (Sesotho)

tsotsi – 'thug' or 'robber' (Sesotho slang)

ubuhle bami – 'a beauty' (Zulu)

ukhuluma isiZulu na – 'do you speak Zulu' (Zulu)

umkhokha – (*Abrus precatorius {L. subsp. africanus Verdc.}*) Common names include coral bead plant, coral bean, love bean, lucky bean creeper, weather vine. (Zulu)

veld/veldt/velt – A generic term defining wide open grass or low scrub rural space in Southern Africa. (Afrikaans)

velskoene/veldskoene/velskoen – Bush shoes. These are suede leather ankle boots, usually worn without socks. (Afrikaans)

verstaan jy – 'Do you understand?' (Afrikaans)

vlei – a shallow minor lake, mostly seasonal or intermittent in nature. (Afrikaans)

wildebeest – (*Connochaetes taurinus*) Also called gnus, grey medium sized antelope.

Witchdoctor's Aloe – (*Aloe globuligemma*) A poisonous plant, the active toxins are aloin and aloinosides. (English)

yebo – 'yes' (Zulu)

Zonke – 'all', a Zulu name (Zulu)

ACKNOWLEDGEMENTS

A huge thank you to my external editor, Glenda Downing, for helping me structure a better book and Annabel Blay, my editor at Harlequin Australia, for always being so patient with me.

Emdoneni Lodge, Animal Care and Rehabilitation Centre (www.emdonenilodge.com). When I did the research for this book I had a million questions for your guides and cat handlers, they never failed to answer anything, always with openness, and never showing irritation. I appreciated that. I love your cat reserve and I hope that your dreams continues to grow and prosper. May you continue your fantastic work within the community for tolerance between wild cats and humans within the growing population of South Africa.

Vincent van der Merwe, Cheetah Metapopulation Coordinator, Carnivore Conservation Programme, Endangered Wildlife Trust (www.ewt.org.za). Thank you for your help in the statistics on cheetah movements and giving me access to so much local information.

Bloggers Inge and Mrad Shahia of South Africa, for your very detailed account of your visit in the 'less travelled' areas of

Mozambique, and for speaking to a total stranger about all things bush, the love of the African land and of the people you meet along your journeys. Happy travels!

Flora of Tropical Africa Facebook Group for sharing a relatively unknown world with me. I love your passion for plants, not only the beautiful but the weird and lethal, too. To the Sangoma Group – I am in your debt for the knowledge shared.

Nicolas Chemin, Regional Sales Director (Asia Pacific) of Textron Aviation, Cessna, Beechcraft and Hawker, for making sure I didn't try to fly one of my heroines in a plane not yet delivered to everyone. I know you weren't too happy I was totalling one of 'yours' in my book.

Gary Fonternel as always, for keeping my birds in the sky, or not …

John the bus driver, this will be the final year that you transport my precious cargo for a school run. I will be forever grateful for the extra four hours a day I gained to write in while you drove them to school and back.

Tess Roesler from Grace Lutheran College Caboolture Campus, for the hours spent allowing me to be the 'silent writer in residence' at the school, while I waited for my boys to finish their day during the writing of much of this book.

To my Daisy Chain Friends, sorry the feather scene had to go … perhaps it might find a home in another book.

To my beta readers, Petro Grobbelaar, Siobhan Graham and Sam Eeles.

The Romance Writers of Australia fraternity, for the wonderful opportunities you create for your members. At one stage of its life, this book was mentored by the amazing Marion Lennox during one of the 5 Day Intensive programs I attended. Thank you, Marion, for your patience and time in helping me not only learn my craft, but also to find where I fitted in the writing world.

Amy Andrews, who read this book in many forms, for always believing that it would be published, for pushing me and not letting me give up on it. Robyn Grady and Rachel Bailey for cheering this book on, and Gayle Ash, who was with me every step of the way.

To Alli Sinclair, stable sister and friend, who's always at her computer, no matter the time, to chat, inspire and kick my butt, even after midnight!

Cherry Adair, fellow South African and amazing author, for your awesome cover quote.

To Lauren Saberli, who didn't object to being killed after agreeing with my sons that I was being a bully! Thank you for the privilege of being the first reader I've ever killed (in literature)!

Last and probably the most important: My darling husband, Shaun, because without your help, my books would still be in incoherent English, and my poor editors would have an even bigger task than they have already! You are the best partner I could ask for. Thank you!

talk about it

Let's talk about books.

Join the conversation:

 on facebook.com/harlequinaustralia

 on Twitter @harlequinaus

www.harlequinbooks.com.au

If you love reading and want to know about our
authors and titles, then let's talk about it.